These Violent Years

Look for these exciting Western series from bestselling authors William W. Johnstone and J.A. Johnstone

The Mountain Man

Luke Jensen: Bounty Hunter

Brannigan's Land

The Jensen Brand

Preacher and MacCallister

The Red Ryan Westerns

Perley Gates

Have Brides, Will Travel

Guns of the Vigilantes

Shotgun Johnny

The Chuckwagon Trail

The Jackals

The Slash and Pecos Westerns

The Texas Moonshiners

Stoneface Finnegan Westerns

Ben Savage: Saloon Ranger

The Buck Trammel Westerns

The Death and Texas Westerns

The Hunter Buchanon Westerns

Tinhorn

Will Tanner: U.S. Deputy Marshal

WILLIAM W. JOHNSTONE
AND J.A. JOHNSTONE

These Violent Years

PINNACLE BOOKS
KENSINGTON PUBLISHING CORP.
www.kensingtonbooks.com

PINNACLE BOOKS are published by

Kensington Publishing Corp.
119 West 40th Street
New York, NY 10018

This book is a work of fiction. Names, characters, businesses, organizations, places, events, and incidents either are the product of the authors' imagination or are used fictitiously. Any resemblance to actual persons, living or dead, events, or locales is entirely coincidental.

To the extent that the image or images on the cover of this book depict a person or persons, such person or persons are merely models, and are not intended to portray any character or characters featured in the book.

PUBLISHER'S NOTE: Following the death of William W. Johnstone, the Johnstone family is working with a carefully selected writer to organize and complete Mr. Johnstone's outlines and many unfinished manuscripts to create additional novels in all of his series like The Last Gunfighter, Mountain Man, and Eagles, among others. This novel was inspired by Mr. Johnstone's superb storytelling.

All Kensington titles, imprints, and distributed lines are available at special quantity discounts for bulk purchases for sales promotion, premiums, fund-raising, and educational or institutional use.

If you purchased this book without a cover you should be aware that this book is stolen property. It was reported as "unsold and destroyed" to the Publisher and neither the Author nor the Publisher has received any payment for this "stripped book."

Special book excerpts or customized printings can also be created to fit specific needs. For details, write or phone the office of the Kensington Sales Manager: Kensington Publishing Corp., 119 West 40th Street, New York, NY 10018. Attn. Sales Department. Phone: 1-800-221-2647.

PINNACLE BOOKS, the Pinnacle logo, and the WWJ steer head logo Reg. U.S. Pat. & TM Off.

First Printing: January 2023
ISBN-13: 978-0-7860-4947-9

10 9 8 7 6 5 4 3 2 1

Printed in the United States of America

CHAPTER 1

"Pardon me, big boy, but ain't you known to the women of this town as a stud horse?"

The craggy, falsetto, and distinctly un-female voice that tried and failed to sound coquettish dissolved into a braying laugh before tailing off in a wet, phlegmy, coughing jag.

The man to whom the comment had been directed closed his tired eyes and gritted his teeth. His cheek muscles bunched and rippled in his bony jaw.

"Oh, don't pay him no mind, Hoke. Man's a fool." This time the voice in his ear was decidedly that of a woman. A fine-looker, too. She gripped his buckskin-fringed sleeve and tugged. "Come on, before you lose any more money."

"Yeah!" brayed the hoarse voice. "You keep on playing the way you always do and you won't never get any tonight! Or any other night!"

With a speed that forced looks of surprise on the faces of the patrons in the Top Dollar Public House and Gambling Emporium, the wiry man in the buckskins and low-crown, green felt topper with the coon tail whipped to his feet. He shoved back, spinning from the baize table where he had, indeed, been losing most of the cash he'd earned in the past several weeks working the freighting trail for Jasper's Hauling out of that very town of Denver City.

Most of the time it was lousy, snoozy work, but it kept Hokum Boone and his trail pard and best friend, Keller "Mac" MacCoole in spending money and out of trouble. Well, some of the time. While Mac was good about keeping to himself, laying low and living a quiet life when in town, Hoke wasn't keen on a life of fine dining and contemplation. Not while there were games tables to be tried, ladies to be wooed, and liquor to be sampled.

It was as if the whip-thin Hoke had somehow levitated and spun on an invisible string as he snatched the shirtfront of his tormentor. His quick moves and hot words commanded full attention.

"I know that every time I set down at the baize table, I'm fixing to be a pauper afore the night's out! And everybody else at the table knows it, too! But dang it, if I don't need to be reminded of it by some gap-toothed, knob-headed, unwashed, verminous, no-account, hair-faced, homely-as-homegrown-sin, sack of trash as you, Wallace Sturgis!"

Though Hoke was a solid head shorter than the big, wide-eyed man whose shirtfront he held balled in his ample, bony fist, there was no denying who had the upper hand. Hoke's sneer was steel and his eyes radiated a cobra-like gaze that rendered his opponent immobile, save for his quivering bottom lip.

The big man, Sturgis, slumped a little and his knees shook as if he were about to collapse from terror. His wide, fleshy face looked to be made of India rubber. "Aw, Hoke, I . . . I was funning you, Hoke!"

"Fun or no, you uncorked this bottle, and I aim to guzzle it down!"

Instead of jumping in to peel the spidery little man off the immobilized Sturgis, the two-dozen bystanders shoved back from tables, their chairs squawking. The piano stuttered to a halt as Abe, the player, responded to the tone of the room.

Chatter ceased and chips stopped clinking. Glasses were gripped tight. Manny the barkeep paused in his endless wiping of bar top and beer mugs.

This was not an unknown occurrence, though it never failed to surprise onlookers. Hokum Boone was generally a mild fellow of more-than-temperate demeanor. It took a whole lot of pushing and prodding and tugging and mocking and jeering and general annoyance before any response other than an aw-shucks smile and a roll of the eyes would be enough to prompt the man into a reaction.

But they all knew, too, that once he'd been nudged over that unseen edge, Boone's was a tight fist of rage all-but unstoppable. In fact, the only way to simmer him down was for his pard, big, calm Mac MacCoole, to step in.

"Somebody fetch Mac," mumbled Manny. But when he said it, he directed his gaze at Abe, the piano player. The arm-gartered man nodded, eyes wide. He made haste, the batwings swinging in his wake. He didn't want to miss out on a moment of the proceedings—Hoke's rages were infrequent but infamous.

Abe knew where to go to find Mac MacCoole. Two blocks over and one block east sat Marta Mae's Café. Everyone joshed that Mac was sweet on Marta Mae—a notion laughable because she was at least thirty years his senior.

What he did like, even more than her conversation, was her cooking. Most folks did, but Mac took all his meals there when he was in town, frequently joined by Hoke Boone when the wiry man had tired himself out at tables, at the bar, or in the beds of one of several doves of whom he was mighty fond.

Marta Mae, a buxom, red-face matron whose graying chestnut hair, piled high and lacerated with pins and sticks to hold it in place, doted on Mac perhaps a bit more than her many other regular customers.

She was forever smiling and shoving wisps of rogue hair from her face while she stirred, chunked wood in the stove, ladled up bowls of hot stew, or seared beefsteaks in a huge cast-iron pan perpetually sizzling and smoking. She kept a crew of four young women in motion as a conjurer might a handful of colored balls, all the while holding conversation with whoever was seated at the counter.

Mac always sat at the same corner table, away from the action. Throughout the day, if she saw Mac there, Marta Mae would bustle over to his table and plop down. He would always return her smile and mark the page in his book and resume whatever conversation they'd been having before her kitchen duties had pulled her away earlier.

Abe, the piano player, knew Mac would be there because it was still about dessert time, and everyone knew that Mac liked to wind up his day with a slice or two of pie and several cups of coffee.

Sure enough, he spied Mac across the room as he tugged open the door with the red-and-white checkered curtains. The little brass bell at the top jingled, and several heads swiveled about to see who was coming in.

Abe blinked at the brightness of the place. He spent most of his time in dark saloons. He played at three in town, and kept telling himself, even after six years of doing so, that he was saving up. One day soon he would open his own music conservatory to teach the promising—and less so—offspring of the town's wealthiest citizens the finer points of classical piano.

That he somehow found himself nearly penniless within a day after each wad of pay was handed to him did not seem to deter him from that dream. Each day, as he trudged home before dawn, he called up that long-ago ambition and, sighing, he'd doze off in his rented room.

Abe spied Mac at his usual table and had to walk right over to the big man to get his attention. Mac was the only one who'd not looked up to see who might have entered the café when the bell jingled.

Abe stood there and assessed the situation—Mac's pie plate was empty save for a few scant crumbs. His coffee cup was nearly empty, too, and his book, something by Dickens, he saw on the cover, was drawing close to its end, as well.

Might not be so bad to pull him away. Everybody knew how stone-faced he could be when he was called away from his pie, coffee, and book.

Without looking up, Mac said, "Hello, Abe. Hoke at it again?"

"Oh, hello, Mac. Uh, yeah, yeah, he is."

"Who with?" Mac slid a big finger in the book's pages and closed it, and looked up at the piano man.

"It's Sturgis again, Mac. Hoke, well, he lost a pile, which isn't a surprise, but Wallace, moron that he is, called Hoke on it, mocked him."

"Oh boy," said Mac. "Well, I have to talk with Hoke anyway."

Abe nodded. "Yeah. Last I saw, Hoke had Sturgis by the throat."

By then, Mac had set money beside his empty pie plate and was halfway to the door. Abe had been on this errand enough to know he wouldn't easily keep up with Mac as he scissored his long legs toward the saloon, so he lingered a moment, giving thought to a slice of what smelled like pecan pie. Oh, that would be lovely, all right. And then he remembered he was stone broke.

And besides, he'd miss out on all the fun. He made for the saloon, too, with Mac's big shape already far ahead in the gloom of the low lamp light of the street.

Abe arrived at the saloon in time to see Mac laying a hand on his pard's shoulder. "Hoke."

The whip of a man flinched and shrugged off the hand. "Ain't none of your affair, Mac."

"It is if I have to bail you out of jail. You're already into me for plenty."

"This rascal called me a . . . Oh, I don't recall. But he mocked me, that's the point. And a man can't let such things stand."

"I can't say I disagree with you, Hoke, but Sturgis here, you know what a lout he is. Right, Wallace?"

The struggling man nodded his purpling, fat face.

"And besides," continued Mac. "He's about passed out as it is. You want to have to pay him restitution on top of spending a night in the jail and paying those fees, and suffering through his mockery, too?"

Hoke adjusted his grip on Sturgis's collar. By then his big, shaggy opponent was all but prone on the grimy floor.

Abe could see that Sturgis wasn't quite unconscious. Yet. Another few seconds and he'd be there. The piano man couldn't say he was sorry to see the big, hairy, smelly fool get his comeuppance. And if he had to wish it from anybody on the man, it would be delivered from the mighty capable hands of Hokum Boone. Part of Abe wished Mac would leave well enough alone and let Hoke and Sturgis have at it, stacked fight though it was.

But he knew there would be no duking tonight. Hoke had gotten the upper hand early in the tussle, and Sturgis was too far in his cups to put up much of a fight.

In the end, it wound up peaceably, with half the room secretly hoping Mac would not have been found. Abe knew that a couple of them would whine at him later for being so diligent in tracking down Mac.

He'd ignore them like he always did and go back to pounding out lousy sing-along songs on the barely tuned piano and nothing much would change. Hoke would play poker again tomorrow, Trissy would dote on him, and Wallace Sturgis would be annoying people, his big shaggy face lapping up beer. Nothing changed.

Abe sighed and somebody shouted for a fresh round and the evening's former jollity kicked back in and soon the place was hopping once more.

Mac steered Hoke over to the bar and the two men leaned, commiserating. As well as anyone in town knew them, or thought they knew them, nobody really knew the odd pair. They were a mystery to everybody in so many ways. And yet it seemed that everybody in Denver City knew Mac MacCoole and Hoke Boone.

One thing they all knew for certain was that, for a fee, the two men could be hired, and frequently were. They'd be about town one day and night, then come the next night somebody wouldn't see Hoke in any one of several bars, or Mac would be missing from Marta Mae's Café.

Then news would filter out that "The Boys," as some folks, mostly women, referred to the two men, were out of town on some mysterious job somewhere. Folks rarely knew where the two went, or who they were working for until they returned, sometimes in as little as a week or sometimes not for a few months.

Once, about a year before, Abe recalled Mac and Boone had been gone nigh on six months. Then . . . bang, there they were one night, sitting in their usual places in the bar and at the café. Only difference that time was that it took Hoke longer than usual to blow through his earnings.

That and they both looked to have been dragged through a knot hole or two. Whatever job that had been, neither man spoke of it as they sometimes did in an off-handed way. That time, though, they were mum and seemed to linger about town longer before taking on a new job. As if they were healing somehow.

Abe didn't much care, but like so many other folks, he was fond of the two fellows. They were decent men, that's about the best way he could put it. He figured that was the best that could be said of anyone in their lives. He hoped he was thought of that way one day. He didn't think it likely, not that he was a bad fellow, but he didn't carry himself like those two.

Hoke and Mac were free with a smile, always willing to listen, always there should someone need extra hands to help with a task, and always the first to offer to buy you a cup of coffee or a glass of beer. As his own sainted mama would say, they were good peoples.

All this and more flitted through the piano man's mind as he pounded out yet another rendition of "Oh! Susannah," for the increasingly drunken crowd at the Top Dollar.

He didn't notice when Mac and Hoke slipped out. But he would notice, as would everyone else in town, the next night when neither man was amongst them. Nor would they be for some time to come.

CHAPTER 2

Mac and Hoke were an unlikely pair. In fact, rumor had it there was a time when they were not only not the best of friends as they were now, but sworn, mortal enemies. On the day they met, they circled each other and clashed in combat. Like death-seeking wolves, they were foamed at the fang and lathered in one another's gore, each desiring to end the life of his adversary, knowing they would also expire in the task.

Nobody in Denver City, home to the pair of town tamers—though the two bristled at that foolish title—knew the full story of the meeting of the two men. No matter how deep in his cups each of the men dove, neither spoke lightly of the other, and hardly ever of their past dealings. In that they were alike. In most other ways, Hokum Boone and Keller MacCoole were as different as day is from night.

What the nosy denizens of Denver City had to go on was rumor, and a few thin, infrequent utterances stretched and pushed and pulled, and used by the townsfolk to stitch together the fabled meeting of the two disparate characters.

Manny the barkeep told Abe the piano man, who told Starr and Beulah and Trissy, the floor ladies of the Top Dollar, that he'd heard from Shinny, over at the stage depot, that Hoke and Mac had met as enemies, Hokum Boone of the gray and Keller MacCoole of the blue, in a swamp at the Battle of Dunklee Ridge, one of the last, little-known clashes in the war . . .

A thick, blue fog, part gunfire stink and part cannon smoke filled with the echo of screams, crept in close, hugging low to the fetid muck and rotting stumpage. It served to mask the men from each other's sight, if not from their hearing. Each knew an enemy lurked in there, somewhere, and each was determined to do his duty.

It took the better part of an hour for them to close in on each other, each as wary as a cat-stalked rat.

The blistered mess of the battle in which they had both earlier fought, a battle still waging, left them ragged and wounded, with chests heaving and gore-slickened bodies trembling with fatigue. Yet each had pursued the enemy in great numbers along the battle's periphery. And these pursuits led them to the far western edge of the battle proper.

They realized that the sounds of the fight—thundering cannonade, screams of agonized, terrorized horses, howls of men, the ripped apart and the dying, the blinded and the addled, the *pock-pock-pock* of random rifle fire—had dwindled and all but pinched off the deeper they ventured into the dank, dim swamp.

Mac MacCoole knew with trusted instinct that an enemy lurked nearby in the death fog.

Hokum Boone knew the same, felt it in his gizzard, a quivering that had never played him false.

Both were seasoned fighters, and promotions in rank had

several times been offered to each man, each time refused, the distinctions as lost on them as their own families had been lost to them in the war, this reviled, protracted litany of blood lettings.

On that fateful day, each took his time, vowing to not let the other live, even though each doubted he himself would live to see the sun grow dim. They accepted this and advanced on each other, slowly stalking, minute after silent, dripping minute.

Their weaponry had been reduced to a belt tomahawk for Hokum and a dagger-blade hip knife for Mac. Step after squelching step, muck pearling and dribbling as they each moved in the stealth of a born stalker, each closed in on the other.

A water moccasin slicked its way, switchbacking in silence, making for Mac. He saw the dull glint of its watery trail and paused, waiting.

Light in the swamp was scant, and though a towering man, he bent low, eyeing above the water's surface for any tell-tale movement of man.

The snake only knew its urge to feed, to defend, to kill, knew the big beast offered something, somehow, and made for the rippling movement of the creature before him.

The snake held a moment and raised its meaty, blunt head, tongue flicking, and worked it side to side, sensing with predation. It pulsed forward.

Mac waited for it to drift closer, waited for the head to show itself within reach.

He struck with the speed and accuracy of a tensed arrow released. The snake's big head grinned even as its maw widened and its fangs flexed and glistened. And then the head *blupped* below the surface of the thick water.

The slight splashing sound caused Mac to wince. He knew it would enable his enemy to find him as sure as if he had taken up whistling. He guessed that his enemy, who by now he had come to think was as adept at stalking as himself, would circle wide to the southeast, given the terrain surrounding the swamp, and come up on him from behind.

This would not do.

At the same time, through the thick gauze of smoke and fog and humid stink that clung low like a sopping clot of wool, the other living man in the swamp—for there were a number of Union and Confederate dead from the days-long skirmish, their bodies bloating and bled out and floating, barely—seized in place when a slight splashing sounded somewhere ahead.

It was low, soft, and quick . . . and human. Hokum Boone knew he would soon meet the maker of this sound. It told him a great many things, most of all, it told him to alter his stalking route. He would cut southeastward and around, wide, and come upon his foe in that manner. No doubt, though, the man would be aware of this. So be it.

The water was thick, as though Hoke were wading through drool. He had one hand on the head of his belt 'hawk, one held out before him, palm down at gut height, feeling for anything that might strike, snag, or otherwise interrupt his hunt.

Oddly, and yet he knew he would feel this way when his time came, Hokum Boone was calm and cool about the impending battle with this mystery foe. It would be a fight to the death, and he would give no quarter.

Hoke bent lower and peered between the foul swamp water and the sag of thick fog. He saw nothing save for the same low glow of daylight somehow allowed to illumine this dreary place. He had not expected to see much other than the dark shadow of a mossy snag, or the ropy, green-wet hide of a swamp tree jutting through the fog.

He marveled now there were no sounds to speak of from

the battle, east of the swamp. Why was that? When he'd menaced his prey in this direction hours before, he had expected to make his way back to the pulsing heart of the battle. And yet he was still here, and the battle was . . . what? No longer? Had it moved away so swiftly that sound no longer carried?

Was the swamp so engulfed by this awful stinking fog that it clouded out all sound? It was true there was no birdsong. Then again, he reasoned, were he a bird, he would not venture near so desolate a place. But not even the occasional rattle of sticks or slide and splash of snakes or gators or rats?

A slight sound, perhaps not even that, perhaps it was only a movement, the still air agitated enough to shift the foggy cloud, pulled Mac's attention. He smiled, for he was correct. His foe was not so skilled that he could not be counted on to do something predictable. The man was circling wide.

Without further warning or thought, he sensed the appearance of the man behind him. The foe was still too far to see him, of course, but he was there. This impressed Mac because he had counted on having more time to fully turn, to swing his gaze. He'd given himself away, he knew, by slicing off the head of that damned snake. But there was nothing for it. It had to be done.

Mac sensed the man closing in. Too close to shift fully around and face him. He'd sold the fellow short but moments before. Good to know—he wouldn't do it again.

He palmed the thick bone handle of his broad-blade hip knife, a modified Bowie he kept keen-edged and gleaming. It had been made to his specifications by an old, blind blacksmith two years before the war and it had served him well since.

And then the mysterious presence was there, to his left, emerging from out of the fog, a slight, steely figure, moving through the water with nary a sound.

"Waiting for you," said Mac, in a low voice that the smoke of battle had reduced to a deep, ragged growl—gravel ground against steel.

"Likewise," said the stranger, his own voice equally filled with cold menace.

Mac had intended to make the first play, but the stranger surprised him and lunged, a tomahawk gripped in his hand.

The move was effective, nearly catching Mac in the left arm, but it was clumsy, too. As Mac spun, the knee-height water swirling as he did so, he guessed that even after all that stealth that brought the stranger to him, the smaller man had likely snagged a boot on something unseen below the water's surface.

Mac dealt a nick high on the man's left side, but he didn't think he'd drawn blood. In the dim light of the afternoon sky that made its way through the gnarled, mossy trees and down to the swamp, Mac saw that the man wore not the standard gray Confederate uniform he'd expected, but a tunic of buckskin. That told him the wiry Reb was likely a backwoodsman, hard and keen and schooled in the ways of the woods.

The Reb's leathers couldn't be any heavier, soaked as both men were, than Mac's blue wool garb. He dispensed with his jacket back in the field, and had been mostly pleased at not wearing it, so hot and heavy was it. But now, in a hand fight with blades, perhaps to the death, he wished he had the thick garment as armor.

The smaller man was quick, Mac would give him that, but he didn't seem to think out his thrusts and attacks, nor did he keep in mind that Mac had a longer reach.

Early on this helped Mac's blade taste buckskin and he was certain, blood.

Then Mac's right boot heel fetched on a root or some such, and he foundered, his left arm windmilling. The smaller man used this moment to dart in on Mac's flailing left side. He shoved Mac's arm aside and lunged, earning a gash in the big man's grimy shirt through which blood flowed down the left side of his chest.

"Gaah," growled the man, clenching his teeth and regaining his footing and setting himself for an attack. He was angry but he knew that attitude, if not tempered with careful thought, would earn him nothing but pain and death.

As the fight wore on, they circled, slowly losing their concern about stealth and tactics. Over the long minutes of the back-and-forth fracas, in which neither man felt himself the superior fighter, they roved, as if by unknown mutual consent, to higher ground.

Soon they stood atop a small island large enough to continue their death match. And so, minute on minute, hour after hour, the fight ground on.

"Enslaving another man? You call that just?" MacCoole lunged once more, knowing it was a foolish move, his strength all-but spent, yet his sputtering rage allowed for no less an action.

Luckily for him, Hokum Boone was equally as knackered. The buckskin-clad man did his best not to wobble on his wiry legs, despite his muscles twitching and jerking on their own.

The big man's comment rankled him and prodded him, parrying his foe's weak thrust with an equally flaccid move of his own, his 'hawk now as heavy as a bar of lead. "You Bluebellies . . . you all think we're fighting to protect slavery? I look like a slave owner to you?" Boone dropped low, the heat of his argument spicing his move, if only for a moment.

It was enough. He landed a gash—lucky, but he'd take it anyway.

The big Northerner sucked in a quick breath, gritting his teeth. "Damn," he hissed, his free hand jerking of its own accord to clap on the fresh wound. It was the worst so far among the half-dozen smaller, slighter cuts the wiry little Reb had dealt him.

If he hadn't also landed an equal number on the Grayback's body, puncturing those odd buckskins, he might have been more worried. They were well matched, though perhaps not equally exhausted. Hence, the fresh wound. Mac held his ground, giving in to the fresh wash of hot pain . . . and made as if to wait for it to pass.

The little man made his move, as Mac knew he would. He knew this because were he in the same situation, had he dealt a decent blow to the Reb, he would have not wasted time, but would have darted in, albeit with wariness, and would have tried to finish off the fellow.

Mac didn't have to wait for long. The Reb leaned back, then swung wide to Mac's left and tried to deliver another gash with the little belt axe.

Mac guessed this might happen, and, gripping tight to his knife's handle, he feinted low to his left, then he struck. The upward swing he gave the knife should have been enough to drive up and in, high under the wiry fellow's breadbasket.

But two things happened—his strength was more sapped than he thought, and the smaller man, the Reb, in his attempt to get closer, had tried to duck down and scoot to the side at the same time.

Mac should have known this, should have seen it coming, but between the damnable fog, the pain, and his lack of strength, his blow did barely half of what he'd intended. As it turned out, it was enough.

The smaller man howled, a blood-stilling sound meant for the mouth of a cave-dwelling savage, and sucked in a breath, halted well within striking distance once more. The men held their latest wounds, chests heaving, limbs trembling, sopping wet with hot sweat, and there in the fetid swamp, they stared at each other.

There was less vitriol for the other than there might otherwise be, less raw, animal anger at the general foolishness of the protracted mess someone who'd never set polished brogan on a battlefield had dared to call a "civil transaction."

For that brief time, there was none of that. Instead, this was a fight between two men who knew they had each met their match, an admirable adversary.

Neither man could continue, at least not until he'd rested, but neither were they fool enough to turn their back or even lower their eyes, not for a moment. And so they each heaved out big, trembling breaths, eyed the other, and let slow minutes work their even slower temporary cure.

It would have to be enough to let them resume their death match, for they regarded this fight as such. One in which neither man would survive. They eyed each other on that muck-punched island in the midst of the swamp.

Then they each heard a lone voice shout, from east of them. It drew nearer, then other voices, and shots resuming—volleying, scattered sounds, some drifting away, others closing in.

For the last half hour of their fight, during which each man had grunted and lunged, panted and gasped, there had been no other sound, save for their own squelching bootsteps. No far-off battle sounds had reached them. But now they had resumed.

That didn't solve the mystery of why it had grown quiet for so long, but it did ease Mac's mind to know something outside of the swamp was alive.

Hokum Boone risked a glance eastward and swore he caught sight of a body moving through dim light at the swamp's edge. He cut his eyes back to the big man, who also had looked to the swamp.

"What's that, you suppose?" said Hokum.

The voice from the swamp's edge became two, then more. But they were not the sounds of anger, of battle, of killing, of bloodlust. They were . . . shouts of joy? How was that possible? Were those men demented?

Mac had seen such, soldiers losing their minds in the midst of battle, giggling without control. He'd seen more than one wander out, unarmed, into the thick of the fracas and, of course, get shot for that moment of madness. But several men at once?

"It's a Reb . . . and a Bluebelly! Standing beside each other. See 'em?" Hokum raised a trembling hand and pointed.

"My word," said Mac. "But . . ."

He had no time for anything else because one of the men, hands cupped before his mouth, shouted, "You men there!" He waved at them. "Cease fire! Cease fire! The war has ended! I repeat . . . the war . . . is . . . over!"

If there were words that each of the two bloodied combatants had longed to hear it was those. An elusive wisp of hope that had haunted their dreams, peppered their weary thoughts, day on day, week after week, month on year. And yet, how could it be true?

Hoke looked at Mac, eyes narrowed. "You heard what I heard?"

Mac nodded. "I think so."

"You reckon it's a game? A trick?"

"I know what you know, nothing more."

As if in response to their disbelief, the other of the two newcomers raised his hands and shouted through them, "It's true. We've come to terms! The war is over!"

The first man shouted, "Come on up here, men!" He beckoned with an exaggerated arm gesture then stood conversing with the other man beside him, one with arms folded, the other with his hands on his hips.

Mac and Boone straggled up out of the murk of the swamp's edge. The two men awaiting them were haggard, muddy-faced, and bloody-handed.

One, a Union officer, though Mac wasn't certain he knew the man's name, so begrimed was the fellow, eyed them up and down. "I'd heard there were men in the swamp. Then a pair of scouts from each side, sent to locate survivors in the environs of the battle, came back with reports of seeing someone scuffling down there. As Colonel Shanks here and myself had matters to discuss anyway, we used the time walking down here to talk."

"You . . ." Mac swallowed and tried again. "You two are not fighting? One side won and the other is what? Taken prisoner?"

The Confederate officer beside the Union officer sighed and dragged a hand down his face, his fingers scratching at his unruly matted beard. "Yes, yes, I expect I'll be his prisoner soon enough."

"Not right now, sir," said the Union officer. "Now." He tugged out a battered flask from his tunic. "Now we toast to the end of the vile war, praise God."

The Confederate officer nodded wearily, and a half smile crept onto his face. "If I've ever seen men looking worse off than the two of you and still alive, I can't recall it." He rested a bloody hand on his sword's hilt.

Hoke half expected him to draw the blade and lay low the enemies about him. But he didn't.

The Union officer also rested his hand on his sword's hilt. Neither officer made a move to take anyone as prisoner.

"This for real, sir?" said Hokum to his Colonel, seeking the truth in the man's eyes. He'd always felt certain he could determine a man's honest state of mind by looking hard into the man's eyes.

"Yes, Boone. Yes, it is. We learned of the ceasefire some

time ago, hours back. Didn't you men notice the fighting had stopped?"

Mac and Hoke both shrugged at the same time, saw the other doing so, and could not help themselves. They each smiled a tired smile at each other.

"I don't know," said Hoke. "I guess. I …"

"It got away from us."

"Yeah, that's about it."

Neither Mac nor Hoke had to ask who it was who'd taken the day on the battlefield, nor who had taken the full war. The Confederate States Army had been losing ground for a long time, and this, they supposed, was the inevitable outcome. Still, it was odd, all so odd. It would take time to think through.

"Are there others down there?" The Union officer nodded past them toward the swamp.

"Not alive, no sir," said Mac.

"All right, then. We'll send men down tomorrow morning to retrieve what bodies we may. For now, we best get you two up to our respective camps. There will be quiet revels, but there will be no celebration. Not while we are in the presence of our dead."

Neither man would debate that.

The officers walked ahead of them back up the long hill.

"Oh my," said Hoke, wincing as he picked his way up the slope, doing his best to avoid looking at the sloppy heap of two dead soldiers, one from each side. They were piled against a boulder, looking as though they had tumbled together, locked in combat, down the pocked pasture, only to die in each other's arms somehow—enemies in life, tangled together at their last.

"Could have been us," said the big man to his right.

"Yeah." Hoke forced his legs to work another two steps upslope. "Course, there'd only have been one of us. I'd have walked away from it." He cut his eyes to the big man's face. He was rewarded with a surprised look.

"Oh, not hardly," said the big Union soldier. "I don't lose a thing when I set my mind to it."

"Always a first time."

The big man offered up a tired chuckle. "Guess we'll never know."

"The day ain't over yet, fella."

Mac looked at the wiry Reb, not certain if he was joshing him, wondering if the little man was going to resume their fight right there on the slope, peace or no. But the buckskin-clad fellow was grinning.

"Tell you what, big boy," said the wiry man in buckskins. "You're lucky I hadn't yet called up my reserve strength. Was saving it to polish you off." He nodded.

Mac paused, readjusted the hand holding the kerchief to his wound. "For a scrawny fellow, you sure are chatty. And full of beans."

Hoke winked. "Yep, and don't you forget it." He offered a bloodied hand. "Name's Hokum Boone. Friends call me Hoke."

Mac took the hand with his own equally bloodied paw. "I'm MacCoole, Keller MacCoole. My friends call me Mac."

Hoke nodded. "Okay then . . . Mac."

"Good to know you, Hoke."

CHAPTER 3

"Lucky for you I let you live." Hokum Boone sluiced a rope of thick brown chaw juice out the right side of his begrimed mouth, then dragged an equally begrimed cuff of his buckskin tunic across his beard.

He smiled in appreciation of the offended look the diamondback flashed him as the spittle spattered the dusty sandstone on which it rested, soaking in the August morning's steely heat.

"Who are you talking to, Hoke?"

Mac stood from bending over the boulder where his shaving mirror was propped, patting himself dry with a small towel he kept in his traps for that purpose.

Rigorous attendance to his daily ablutions was something his pard, Hokum Boone, never understood and frequently chided him about. Hoke's idea of bathing consisted of splashing a hand scoop of water over his face and letting it trail down, once every couple-three days. Whether he needed it or not.

Mac was of the opinion that Hoke needed such water-based frolicking on a daily basis, and then some.

"That ol' snake yonder. I normally would take him for grilling later, but as it's early and I am already stretched tight to the hide with biscuits and meat, why, I felt kindly toward him." He stood full height—still a good head shorter than Mac, and puffed his bird chest. "Never let it be said of Hokum J. Boone that he was not a kindly soul."

Mac shook his head. "J.? I thought your middle name was Felton?"

Hoke shrugged. "Might be it is, might be it ain't."

"You aren't sure?"

"Never said that. But now you mention it, it ain't a crime not to have a middle name, is it?"

"No, no, I'd guess not." Mac drained the last of his cup of coffee, gone mostly cold. In their years riding the trail together, in all manner of scrapes, he had never grown tired of the frequent, strange conversations he had with Hoke Boone. Frustrated, annoyed, bewildered, sure, but never tired or bored.

"Glad you liked the biscuits," said Mac. It was something he never tired of making or eating on the trail. Hoke was a good meat-maker and a passable cook, but his heart was not in the task of cooking. He could, by gaw, eat, as he put it, and proved it, every day.

While Mac was a large man with a large and discerning appetite, Hoke was smaller, thin, and wiry, with an appetite at times as robust as Mac's. At other times, he would take nothing but water, coffee, perhaps a bite of elk jerky. And that would last him for days.

"Time to saddle up," said Hoke, stuffing back into his floppy saddlebag the sleeve of his spare long-underwear shirt.

"Why do you bother lugging along extra togs on our forays, Hoke?" Mac already knew the reply. It was the same question he asked early on in each outing. "You never change your clothes anyway."

Hoke rolled his eyes and let his hands drop. "If I told you

once, I told you a hundred and four times, I wear buckskins."

He didn't continue, as if the response had settled the matter, so Mac pressed the point, as he always did. It had become a ritual conversation for them most mornings on the trail as they packed up and saddled their mounts.

"Wearing a full suit of buckskins does not exempt you from bathing, you know."

"Ha, now see? There's where you are wrong, mister smarty book-reader!" Hoke smiled and shook his head. "Seems to me a fellow who's spent as much time as you have in and around books ought to know by now of the natural stink-killing properties of buckskins."

Mac said nothing for a few moments, long enough to get on the far side of Lincoln, his tall Appaloosa stallion. It wouldn't do to insult Hokum Boone and not be able to hide behind something as substantial as a big horse when the squawking little man cut loose.

"Somebody forgot to tell your buckskins. Then again, maybe yours are faulty."

Their battered gray coffee pot sailed over Lincoln, who flicked a long ear. The pot missed Mac's ducked head by a good six inches. It clattered on the ground behind him. "You're the reason we go through so many coffee pots."

"I always pay for a new one, don't I?" Hoke smoothed a striped blanket on the back of his paint, Chummy, who danced and offered a slicing hoof at whatever might be dumb enough to stand behind him.

"Mmm-hmm, with money you borrow from me."

"Well. I pay you back, don't I?"

"Sometimes." Mac could care less about money he lent his pard, for Hoke mostly kept a tally and repaid him, if not in cash, in kind. Besides, there were far more important things in life than money, especially between friends.

Hoke was a lightning-fast hand with a weapon, especially

one of his hideout pistols. Mac wasn't certain, even after all these years, how many the man carried. He thought maybe Hoke carried three little derringers about his person.

And then there was his hip knife, his single-barrel, sawed-off shotgun, a blunt, modified thing Boone had toted for years. And of course, he couldn't forget what Hoke called his "widowmakers," a perennial assortment of dynamite sticks. He generally kept a few here and there in his gear and in his tunic, "in case." Those deadly things had saved their bacon more than once.

As for Hoke's part, he never had cause to worry when Mac was around. The big man was armed with that same big, bone-handle Bowie he'd had when they first tangled in that swamp. Hoke had felt its deadly bite. Plus, Mac had added a Henry repeater and a Colt's Dragoon hand cannon to his arsenal.

And of course, they both lugged enough solid, hempen rope for nooses, or what Hoke liked to refer to as "dance partners."

And of course, Mac was smart as a building full of books, though he'd never tell him such. Seemed like that big goober could spout something fancy some long-dead fellow had said, and dang if it didn't apply to their situation nearly every time. It was an amusing trait.

Sometimes Mac recited poetry, though most of that wasn't to Hoke's taste. Too many flowery words that meant less than nothing. Why not say a thing and be done with it instead of perfuming the air with silliness and foofaraw?

More than once, Hoke openly lamented for the world. Mostly the people in it. He had known a good many of them and a good many critters, too. He had to say that without a doubt, the critters that didn't walk on two legs (and weren't birds) were far smarter and happier than people ever would be.

Hoke had a head full of songs and poems, too, naturally,

but mostly they were bawdy tales of flirtatious women and their various misdeeds. He swore he knew half of the ladies in those ditties. Still, he'd offer the songs up now and again, and Mac never seemed to tire of them.

These were Hoke's favorite times, away from town and all its temptations once again, making for a brand-new, never-known-to-them situation that required their eyeballing and tough-dealing.

They'd never advertised, never sought the reputations they had earned, certainly never wanted to be called "town tamers," which the weak-minded citizens and newspapermen all insisted on calling them. Foolishness for the most part, but it was good when they were able to genuinely help folks out of tough situations. And even better when folks felt all warm and grateful and paid them more than their agreed-on price.

Not like that last job, hired guards for that freighting outfit, Jasper's Hauling. Bah, nothing but boredom and more of the same, riding on a spine-wracking freight wagon for three weeks, hauling junk for folks in one direction and ore and payroll and sacks of meal and kegs of nails in the other direction.

Still, Jasper himself was true to his word and paid their rate. He'd hired them on because he'd been given what he called "trustworthy information" that somebody was set on robbing him blind one of these days.

But the rate he paid them wasn't one that could be sustained, no matter how good business was for the freighters these days. Still, their presence for three weeks made Jasper feel like he'd solved his problem.

Afterward, they agreed Jasper was mad in the head and would likely be robbed one of these days just the same.

"Speaking of money," said Hoke, long minutes after Mac had thought they'd left that topic behind.

Mac suppressed a smile and rooted in his breast pocket for a cigarillo.

"I have got to stop squandering all my hard-earned cash at the games tables." Hoke rubbed his head and readjusted his hat. "I don't have a concern where the wine, women, and whiskey are concerned, but that faro will be the death of me."

"Not to mention poker."

"Oh, now, poker, that's Satan's own game!" Hoke shook his head in disbelief. "I ain't smart enough for poker."

"You're smart enough, all right. You're just not patient enough to pursue the nuances of the game."

"Oh, and you are?"

"Yep."

"Then why don't I ever see you settin' around the baize?"

"I choose not to waste my money on games of chance. I'm saving up."

Hoke snorted. "What are you saving for?"

"You know." Mac smiled and sighed. "A fine place in the mountains by a lake where I can fish and hunt and spend my time enjoying quiet, cerebral pursuits."

"You are an odd one, Mac MacCoole, and no doubt."

"You know, if you saved your money instead of squandering it on fleeting passions, you'd be better off in the long run. Why, you could buy the neighboring property and we could visit and discuss matters of import."

"Oh, Lordy, take me now," said Hoke. "I'll keep on as I am, thank you. And at the end of my days, I'll have something to recall that'll bring a smile to my face. But what will you have? Memories of long, boring days reading books and fishing and . . . thinking? Pah!"

Mac smiled. They rode in silence for a few minutes, then Mac said, "You know, I had to send a telegram telling them we were taking the job."

"Yeah, you said that already."

"While I was there, I happened to see another one, in the outgoing stack."

"Well, that's what made you a good spy in the war. You're nosy."

They were quiet once more, then Hoke said, "Well? You didn't tell me that for no reason. That ain't like you."

Mac smiled. "The telegram I saw was addressed to a Mrs. Dorinda Cutty."

Hoke stiffened and looked ahead.

Mac continued. "Don't you have a sister named Cutty?"

Finally, Hoke said, "What of it?"

Mac shrugged. "Oh, no reason."

"Ain't there room in your head for coincidence?"

"Sure, there is, sure. It's that this telegram was sent from one Hokum, signed, 'your loving brother.' Hmm, wonder how many folks are named Hokum in Denver City. Now, if there was another one, that would be quite the coincidence, wouldn't it?"

"Oh, all right! You know I send my sister money! You know I do. Why, she's got all them squallerin' mouths to feed and that useless slug she married went and drowned himself doing one of those things you love so well, fishing. Ha! See what that'll get you?"

"If you're not drunk, it will get you a full belly," said Mac. "And I'm only joshing you about the telegram. I admire the fact that you send money to your kin. It's an admirable trait, Hoke. About the only one you have . . ."

"Well, it's one more than you have, you muscled-up ox."

Both men smiled.

Long, silent minutes passed as they rode. Then Hoke spoke. "Hey, Mac, speaking of that telegram, what's this job about, anyway? What'd that first telegram say again?"

Mac nodded, knowing his pard had been too deep in his

anger and in his cups to have paid attention to what he'd told him that night at the bar.

Mac sipped from his canteen and recorked it. "Hang on." He reached into his left vest pocket and lifted out a thrice-folded yellow piece of paper. He unfolded it and read:

> *To: Messrs. Boone and MacCoole STOP Services required immediately STOP Brimstone, northern Utah Territory STOP Double fees plus bonus on successful completion STOP If you agree, more to follow STOP*

He paused, reread it again in silence, then held it out for Hoke, who shook his head and sneered at the paper as if it were something contagious. Mac refolded the telegram and tucked it into his pocket.

"That's it? That's all they said? Nothing else?" Boone had stopped Chummy in the trail and looked at Mac.

"Yep. Except for the follow-up, which was rough directions to get there, precious little else. What were you expecting? We don't usually get more notice than that anyway."

Hoke urged Chummy into a walk once more and shook his head. "We're getting soft, I tell you. Letting folks take advantage of our good nature."

CHAPTER 4

The second morning on the trail promised to be another fine blue day from first to last. Other than stopping for water and to rest the horses, plus their midday coffee break—neither man would forego a cup of hot coffee of an afternoon—they usually rode on through, until by an unspoken mutual agreement they drifted to a halt for the evening.

It was still morning, another hour or two before they paused for coffee. In the midst of their usual trail silence, Hoke said, "War's been over how long?" He squinted over at Mac.

The tall, raw-boned man beside him drummed his chin and was about to reply when Hoke again spoke. "Exactly."

"You didn't let me answer."

"No matter, we both know the answer."

"You know," said Mac. "Talking with you is like trying to convince a ringtail with hydrophobia to take up knitting."

"That don't make no sense."

"Exactly."

"Well," said Hoke, eyebrows drawn in thought. "I'll take it as a compliment, then."

"You would," said Mac, smiling and tugging out a cigarillo.

"Gonna fire up one of them stinkers, eh?"

"Yep, I planned to. Problem?"

"No, no. Not if you want to drive off any game we might scare up for suppertime."

Mac set fire to the cigarillo, puffed voraciously a few times, then plumed the blue cloud over at his friend. "The way you shoot, it won't much matter."

A little while later, with a fresh quid of chaw bulging out his cheek, Hoke said, "How did you come to smoke those things, anyway?"

Mac pulled the thin brown cigar from his mouth and regarded it. "Developed a taste for them, that's all. Why do some folks prefer whiskey over beer?"

"Or big women over them with matchstick legs."

They rode in silence a moment longer, then Hoke said, "You can't really like them things, now, can you?"

Mac sighed. "You got me. I only smoke them because they annoy you so much."

"See? I knew it, I knew it. You ought to try yourself some chaw. It's far more civilized and don't stink at all."

Mac puffed a moment. "If your idea of civilized is drooling all over yourself, I will kindly demure. Besides, if I want civilized, I'll puff my briar pipe, which I normally save for reading. But I thank you for the offer of chaw."

Hoke let loose with a long sluice of spittle and dragged a cuff across his mouth. "Some folks got no sense."

After four and a half days in the saddle, they came within sight of the town they were aiming for. "There it is," said Mac. They'd both reined up atop a low rise and gazed down the valley before them. "Brimstone. Utah Territory."

Boone whistled, then spit. "Wow, that is one purty little valley. It's like a painting."

Mac nodded his head. "Yes, yes, it is. I know it's August, height of growing season, but I don't believe I've seen a greener or prettier little farming set-up before." He looked at Boone. "What say we ride on down there and see what the worm is in this shiny apple?"

Boone smiled. "Don't mind if I do!"

They heeled their mounts into a trot and wound their way down a long, wide trail from the east that married with a similar trail from the southeast. Where the two tracks converged, they widened into an even broader roadway that, judging from the wheel ruts and fresh mounds of horse dung, appeared to be well used.

To their right and left stretched vast fields of crops, northward to a river running east-west. Beyond the fields, the land rose on both sides in forested slopes that bore sign of timber harvesting. All about them, as if they were riding through a vast, green bowl, close-up and far-off hills became mountains topped with peaks jutting high and hazy.

"Look yonder," said Boone, nodding ahead.

Mac followed his pard's eagle-like gaze. Hokum Boone was blessed with eyesight far keener than any Mac had ever seen in a fellow, and certainly better than his own average ability.

After squinting a moment, sure enough, he spied dark and light shapes that moved among the tidy rows of corn and what appeared to be squash and greens of some sort. The more he looked, the more he saw there were many other types of crops, including grains.

As they rode, they saw more shapes that turned out to be people, adults both male and female. The men wore black trousers of rough, thick cloth, and white shirts with sleeves worn full length and buttoned at the cuffs. Black braces striped up over their bent shoulders. Their faces all wore full beards and their heads were topped with wide-brim black hats.

The women were garbed all in black, long dresses that showed little flesh save for quick flashes of the backs of hands as they stooped to tug out errant plants, pick off dead leaves, and hoe between the rows. The heads of the women were swaddled in large bonnets pulled tight, hiding their faces so that neither Mac nor Boone were able to glimpse a female face.

Several times one of the men stood, as if to stretch his back, and visored his eyes, staring at the newcomers.

Boone waved. "How are you on this fine day?"

Mac looked at him, brows drawn. "What did you say?"

"Thought I'd try to say something you might say. Beat you to it, didn't I?" Boone smiled and nodded. "You're slowing down in your dotage."

"I noticed you didn't get a response." Mac gestured before them. "Let's ask this fellow."

About fifty feet ahead, a man stood by a barrel atop a sturdy wooden table. He dippered a ladle of water from the barrel and drank it down. They were abreast of him before he noticed them.

"Howdy, fella." Boone nodded. "This here Brimstone?"

The man looked at them with alarm, then quickly replaced the wooden lid on the barrel, hung the dipper on a peg, and hurried back into the crop rows.

"Well," said Mac. "That's interesting."

"What's it tell you?"

"It tells me the mystery has already begun. It's too early to speculate, though. But at least one thing's answered for us." Mac pointed a big finger ahead.

Boone and Mac passed a demure signpost with the word, "Brimstone," and an arrow pointing in the direction they were headed.

"Good," said Boone. "As shut-mouth as they all are, I thought for a minute there we'd found the wrong town."

They rode on in silence for a few minutes more, then, in a low voice, as they were still within sight of yet more folks bent over and working the crops, Mac said, "Boone, what do you make of these folks?"

Boone shrugged. "Hard to say. Religious, I'd say. Mostly that's a good thing, though sometimes it can take on a stunty angle. I seen all sorts. Remind me to tell you about my cousin, Hod, some time."

"I thought you did. He was the one with the snakes, right?"

"No, no, weren't you listening? That was Hoddy."

"Oh, I hear the distinction now, sure."

"Darn right you do . . ."

But that was all the squabbling they had time for, because they rounded a bend in the roadway and took in what they found. Where before the roadsides were lined with crops, they now gave way to unpainted two-story cottages fronted with unpainted picket fencing and walks leading to plain-face doors.

As tidy as the homes looked, they bore no adornments, no ornamentations to show the occupants had individual tastes. And for all the agricultural skill the citizenry of Brimstone obviously possessed, the front yards of their homes were bereft of shrubbery, no flowering bushes as the two men might expect to see, given what bountiful fields they had ridden among.

"Odder and odder," mumbled Boone.

"Yep," said Mac.

The cottages, far between, soon gave way to larger buildings, more numerous, and fronted with signs the men were most familiar with: Gristmill, Smithy, Joinery, Bakehouse, Mercantile, Stable, yet none were personalized to show who owned what. As if they were all owned by no one and everyone at the same time.

Mac heard a low, thin groan rise up from Boone's lips.

"I don't see a saloon," said the wiry fellow.

Mac smiled, but he, too, felt a twinge of concern. If this job carried on for some time, well, that would be a mighty long dry spell for his pard. He was not concerned so much for himself as for what he would have to endure from Hoke, who was not used to life without a nip at the end of a long day.

Tucked back on a lane behind what was now obvious to them as the main street stood a plain-wood building with a bell on top and broad steps. Two doors at the top of the steps stood propped half open and they heard the drone of voices from within.

"Schoolhouse?" said Boone.

"Must be," said Mac. "Because there's the church." He nodded across the way, to their left. Set back an equal distance from that side of the main street stood a large timber building, also unpainted, with a bell tower atop.

Boone whistled low once more. "That's one big ol' church."

"And that," said Mac, nodding ahead once more, this time at the far end of the street. "Is a big ol' house."

Boone's gaze settled on a massive mansion squatting there, as if daring anyone to venture past. Though at first glance a completed structure, the north side and part of the east side, facing them, wore scaffolding, indicating the big building was, perhaps, a work in progress.

Unlike the other structures in town, this one, at least in comparison with its plain siblings, was an ostentatious affair. It was painted a deep brown, perhaps stained, Mac couldn't be certain, and the shutters and all trim work were deep black, accented throughout with wrought iron.

The building sported three stories with two towers anchoring the front, square affairs with mansard roofs surmounted with steel crosses. The windows, of which there were not many, boasted stained glass. As they rode up to the wide, front steps, they noted that the largest windows showed scenes of suffering and torment.

"Dark deeds," said Boone.

"The wages of sin," said Mac, guiding his horse to the hitch rail. He slid down and stood off to one side of the wide staircase, gazing upward at a wide front porch supported with vast columns entwined with carved serpents.

As he stepped down out of the saddle, Boone said, "My word, but this place is grim."

Before Mac could respond, a man's voice, from above, spoke. "Indeed, sir. And that is as it should be—for is not life but a vicious journey of vileness and treachery? Wickedness and degradation?"

They looked up to see a portly man dressed in black emerge from the shady depths of the porch. He stood at the top of the steps, hands clasped behind his back, staring down at them. His form was fleshy, with the look of not having had to work hard in some time.

Unlike the other men they'd seen on their way in, this one didn't wear a beard or completely black clothing—his vest bore blue striping. He also didn't appear to be red-faced and overheated by hard work, as did the other men.

"I had prayed," said the man in a raised voice equal to his raised hands, "that you would arrive, gentlemen. And my faith has been rewarded with your presence."

"Well," said Mac. "I'm glad we could accommodate you."

The man nodded, not quite smiling, and regarded them for a long, awkward moment. Finally, Mac broke the silence. "I'm Keller MacCoole, folks call me Mac. And this is Hokum Boone, my business associate."

Boone smiled. "Folks call me Hoke. If I like them, that is." He winked.

The man did not smile.

"We saw some folks in the fields on our way in." Boone looked behind him up the long, broad street. "But where is everybody else? Town looks deserted."

"We have completed a prayer service. Soon you will see Brimstone begin to stir once more."

"So them folks out in the fields, they're not the praying sort?" said Boone.

"On the contrary. They spend the entire day in silent, working prayer. Tomorrow they will tend to the town's affairs while the people in town today will work in the fields. The church is rarely unoccupied."

"Sounds like you have an equitable arrangement, then." Mac continued to stare at the man.

This comment appeared to unnerve the pudgy fellow. For a moment, his unemotional demeanor faltered and a look flashed across his face—Annoyance? Anger?—before disappearing once more. "You men will follow me, please." He turned as if to go back into the house.

"Hold on a second there, fella. Who be you, anyway?"

The pudgy man turned to face them once again. "Why, Mr. Boone, I am the man who summoned you. I am"—once more he raised his arms, hands palms up—"Hezekiah Creed. Also known as the Appointed One."

"Huh," said Boone. "Appointed to what? And by who?"

"Hoke," said Mac in a low voice, still eyeing the man. "Simmer, will you?"

The man at the top of the stairs turned and beckoned them to follow him into the mansion.

CHAPTER 5

As they trudged up the stairs, both men looked about them, hands on their sidearms. Wariness was a given in their line of work.

Hoke said, "No saloon means no fancy ladies, no cards, no nothin'."

"That also means no way for you to lose your money."

"What money? Ain't seen none yet." Boone flashed Mac a grim look. He held the sneer as he sampled a discrete slug from his hip flask.

The two men found themselves ushered through a wide, double door, the top halves glassed with leaded panes. Beyond this, a dark, cool foyer revealed the most surprising element so far—they were surrounded by several bonneted, black-clothed women, bustling about in the dim interior of the grand entry hall.

Their eyes were downcast, though as Mac and Boone's eyes adjusted to the darker interior, they were able to make out the lines of jaws, chins, noses, the careful, quick looks of the women.

"Lead them into my study. Now."

Creed's voice now carried a hard, cold edge, and two of the women hustled to accommodate.

A wide staircase rose before them, and while Mac and Boone looked about, two of the dark-clothed women stood waiting for their attention to drift back to them. When it did, Mac and Boone were led through another set of double doors to their left.

The room they entered was equally grand, with tall bookcases and a massive desk covered with tidy stacks of papers and two glowing oil lamps anchoring the corners. Creed stood behind the desk.

"Huh," said Boone. "I do most of my studying in the saddle."

"Or at the saloon," said Mac under his breath.

But Creed heard him. "We do not allow drink nor gambling nor illicit pursuits of any sort in and around the environs of Brimstone, gentlemen."

"So, Creed, was it?" said Boone, swallowing back the urge to berate the man for calling the few of life's pleasures illicit. "What else do you folks get up to in Brimstone besides praying and working?"

The man regarded Boone as if he'd been asked to stand on his head. "I don't understand your meaning, Mr. Boone. What else is there besides work and prayer?"

If the question required an answer, Boone was not inclined to give one, but he did jump into a new topic. "And that's another thing." He narrowed his eyes and jutted his whiskered chin. "How did you come to hear about us?" He leaned forward. "I don't believe we've ever met."

"No, Mr. Boone, that I would remember." Hezekiah Creed indulged in a slight smile. "As the father figure of Brimstone, it is my duty to ensure that anyone who sets foot on my soil, either invited or otherwise, is known to me."

Mac folded his arms across his chest. "Then perhaps you can tell us why we have been summoned here. After all, it appears that as the father figure, as it were, you are doing a bang-up job of keeping Brimstone and its denizens orderly, quiet, tidy, and law abiding. Your telegram made it sound as if you were on the brink of a catastrophe."

"You are perceptive, Mr. MacCoole."

"Call me Mac."

"I think not," said Creed. "As to why you are here, I must first edify you as to the town itself and of our way of life, for it has great bearing, indeed, the only bearing worth discussing, on the matter at hand."

"I wish he'd get on with it," mumbled Boone looking to the side.

Mac gave him a quick, hard look.

Creed cleared his throat. "I'll not be rushed, Mr. Boone." He clapped his hands and a dark shape, one of the women, appeared, bustling past the two men. She stood, head bowed, before Creed's desk.

"Bring us libation and something edible." He ended the directive with a shooing motion and looked back to the men. "As I mentioned before, I am Hezekiah Creed, known to the residents of Brimstone as the Appointed One, which makes me leader of the Kindred, my people, as it were."

Boone whistled low and grinned. "They ain't like any kinfolk I ever had."

Creed sniffed and continued. "We are a sizable and growing group of individuals who have sworn fealty to the Giver of All—"

"You mean God?" said Mac.

"Eh, that is one name I have heard given to the all-powerful deity, though I dare say ours is the Supreme Giver of All. You will also meet shortly members of my elite guard who report to me and only to me. They are my Acolytes. You will know them by their appearance."

Mac and Boone said nothing, but looked about themselves once again. A dark shape emerged from the doorway while Creed continued his explanation.

"I settled this town some years ago—"

His utterance was cut short by a quick cough.

Mac realized it had come from the woman who'd entered bearing a tray on which sat a stoneware jug and a plate of small rounds of sliced bread and cheese.

"Oh, yes, well . . . here are our refreshments." Creed eyed the woman with a narrowed gaze as she set down the tray on his desk. Though she had already turned to leave, in a tight, low voice, Creed said, "Leave us now," once again shooing her off.

He turned his gaze on them once more, showing a forced smile. "Now men, pour yourselves a cup of cheer and enjoy something to eat."

The last few hours of the trail had been dusty and dry and Boone tucked in, palming two slices of bread and several wedges of cheese before pouring two cups from the jug, and handing one to Mac.

"Our horses," said Mac, "will be thirsty and hungry as well."

"Never fear, Mr. MacCoole. They have already been brought to the stables and will be tended well, I assure you. And your gear will be taken to the accommodation we have reserved for you—a cottage one street behind the church, reserved for visiting dignitaries." He ended with a stiff bow from the waist.

"No need to butter us up, Creed," said Boone through a mouthful of food. "And speaking of butter, what's the story with this bread?" Boone looked as if he were gnawing wood.

"The bread is plain—"

"I'll say," mumbled Boone, swallowing hard.

"—and of a grain we grow ourselves. The libation is special for such occasions." Creed smiled and poured himself a cup.

Mac and Boone both sipped. Boone's mouth pulled wide in a leer.

"Chilled water with a touch of rosehip, in honor of your arrival."

"Gee," said Boone. "You went all out."

"Brimstone is a place of pilgrimage for the newly ripening believers."

"Believers in what? Strange food?" said Boone, cackling.

Creed ignored the remark. "Soon, even greater numbers of the hopeful and eager will journey here from the world over. I know this as a truth, for I have received a sign. Here they will find the one and only true god of all gods, the Supreme Giver of All."

"How long?" said Boone.

"How long?" said Creed.

"Yeah, how long has he been missing?"

"I . . . I don't understand."

"You said they will find him, so I wonder how long . . ."

Mac set down his cup and rapped Boone on the arm, then said, "Why name it Brimstone?"

"Why? Well, it's to remind one and all that this world is nothing if not a place of anguish and hardship."

Boone looked about the room, admiring the artwork and bookcases. He leaned over to Mac and in a low voice said, "Seems to me the Appointed One has figured out a way to avoid the hardship part, eh?"

"Mr. Boone," said Creed, puffing his saggy chest and standing full height, his fingers steepled atop his desk. "You have made a number of comments that, while I am certain you find them clever and amusing, do not bode well for our working relationship."

Before his sputtering pard could jump into the slim conversational gap, Mac said, "Perhaps you could tell us what it is we are here for, Mr. Creed. It has been a long few days' journeying for us. And on very little information, I might add."

Mac reached over and wrapped a big hand around Boone's stringy forearm and squeezed a moment. It was a silent warning to cool himself down, something Mac had had occasion to do a number of times in the past.

"Yes, yes, quite right." Creed pulled in a deep breath. "You have been summoned here to deal with a diligent and worrisome faction of interlopers known as the Outcasts. And that word is a kindness on my part, I assure you."

"Why are they called that? Were they initially from here?"

"They are not of our faith. Until they embrace it, they are forever cast out."

"Then it is because they are from here."

Creed shrugged and did not reply.

"What is it they're doing, exactly?"

"They have seen what it is we have built up here, the gristmill, the homes, the crops, the communal bakery, all of it, and they wish to take it for themselves. I have seen them with mine own eyes, and the greed in their bearing and demeanor is obvious. They routinely send into our midst some of their own ilk, non-believers, people to disrupt, to corrupt, and to lay to waste all that I . . . and the Kindred, of course, have worked for. They are doing their best to disrupt the law-abiding citizens of Brimstone and take the town, and the lives, the very souls, of the Kindred!"

"How would we know them? How might we find them?"

Creed looked at Mac with raised eyebrows. "Why, they will be the non-believers, of course. People such as yourselves."

"So they'll be normal looking," said Boone.

"No. Well, yes. That is to say they dress as do you, but as with you, they will have the distinctive aura of hellfire about them."

"Aw, no, that's my natural scent." Boone smiled. Nobody else did.

"Haven't you tried to bring in the law?" said Mac, changing the subject.

Boone nodded. "That'd be my first thought."

Creed sighed and smiled as if he were explaining, once more, a complex task to a child. "Of course, I made every effort to do that. Unfortunately, those efforts were snubbed."

"Why?"

Creed spread his arms wide. "For our devoutness. Our beliefs, of course. We must walk with burden all our earthly lives, enduring hardship and pain."

"I only feel that way after I've been on a rippin' toot for a few days."

Mac gave Boone another hard glance and once more jumped in with a question. "How did you come to find out about us?"

"You were recommended by an acquaintance."

"Anyone I might know?"

Creed offered another of his half grins, which by now were becoming infuriating to both men.

A quick, two-knock rap sounded from the closed study door. "Enter."

Three men strode into the room, each wearing black frock coats, black broad-brim, flat crown hats, white shirts, and black trousers tucked into tall black boots. Each of the three were of above average height, taller than Boone but not as tall as Mac, and wide of shoulder. They were also unsmiling.

Other than sharing the same style of wardrobe with the men in the field, these three didn't appear to have anything else in common with the workers they'd seen earlier. Certainly, they did not evoke friendliness. They did, however, show no fear as they looked at Boone and Mac full-on, their dark eyes drawn in silent challenge.

The only thing truly different from the other men they'd seen, apart from their glowering demeanor, were their beards, which were long, reaching to mid chest, and worn forked, combed and separated into twin tufts, tied at the ends with bits of black rawhide.

It was an odd look, to be sure, but then again, nothing about Brimstone had been normal to Mac and Boone since their arrival.

"How do," said Boone, stepping forward and offering a hand. The three newcomers did not return the gesture but kept their hands behind their backs, as they had been when they filed in and stood in a line.

Mac kept his hand resting atop the butt of his Colt Dragoon.

"Gentlemen," said Creed, to Mac and Boone. "Please allow me to introduce three of my Acolytes. I mentioned them earlier. They . . . keep the peace here in Brimstone."

Boone let his hand drop. "Why invite us to town if you got these surly looking gents lurking about the place?"

Mac nodded in agreement.

"A logical question, to be sure." Creed stopped there, not offering more of an explanation.

"You know, Mr. Creed, this"—Mac raised his hands in a gesture meant to take in the entire room, and beyond, the town of Brimstone—"is interesting, certainly, but I think you might be better off calling in someone else. We're not used to dealing with folks who flat-out refuse to answer the simplest questions."

"I wasn't aware I'd refused to answer anything you've asked."

"Well, you have, and you're mighty cagey, to boot, mister." Boone stepped forward, rested a hard-knuckled hand atop the desk. The gesture stirred the Acolytes to also step forward.

"Easy boys," said Mac.

"Look, gentlemen, the Outcasts simply won't let us live in peace, to worship as we so choose. I wish them dealt with once and for all. Is that too much to ask?" Creed looked from Boone's tight fist resting atop his desk to Mac's face. "I'll triple your usual fee."

"You don't know our usual fee yet."

Again, Creed's annoying smile crept onto his face. "I have been informed."

"By the acquaintance, eh?" said Boone, shaking his head.

Mac glanced at Boone and raised his eyebrows in question. Boone shrugged. To Creed, Mac said, "We're intrigued enough to give this a go, a trial of a day or so, then we'll make our decision."

Creed pooched his bottom lip, stared at the ceiling, then said, "Fine, fine." He leaned forward in what Mac assumed was what Creed intended as a menacing posture. "I will, however, have to ask you men to disarm yourselves while you are in Brimstone, however."

"Nope," says Mac. "That's not how we operate, and not why you called us here. If that's the way you want it, then we'll take our leave right now."

As Boone reached for the door handle, Creed said, "Wait, wait, wait. You are correct, of course. After all, I did call you here to be enforcers of a sort." He sat down heavily with a sigh and nodded toward the still-silent Acolytes.

They returned the gesture and bowed and backed to the door as if Hezekiah Creed were royalty. Mac and Boone watched this with raised eyebrows.

Creed looked up at them, surprised to still see them there. "They will show you to your quarters. You will want to rest after your journey, I trust. You will be summoned in several hours for evening prayer and repast."

"Prayer?" said Boone. "I guess not. But I will break bread with ye." He nodded at Mac, who nodded back.

Another sigh from Creed. "Fine, fine." He gestured at them, shooing them away like flies.

Boone was about to begin another round of sputtering, but Mac rapped him on the arm and gestured with his chin toward the retreating forms of the Acolytes. They filed out, with Mac knowing he would soon hear an earful . . . and then some.

CHAPTER 6

Mac leaned against the doorframe of their guest quarters, a small, tidy cabin, and eyed the town. "I'm intrigued enough by the sheer oddness of this place." He looked over his shoulder at Boone. "And you can't tell me you don't want to know more about Hezekiah Creed."

"Know more? Nah, I know all I need to know about that pompous windbag. What I want is to button up his eyes with a couple of fists."

"Hold that notion a while. I may want to join you. But until we recoup our expenses, we may as well see what's what about Brimstone."

They took to the tidy street, strolling slow, each keeping a watchful eye for anything that might appear even odder about the strange place and the people in it.

"You notice how that fool clammed up when that bonneted woman with that tray of godawful vittles coughed? Seemed to me he got caught in a fib."

Mac nodded. "Right, that was when he told us he'd founded the town, practically claiming credit for birthing the entirety of Brimstone, buildings and all. Though it is pretty impressive, I have to say."

"Bah! The original creator, he fancies himself."

"If there's one thing I have never been able to stomach," said Mac, "it's someone so bent on religion that they become blinded to everything else, including common decency and good manners."

Boone nodded. "I know all about folks like Creed and his flock of sheep. You forget I was born and bred down in God's country itself, a little vale of heaven known as Hoddy's Gulch, Hoddy being the name of my grandpappy twice back on Mama's side."

"You don't say."

"I do say! And what's more, ol' Hoddy the second, my cousin once removed on Mama's side, whelped out of Aunt Bertie, he went off for a spell and when he come back, he was in the grip of a fierce passion for the Lord himself."

"Not so unusual."

"You're right there, but what is a little odd, and I wager a beer you'll agree with me, is how he went about showing that passion. He got himself a sack of vipers, them being plentiful in Hoddy's Gulch."

"Sounds positively heavenly to me," said Mac, stifling a grin.

"Hush your mouth now or we'll have a set-to right here. I've a mind to take a round or two out of you all the same, but let me commence with my tale."

"Does it have a point?"

"You damn right it does."

"Then get to it. We have a town to see."

"You . . . you . . . oh, all right. So Hoddy, the cousin, not my great-great grandpappy."

"I gathered that."

"Good. He used them vipers as a way to attract attention

to himself and his calling. Went around all the hill communities thereabouts and he'd set to swaying and whatnot, then he'd reach right into that sack of snakes and yarn out a handful in each fist and hold them up."

"Lucky fellow."

"Yeah." Boone nodded. "For a while."

"Don't tell me—the odds caught up with him?"

"Yeah, they did. Killed him deader'n dead on his sixth or seventh such revival. Snakes went everywhere lashing out at whatever they could, notably people who were also running about everywhere. It was a scene, I tell you. I was up a tree with my other cousin, Merle. It was a good time. Best church service I ever been to."

"As interesting as the story was, what was the point, Boone?"

"Why, I should think that was obvious. I've seen such behavior before, and worse. Might be we ain't seen the whole of it yet. You know, the eye rolling and twitching, all of it, except for the lack of snakes. Only trouble is, ol' Hezekiah Creed, he's intelligent enough to know that snakes will turn on a man any ol' time for any ol' reason. So he stays away from them."

"Creed is about as low as a snake, I'll grant you."

They walked on in silence for a few minutes more, then they passed the bakehouse and saw two women working inside, their sleeves rolled up, kneading dough on the low work table.

Mac said, "Even if we disagree with the way the Kindred live, they should be allowed to live, unmolested by others."

Boone nodded. "Yeah, such as those so-called Outcasts."

"Exactly. They're entitled to whatever lawful protections, hired or no, that anyone else might have. But I don't want us to cross the line that I bet Creed wants us to cross."

"You mean killing off the Outcasts once and for all."

Mac nodded. "Mm-hmm. No matter the cause, no matter the consequence."

"I hear that fine. It's a line we have never crossed, and we never will." Boone shrugged. "Okay, we'll give it a go, then. Hope it don't take too long. My flask and my emergency bottle ain't going to hold out forever."

CHAPTER 7

"Don't you remember how it was, brother?"

The man on the receiving end of that question, one Roland Toomey, turned on the speaker with eyes the color of worn leather, grown narrow and cold. "You stand there and dare ask me if I remember how it was?" He flexed big hands in a useless grab for something, anything.

But there was nothing there. Truth be told, there was less now than ever—less food, less men, less will to fight.

In their lightest moments, which were all but gone, the thing they'd lamented most was the last of their tobacco. Nothing brought a fellow comfort quite like a silent smoke by the fire. Especially when he was bereft of that which he loved most dearly in life, his kin.

This many of the men knew well, considering they'd spent such anguished moments, more than they cared to remember, huddled about small watch fires in the war. In the company of their fellow soldiers, to be sure, but each man alone, a statue of stony fear lost in his own thoughts.

"Been three years now, Roland. I'm all but done in."

Instead of once more losing his temper with his brother-in-law, Paul, still sometimes annoying to him after all these years, Roland nodded, knowing how the man felt. Roland once more reminded himself that Paul had been here the entire time, too.

He nodded. "I know, Paul. I feel it, too."

The younger man must have sensed the misery and exhaustion in Roland's voice, for he said nothing, out of character for him, and prodded the blackened, cold embers of that morning's small fire.

Paul's sister, Ruthie, and then by marriage, Roland, and their daughter, Emma, were all the family Paul had left in the world. Of course, the man would stick with him. What choice did he have? What choice did any of them really have?

Roland thought back to how it was before, when he and his Ruthie and Emma, and even Paul, were all still truly a family. He had never quite gotten along with his brother-in-law, but for Ruth's sake, he'd tried.

He'd do anything for that woman. Still would. And that's why he was living like a starved rat in the hills, keeping watch on the town he'd helped to build. A town he no longer recognized.

Roland looked westward, as if he could see straight through the boulders heaped about them. He looked toward Promise, now Brimstone, and he thought back to the time before Brimstone, before the Kindred . . . before the coming of Hezekiah Creed.

Ten years before

Roland Toomey stood in the field and stretched his back. The big straw hat might well keep the sun off his pate, but it did precious little to protect his neck and back from the heat when he was bent over in the field, sowing seeds, tugging weeds, or picking the harvest. Still, he thought, looking about him, if he had to bake somewhere, this was the place to do it.

Roland still marveled at the raw beauty of this unlikely spot. Think of it, a green, vast valley that lay smack in their path on their trek westward but a few years before. Their unintentional discovery of it had been the best thing to have happened to them on their trip West.

The worst, though no less a surprise, had been the appearance of that bull grizzly way back east of the Rockies. It had thundered in on them from what had seemed nowhere at all. With a gut-charged roar and a thwack of a meaty, claw-tipped paw, it had laid low their yearling heifer, Bonnet. Following that, finding their new valley home had been most welcomed by the weary travelers, who had spent the remainder of the journey jumpy and regretful.

They had intended to venture farther, northwestward, toward Oregon Territory, but the splendor of the valley had stopped them as no sign from the hand of God could ever do, no utterance from a voice on high.

After so much skin-puckering sun and sand and rock and unforgiving heat, to find this vast, long, green valley cut through with a clean, clear river that coursed with fish was a pure wonder. There were timbered slopes far to either side, but not too far to harvest from. It was all far too precious and perfect to leave. As soon as he'd seen it, a voice deep inside told him to let others have Oregon Territory. Roland Toomey had found his paradise on earth.

Ruth had teased him about his stubbornness and wanderlust, but she had always gone along with his ideas, including uprooting their lives from Ohio and venturing westward.

Along the way, Roland had studied their modest and poorly rendered maps and decided to veer from the beaten, too-traveled trail. For a time, it had seemed as if that wanderlust and stubbornness had crippled them. And then they found the valley. Roland supposed that if anyone had to, he was the one to take credit for it, but could a man claim credit for something if it was tripped over by accident?

And so they had stayed. Roland, Ruth, and up to that point, their only child, six-year-old Emma, as well as their dog, Sass. And then there was the assortment of chickens, and Bonnie, mother of Bonnet, plus two brace of oxen and two horses.

And of course, there was Ruth's brother, Paul, a quiet, hard-working fellow who, though a young sixteen at the time, was already seasoned in battle with other men at the tag end of the war.

Despite Roland's silent hopes, their valley, which they named Promise, was too fine to remain theirs alone for long. They had been there for nearly a year of seasons, and had built the beginnings of a life with a cabin, a stable, gardens, coops, and more, when he began to sense that others would soon arrive. As Roland well knew, once a trail has been seen, others will follow it.

He had always believed it is satisfying in life to be the first to do a thing. It was far less satisfying to be the second, less so the third, and so on. And yet, most other people he'd met in life seemed satisfied with not being the ones to discover a thing, to blaze a trail, to explore untrammeled ground.

That was something Roland could never understand. Still, if he was one of life's few path makers, he must accept the fact that others would use the path he created, the path that led to his valley, his family, his new life.

When the newcomers began dribbling in, he could do nothing more than sigh and offer a handshake. It annoyed him to admit it, but it was with some unspoken relief that they welcomed the first of the new families, other similar seekers. Roland supposed it was that notion of safety in numbers, some hearkening back to a tribal instinct.

And so over the next six years following their discovery of the valley, a couple of dozen families made their way to the lush, green valley. People brought with them needs and skills to help fill the needs of others. There were two blacksmiths, plus bakers, joiners and carpenters, and a number of women who were adept at sewing everything in the way of garments and tarpaulins.

Another fellow was not only a skilled hunter but knew more than anyone else about tanning hides and making of the leather useful goods, from winter wear such as fur-in mittens and hats to harnesses, knife sheaths, vests, moccasins, and in time, shoes and boots. Still another young couple had a fortunate expertise in foraging for edible plants and healing herbs.

Children came with many of the newcomers, and Emma had new friends her own age to play with. Soon thereafter, the need for a school became apparent.

A young, unmarried woman named Demelza Schmidt, unmarried cousin of a couple with three children, had come along on a trip West with her cousin and her cousin's husband. She had paid her way in kind by helping with their three children. Demelza had been educated back East in Providence, Rhode Island, and was rarely seen without a book in her hand. Soon enough, the townsfolk knew they had found their schoolteacher.

Roland became the town's unofficial and reluctant first leader. Ruth convinced him that since they were the valley's first settlers, they owed the rest a debt in the form of stewardship. Roland did not agree, but for the first time, and much to Roland's annoyance, Paul took his sister's side in the argument. Roland soon learned why: Paul was sweet on Demelza and Ruth had promised to talk with her on her shy brother's behalf.

And so, Roland had relented under the double-barrel assault of wife and brother-in-law. To his surprise, Roland had, at times, come to enjoy the challenges the role of town leader brought with it.

He and several other men formed plans for the various emergencies likely to befall the fledgling town. Not the least of these was the notion of attack by Indians. This seemed to them not fanciful thinking, since they had often seen braves riding the low grassy hills about town, skylined and armed.

Though they never made a move to trek down to town, the Indians would sit their horses and watch the townsfolk work their crops or go about their daily lives. No attacks ever occurred, for which they were all most grateful.

The growing number of Promise's log buildings included houses, barns, shops, and the meeting house. This doubled as the town church and schoolhouse, though it was soon agreed that children would benefit from their own building, and a schoolhouse was built.

Along about that time some six years into the life of the budding town, trade from two directions east and west, came in, irregularly but more than there had been. The pathway Roland had carved through wildlands was now a roadway delivering goods and commercial traffic in both directions, to and from the town.

Those early years were good years, filled with surprising growth, and with more people coming in all the time. They were boom years during which their crops—grains, vegetables, fruits, nuts—and livestock were becoming known far and wide, from long-established towns and newer settlements in all directions.

Even Roland, who still quelled a throbbing streak of discontent and unease at the very busy-ness of the Promise had, nonetheless, also felt a quiet pride in seeing the first of the plank-sided homes, businesses with painted signs, goods from far and wide available to them right there and not at the far end of a four days' ride. But those boom years were to be short lived.

For there came the day when a congenial, not-quite-young preaching man by the name of Hezekiah Creed rode into their midst. He ingratiated himself into the very heart of town politics, but as he was a man of the Good Book, few found fault with him early on.

If they did, they felt they could overlook such petty grievances as the slightly uncomfortable jokes and innuendoes he made regarding the fairer sex, the fact that he did like to occasionally indulge in the drinking of liquor and the taking of tobacco.

His sermons were always well attended, though far too fiery for Roland, who preferred his biblical teachings to be of the quieter sort. He always thought that what occurred between a man and his god should be just that, between a man, or a woman, in silent prayer, and living in prayerful ways, as a way of holding a conversation with the Almighty.

But that was not the case with Hezekiah Creed. From the start, he vowed that the fine folks of Promise would roast alive forever if they did not see the error of their ways. Their very skin would blister and pucker and crackle and, in flame, the fat would bubble and the meat would slide from their bones. Their hair would torch and smoke away and still they would not know the extent such agonies as an eternity in the hell fires of damnation might bring them.

Lashing fears upon fears only made the people of the town quiver and shake. And the more they did so, the more Creed seemed to enjoy his role as their tormentor and the sole source of a potential path to salvation.

Only after he had all but laid them low with knock-kneed frights day after day did he deliver the slimmest glimmer of hope. By then he had held daily services and taken over the entirety of the meeting hall, making it nothing other than a church. Within that space, he held the promise of salvation before them as a drop of water to a parched and dying man.

Yes, yes, they cried, save us! Anything you say we will

do, only don't leave us to roast in the fires of agonizing hell forever and a day. Anything, they had seemed to say.

About that time, Roland noticed a wave of newcomers, many who seemed to know Creed from the outset, deferring to him in a way that suggested they were familiar with him. They settled in Promise, doubling the town's population within a couple of months.

On arrival in Promise, they were already more pious and devout than the original, and recently converted townsfolk. These newcomers were unsmiling, garbed all in black, and the dourest yet most hard-working people Roland had ever met.

But they were not the worst to arrive. That distinction went to the two-dozen black-garbed men who rode in soon thereafter. They were well armed, well provisioned, and as unsmiling as had been the previous wave. But this new batch wore menace like a cloak. Roland recalled the storm clouds of anger, hatred, doubt, and malice in their dark eyes.

They were different in other ways, as well, easy to tell apart from the other men. These newcomers never worked the fields. They rode their horses or walked the streets toting rifles, their peculiar beards, parted in the middle and tied in two long tufts, ending with wraps of blackened rawhide strips. But the oddest and most frightening trait these menacing men shared? None could speak. It would be some time before the townsfolk found out why.

Within a day of their arrival, it became apparent they were in the employ of Hezekiah Creed, who by then had become far and away the most important, powerful, and revered figure in all of Promise. More so than the town's silent, doubting founder, Roland Toomey.

Roland would look back on those days before Creed arrived with fondness, for he and Ruthie, as his long-dead father used to say about a good marriage, were both pulling in the traces, making for the same dream. They were young, happy, healthy, and they had two children by then, too—young Emma, and the baby, little Shane.

Roland had been happy then, perhaps happier than he'd been in his entire life. At the same time there was something bothering him that he'd never told Ruthie. He couldn't shake off the feeling that it was all going to change, and not for the better. Sure, change happens in life. Maybe life is all about change, he'd reasoned, over and over again to himself in the years since those glory days, but not the sort of change that Creed brought to Promise.

At first, those who didn't find his preaching of interest tolerated him. Then members of the town's overseers began meeting several nights each week in secret at Roland's house, as if they had something to hide. By then the Acolytes, the name Creed had given to his silent, split-bearded guards, were nosing around town as if they owned the place.

Rumor had it they would report back to Creed any behavior that didn't fit in Creed's narrow definition of how folks should live their lives.

One particular night in autumn, the leading townsmen had gathered. Roland remembered the cold air and the smell of snow on the wind. Nothing much had been decided among them that night.

They had been drawing up a letter and a list of complaints, still trying to think of a kind way of telling Creed that while they respected him being a man of the cloth, they did not think his heavy-handed preaching and frightening, threatening tactics had any place in the lives of the people of Promise. A town, Roland insisted on putting in the letter, that had thrived peaceably long before Creed ever arrived.

At the insistence of their wives, notably Ruth, they'd been polite about it, and had taken their time to make certain their arguments were well reasoned and soft-edged. Ruth kept insisting that if they began ousting people from town,

Promise would gain a reputation for being an unwelcoming place and would eventually wither and die.

In an attempt at being understanding toward his wife, something he did not particularly feel, Roland admitted as to how that had some merit to it, so they'd been cautious in their choice of words.

But the letter hadn't been received well by Creed, and as it turned out it wasn't enough for Ruth and the other wives, either. And then one of his best friends in town, a blacksmith named Joby, agreed with the women. Then another man did, and another. Pretty soon there was but a handful of men in town, and no women, who hadn't gobbled up what Creed was serving. The one Creed convert that wounded him the most, though, was Ruth.

She'd always been a wise woman, independent to the point of being frustrating to talk with at times, so bold had she always been in her thinking. But that also was one of many of her traits he admired. Then Creed came.

How in the hell such a strong-minded woman could be taken in by him baffled Roland. Did she find her own life so unfulfilling that she would fall prey to whoever came along selling nostrums and tinctures? For Hezekiah Creed was nothing more than a seller of snake oil, scented lies, and false hopes.

It didn't take long for their lives to peel apart. There came a day when Ruth refused to talk with him, and even forbade the children to play with him. He tried to see things her way, to bargain with her. Heck, he even attended a service with her.

Once there, he found the piggish Creed, who had grown fatter since moving to Promise, spouted little more than windy, tired stories with the thinnest of connections to anything remotely biblical. The experience only strengthened his own resolve to oust Creed and his followers or take his family—bound and gagged if need be—away from there.

Roland put up with these increasingly hostile conditions for nearly two months as did the few others who felt as he did. They felt helpless to act as they watched their lives, their families, their town, being thieved from them, while they, so outnumbered, could do nothing about it.

Then came that night in November, when the Acolytes paid the Toomey household a visit. He met them at the front door of the home he and Ruthie built together. He met them while holding his hunting rifle. They swarmed through the door and over him before he could squeeze off a shot.

Ruth watched them beat him, then haul him away. She watched, holding little Shane, his four-year-old son. And, standing beside her, their Emma, a twelve-year-old little lady herself. She, too, stood by and watched her father overcome by the brutes.

They watched with no surprise on their faces and without attempting to stop them. That hurt Roland more than any of the blows they drove down on him, bloodying his face, the kicks that snapped his ribs. Ruth stood there cold and free of any outward sign of emotion, the woman he pledged to live with, to live for, forever.

Oh, but he fought, fought as a weakened, canyon-trapped lion snarls and lashes out at the pack of winter-starved wolves that have cornered it, even though it knows this will be its end. Roland fought those devils with every thrust of his will and muscle he could muster, landing hard blows and making the near-silent brutes groan in their beastlike way.

It was during this melee that he saw why the Acolytes never spoke. As they tussled, raining blows on Roland, he saw between their parted gnashing teeth not pink tongues in their foul mouths, but puckered, scar-welted nubs where tongues once had been.

It came to him then that they must have had their tongues cut out. Or worse, he thought, as they kicked and punched him before his family, had these men performed this mutilation on themselves? And if so, why? For Creed? The very thought of it shuddered him to his core. It was the last thought Roland had before the blackness of unconsciousness dragged him deep.

When he came around, Roland was surprised he was not dead. He hurt like the hounds of hell had savaged him—and he reckoned that was more the truth of it than not. His head throbbed, his chest ached, sharp needling pains lanced through him when he breathed, and he had at least two broken fingers. He was soon also surprised but relieved to note that he was not alone.

All about him lay groaning or unmoving men all familiar to him, his comrades in opposition to Creed. Among them were a few youths not yet old enough to shave, several men his age, and a few old timers. All men, though. No women.

It would take long hours before any of them were revived enough to stumble about their new environs. And when they did, they all knew it for what it was and where it was. The base of the rocky hills to the east/southeast of town. And the message was obvious—get gone.

To a man they wore the shame of the attacks like heavy cloaks, weighing them down in those early days of exile.

They had expected their belligerence and refusals to conform to Creed's way of doing things, their refusals to take the oath to become a Kindred and swear fealty to Creed would make them targets. But they had not expected it to happen so swiftly, nor so brutally. And not in front of their wives and children, their mothers and fathers, their neighbors and friends.

The men buried their dead, for two of them soon expired of their wounds. One, Jose, was addled from kicks to the head and died drooling and raving. It had been fortunate for the others he was unable to rove about because of damaged legs—a broken ankle and a smashed kneecap.

The second man to die was a quiet, older fellow, Walter,

who showed up in town with his wife only months before Creed arrived. Within weeks of arriving in Promise, his wife died suddenly. The old man stayed on and became relied on for sage advice and kindness.

He was quietly resistant to the incursion of Creed and his followers and he paid the price for this by dying as he had lived, quietly and without complaint. The men could do little to ease Walter's passing, as his injuries were deep in his gut, likely caused by an Acolyte's boot kicks. His belly and ribcage were pocked with foul purple welts and large, blue-black bruises.

At the last, he whispered to Roland, "I am grateful my Sadie was gone. She would have seen through Creed's lies. She was a wise one, was my Sadie."

Then he'd grasped Roland's arm and looked with intensity with his old, watery eyes. "Your wife, your family, they are worth fighting for. This will not last, but love . . . that is forever . . ." And then the proud old man had died. But his last words lived on in Roland, and in most of the other men, too.

They counted up the meager items among them, bits and bobs on their persons when they were cast out—matches, folding knives, tobacco, hard tack. For a short time, they were able to climb higher into the hills to lick their wounds, heal up, and snare rabbits and rock rats. They broiled the hairy carcasses over flame, and tried to figure out what they were going to do.

"What's Creed getting out of all this?" said a thin, whiskery man named Zeb. "You think he buys what he's peddling?"

"No," said Roland. "I think he's setting himself up to be head of his own church because he wants to live in fine style. What better way to do that than to have other people do your bidding for you? And what better place to do it than here in our pretty valley."

"Makes sense," said Zeb. "Back when me and my Margaret was still speaking, she told me that Creed let slip he had other churches already stocked with Kindred. Said soon they'd be popping up all over the West."

"And all of them paying his 'tithe,'" said Roland.

The men all groaned and mumbled. They'd heard that word plenty from Creed and then from their wives and children.

"It's nothing but a blackmailer's fee," said Roland's brother-in-law, Paul, himself still nursing a limpy leg and an aching head.

Roland nodded. "Yes, we pay him to sit on his backside and get fatter."

"You ever seen the like?" said Zeb. "He's getting to be a prize piglet, is that bastardly Creed."

Their conversations in the early days ran on in such a manner, fueled by anger and exhaustion and little else. But it was enough to keep them keen and hungry for revenge, in whatever form it might take. But it would be pursued, on that they all agreed.

It was obvious to them that Creed and his filth intended that they leave and never return. They knew if they were seen again, they would not be allowed to live.

They also knew that save for a couple of them, none of them were interested in venturing away from their lives, their families, their homes, their businesses. Where would they go? To what purpose? No, they'd agreed, they were men, were they not? They would not, could not tolerate this outrageous theft of their lives and the lives of their hoodwinked loved ones.

But what to do? And how to go about it?

As Roland had been the founder of the town, all eyes fell on him. On a cold morning in those early days of exile, he pulled in a deep breath then let it out. "The way I see it, we have no choice. I want our town back and I will fight to the last breath for it."

The group of ragged men cheered. They were in little danger of being seen or heard, as they had ventured far into the hills, a place many of them were familiar with from hunting forays in the past.

Those early days were tense, tight times while they decided their next steps. Finally, Roland said, "Well, men, there aren't enough rabbits in these rocks to feed us much longer, at least not by using snares. We need tools, guns, and bullets. And we need clothing and shelter. Then, when we are stronger and healed, we can take back what's ours."

Paul snorted and threw a stick into a nearby jumble of boulders. "Where do you think we're going to get ourselves guns and clothes and houses? Huh?"

Roland nodded, flexing his jaw muscle and forcing a smile. "I've been thinking about this. I think the strongest of us can sneak back into town. Make a unified effort of it."

"Those tongueless devils will be waiting," said Zeb.

Roland shook his head. "I doubt it. My guess is they think we're long gone by now, dragging ourselves off to Pennerville to lick our wounds and get help from the law."

"We'd never make it."

"That's why we need to act right away. Now, I'm hoping they haven't been appropriated, but does everybody have a clear idea of where their horses might be. And where their guns are in their houses. And their money, matches, anything else we can carry that we will need. Clothing, to be sure. Socks and whatever else we might take."

"Do we go in at night?"

"No," said Roland, surprising them all. "That's when everybody's at home. No, we go in the middle of the day."

Paul snorted again. "Yeah, that's when they're all praying and swaying, listening to Creed flap his gums."

Roland ignored him. "Anybody with a better idea is welcome to share it."

Nobody said anything.

"Good. Then I say." He looked up at the sun, visoring his eyes. "We choose who goes, then make our way down in the next hour or so. That should put us behind the Colters' barn about when everybody is heading to church."

And that is what eight of them did, surprising themselves more than anyone by making it into town, into their homes and businesses, and out again with as much useful gear as they could carry. Not one Acolyte had been spotted, not one member of the Kindred. One dog barked, but it was ol' Useless, a decrepit town hound, and everyone was used to his random outbursts anyway.

To the collective surprise of all the Outcasts, their horses and mules were no longer kept at their home stables but had been commandeered by Creed and kept close by his church and home, at a new stable, what had been a smithy and town animal pound.

Nonetheless they made it back out of town with a solid supply of goods. Two of the men commandeered handcarts and another found a wheelbarrow. They raced for the far, high rocks, spelling each other with turns on the carts and swapping out on gun toting and eyeing their backtrail.

Roland had warned them that their thefts, thefts of their own possessions, no less, would not go unnoticed. There would be retribution, for the Acolytes now knew the cast-out townsmen had not crawled away, but were now somewhere close by, and armed and angry.

Despite this suspicion, they saw no sign of Acolytes sniffing about their rocky locale. A couple of busy weeks passed. They found an ideal spot at which to set up a camp. It was easily defensible and there were enough old caves and grottoes they could incorporate into shanties.

Heat would be a top concern in the coming winter months, but they laid in an ample supply of wood. They did likewise with game. Despite this, it was a dismal time during which few men spoke, and when they did it was to curse Creed and their own bleak misfortunes.

Once they were settled in their mountain haven, Roland proposed the idea of another raid through town. "We'll need more food and blankets. And we need a horse to carry one of us to Pennerville to fetch the law."

"I'll go!" said Paul, standing and raising his hand.

They did manage to find food and two more blankets. But all the horses and mules were watched over by Acolytes or townsfolk. The Outcasts headed into that winter feeling more desperate and forlorn than they had been.

The surliest among them, Roland noted, was his own brother-in-law, Paul. The other men tolerated the young man, but his attitude was poisonous. From his time in the war, Roland knew that it didn't take long for one spoiled apple to taint the barrel full.

Not long after, some of the men began to leave, stealing into the night and taking precious food with them. Roland could do little except to bid them a silent wish of good luck the next morning when their disappearance was discovered.

On a spirited horse, and in foul weather, it was possible to make Pennerville with two long days of hard riding. But on foot? Roland doubted any would make it halfway, given the weather and their weakened state.

He hoped he was wrong, but he was proved correct—and never was a man more disappointed in being correct. Over the next two years, no help came, even when they sent men in high summer.

The following June Paul did steal a horse. He'd been watching the nearest barn for a couple of weeks and one fine afternoon, he crept up on the tethered beast, a solid brown cropping grass. He filched a latigo from atop a post and was leading the horse away, eyeing the barn, but he saw no one.

He mounted, bareback, and had gotten far enough from town that he felt certain he had made it away to safety when a shot cracked the blue afternoon.

By the time Paul heard it, the horse had already fouled its feet and pinwheeled forward, slamming hard to the dusty earth. He was thrown and landed hard on his left shoulder. He heard something crack as he fell and he lay motionless for a moment, the sky spinning about him.

Close by, the horse whinnied and thrashed, mortally wounded but not willing to give up.

Paul knew, despite the fact that he was armed with a revolver, that he would not be able to defend himself from whoever had unleashed such a distance shot. He raised his head and squinting, looked toward the far-off barn and the town beyond. Of movement, he saw nothing. Nobody stalked him. Whoever it had been was now waiting for him to make a move.

A boulder half as big as a wagon lay beyond him, toward the hills where he was supposed to be. None of his fellow Outcasts knew he had been planning his singular raid. He had expected to surprise them with his theft of the horse, and then Roland would have to shut his big mouth and let the men listen to Paul for once.

But not now. Now all he could think to do was make it to the boulder. Somehow.

It took him two hours, lying face-up in the hot June sun, seeing the high-up, slow gather of wheeling buzzards and feeling the gut-heaving pain of his broken shoulder become unbearable before he dared make a move.

He began to slither, revolver in his one good hand, his wounded arm angled higher than he'd like, dragging his way with his elbow and knees, toward the boulder.

No shots chased him. Paul had the rest of the day to think, leaning in the pounding sun with a broken shoulder against a skillet-hot rock. He knew he was lucky, knew he should have made this an effort by them all, then it might have turned out differently. It bothered him to think it, but, as Roland had often said, the truth stung like an arrow.

Under cover of darkness, Paul staggered back up to the high rocks, and his few fellow Outcasts tended him as though he were family. Roland surprised him most of all by saying nothing harsh about Paul's ill-fated foray.

After he'd been plied with food and water and a small sip of their precious medicinal whiskey, Paul began to lose his fight with sleep. But he could have sworn he saw a tear slide down Roland's cheek as the man sat watch by his side.

CHAPTER 8

Neither Mac nor Boone had slept well that first night, in part because the beds in the little hut in which they were lodged were barely padded. Creed had mentioned that they were plush compared with the beds of the Kindred.

"Can't imagine anything with less padding than that plank. Why, I gave thought to bunking outside like we do on the trail."

"What stopped you?"

"The thought of all those Kindred folks wandering around, not looking up when you say howdy, scurrying away like mice and I'm a cat. It ain't like I'm carrying a disease!"

"To them you are."

"Huh?"

"The disease of the Outcasts."

"Oh, bosh!"

As they spoke, they were setting out once more from the hut, which thankfully had been equipped with a small woodstove. The first thing they did on waking, of course, was see to their horses, Lincoln and Chummy, as they had the night before.

True to Creed's word, the beasts had been nicely looked after and fed well, even brushed down and given adjoining stalls. They'd also been impressed with the state of the stables and the healthful look of the other livestock under the care of the Kindred.

Of the stable caretaker, they saw no sign. "It's as if this entire town is run by ghosts."

"Not ghosts." Mac winked. "Prayer."

They'd managed to brew up a pot of bold morning coffee and now were off to find trouble—and figure out if this trip was worth their time.

Their slight plan was to split up to see more of what they faced in Brimstone, and would compare their findings later. They'd made it down one of the few streets, when they heard the quick, clipped scream of a woman.

"Came from up there," said Mac, already legging it ahead. Boone doubled his efforts, and soon they were side by side once more.

At the far side of the schoolhouse stood a young man in haggard farmers' clothes—beat-up straw hat, a blue shirt with brown leather braces, and brown wool trousers with more patch than cloth, tucked into tall, worn, dogear boots.

Before him stood a young Kindred woman, all in black, but her bonnet had tipped back enough that they could see her smooth, unlined cheek and wispy golden hair. He held her by one arm and was trying to pull her close.

They both were shaking their heads at each other, and he spoke sharp, urgent words, none of which they could make out as they were still too far off.

The young woman let out another quick shout, and Mac bellowed, "Hey!"

The young man turned, eyes wide, and backed up a step, staring at them as if they were spirit. He still held the woman's arm, as if he might drag her away, then he looked at her and said, "Eliza—come on! Come on, girl!"

She shook her head and jerked free as the young man stumbled backward, nearly losing his footing, before Mac lunged and laid a hand on him.

Boone approached the young woman, who backed up, watching all this in horror. From around the near corner of the school building, two Acolytes, forked beards wagging, bolted for the young man. One faced Boone and pointed a finger at him and shook his head as if to warn him against touching the girl.

Boone growled and took off after the young man in the blue shirt who had outdistanced Mac.

"Get him!" Boone shouted, but it was too late, the kid had bolted, cutting across lots and leaping fences like a stag pursued by hounds. Mac and Boone pulled up short and the two Acolytes continued their jog in the same direction as the kid, though he was now gone from sight.

They ran as if they were in no hurry, as if they had all the time in the world. Odd, thought Mac.

They both looked toward the girl or where she had been. No one was about.

"Why'd you not run full out after him? I've seen you run," said Boone, hands on his knees as he pulled in a few deep draughts of air. "Only one ever faster was me."

"Oh really?" said Mac, looking at the receding backs of the Acolytes. "Nah, I pulled up."

"Why? He was likely one of the Outcasts Creed is so bothered about."

"Likely is, but he's also a poor farm kid, and not much of a threat, if you ask me. Did you see the way he was dressed?" said Mac, shaking his head.

"Yeah, and the fear on his face. Ain't seen that since the battlefields of that damnable War of Northern Aggression."

"Don't get started on the war, Hoke. We don't have time to listen to your usual rant." Mac strode past him.

"Where you headed?"

"To find that girl. There was something more to that little encounter than religion."

"Yeah, like young love, maybe."

"Maybe. And Eliza's the one to tell us about it."

"That's right," said Boone. "He did call her that. Said, 'come on, come on,' something like that, too."

"Let's split up, see if we can't track her down." Mac veered to the right, in the direction of the church, which left Boone making for the left and the tidy cottages lining the lane leading into town. He hadn't run fifty feet when he saw, from around the corner of the nearest building—the bake house, if he wasn't mistaken—the shape of a woman in a dress, head down, rushing into the front yard of the third house on the left.

"Hey!" he shouted and she looked toward him. That blasted big black bonnet was in the way, but he swore it was the same girl who'd been man-handled by the Outcast kid.

If it was, she wanted no part of him and fairly sprinted to the house, wrenched the front door wide, and disappeared inside with a slamming sound.

Boone didn't let up until he was at the gate of the cottage. He was about to lift the latch and bull on through when he heard footsteps behind him and turned to see the two Acolytes bearing down on him. He spun and squared off, right there in the dusty lane.

"What's the story, fellas? You think you can point at me and scare me off? Me and my pard are here by official invite to figure out what ails this little town of yours! Seems to me we was called in to do what you fork-beards can't figure out how to do."

The two black-clad men separated and came at Boone from each side.

He held his ground, feet spread and hands raised. He still hadn't palmed a weapon, but only because he didn't see any weapons on the Acolytes, not even sheath knives under their flapping frock coats. But he well knew that didn't mean they didn't have them concealed.

He'd faced down more innocent-looking rogues than these, and some, a good many of them women, were anything but innocent. And they produced the darnedest weapons imaginable—hat pins, pocket knives, jagged bottle necks, poison-tipped fingernails, let alone little one- and two-shot hideout guns—and from the most frightening of places, too.

No sir, Boone knew to keep his hands free, ready to drag on either his knife, one of his own derringers, or his sidearm. But for close-in work, he preferred to keep it to bare knuckles and quickness of foot.

The one to his right, who he recognized as the very man who'd given him the rude pointing business a few minutes earlier, darted in and Boone saw it for what it was—a maneuver of distraction. The man stayed out of solid swinging range and feinted left, then right.

Boone was no wet-nose pup, and he sprang one side-step to his left and met the other, sneaking Acolyte square on with a quick, tight jab to the snot locker.

It did what Boone's Pa had taught him all those years before that a good solid punch should draw quick, easy blood. And the nose was the way to do the job.

"Fastest way to end a fight is to show a man his own life juice leaking from his face, boy," his Pa had said. "Never you let me hear you started a fight, but never let me hear you weren't the one to end it, you hear me, Hokum?"

It was something Boone had tried to keep in mind over the years and succeeded at some of the time.

That was one of many slices of raw, pure inspiration and wiseness from his Pa, rest him, that Boone carried with him like an heirloom knife.

All this and more flashed through Boone's mind quicker than his own fists flashed outward, lacing the fool Acolyte's hairy face with a flurry of blows.

Why, the idiot split-beard barely landed but one hit himself, a quick, glancing shot to Boone's left shoulder. Along about that time, the second man, the pointer, finally decided to make his own move. He whipped in left, then right, landing what Boone had to admit were decent blows. But Boone had been in plenty of scrapes and he knew how to take a hit, and in so doing, he knew how to fold around it and at the same time draw himself backward, sort of gather himself for a renewed effort.

And that's what Boone did. He whomped the finger-pointer once, twice, and set the man's teeth to rattling. His head pivoted back, clacking teeth and all, blood spraying from a split lip and a buggered nose.

Boone felt a finger snap of a moment of satisfaction knowing he'd not opened the ball but he damn sure did Pa proud and drew blood on the two rascals. And then he had to snap another shot at the chin of Pointer. The man was bigger and tougher than the other fellow and didn't know enough to back off.

That's when Boone saw something he hadn't expected to see—the man's mouth opened wide as his head jerked backward from the last punch, and behind the bloodied lips and red-rimmed teeth, there was a tiny, wagging, wet, pink stump where the man's tongue should be.

The shock of what he'd seen seized Boone in place a moment too long. That was all the opening the Acolyte he'd forgotten behind him needed. Hc barreled forward and flailed into Boone with the reckless thrown swings of a punch-addled man.

A hard-knuckled fist crunched against Boone's right ear, and set his head to ringing like a church bell had been set loose, rattling around inside his pate. The blow whipped his head to the left, and he twitched a second, thinking maybe he'd been paralyzed by the lucky shot.

But now, it was the shock of being caught unawares that dazzled him. He growled and spun and pummeled the attacker who'd launched at him from behind, an unforgivable play. That was another bit of advice that Pa had doled out to him long ago—always fight from the front, never weasel up on anything, be it a man, a beast, or a task. Face them all head on, and you'll never go to bed ashamed of yourself nor regretful of your actions.

His rallying round of shots caught the man in the chest and the shoulder. One side-long glancing blow on the brute's chin dazed the fool.

To Boone's horror, this man's mouth, also bloodied, opened wide for a moment as the man staggered back. There wriggled a badly healed, knobby clump of pink, wet flesh where a tongue should have been.

"What . . . ?" Boone took a couple of steps backward, his fists clawed tight and balled before him. He looked from one to the other. "Cat got 'em?" he said, between gasps, not taking his eyes off the savage bastards.

He hadn't meant it as something hurtful or malicious, almost as a joke to himself, and yet it was a sincere question, too. Surely this was no coincidence? It made some sense though, since none of the blasted Acolytes had uttered a danged word, other than a few grunts in this fight, in his or Mac's presence. But no tongues?

"Hoke!" bellowed a voice.

Boone cut his eyes to his right, upstreet, and saw Mac barreling toward him. The big man reached the three fighters, two of them still with chests heaving. Even before Mac reached them, he shouted, "What's the game here?"

"Easy now, Mac," said Boone, feeling oddly as if he needed to protect the two Acolytes, for some sliver of a reason, though he'd be hard-pressed to say why.

"Ain't no harm done, these two fellas were . . . ah, concerned that I was out to do harm to Miss Eliza, I guess."

At the mention of her name, the two battered, faced-bloodied men glared afresh at Boone and Mac.

"Calm yourselves, you fools," growled Boone. "I ain't never harmed a woman, and I ain't about to start!"

Mac stood by Boone's side, glowering, his run down the street having barely winded him. "I think we need to have a chat with your boss, Mr. Creed, or whatever he calls himself. What was that name? The Anointed One?" Mac looked at the men, who glowered at him and brushed the dust from their coat sleeves.

Mac looked at Boone. "Something I said?"

"More like something they didn't," said Boone, offering the Acolytes a half smile that quickly faded. Out of the corner of his mouth, he said, "They can't talk to you."

"Why not?" said Mac. "Too holy for us common folk?"

"Settle down, man," said Boone. "They . . . can't speak, is all."

"I don't understand."

Boone sighed. "My word," he said, at full voice. "For a smart fellow who spends more time with the fake dead people in books than he does with living folk, you'd think a body such as yourself would savvy when a fella's trying to tell you these two poor saps ain't got tongues!"

Mac's eyes snapped wide and he looked from Boone to the two men. "Oh," he said. "Oh."

The two scowling Acolytes shook their heads and stalked off up the road, in the direction of the big house.

"Well," said Boone. "Ain't no doubt about one thing. If they plan to blather to the boss man about whatever it is that happened here, he's gonna have a time getting it out of them." He glanced at Mac, then broke out in a wide grin and smacked his thigh. A cloud of dust rose up from his buckskins and set him coughing.

"What was that all about, Hoke?" said Mac, watching the

two men disappear up the street. They were indeed making for the mansion and Creed's study, no doubt.

"Oh, like I said, they was all riled that I was chasing that girl. I had to set them straight on the matter, though. Bloodied their noses and lips for them, I did. Done Pa proud, I reckon." He pointed a finger at Mac. "And they started it."

"I am quite certain of that, Boone. You are nothing if not a man of your word and honor."

"Damn straight. I think. Funny thing, Keller MacCoole, I can't never quite tell if you're funning me or flattering me."

"Maybe it's a bit of both."

"Huh."

"So the girl, where did she get to?"

"Oh, in there." Boone pointed at the cottage they stood before.

"Well, let's go," said Mac and popped open the simple wooden slide latch on the gate.

"Now, now, I don't think that's a good idea."

"Why not? Don't tell me those Acolyte fellows have gotten to you."

"What now? No, no, no, it's that, well, that girl, there, Miss Eliza, I'm guessing she's been through the mill already, what with being mauled by that kid and being chased by me. She looked right weepy when she stomped on in there."

"Why, Hokum Boone, I do believe you've become an old softy."

"What's that now?" Boone backed up and squared off, fists rotating and jaw jutting, looking not so much like a pugilist as a worked-up rooster.

Mac regarded his friend, then said, "Fine, but we're going to go see Hezekiah Creed."

It didn't take them long to make their way to the big house. As it dominated the western end of Brimstone's main street, they kept it in sight the entire walk up there.

Neither man spoke, knowing there wasn't much else to say. They needed more answers to questions they knew they were as yet unaware of.

They mounted the steps, and Mac rapped on one of the double doors at the top, half-shaded by the broad porch's overhang. His knuckles met the door's solid oak a second time, then the door swung open hard and two more Acolytes, neither were men they had seen before, stood shoulder to shoulder, glaring at the men.

"How many of you scowling goobers are there, anyway?" said Boone.

The comment did nothing to lighten their obvious dark moods.

"Where's your boss?" said Mac, using his impressive height to look over their heads, but the inside of the entryway was dimly lit and revealed little.

The two strongarms glowered.

"Creed!" shouted Boone through cupped hands. "Creed, come out, we want to talk."

One of the Acolytes surprised them and shook his head and made walking motions with the fingers of one hand across the open palm of the other.

"So Creed's gone off on a walk, eh?" said Boone. He looked up at Mac.

"Let's go. I got me an idea."

They departed and instead of walking back down the main street, they made for the bake house where a handful of women were still working away, engaged in various elements of the fine art of bread making.

Without knocking, Mac opened the door and he and Boone piled in and shut the door behind them.

The warmth of the room was nearly stifling, though the big door at the rear of the communal kitchen was wide open, as were all the windows.

Four women swung startled, bonnet-shrouded faces up to look at the newcomers.

Boone thought they all looked far too hot to wear bonnets, made for keeping the sun off faces. "I don't see the sun blazing too heavy in here, ladies," he said.

Both men held the brims of their hats in their thick hands.

"Ladies," said Mac. "We need to talk with somebody in this town who has a tongue and answers."

The women, as if on cue, dropped their startled eyes and bent their heads and resumed their various tasks.

"Ladies, as I expect you all know, Hezekiah Creed hired us to deal with the Outcasts who have apparently been molesting you all and doing their best to disturb the good works of the Kindred."

Mac let that hang in the air a moment, hoping that bit of fawning might persuade them to chat. The two men waited.

For nothing.

As they left the bakery, hotter, hungrier, and with as few answers as they went in with, Boone said, "You don't suppose they all lost their tongues, do you?"

"Not hardly," said Mac. "If I had to guess, I'd say those foolish Acolytes did that as a ritual of some sort."

"Yeah, I wondered that myself. You think all the Acolytes are tongueless?"

"It's a safe guess. Not a one of them has spoken in our presence yet. Heck, we don't even know how many of them there are."

"What a crazy town," said Boone, shaking his head. "What say we walk back to that girl's house?" He shrugged. "Might as well give it a go."

"I think, given how the Acolytes feel about us, we might get her in more trouble than she needs."

"Oh, good thinking. Well." Boone smacked his belly. "I would like to find something in this town worth eating. The bread smells fine, but like everything else here, it's afraid to flavor up."

Mac nodded. "I do believe we still have enough flour for biscuits and a little bacon, too."

"Now you're talking my lingo, pard."

That same morning, the two men once again walked throughout the town. They figured they'd stick together, as they had more talking to do.

So far Creed had not only not been helpful, he'd all-but disappeared. Either he'd taken a buggy trip somewhere or, more likely, he was holed up in his mansion, doing whatever it was that suspicious religious leaders do.

The one thing they could set their pocket watches to were the times of the services in the church. They had expected Creed would be there for every one of them, and that morning they heard a voice they thought was his coming from inside.

When they tried to enter, seven unfamiliar Acolytes had blocked all the doors and stood with their hands folded across their waists, shaking their heads, their odd parted beards wagging.

"I aim to talk to that rascal," said Boone, a few feet away from the latest Acolyte to bar their entrance to the church. "But even I ain't crass enough to barge in on a service of worship."

Mac smiled. "Hoke, I'd normally be inclined to go along with such a sentiment, but at this moment, we really need answers. So if he doesn't show his face soon, I say we leave. And take a loaf of bread or two with us as payment."

They walked toward their tiny cabin. "Yeah, I hear you," said Boone. "What I don't understand is why he called us here anyway. Seemed keen as heck to get us on the case.

Then once we're here he doesn't give us any help, and sends those tongueless devils after us every time we try to make a move! I'm about done with this. I'd rather go back to guarding Jasper's freight runs, and you know how little I thought of those."

Mac nodded. He felt the same way. Jasper's was a long, boring bit of work, but it paid well, and best of all, there wasn't a whole lot of mystery surrounding it. You guarded the freight, winging anybody who tried to make off with it. Simple. But this? This had quickly become a confusing waste of time.

"And this blasted town's dry as a cork, to boot!" growled Boone, kicking at the dusty lane at the end of the rows of houses. Before them lay fields of vegetables, with grains to the left, along the north side of the road. To the south of the roadway sat broad strips of pasture land in which grazed beef cattle, and in an adjoining pasture, sheep.

It was still early, but they were hardly the first folks in Brimstone to be up and out their doors. Most of the town's residents had already crammed into the church for their early-morning service. Mac and Boone ventured down the long lane toward the fields, enjoying the newly risen sun lighting the land before them.

"What's that, yonder?" said Boone, gesturing with his morning cigarillo. Thick, blue smoke parted before him, and they saw a dark shape humped twenty yards before them in the roadway.

Mac squinted. "A dog? Calf?"

"Nah, no dogs in town that I seen yet, and a stray calf would be bawling for his mama. No, it's something else."

Mac shrugged and they walked toward it.

"Oh no," said Boone, his excellent eyesight allowing him to see what lay ahead a couple of seconds sooner than Mac.

Boone bolted forward, with Mac close behind. Within

two steps, the big man saw what Boone had seen—what looked to be the young man from the day before, the Outcast.

He lay in the middle of the road, at the end of the lane, the very lane they'd ridden in on, the one that led right out of Brimstone and stretched toward the near and far hills. A trail, overgrown for the most part, was visible angling out, and upward, into those hills to the southeast.

But it was not the hills that concerned the men at that moment. They saw that the kid was sprawled on his side in the road, his back to them. Before they reached him, each man muttered not-so-silent prayers, hoping against blind hope that the youth was merely unconscious, nothing more.

Boone reached the kid first, dropped to his knees, and grasped the young man's jutting shoulder. "Hey, fella!" He shook him, tugged him lightly toward him, and the man flopped backward, his head and shoulders slopping awkwardly into Boone's lap.

Boone screamed.

Mac said, "Dear God . . ." and turned away, a big hand over his mouth.

Where the young man's eyes should be were two swollen, red-black, clotted wounds. Someone had plucked out the kid's eyes.

"Son? Son?" whispered Boone, shaking the boy by the shoulders. The movement jostled the youth's head and his lips sagged open. Inside his mouth sat another fresh wound, a clot of blood that did not quite hide the rough stump of a tongue, now blackened and pitted.

The front of the young man's once-blue shirt was now stained dark with blood, not only from the wounds to his face but also from the three gashes as wide as the blade of a hunting knife.

"Just a kid," growled Mac through tight-set teeth.

"I didn't think even they'd be up to this sort of thing." Still cradling the boy's savaged head, Boone looked up at Mac. "This is unthinkable, Mac."

Mac nodded in agreement. "Hezekiah. We need to find him."

"What about him?" said Boone, laying the kid down on the road, face up, gingerly.

A man's voice from the field to their left said, "Leave him there."

Boone and Mac spun. The big man already had his Dragoon palmed and cocked, and Boone's right hand had clawed free the hideout gun closest to it, from a discrete pocket on the side of his buckskin tunic.

The man stood in the field, twenty feet from them, his hands held at shoulder height. He wore the black hat and beard of the Brimstone men, white shirt, braces, trousers, and boots. But he was old, as old as the rest of the men they'd seen in town, anyway. That there had been precious few younger men about the town had been another point of concern for them.

"Explain yourself, mister!" Boone sneered at the man. "Or you'll end up like him!"

"Not that we are responsible for this man's death," added Mac.

"I know you are not," said the man in the field. "I know who did it."

"The Acolytes," said Mac, rasping a thick hand across his stubbled chin. He knew he was right, and from the lack of aggressiveness on his part, and his downcast eyes, this man agreed. "How long?"

"What?" said the man.

"How long has this foolishness been happening?"

But the man's response didn't answer the question. "They are following the Will of the One. It is His Will that brought about the death of the Outcast. He was displeased with the boy's behavior toward one of the Kindred. There are consequences. There are always consequences."

"What foolishness are you spouting at us?" shouted Boone. His voice shook but his gunhand held steady.

The Kindred man in the field did not flinch, did not move save for a squint. He showed no fear of them or their guns. "The boy's fellow Outcasts will retrieve him. It is the Will of the One."

Mac and Boone did not move.

"Leave him, I tell you," said the man once again, then turned his back on them and walked away, into the chest-high crop of corn. In moments he was gone, a shadow among shadows in the early-morning sunlight slanting in on the green crop, the leaves of which rustled gently on an unfelt breeze.

CHAPTER 9

Not long after they left the dead young man in the road, they made for Creed's mansion. They were not allowed entry by yet more Acolytes. As they walked away, toward the stable, Boone gave voice to what they were both thinking. "How many of those devils you think he had working for him?"

Mac shook his head. "Good question. Hopefully not more than we can handle at one time."

Mac took his leave of Boone at the stable. They conversed in low whispers and the head nods of men familiar with each other's habits through long years together on the trail. They agreed that Mac would be the one to ride off into the hills and find the Outcasts to find out their side of the story.

Boone was up for it, but he wasn't as good at tracking as his large companion. But he was smaller, sly, and sneakier, and so that made him ideally suited to staying back in Brimstone and sniffing about the odd place.

Lincoln, Mac's trusty Appaloosa, had been with him nearly as long as had Boone. "Sometimes, horse, you're a whole lot easier to take than Hokum Boone. But don't tell him I said that." He patted the big horse's neck, then rode out past the spot where, but a short time before, the dead Outcast kid had lain.

As the older Kindred man had said would happen, the body was gone. Mac presumed it was the Outcasts' doing. If so, that would make his job of tracking them far easier, for whoever retrieved the kid's body had used a wheeled cart, not a beast of burden. Well, in a situation involving a hand-cart, the man is the beast of burden.

Judging from the tracks leading to the spot where the kid had lain, Mac saw there were two men involved. One to keep guard, likely, and one to push the gruesome load. Leading away, the prints of one were heavier, the stride shorter, indicating they'd left with the kid's body.

Their trail was easy to track, as it followed the roadway out of Brimstone and into the hills to the southeast of town curved with the slow rise of the land. It never was steep, but he sensed they were climbing. The higher up they climbed, the more switchbacks the lane took. It also quickly narrowed to little more than a single-track hunting path.

Mac guessed it had once been—and maybe still was—a game trail. Wild critters were no different from their two-legged kin in towns in that they always made for the easiest route. Why fight the terrain any more than you had to?

It was a good lesson he'd learned early as a kid hunting the hills of Vermont, bagging squirrel and rabbit for the pot. Sometimes, if he was lucky, he'd nab what he had then called a dummy bird, because they would stay still, as did deer and most game, hoping not to be seen. All the while you were sighting in on them and about to touch off the trigger. He later learned from Gampy, his grandfather on his mother's side, who lived with them, that they were not dummies at all.

They were intelligent birds, he'd said, but the unfairness of guns hadn't worked its way into their critter thinking. Gampy had thought it might take many hundreds of years, maybe even longer, before it would. He also taught young Mac that the dummy birds that weren't really dumb were called grouse.

Mac had been riding for more than an hour, slowly climbing higher, deeper into the high rocks, when he caught himself musing. He was about to half-cock the rifle he'd laid across his thighs as he rode, when he spied the first shack.

It was a surprise to see such in the sparsely treed, rocky place, but it was even more surprising to see how cleverly disguised it was. Part rock, part plank, part small log, the shelter was a sight he could easily have ridden on by had he not had so much experience in tracking while in the war.

He'd learned to see all about himself even when he wasn't looking. Even that skill didn't warn him in time of the man peering at him from up the trail, to his right. Peering at him down the barrel of a rifle.

Mac halted Lincoln and eyed the man a moment. He judged he'd have but a second should the man tense that hand on the rear stock, which Mac could see, given the angle of the man's stance.

It would be enough time to pull low and drop to his left, yanking the rifle with him. He'd roll with the momentum and come up firing.

Then the man cocked his head as if he had been told something. Without taking his eyes from Mac, he eased, and the rifle barrel lowered an inch or so.

Mac held his pose, still plenty ready to swing up his own rifle. He was about to shout, "Ho there," when a second man stepped out from behind the gun toter and into the trail.

This man looked similar to the first. Mac studied them both and saw thick beards streaked with gray, growing out of gaunt faces beneath flop-brim hats. Their clothes were layers of well-worn cloth, patches on patches. Their worn boots were poorly mended with thick wraps of rawhide. This second man, as with the first, carried a rifle. The other joined him in the narrow trail, neither scowling nor smiling, merely staring. And blocking the roadway.

Finally, the second man said, "What's it going to be, then?"

Mac adjusted himself in the saddle. "I'm here to . . ." What was he there for, exactly? To roust them? To shoot them? No, to find out about them, that was all. Then figure it all out from there. They hadn't been hostile to him. Yet. So no need to jump to that notion yet himself.

"I'm here to talk with you, if you be the Outcasts."

The comment made the man react in a way Mac had not expected to see on so dour a face. The man smiled. The other chuckled and shook his head.

"Yeah, we figured. Only a stranger to Brimstone wouldn't know such a thing." The man walked forward, the other followed. About a dozen feet before Mac's horse, they spread apart, as much as the trail would allow, and held.

The one who'd done the talking so far nodded. "We invite you to step down. And make sure to slide that rifle in the boot. Then you can walk with your reins in one hand and the other up away from that holster. Okay?"

Mac nodded. So far, the fellow was friendly, if tired looking. In fact, they looked like little more than worn-out farmers, ill-equipped and ill-suited to living in a settlement of rag-tag shacks wedged into the scraggle-growth hillside.

Soon, that suspicion proved all the more truthful. Another dozen men stepped without sound from out of the surrounding landscape. They were of varying ages, from a couple in their late teenage years to a few old limpers, and they all shared the same gaunt-faced, rough-beard, ratty-clothed look.

He didn't question where they were leading him. He felt somehow as though they were trustworthy, and he felt as if they had been expecting him one of these days. None of them looked surprised to see him.

They walked with a slow, steady gait, their feet and hands swinging as if they were burdens that relied more on momentum than strength to keep moving. Some of them carried weapons. Most of the guns were older, but serviceable, and he spied one or two brass buckles that bore the tell-tale letters "US," and one with "CSA," remnants of the foul war they had also somehow survived.

After a solid ten minutes of walking, cutting left then right along branches of trail that veined away from the main path, trails that even Mac wasn't certain he could follow back to get out of there, he asked of no one in particular, "Where are we headed?"

About then they rounded a boulder, and in a clearing before him he saw the source of the tickle of campfire smoke his nose had detected some minutes earlier.

"Yonder," said the man, nodding, walking off Mac's left side.

By the smoking campfire in the midst of the well-trampled clearing stood a broad-shouldered man, easily Mac's height, hair nearly to his shoulders, beard halfway down his chest. There was more pepper than salt to his beard and his broad straw hat shaded, but did not hide, a strong, bony face and two glinting gray eyes.

Poking from the ample shrub of beard was a bent-stem briar pipe clenched in the hidden mouth. No smoke drifted from the pipe.

They came to a stop on the other side of the smoking fire. The man across from him regarded him a moment longer, then nodded. "Keith there will take your horse, see that he's watered."

Mac looked to his side, saw a haggard but kindly looking man standing nearby, holding an arm extended as if to take the reins from him. Mac considered a moment longer, then nodded once and handed over the reins. So far his trusted instincts, or as Boone called them, his "gut flibbers," weren't telling him much of anything in the way of danger signs.

Mac eyed the man across the fire.

The man with the pipe said, "You arrive in our midst at an interesting time."

"How so?"

"We brought home the body of one of our own not long ago. But then you knew that."

Mac nodded. "Yes. The young man. We saw him alive yesterday."

"So did we," said the pipe smoker.

"Yes," said Mac. "He was bothering a girl down there in Brimstone."

"What girl?" said the man, but he asked it in such a way that made Mac think the man already knew the answer.

"I believe her name was Eliza."

The man with the pipe nodded, as did several other of the haggard men. "I reckon he had a right to bother her."

"How do you figure that?" said Mac.

The man looked him in the eye. "She was his sister."

"What?"

The man didn't answer, but made a show of poking the fire's dwindling embers with a long stick, the end charred where it had poked countless coals before. Finally, he drew a deep breath and pulled the pipe from his mouth. "What is it you think we're doing up here?"

The man's tone was not as friendly as before. There was nothing specific about his change in attitude, but Mac saw it for what it was. And what's more, he felt certain he was about to learn a little something.

"So you're the Outcasts," he said.

Another man snorted, shook his head, and dragged a hand across his bony jaw. "That's rich," said the man.

He reminded Mac of Boone in appearance. Even that mannerism was Hokum-like.

"How so?"

The man with the pipe said, "How would you like to be called an outcast in your own home?"

"Not sure I understand your meaning."

The man who looked like Boone said, "Damn right, you don't."

"Easy, Zeb." The man with the pipe nodded to a thigh-height boulder beside Mac that he now saw had been chipped away somewhat in the middle to better accommodate sitting.

"Have a seat and I'll try to explain."

Mac did as he was bade, keeping his weapons ready to bear should the need arise.

"I'm Roland. Roland Toomey, by the way."

Mac nodded. "Keller MacCoole. Folks call me Mac. Pleased to meet you all."

The assemblage of grim men stared at him, not one offering a nod.

Roland Toomey cleared his throat. "I'll explain the situation to you, to sort of balance the lies you've been told by that jackass charlatan, Hezekiah Creed. But tell me one thing first—I take it you and that little fellow in the buckskins are hired guns."

Mac's surprise must have shown on his face.

"Yeah, we seen you both. Don't know your names, but we've marked your comings and goings. So, as I say, I expect you are hired guns brought in to deal with the likes of us. Am I right?"

"Yes, that's about the size of it."

"Well, that's not a new notion to him nor to us. But I will say you're the first with gut enough to seek us out. For that, we'll listen to you. But first, you'll listen to us."

"Fair enough."

"Everything down there?" said Roland, gesturing with his pipe. "Everything you came from? The town that jackass calls 'Brimstone'?"

Mac waited for more but the man let it hang, awaiting an answer. "Yes, what about it?"

"He stole it."

"From who?"

"My God, man," said Zeb, reminding Mac more than ever of Boone. "If you ain't the thinnest flame I ever seen."

"Easy, Zeb." Toomey placed the pipe stem back between his teeth. "This one isn't as dim as he seems. He wants the full story from us. Am I right, mister?"

"That's about it," said Mac.

"Okay then. Creed stole it from us. We founded the town, named it Promise, too. Not this 'Brimstone' foolishness. We all settled this valley years ago, came here with hopes and dreams and all that happy codswallop. Back before we knew better, we built this entire valley into a respected, happy, family-filled center of agriculture." The man warmed to his topic and waved an arm. The rest of the men nodded.

Mac thought briefly of Creed and his similar movements and mannerisms, of his proselytizing.

"We built it up, the whole thing. Then Hezekiah Creed showed up and commenced his preaching. Nothing wrong with that, at first. But soon enough, he began convincing people to join his so-called church. Then everyone in town succumbed to his smooth, silvery tongue."

"Not everyone," said Mac.

The man nodded. "True. We're the only ones with sense enough to see through his ways. The rest of them you saw down there are stuck in Creed's muck up to their arm pits."

"What about choosing for oneself?"

"Sure, I hear what you mean, but that isn't the way all this works." He gestured wide. "It isn't the way the world works. You know?"

Mac nodded.

"Those who didn't join were forced out, as you can see. We're a worn-out band of fighters, all right. Problem is, we have to pick and choose our fights, lest somebody gets hurt."

"Why would you care?"

"Oh, we don't care about the Acolytes, and certainly not about Creed, but they're wily and we aren't well armed. Don't forget, we were farmers."

"Still are!" said Zeb, the man who reminded Mac of Boone.

Roland nodded. "God willing." Then he looked at Mac and smiled. "The real God, that is. Not the clap-trap that fool peddles."

"We make raids down into town in hopes of convincing the Kindred to leave the church."

"Because the Kindred are your, well, your kin, am I right?" said Mac.

"Got it in one." Roland shifted to his other foot and rubbed his upper arms as if he were a cold, old man. "They're our families. Our children, brothers, sisters, uncles, aunts, parents . . . and wives."

The group was silent. Mac wasn't too certain what to say next.

Roland broke the gloomy spell. "That son of a . . ." His voice trembled with rage, and he tugged the pipe from his teeth. "He's bedded my own wife. My wife! I'd ride down there right now and take him apart finger by finger if it got me my Ruthie back. But it won't."

"How many . . ."

"Wives has he claimed?" said the skinny man, roistering up his chest. "Who knows? More than is right, that's for damn certain."

"So now you know why we're called 'outcasts' in our own home." Roland spat. "So be it. Now we the Outcasts want it back."

"Why fight for it for so long? Why die for it?" said Mac. "Wouldn't it be easier to move on, call it a loss, and admit the bigger force won the battle?"

"Yeah, sure it would," said the man with the pipe. "Except for our families." Roland nodded to his right once more, in the general direction of Brimstone. "We can't leave them behind. We won't leave them behind."

Mac saw several of the men in the ragged cluster about him squeeze their fists in impotent rage, their gray eyes rheumy with fatigue and helplessness. But he saw something else there, too. He saw the flicker, faint, to be sure, but still there, of a dim hope.

"They are our children, our brothers, sisters, uncles, aunts, parents . . . wives." The pipe man didn't appear to realize he was repeating himself.

Mac let out a long breath. Creed's was, as he had strongly suspected from the start, a cult of sideways religion. Some sort of stunted worship that maybe had begun innocent enough, as most churches seem to, but then grew a freakish limb. From what Mac could see it now served no purpose but to enrich the jowls, the self-importance, and likely the coin purse of Hezekiah Creed. He wondered if Creed even believed the palaver he spewed.

"So your own wife joined up?"

The man nodded. "Yeah. I warned her, tried not to let her mix with them that began to feel his strange powers. Hell, we all tried." He gestured at the others, shaking his head. They were all silent. "He was a traveling preacher who came to town one day. He didn't have much in the way of possessions, but he sure had a way with that tongue of his. Convincing folks left, right, and center of the wickedness of their lives and all. Hell, before we knew it, he had half the town doing his bidding, all out of fear."

"Fear," repeated Mac.

"Yeah. Creed got them all so riled up into believing that the devil himself was waiting around every corn stalk and house corner. And that he, by good fortune, was the one man on the whole earth who knew a way to keep us all from slipping into a world of pure fire."

Roland shook his head, a grim grin marking the memory of that foul time. "By God, but we tried. In the end it wasn't enough. Somehow, he got to them all. Got right inside their heads."

He tapped a blunt, callused finger against his temple. "I still don't know how he did it, but you be careful yourself, man. That Hezekiah Creed, he's wily. He took my wife for his own, to live in the big house with him and the rest of his women."

"How many wives does the man have?" Mac couldn't imagine wanting or needing any more than one spouse in one's life. No, this Creed's so-called marriages were not based on love. It was the other thing, the unspoken part of all this, that kept these men at the boiling point.

Toomey shrugged. "I don't know for certain. Must be at least a half-dozen, maybe more by now. For some reason people keep on showing up and settling in Brimstone. I reckon they'll get powerful enough to run us out of these hills one day, too."

Mac was about to ask why they didn't fight back in a bigger way, instead of little ineffective forays in ones and twos such as the boy tried, desperate weak attempts to take back their lives. But the tiredness he saw on their faces, and the fact that there were so few of them in number, answered the question.

"Ask your new friends why Hezekiah Creed won't allow people to leave his fold."

"At all?"

"Well, Creed will let them leave, sure. In fact, he encourages them to leave if they're not happy. But somehow they never make it out of town."

"What happens then?" said Mac, though he knew the answer right enough.

"Then," said Roland Toomey, sighing. "Then they are hunted, run aground like rats, like mangy foxes fleeing a hen house. Only there's no struggling hens in their jaws, only a desperate need to get away. Many times before, bodies have been dumped at the edge of town, bodies of our kin. Today, it was the boy."

Mac winced at the word, so similar to "kindred," but said nothing.

"A few of them weren't quite dead. We did our best to nurse them. We don't have much up here. Both times they died, but not before they told us things. Terrible, terrible things.

"So, to answer your question," said Roland. "No, not really. They never let anyone leave the church. At least not alive and unmutilated. They are hunted, savaged, then dumped outside of town. Most are dead, but a few told us of terrible punishments and rituals taking place in that hell hole before they died."

"What sort of punishments?"

Roland took a deep breath. "There are unwanted children who are never allowed to romp and play. There are the sick and infirm born to unmarried women. Some of them not far beyond childhood themselves. And when you go back there, Mr. Hired Gun, ask yourself why there aren't many old folks.

I'll tell you why, save you the trouble of figuring it out. They're sacrificed and then dumped in a mass grave beyond the church."

The man with the pipe poked at the smoldering coals while another man dumped a small armload of sticks beside the fire ring, then bent low and began slowly to rekindle a blaze.

There was an awkward, long silence, then Mac stood. "I brought a few things," he said. The stone was cold on his backside and he didn't need to usher rheumatism into his life. It had laid low plenty in his family in the past. "If you'll let me at my saddlebags." Lincoln stood tied a dozen feet away.

"Seems odd you'd travel up here with provisions."

"Not so odd," said Mac, unbuckling the near bag. "Considering I didn't know who or what I'd find. I was hoping to use them as peace offerings."

The men, despite their efforts to remain cool and standoffish, eyed with keen glances what Mac brought forth from the bag. "Coffee," he said. "And some corn meal, not much, but it'll make a batch of fritters."

He pulled out another, smaller bundle. "And here," he said, tossing it to the man with the pipe. "Tobacco. I noticed you haven't lit that thing once while we've talked. I'm partial to a pipe now and again, especially when I'm thinking through a thorny problem."

The men, Mac counted fourteen of them—no doubt there were others keeping watch—had fetched battered tin cups from here and there, and gathered around the crackling little campfire. He guessed this was the whole lot of them. A ragged, sad lot it was.

As their leader packed tobacco in his pipe and passed the sack of tobacco around to the others, he spoke. "Ask your new friend, Creed, about the children, the ones who are born to women not yet married. Ask about the sick and the infirm. Ask yourself why everyone in that blighted town seems healthy and on the younger side of life. Where are the truly old ones?"

Mac knew he wasn't expected to respond.

"I'll tell you where—look past the old tree line, out behind their damnable church. You'll find graves. Or more to the point, you'll find one grave. It's a big pit they keep opening along the far edge, enough to dump in someone else. Somebody's mother or father, grandfather or granny.

"As I said, others have tried to escape, to expose them, and they are killed for the effort. That cult has blood on its hands, more than can ever wash away."

They were silent as they ruminated on what Roland Toomey had said. None of it was new to the Outcasts. It was all spoken for his benefit. The wound was always fresh, thought Mac, never allowed to heal for these poor bastards.

"We're about to give them what-for, though," said a voice to Mac's right.

This new voice surprised Mac and he looked at the man, a young, wolfish, haunted-looking fellow. Then Mac saw Toomey glaring at the speaker, as if to shut him up. It worked, for the young man said no more, though the flinty look in his eyes spoke much.

They passed around one of their few tin cups with coffee and he accepted it when it came to him. He sipped, not wishing to insult them.

In the silence, Mac said, "Why haven't you tried to get help from the outside before now?"

"Who, us?" Toomey laughed. "What makes you think we haven't tried? But who'd work for nothing? Which is exactly what we have here. Look around, man." He spread his arms wide, in a gesture that reminded Mac of Creed. "We're poor as outhouse rats. Barely surviving as it is. Besides, look at them down there in town, and then look at us. Who would you believe? Hezekiah Creed is a controlling tyrant, but he isn't stupid. We've learned he's a powerful and wealthy man in Utah Territory."

"At the risk of insulting you men, it doesn't look like you're doing such a good job of it."

None of them looked insulted at his statement of the obvious. Finally, Toomey said, "Well, maybe not, but we aren't waiting much longer to avenge the boy. You hear?"

Mac nodded, seeing the man's temper rising—and for good reason. "Let me try something first. Me and my friend. If you don't hear from me in two days, then you do what you feel you need to. But understand this, I won't stand by and let you harm innocent people."

"We only intend to harm the ones who took our kind, the ones who keep them from us, who keep us from them. The ones Creed calls his Acolytes."

"What do you know about them?" said Mac.

"Mostly that none of them were here before, when things were good, back in our old lives. Creed brought them in later."

"You know they do that," Zeb spoke up, and gestured with a grimy finger at his own mouth. "To themselves!" He nodded.

Toomey continued. "It's to prove what Creed calls 'unspoken loyalty to The One.' What that really means is to him. And it's mighty convenient to have the men who commit the biggest sins on your behalf unable to speak."

Mac regarded the group a moment longer, then said, "I expect we'll meet again."

Roland Toomey shook his hand. "I expect if you aren't successful, which you won't be, and if you defend him from us, we'll have to kill you one of these days."

"Don't count on it," said Mac. "I want to see if I can make this right, Roland." Mac eyed the man as he said it.

Toomey's hard, gray eyes never blinked. Finally, he said, "If you do, you'll be the first."

Mac knew there was little else he could do here, no other information to be gleaned from these starved surroundings. He turned to Lincoln and grasped the reins once more. "Promise me one thing—you won't venture a fresh attack until I try something of my own first. Two days."

Toomey eyed him, puffing out a thinning cloud of smoke, then nodded. "Two days."

Mac nodded, touched his hat brim to the men, and swung up into the saddle.

"Hey," said Toomey.

Mac looked over at the man with the pipe.

Toomey knocked his dead pipe on his callused palm. "I told you my name, but you should know the rest of us. We're men, not criminals, not outlaws, nor outcasts, either." He looked to his right and nodded. and the rest of the men, one by one, spoke their names, looking Mac in the eye.

When they'd finished, Mac said, "Pleased to meet you all. As I said, my friends call me Mac. My pard is Hokum Boone, but you can call him Boone or Hoke, he answers to either." He smiled. "And sometimes he shows up, especially if he smells food."

He felt bad about his joke as soon as he said it. He'd meant little more than to leave on friendly terms, but these men didn't look to have had a solid meal in some time.

"One last thing, MacCoole," said Toomey. "As far as Brimstone goes, Creed lets very few folks in. And then the ones he does are hardly ever seen again outside of town. You and your pal ought to sleep wide awake, if you take my meaning."

He nodded to them once more and slowly guided the big horse downslope, retracing his route. None of the men had offered to guide him back down, but he figured he knew the way.

He wished he had had more to offer them, but he vowed to himself to bring them more goods, whatever he was able. If, that is, he was allowed to return. He had a feeling those vicious, split-bearded, tongueless Acolytes were fixing to give them trouble, and soon.

"Let them try," he muttered as he angled Lincoln back down the long hills to the gaping maw of Brimstone.

CHAPTER 10

Boone waited in the stable until he heard the now-familiar sounds of many voices repeating what one voice was saying, all coming through the open windows of the church not too far away. “Bunch of yowling thumpers,” he mumbled to his horse, Chummy, standing hipshot in his stall. “But at least we know where most of them are about now.”

He didn’t waste any more time, but made his way out the far, western end of the building, and catwalked low through the corral, ducking between rails. Yonder sat the massive mansion he was headed for. He only had to get there, then get inside without being seen. If he was caught, he would claim he was trying to get hold of Creed because he had been avoiding him and Mac. That part wasn’t a lie.

He’d seen the back of the place from a distance, when he and Mac had roamed the town, gawking at whatever they might. Funny that they’d decided to ride on out of here and wish them all good luck when circumstances changed their minds. That poor kid went and got himself killed for handling that young woman.

The thought of the kid’s mutilated face and beat-to-hell

body, knifed and bled out in the dust, kept Boone's eyes skittering and his hand resting easy on his sidearm.

"Ain't no way I'm going to let one of them no-tongue, fork-bearded scum have at me. Leastwise not without a fight." He often whispered to himself, and found that the thing his dear old Granny used to say about such doings was correct: You talk to yourself, you meet a nicer bunch of folks that-a-way. She should know, as the old girl was one hell of a chatty lady, most notably when nobody else was around.

It took him a couple of minute's worth of low-walking and whispering and scouting, as if his head were on a swivel, to make it to the back door. From what he'd seen of it from a distance on their few walks about the place, the little, uncovered porch he had reached topped a rise of four steps. If he had to guess, and that's all he could do at this point, he'd say the kitchen was inside there. Funny, no sounds came from in there, though. And so far, he'd seen nobody about.

He didn't trust those Acolytes a whisker, but it appeared that nobody was around, despite the fact that it didn't seem likely the whole town was crammed into that church. But he wasn't going to wait around long enough for someone to discover him.

At the top of the steps, he whiskered past a churn and a raised trough for washing various kitchen implements. He didn't know what half of them were for, but they were all arranged tidily.

Boone swung wide a screen door. It leaked out a low squawk. He thumbed the latch on the inner door and pushed it inward. He swallowed, poked his revolver's sniffer inside, and followed it with his own. Nothing.

He glanced behind once more, then stepped in.

He was relieved to see it was indeed the kitchen, and it appeared to be empty of people. He wasn't much of a hand at formal kitchen work, nor much use at informal, either. He could, by gum, make a dandy batch of biscuits, beans, and bitter-as-an-old-shrew coffee on a campfire, though. And he could fry up a hunk of fresh-killed meat and it usually didn't come out so bad.

He had no problem eating it, and most of the time Mac was too polite to complain. He knew that when Mac pulled a face and hemmed and hawed about the edible qualities of the meat, that the meal wasn't Boone's most toothsome culinary effort.

As he stepped deeper into the room, Boone wondered about Mac's whereabouts, and hoped he was faring okay in the hills with that Outcast lot. Nothing for it, as they often split up in their investigations on the tougher jobs. It was the only way they could get anything done.

He glanced around. "Hello?" he said, in a low voice. "Anybody about?"

The room was silent, and somewhat dark, as most of the place seemed to be. He recalled there weren't all that many windows on the place, and those he saw, most of them of the fancy stained-glass variety, were either shuttered or had thick curtains drawn.

"They afraid the sun's going to cause them to sin?" he muttered, fighting down the urge to cross the room and tug the curtains wide, but he didn't see a window.

The dark would work to his advantage, anyway. He closed the door behind him and shifted his gaze once more to the room. It was the tidiest kitchen he'd ever seen.

The long work table that dominated the middle of the room was a well-used surface, smooth wood from years of womanly efforts, such as slapping and pounding away on bread dough. Above it hung a suspended rack with a number of large copper pots and an assortment of cast-iron pans. He'd hate to be strapped to the table and have that lot drop on him. Crush a fellow if he wasn't cautious.

Behind him, in the middle of the wall that faced the

church, a dry sink held nothing more than two folded and hanging towels from its front edge.

The cookstove hugged the far wall, closer to the innards of the house, and likely shared a chimney with some other room heater. But this one gave off a faint warmth, dampered down as it was, awaiting someone to return from church and attend to it.

That thought got him moving once more. There was plenty in the room to explore, to sniff at and rummage in, maybe even some toothsome treats to sample. Though from the paltry and nearly flavorless meals they'd been fed, it seemed that even if he did find a snack, he'd regret taking a sample of it.

Still, he did sniff something savory and moist hanging in the dim air of the kitchen. Smelled like a cut of charred meat of some sort, but clouded with a light hint of gravy, enough to make his mouth water. Might even be a bird of some sort. Boone heard his stomach gurgle. He'd need to eat soon. But he reminded himself he was no thief, much as he sorely wanted to be at that moment.

This was too much like thief's work, he thought as he crossed the room and made for the one other door. It had to be the magical way into the place. Again, he paused. This door was gappy about the edges and hinged such that it swung to and fro, like batwings in a saloon, but it was full height. He reckoned it made lugging food in and out easier. If you met someone halfway through and collided you were bound to drop a tray of food or dishes.

It made Boone smile to think something like that might cause Hezekiah Creed discomfort. He poked his nose into the next room and saw it was a dining room, complete with a long table bordered with chairs. There was one place set, at the far end, facing this way. Had to be where Creed set himself down to be waited on by all those women they'd seen when they first met with Creed.

Boone looked about again but saw no one. Several doors led off this room, one in particular caught his eye. It stood on the side wall, at the far end of the table and thus the room. It was not a swinger, but it had a latch. It also fronted the wall that led to the main part of the house, not out toward the front foyer, and if he recalled correctly, beyond to Creed's office.

Boone had done this sort of snooping around long enough to trust his gut flibbers, as he called them. They rarely led him down an odd path. And that door was chiming his gut something fierce. He catfooted down to it and tried the handle. It resisted him. He tried again, and it still put up a fight.

Boone grinned as he reached into his tunic and tugged out a rawhide pouch slung on a thong about his neck. He carried various essential items in it, as he did all over his person, in fact.

A clock on a mantel above a fireplace set in the dark-paneled wall behind him chimed softly, clanging a low, brassy, warm sound. Nonetheless it nudged his heart up his throat. He paused. No feet sounded anywhere in the place that he could detect, and he prided himself on having ears the equal to his eyes. He could see the whiskers on a skeeter at a hundred paces.

Alternating between glancing at his nimble fingers as they rummaged in his sack and looking about the still too-quiet room, Boone managed at last a grim smile as he tweezered out a couple of long, slender, stiff, oddly shaped lengths of metal no longer than his pointer finger.

He squatted before the door's lock mechanism and, with one eye squinting and the tip of his tongue gripped between his teeth, Boone thrust the two odd-shaped pieces of steel into the skeleton-key's hole and worked them, angling to the inside edge of the diminutive mechanism's interior.

Boone's face scrunched, he held his breath, working the two bits up and down, in tandem and then apart, hearing clicks and pops, no louder than sounds a mouse might make. He smelled the dry, dusty tang of unoiled metal and silently cursed whoever should have been maintaining such expensive door hardware. Wasn't often that he had come across a quality steel lock out here in the wilds of the blooming American West.

Last time he'd had to work a lock like this was six, no, seven months back, when they were caught up in that Hazlitt affair, with the widow in her musty weeds stalking after him wherever he went in that blasted rich-folks' hotel.

Couldn't get a wink of shut eye while they were there, but they'd signed on to do the job that needed doing. They'd found the culprits and proved the rascals had done what everybody figured they'd done anyway.

But it had been the crazy old widow who'd taken a shine to him, even though she'd seen Mac without a shirt and all. For some reason she set her silly little feathered topper on Hokum Boone and wouldn't be deterred. It got so bad he had seen her trailing after him in the hotel's hallway in the middle of the night when he went to answer nature's call.

No widows here this time, though. None that he was concerned with, that is. A crazy thumper and his equally odd followers. Boone had a feeling that any second now he'd find out more of what they came to town to learn. All without knowing that's why they'd come to town.

Any decent feelings and tolerant attitudes he and Mac had toward Hezekiah Creed and his way of doing things had dried up when the very man who'd hired them had refused to answer their questions, then sent his hounds after them.

It had dawned on him and Mac early on that as far as expectations went, they weren't impressed with who'd hired them or his reasoning. Creed, for certain, had to feel that way about them. He'd only wanted hired guns to kill the ones he called the Outcasts. And that made him and Mac angry and suspicious.

The tell-tale double click, then the turn of his tiny tools brought a smile to Hoke's face. He continued the motion to its logical end and then, holding the metal bits in place with the fingers of his left hand, he turned the knob with his right hand, and the door latch clicked back. He ducked behind the frame and nudged the door open wide with a big knuckle.

It swung halfway, offering up a long, loud squawk from the metal hinges. He winced and grimaced and cursed once again whoever hadn't oiled the door. He thought for certain he'd land a square punch on the nose of whatever fellow should happen to show himself and fess up to such negligence.

Nothing moved inside there—wherever and whatever that room beyond was.

Boone poked his reedy neck around the doorframe and looked in. The space was as dark as the rest of the house. Maybe more so. Nobody shot him yet, so he figured he was in the clear. Boone gained his feet and stuffed his tools back in the pouch as he walked into the room and shut the door quietly behind him.

CHAPTER 11

"Too blasted dark in here." Boone whispered his thoughts so low he could barely hear them, as he walked, with caution, forward. He was rewarded with a knee clunking into something hard and unmoving. "Gah," he growled, and felt for the offending object.

As soon as his fingers touched the edge of the thing, he knew what it was, a billiards table. The baize, the polished wood, and there, to verify, a woven pouch with a ball hanging in it.

"Well now," said Boone, cracking a smile. Along about that time his eyes adjusted to the room's dim light about as much as they were going to.

This is one interesting little situation, he thought. What else you got to hide, ol' Hezekiah Creed? Didn't know that billiards had become an official church-approved pastime. Maybe it helps calm his mind after a long day of hoodwinking all these people.

As he thought all this, Boone roved the room, avoiding further knee-cracking. Then he stopped. He'd caught a whiff of something. Something familiar. He sniffed again, raising his head and closing his eyes like a dog will do when he's caught the far-off drifting scent of a decaying critter in the brush.

Then Boone smiled as he moved forward, letting his nose—and his eyes—guide him. He reached out toward what looked to be a massive desk, bigger than the one they'd seen in Creed's office that first day.

This one, too, was piled with all manner of papers, a number of them scrolled and tied with lengths of rawhide and ribbon. But it was what anchored the near corner of the desk's broad surface that drew Boone's hand forward. Sure felt like a humidor.

His fingers crept around the edges of the wooden box. Then they found a small, rounded lip jutting from the rest of the box, about an inch-and-a-half or so below the top. He lifted it and the box's top rose on hidden hinges to reveal very little Boone could make out in the dim light.

But the scent that rose with it did not disappoint him. It verified what he suspected—here be tobacco. If he wasn't mistaken, it was an exotic blend from several tasty varieties.

He looked in and saw a stack of cigars, piled like logs beside a trestle. Would Creed miss one? Likely not, but Boone had never been a filcher and he wasn't about to begin, even from a liar such as Hezekiah Creed.

What else was there to see? He'd already found enough to convince him that their guesses were right—Creed was a fraud. But what to do with that information? He'd need to confabulate with Mac on that one.

He cocked an ear, thinking he'd heard a sound. He waited a few seconds and heard nothing more, but it reminded him he needed to get a move on.

What else was there to see? And there, behind the desk, at the end of a mote-filled sliver of light, was a bottle of some sort of honey-colored liquid. Hmm. He rounded the desk and took a closer look. Yes, indeed, it was a decanter of cut glass. Too fancy for a preacher.

He licked his lips. Now, then, a quick sniff wouldn't hurt, would it? He glanced around the dim room. Slippery path, Boone, he told himself. But the look of that pretty liquid was too much, and he gave in and lifted the nested bottle stopper.

It clinked and he held his breath as he looked around again. Nobody nabbed him. He hefted the bottle and gave the neck a good, long sniff.

"Oh boy," he said, recognizing the quality of the whiskey within. He licked his lips once again and hoisted the decanter, glugging back a couple of swallows. That there is payment for putting up with all these shenanigans, he thought.

He set down the bottle, wiped the rim with a thumb, and set the topper back in place. "Now then," he said, emboldened by the hot trail the whiskey laced down his throat. "Let's look at this desk."

He unrolled a couple of scrolls of paper, saw deeds for properties all over the United States, one from back East, in Providence, Rhode Island, plus shares in a railroad line in Pennsylvania, and a tobacco plantation in Virginia.

But they all bore the name of someone called "Melvin Whipple." Hmm, he thought. Could that fella and Hezekiah Creed be one and the same? I bet so, I bet so.

The more papers he looked at, the more impressed and confused he became. They all bore the name of this Melvin Whipple, and they were stocks and bond certificates, more deeds to various properties and businesses, and all manner of fancy papers with fancy scrolly writing.

Regarded together, plus the bundles of cash and sacks of coins that Boone happened to see in the drawers of the desk, all led him to think the inevitable: This Melvin Whipple fella was one rich and powerful gent.

And if it was Creed, he was as far from being a preacher man as Boone was. If he weren't so powerful and slimy, Boone might almost admire such a fellow. But no, that would be wrong, even if the rascal did have decent taste in whiskey.

Boone nudged the papers back into a similar arrangement as he'd found them and turned his attention to the rest of the room, knowing he had to get out of there soon. He'd neglected the bulk of the room, seeing now that it led, via a tasseled doorway, to another room beyond. As he skirted the billiards table, to his right, he noted that the wall to his left was filled with shelves of books as well as . . . "And what's this?" he said, eyeing row on row of booze bottles with fancy labels and names, most of which he'd never seen before, but all looking pricey. And a good many of them had been sampled from, some much more than others.

Beneath them, nested many rows of wine bottles laid on their sides with their snouts poking at him.

They, too, looked fancy. And expensive. Boone whistled low and continued on.

Dead ahead stood the doorway in which hung the thick gold tassels. He made for it, though only after seeing, and stopping to admire, two larger-than-life-size paintings of reclining nude women, voluptuous and apparently all-too-happy to have their portraits painted, by the looks on their smiling faces.

They set Boone to whistling low and regretting he'd not sampled another swig from a different bottle on his way down the long room. It was quite a trek and made for thirsty work.

He reached the doorway and parted the thick, gilded ropes with a poking finger and peeked in. The room smelled of stale whiskey and tobacco smoke.

The room was better lit, though not by much more than a

high-up window with blue and red and gold stained glass with daylight cutting in.

But it was what sat beneath the window that caught Boone's eye. There sat a huge bed, a four poster, the bed clothes in disarray. The fabric of the various layers was of a shiny, slidey looking sort, sumptuous in puffiness, and with all manner of pillows.

It was the biggest bed Boone had ever laid eyes on and was about what he thought the Queen of England might snooze on of a night herself.

He walked closer, noted the two fancy, painted-globe oil lamps flanking the bed, saw liquor and wine bottles like fallen soldiers scattered about on the carpeted floor, and noted that there were two sides to the bed, two dents where heads rested, and saw that on the side at which he stood, men's underclothes were draped on a chair.

On the other side, which he wandered over to take a gander at, there were all manner of frilly, lacey items such as those worn by various women of his acquaintance over the years, usually soiled doves in rooms above busy, boisterous saloons.

"Huh. I'll be," he said.

Then he heard sounds, far off, to be sure, maybe from outside . . . yes, definitely from outside. He cocked his head and listened. If that meant that the church service had let out, then that meant that the mansion would begin filling up. He had to make tracks.

He spun and was about to poke on through the tassels and retrace his route through the rooms when, recalling the general shape and layout of the place, he looked to his left. Sure enough, he saw another doorway there, though this time it was not tasseled but a solid wood panel.

Surely it would lead him to some other way out. Had to. He doubted he'd be able to make it to safety back through the kitchen. At least this way, he thought, as he tried the door's handle, I'll know where I'm headed. Sort of.

Already he was thinking of his intended route. He knew precious little of the house's layout, but if he made for the northwest wall, he should find an exit.

The doorknob, to his great relief, turned in his hand and he eased it open. He stepped in and closed it behind him.

The room beyond was not a room but a hallway, no longer than eight, ten feet, and paneled with dark wood, as was much of the place, but the gloominess of it all would have to wait for his rumination because he heard a sound behind him, as if someone were in that office. He pictured Creed walking around the billiard table, sniffing for intruders much as a dog might.

He reached the end of the hallway, and another door faced him. Oh boy, he thought. If this one's locked, I'm a sunk duck. But no, it wasn't. The knob turned in his hand.

He cracked it open, and light slanted in. He eased it a bit more and eyeballed beyond. There was a long staircase. He thought it might well be the very one that faced them when they had been ushered in that first day. Now he was on the other side of it.

So that meant the entrance was to his left, then straight ahead. And that meant so was Creed's office. Or rather his other office, the one he wanted folks to see.

He'd make for that if he couldn't get out the front door unmolested. And that's what Boone did. Almost. He was rounding the foot of the grand staircase when he heard voices from two directions: outside on the front steps, the low, murmuring voices of women. And the other sound was of Creed himself, coming from beyond the stairs on the other side. Making his way forward to the front of the house from the rear. He'd likely come in through the kitchen. Lucky me, thought Boone. He scooted fast as he could, his boots clunking on the polished wood floor. He cursed the sound as he reached Creed's office door and straightened. He held his hand up as if to knock on the door when Creed saw him.

"What's this?" said the black-garbed man, eyes wide and fleshy face already puffing in indignation.

Two seconds later, as if conjured out of the air, two Acolytes flanked Boone and made for his arms. He spun, keeping the closed office door to his back. He raised his big bony hands, one of them sporting a wide, gleaming, gutting blade.

"You try me, just try, and I'll cut more off you than you brung to the scuffle!"

Neither Acolyte backed off, but neither did they make more of the intention of grabbing him. They stood and seethed, their eyes glowing red, all angry veins. Their forked beards seemed to fluff and wriggle of their own accord.

"Mr. Boone," said Creed, halting before him. "What are you doing in here? How did you get in?"

"Come up the front steps like all good company, didn't I?"

"Hmm."

Creed eyed him for a long moment and Boone cursed the family trait that left him feeling and looking forever guilty whenever he got caught doing something he shouldn't be doing. His face and ears bloomed redder than a hammer-struck thumb.

Then a curious thing happened: A slow smile spread across Creed's face.

Boone's eyes narrowed. "You ain't so concerned about hiding your feelings, are you?" he said to the portly town leader.

"Whatever do you mean, Mr. Boone?"

"Oh, not much, except you look like you had a thought that I might not like to hear."

Creed's smile slipped, but did not disappear from his face. "What makes you think I am about to share any thoughts with you, sir?"

Boone shrugged. "I know a guilty face when I see one." He smirked. "I ought to," he said. "I see one every time I look in the mirror!" He let burst with a hearty chuckle and smacked the thigh of his buckskin trousers. No matter how often he tried to clean them, usually by standing bare-ass and smacking them on a river rock, which admittedly wasn't all that often, there still arose a faint cloud of dust.

Creed did not look amused.

CHAPTER 12

"From what you're telling me, Mac, them Outcasts have every right to be worked up. Anybody rode in and stole my business, my home, my woman, my kids, then run me out of town as if I were a dog in the night, why, I'd . . ."

"Boone?"

"Yeah?"

"You don't have any of those things. You don't even have a regular room you keep. Heck, it was all I could do to convince you we ought to be based in Denver City, instead of riding around hoping people might find out where we were and offer us paying work."

"All right, all right, mister, I know what you're driving at. I'm a rambler, I admit it, but that don't mean I can't think such things. And the me in my thoughts, the thinking me, you see, why, he's riled up."

"Well, that's good, Boone. Because for what I have in mind, we're going to need you to get riled and stay that way for a spell."

Boone puffed up his narrow chest and nodded. "I reckon I'm the man for the job."

"Okay, then, here's what I have in mind." Mac stepped to the door and cracked it and peeked out. Then he leaned over and looked out the small window. He saw no one, but in a strange little town such as Brimstone, where it seemed the air itself had been duped against them, it didn't pay to take any chances, no matter how slight.

He nodded toward the two straight-back chairs and he and Boone took their seats in the middle of the room, facing the door.

When Mac spoke, his voice was low and even. "Since you made up that business about being curious about what Hezekiah is selling, you'll be the one to wander back on into the lion's den."

"Yeah, I figured as much. So what's your plan?"

"Well," said Mac. "Beyond that, I don't know yet. But I do know we have to act fast. These men in the hills have about lost everything they can and still be upright."

"I should say so."

"Yeah, but what that also means is they have nothing left to lose . . ."

Boone nodded, knowing where his pard's thinking was headed. "Yeah, and that makes them dangerous. To themselves and to everybody in this town."

"Especially bad since the people in town are all their families."

Boone rasped a gnarled hand over his chin whiskers. "And here we are in the middle. So what do we do?"

Mac crossed his arms, stretched out his long legs, and crossed his boot at the ankle. Boone recognized it as Mac's thinking pose. He watched his pard, and the big man did what he expected he would next.

He sighed and tugged out his pipe and took a long time stuffing tobacco into the bowl. Then he sat with it in his mouth for a couple of minutes, staring at the wall beside the door, then he leaned out and lifted a match free from the small box of them beside the stove. He snapped it alight with his thumbnail and set fire to the tobacco.

At the same time, Boone tugged out a cigarillo and bit off the end. He also lit a match and then the two men sat still, filling the small cabin with blue smoke, and thinking.

Several minutes passed in silence, except for the slow, heavy footsteps of two people, likely men, walking together outside along the lane.

Mac and Boone paused in their smoking and ruminating and tensed, watching the door, their hands hovering about their waists, fingers flexed and ready to grab at revolvers and knives, dynamite or derringer. The footsteps outside receded.

It had likely been Acolytes.

Finally, Boone sat up and snapped a finger. "I got it . . ." Then he slumped back once again. "Nah." He puffed harder.

Mac looked at Boone and a slow grin spread across his clean-shaven face.

"You come up with something better?" said Boone, feeling more hopeful by the second.

"It's possible," said Mac, puffing the pipe, "that we can pull this off. But we need to act fast. Those men in the hills won't keep. You okay with going undercover? We need to get back in there and get enough proof to show the townsfolk who they're dealing with. It might be enough to cause them to begin to doubt Creed."

"That's all we need to do, ain't it? Plant the seeds of doubt?"

"Mr. Boone, you are a poet and a philosopher."

Boone reddened. "No call to go insulting a fellow now."

"I have a few things I'd like to do hereabouts, which includes disabling a few Acolytes, then I have to go back into the hills. I asked them for two days then they plan on invading.

Sounds like a suicide run to me, so we have to get things tight here before then. You okay if I leave you alone in town tomorrow?"

Hoke pulled back as if slapped. "I look like a wet-nose tot to you? Sure, I'm okay. Go on for a week if you need to. I'll keep this powder keg from blowing 'til you skip on back."

Mac smiled and leaned back in his chair, puffing with furious intensity on his briar and wondering how in the hell they were going to pull it all off.

CHAPTER 13

"Now look here," mumbled Boone, scratching at the dirt before his boot. "You should know by now that when I go in deep, I do it with everything I got." He nodded as if to agree with himself.

Boone thought he was still alone, then he looked up to see a half-dozen Kindred women, not quite averting their eyes from him. That was all the time Boone had for regretting his decision to infiltrate the Kindred.

Two were old, pinch-face things, one was youngish but from her infrequent glances, it seemed as if she'd like to claw his eyes out. Never had he seen so much cooped-up anger on a face before, and the last three were younger things who wore red cheeks beneath those black bonnets.

This could be an interesting time, he thought, then nipped in the bud any stray notions that were popping into his mind with frightening speed. Can't let such ideas cloud my thinker, especially since these women were all wives, sisters, daughters, or sweeties of the men in the hills. Do your job, Boone, he cursed himself, and the sooner you get it over with, the sooner you can get back to the wide-open arms and ample bosom of Starr or Beulah or Trissy.

"Now then, ladies," said Creed's voice behind him. That broke any witchy spell these religion-minded women might have been using to cobweb his mind.

"I think our guest would like some light refreshment, am I correct, Mr. Boone?"

"Oh, ah, sure, sure. Whatever you got is fine. I'm not choosy."

He was about to say he could do with a few drops of that fine whiskey he'd sampled in Creed's private chambers. But that would go over about as well as if he broke wind in church.

The six women bustled off in three directions as soon as Creed finished speaking. He darn sure ruled this roost, confirmed Boone. He had a witchy sort of spell over these folks, notably the women.

Maybe he's quite impressive romping in that big bed Boone had seen earlier. You never would guess it by looking at the paunchy, pious, annoying man before him.

When the women had gone, Hezekiah Creed cleared his throat. "Mr. Boone. You mentioned earlier that you had showed up to talk with me about the Kindred. What are your concerns?"

Boone did his level best to look as if he cared for and respected the man's thoughts. He cleared his throat. "Well, Creed, it's about like this: I am a traveling man, always have been. And my pard, Mac, bless him, he's more of the same. We get along on a pile of topics, but in the important ways, we're drifting. Mostly lately, you get me so far?"

Creed nodded, his brow furrowed as if in deep concentration. Boone doubted that. More than likely he was thinking about how many women he was going to corral in his hidden chamber later on.

"So for some time now, I been looking for something

some place to hang my hat. Some way to give of myself instead of doing something for money, if you get me. Ain't nothing more irksome than a man who lives only for money and power. Unless of course it's a man who does all that but lies about it." Boone offered Creed what he hoped was an innocent look. "That's doubly wrong, in my book."

He knew he was treading mighty close to the riverbank's edge with that, but he couldn't help himself. The pinched look on Creed's face was worth the risk.

The rascal didn't dare come right out and ask Boone what he was talking about, but he surely wanted to. Instead, Creed surprised him. "Brother Boone, I know exactly what you mean. And there can only be one path for you in your life. The rest is death, destruction, and the heat of a thousand suns burning your soul forever."

"Oh," said Boone, a little shocked at what he was hearing. It did not sound pleasant at all. Not at all. He worried the brim of his hat. "What's that mean, Creed?"

The fat preacher smiled as if he were addressing a simple child. "Brother Boone, for that's what you can be if you give yourself over to The One, Brother Boone. You must join us here in Brimstone, Brother Boone. You would be a most valued member of our society here.

"As much as it pains me to say so, I could use a man who is as proficient with a gun as you are as a member of my elite Acolyte squad. I believe you know what I am driving at here.

"You see, the ones who I now have are largely farm-raised, some of them from towns not far from here. The others I have worked with in the past, before I came here. They followed me here. And yet, that doesn't mean they have the experience you have in dealing with, shall we say, trouble."

"Oh, you don't mean you need more protecting from those men up in the hills, do you?"

"Why, Mr. Boone, they are exactly who I mean. Were it

only me, I might consider moving on, trying to find another town in which to proselytize, but curse me, Mr. Boone, I like it here. And I suspect you will, too."

Creed stuck out his hand and Boone, after a slight hesitation, took it and gave it a hearty shake. None of that weak-as-water, dainty handshaking for him. It was one of the reliable ways of judging a man's worth and abilities right-off quick. At least that's what his old Pa told him.

Boone had taken that notion to heart and always tried to size up a man as he was now doing to Hezekiah Creed. He came up with the one answer, unchanged since he and Mac had arrived in Brimstone. Creed was a madman, and one lousy hand shaker.

CHAPTER 14

Millie Taylor had no notion when she awoke that morning that it would be her second-to-last day of life. What she did know was that even though she had been trying to be the sort of young woman she was approved by The Chosen One and her mother and the other ladies, it was a most-difficult thing to do. And she really wasn't certain why it was so difficult. But it had been that way, and more so, with every new day for the past few months.

She was now sixteen, and while she truly understood what was so important about the Word of The One, as handed down to them by The Leader, in the small hours, she had her doubts. They weren't even clear thoughts, just doubts. She wondered if maybe she had come down with the same affliction that caused her father to stray from The Way.

It was deep in the dark, early morning time and she once again lay awake, listening to the breathing of the other women in the sleeping room of the house her father had built when she was much younger. Now only she and her mother and Aunt Nancy and her annoying little brother, Cal, lived in the house. Papa was gone. Long ago he had been found out by the Acolytes and sent away, lest he cause further harm to the Kindred.

Mother had told her that even though she might well remember her father, and she knew by the look in Mother's eyes that she, too, remembered Father, he was gone for good. As good as dead, she had told Millie. He had refused to accept The One in his life. Instead, he had abandoned them and, for that unforgivable decision, he had journeyed beyond death, to a place unspeakable, never to return. Mother had said we must do everything Hezekiah Creed told us to do each day in order to avoid ending up there in that unspeakable place, too.

But then the other day something happened, something she never expected. She had been returning to the bake house for her turn at kneading and working the second oven when she saw the two strangers. The smaller of the two, a funny fellow, wore a suit of greasy buckskin and a green hat with a coon tail atop a bony, whiskered face. He had two gray eyes that seemed to see everything all about him and yet never settle on a single thing. He walked by, right at the side of his partner, the taller of the two strangers.

The tall man, she believed she heard The Chosen One refer to him as Mr. MacCoole, he was very much unlike his friend. The tall man was, well, tall, and broad. Millie wasn't certain she had ever seen such a wide-shouldered man before. But the funny thing was, he had kind eyes.

She wasn't certain she could remember exactly what it was he wore, other than clothes that men outside of those in the Kindred wore, but she recalled his eyes. Even then, in the dark of the early morning, when all the rest of the house was asleep, Millie remembered his gray-blue eyes and how they had smiled. She smiled in the dark thinking of them, of him.

She felt certain that even if she could not see his nose or his mouth, she would know he was smiling because of his eyes. She supposed, now that she thought on it more, that was because nobody else she knew smiled much anymore. If they did, it was something they quickly hid behind a hand and then turned away their faces. It was because there was dire shame in smiling, let alone the utter humiliation of laughing, an act which would heap shame on them all.

But why should it be so? She had asked her mother that question once a year ago and Mother's eyes widened and she seemed so very afraid. Then she looked around them to make certain they were alone and wrapped a work-reddened hand over Millie's mouth, as if to kill her words, suffocate the question she had thought was innocent enough.

She still remembered the smell of lye soap on her mother's hand. It had been the only time in three years that her mother had ever touched her intentionally. That more than any other thought had kept her awake. Well, that, and the memory of the stranger's kind eyes.

She had wanted to ask her mother why she was late to bed one night each week, always on a Tuesday evening, always alone when she returned. But the next night it might well be Aunt Nancy, then Clara Bond, who had stayed with them for a time, until she had begun to feel poorly.

Clara had gone to live in Mrs. McGillicuddy's house, the little place set back from the church, near the burying grounds. Mrs. McGillicuddy was a nurse and midwife. Sadly, Clara had not returned from that little house. Mother said Clara had come down with the "grippe."

After a few weeks were gone, though everyone spoke with envy, including The Chosen One, as if the place Clara went was the best place anyone could ever imagine going.

The Appointed One had told them all that Clara Bond was now roaming barefoot and happy in the green fields of The One, where night never came, the sky was always the bluest of all blues, the grasses were soft and green and no snakes dwelt there.

It sounded nice to Millie. Too nice, she admitted only to herself. And even though it was but a thought, given no utterance, she felt deep shame and vowed not to think such things. But somehow that proved impossible. Still, she prayed and prayed that such evil thoughts would go away.

She had told her mother no, had shaken her head no when her mother had told her when she turned seventeen she would be asked to visit the big house in order to attend special training sessions with The Chosen One.

Something in her mother's voice told Millie that her mother did not like this and had not wanted to tell her about this. Something told her it was somehow part of the reason her mother spent one evening a week away, coming in late, and then looking as if she were about to fall over from lack of sleep the next day.

Whenever Millie asked her what was wrong, Mother would shake her head and say, "The One wills it."

But now Millie's mind, late at night, and during the day, was filled with thoughts of that stranger, the larger of the two, and she did not know why. But he was all she could think about. She was even reprimanded for it, not that anyone knew what she was thinking, but Dolores Quimby had poked her hard in the shoulder, her sneer following as it always did.

She was the woman who ran the bake shop, and Millie had always been afraid of her. She never seemed to get any older, but she was one of the ugliest people Millie had ever seen. She knew that was a terrible thing to say, but Millie could not help it.

Now, here in the dark, when she was thinking of the tall, handsome stranger, she should have been thinking about what her mother said would be her next day's duty. She had been told after evening prayer that she was to undergo a special ceremony the following day. A ceremony so special that only Hezekiah Creed, the Appointed One, was able to conduct it.

When she'd told her this, however, Mother had not looked her in the eye, as she always did. Mother was a serious woman about everything, and she always told her to look someone right in the eye when you spoke to them.

What did it all mean? Was Mother angry with her? And if so, why? Because she was maturing? That was not the most worrisome part of all this, though. That was instead the thought of what The Chosen One would do in this special ceremony. What could it mean? Something told Millie it had to do with the times when Mother and Aunt Nancy and the other women went to see The Chosen One in the big house.

Millie had been in there but only on errands, to deliver vegetables or his special loaves of sweet bread, never for any other reason. She longed to ask others what this ceremony would be like. Would she feel differently? Was she to learn something about being a Kindred that others already knew but were forbidden to speak of?

As dawn approached, Millie Taylor lay wide awake and more nervous than she had ever been in her life. And she still had hours to go before her special ceremony. She tried to concentrate on what The Chosen One might ask of her, perhaps of her readings of the One Book.

Or perhaps he would want to know how she planned on being a more useful member of The Kindred once she became an adult? She knew she would be required to have children, though she was not entirely certain what that involved. It was not something Mother ever spoke of.

Though she tried with desperation to concentrate her thoughts on the One Book, and the words therein, her mind dragged back to the eyes of that man, that strange, tall, and yes, handsome man. She was wicked for thinking so. Wicked, wicked girl.

* * *

"Well, now, Millie, isn't it?" said Hezekiah Creed to the all-but-shivering young woman standing before him in his office. Inside the open doorway, two of the Kindred housemaids lingered, as if daring him to reprimand them.

He obliged with a quick, barked order. "To the kitchen!"

Then Creed turned his gaze back on the girl, letting his eyes travel from her feet all the way up to her bowed head.

"Take off your bonnet, Millie. And follow me."

CHAPTER 15

Millie Taylor barely saw the front steps of the big house as she descended them, the Appointed One's angry, shaming insults had echoed in the hallway and followed her out the big doors and down the wide steps. She pulled her dress close about her, as if to protect herself, and tugged her bonnet down tighter about her face.

She had been crying, it seemed, almost since the Appointed One had taken her into that big room, the Chamber of Iniquity and Shame, as he had called it, shaking his head, but not taking his eyes from her.

Then the most horrible things had happened. A test, the Appointed One had called it, determine her worth as an adult Kindred. He had told her that he had been instructed to do these things, that he had no choice, and that if she failed to endure them, she would become an Outcast.

Millie had no idea how she had endured them, how she had gagged down the proffered glass of the devil's brew, and then came the horror of disrobing before the Appointed One. Then he had done the same, chanting words he said were known only to him, words that would protect them from the wrath of the One should we fail to do all we had been ordered to do.

Afterward, the Appointed One had said she should feel confident that she would become an adult member of the Kindred and not an Outcast. But only if she stopped crying.

She had tried, tried so very hard, but . . . it had all been too awful, and she had cried all the same.

That's when the Appointed One became angry. He said her crying would come to no good end. And then he shouted and shoved her and she remembered flailing her arms, shoving back, protecting herself. And then the Appointed One's face was bleeding.

She didn't remember scratching him, but she must have somehow. He was so angry then that spittle flecked from his mouth and he shoved her again and banished her forever from the big house.

Millie saw few people in the street and she did her best to stop crying and to not run all the way home. But that's all she wanted to do.

She ran toward home with her face down and hidden. Her sobbing grew louder and more forceful. She felt certain she was soon to be thrown out, forced to become an Outcast.

Then she walked right into someone—it was the big stranger with the kind face and gray-blue eyes.

He stepped back and apologized and then saw her crying face and asked her what was wrong. He held her by her shoulders with his two big hands and looked at her face and asked her if she was all right, if she needed help getting home.

She shook her head, could not stop crying, and then beyond him, coming from the big house she saw an Acolyte walking toward them. And he looked angry, though they were always thus.

She pulled away from the kind stranger and ran toward the nearest building, the bake house, full of women she knew who would think her weak for crying. They would be angry with her, too.

It was not where she had wanted to go, but it was close by, and she had to get away, away from the stranger, away from the Acolyte. She did not know what to do. Even her mother would be angry with her, for now Millie would be an Outcast, she was sure of it.

Hezekiah Creed shook his head. "The poor deluded thing took her most precious gift from The One! She smashed it on the floor and trod upon it! She who was lucky enough to be among the Kindred, and she acted this way? Bah!"

The gathered Kindred murmured and covered their mouths and shook their heads in the same manner as the Appointed One.

"And now the thing once known as Millie Taylor has doomed herself to forever be exiled in the fiery roads of damnation! With no chance for salvation from that hellish torment. No chance to walk the Green Fields of Grief!"

An eerie, low-pitched shriek rose up from someone near the front of the crowd. It was a woman's shriek that clipped off and became low, wracking sobs.

The Kindred, all gawking at the limp, slowly spinning form hanging before them, gasped, held hands to their mouths, shook their heads, gesticulated in the various ways Kindred had learned of warding off the taint of such an evil in their midst.

At the back, on the periphery of the crowd, the tallest figure among them, Keller "Mac" MacCoole, held his tongue until his jaws ached from clenching. Only his friend, Hokum Boone could see what the sight of this sad, wilted flower had done to the big man. But Hoke, undercover, stood not at the back of the crowd with Mac, but a half-dozen steps from the left side of Creed, and an arm's length from an Acolyte.

Hoke, too, was doing his best to tamp down the urge to shout, to cut down the girl. What he really wanted to do was to cut down, in a far more brutal way, the Appointed One himself.

He wanted to rip the man's arms off and pistol whip the man about the face. For he knew what Mac knew—this girl, along with that other girl the young man had come to visit, Eliza, was as innocent as a child could be of anything that could incite a devotion-crazed Acolyte to kill her.

Hoke knew with full certainty that he and Mac were the only folks in these parts in their right minds.

Creed dabbed a white kerchief at the ugly, welted scratch that ran from under his left eye down his cheek, then disappeared in the sweaty stubble about his mouth. He raised his arms to quiet his flock and said, in a loud, commanding voice, "By now you are all aware that we are being infiltrated at a more rapid rate by the Outcasts, the hill people who once claimed to be worthy enough to walk among us!"

He surveyed the group with a steely gaze, then continued. "They are, as we can see, a scourge that must be dealt with. They have been among us more and more of late, even as recently as two days ago, when a brute of a young man, more starved wild dog than human, savagely attacked poor Eliza near the schoolhouse.

"It was only due to the quick action of my Acolytes that she was able to escape. This deluded creature, however." He gestured with a quick, careless wag of a pudgy hand toward the drooped body of Millie Taylor.

"This deluded soul was driven to take her own life out of shame. Shame for what she and one of those wild beast men . . . got up to!" He nodded his head with increasing speed, in time with the rising voices of the assemblage before him.

"Yes! Yes, and it pains me to say it, but that is what happened here! Under cover of the moon, that brazen animal coupled with this deluded creature to produce nothing but shame and filth and degradation! The One has seen this behavior, and has assured me it does not bode well for the rest of the Kindred. For if one falls, all shall suffer!"

A moan rippled through the crowd, punctuated with shrieks and tearful wailing.

Mac noticed that the more the crowd lamented, the taller Creed stood, the brighter the gleam in his fiendish eyes, and the more he seemed to fight to tamp down a smug smile of satisfaction.

"That is why I called in to our midst two men who, though they are not Kindred, yet . . ." Creed glanced at Hoke and offered a slow nod, then shifted his gaze back to the quieted crowd, who also were eyeing Hoke.

Hoke felt right odd about this. His face heated up, and he thought for certain his buckskin tunic's collar had shrunk somehow.

"And yet . . ." Creed's gaze swept the crowd, then settled on Mac at the rear. "It appears that our money, our hard-earned money, has been thus far spent for naught, since these two men have done nothing since their arrival to quell that tide of disease that the Outcasts' very presence on earth brings closer to our lives with each day that passes."

Every Kindred eye leveled itself on Mac. His clenched teeth and jouncing jaw muscles leveled out, and his normally kind eyes narrowed. "That poor girl you see before you did not kill herself, and certainly not out of shame. She did not do anything she was responsible for. I repeat: Millie Taylor did not take her own life!"

A woman's low, deathly moan rose up over the crowd as a bleak, dark cloud.

Mac returned the hating stares of the Kindred and shouted at them, "Go ahead! Ask Creed where he got that scratch!"

Even as he spoke, Mac knew it was wrong. For the safety of their plan, it was too soon. He could have gone on, ranting and blaming Creed but it would have killed in the cradle any plans he and Hoke had afoot.

Still, as he spoke, Mac did not shift his gaze from Hezekiah's face. He was responsible for the girl's death and Mac had to prove it. And if Hoke didn't succumb to the zealot's life, he might prove useful in that attempt since he was now closer to being on the inside.

From the front of the crowd rose a deep, heartbreaking sob, one such as Mac had heard a number of times in his life. It always came from women who had lost too much and still faced yet more misery in their lives.

A gaunt, black-clad figure broke from the crowd and staggered forward, wailing and clawing at the air. Mac knew it could only be one person—the girl's mother, the one who had moaned moments earlier. The grief in her wracking sobs sounded as if a village of mothers had been robbed of their offspring.

In that moment, Mac had never felt so low, so helpless. It was nearly too much, seeing the young dead girl, dangling, her thick tongue purpled and bulging from her mouth, her eyes wide and popped, her slender hands swaying gently as her body slowly spun on the makeshift gibbet, her mother sobbing from deep in her body, sobbing as she never had or would again.

Mac walked away from the dismal scene and ground his teeth together until they felt as though they might powder. He knew they must somehow fix this mess before other people died.

There was a cold comfort in the fact that at least now they were doing something, no matter how slight. Hoke was infiltrating Creed's mansion, and hopefully his secret life, so that was a start. Though Mac strongly doubted that Creed was so dim as to believe that a savage such as Hoke would buy into the Kindred mindset.

Never had he felt such a fool, to be taken in by this huckster. He stormed off toward the stables, aware now that everything had changed. He'd stepped over a line back there that jeopardized their meager plan and put Hoke in danger. He had to warn the Outcasts that he and Hoke needed more time.

He also needed to tell them that Creed would be out for Outcast blood, once and for all. They'd outlived their usefulness to him, as scapegoats to keep the fires of fear stoked in the Kindred. Creed had all the flame he needed, now the Outcasts must die.

Deep in thought, Mac strode up the deserted main street of Brimstone, a thin trail of dust rising behind his bootsteps. Far back, from each side of the street, Acolytes, six in all, fell into line, walking slow and steady toward their first victim.

CHAPTER 16

The first of the six Acolytes to land a blow on Mac's person came away with a crushed hand and a shin that felt as if it had been slammed with a stone mallet. The big man's blunt-toed boot drove into the split-beard's shin with enough force to crush the bone.

Though the tongueless brute crumpled in a shrieking pile, the only reason his shin didn't snap is because the other five Acolytes swarmed Mac like flies on a meat pile.

He withstood their assault for much of a minute, but their near-silent attack soon became too much even for the big man and he, too, crumpled. Their blows were savage, their arms pistoning from the elbow, ending in bony fists that pummeled his rock-hard muscles. He doled out kicks, punches, even a couple of bites to zealot flesh that shoved too close to his sneering mouth.

"You . . . snakes . . . gaah!" On it went, with Mac thrashing as good as he got, but by the time even the first one who'd attacked him had rejoined the fray, cradling a shattered left mitt to his chest, Mac succumbed for good in a thrashing, swearing, clubbed pile.

The Acolytes, seeing they had finally succeeded in their appointed mission, climbed off the big man. He was not dead, but they had clubbed him into submission, an unconscious brute whose features were already swelling from the beating they'd delivered unto him.

The Appointed One would be pleased, their glances to each other seemed to say, though their grimaces told a further tale. Though they'd gained the upper hand in the fracas, they did not emerge unspoiled.

There was the crushed hand and cracked shin of the one. Another found that his head smeared with his own blood, pulsing from the place where the top of his left ear had once been. Two others also cradled their heads, unable to breathe through pulped, clotted smears that once were their noses. To a man, their peculiar forked beards had been torn out in great patches, leaving bloodied holes in their faces.

Below their sore heads, chests were tender and breaths shallow. Ribs had been snapped like the twigged branches of a seasons-old pine crackling in a campfire. One of the Acolytes moaned and collapsed to the dusty earth of the paddock as he realized one of his legs might be broken.

To a man they seethed at the sight of the crumpled brute at their feet. Those who were able delivered harsh kicks to his yielding frame. And to a man they wished they could kill the beast and be done with him. But the Appointed One would not like that one bit. And his word—and retribution—would be swift and final should they overstep his wishes.

He had been plain enough in his order, that the man Mac be delivered to him, Creed, alive—in any condition so long as he was alive and would regain his consciousness.

Despite this, they were tempted to continue their beating, and perhaps risk a broken leg to the man or broken arms. How far to go before the pain killed the man? But they were running out of time. They had other tasks that the Appointed One required of them.

The two of the six men who were still able to walk and had at least one useful arm muckled onto the big man's shoulders and, with what help the others could muster, dragged the lifeless hulk toward the rear of the Appointed One's massive house.

They left behind divots where their own boots dug into the dusty earth as if they were a mighty braces of oxen dragging a heartless load. They reached the building and sagged, releasing their hold on the man.

Mac flopped to the earth, still unconscious, his head slamming with a bounce on one of the paving stones that lined the back service entry. Blood from a wound on his head stained the gray rock beneath him, and the same leaked down and dribbled off his arms and cheeks. Gashes along his arms seeped blood through rents in his once-blue chambray shirt.

Each little sign of discomfort the Acolytes caused the flopped man brought a leer of a smile, thin and grim, to faces unused to mirth.

One of them, the widest at the shoulder, if not the tallest, grunted and gestured with his own bleeding head toward the dark shadowed space before them at the base of the house.

One of the others limped into the shadows. He bent and heaved up a creaking wooden door built of thick timbers and wrought-steel hinges that squawked their need for oil in the baking heat.

A second door crashed back and a slight wash of cool air wafted up at the Acolytes, who stood close by the gaping black hole before them gazing into it for a moment.

The cool air might have been a welcome thing, however slight, were it not for the waft of stale breathless air, reeking of decay, of brittle things long dead now powdering in the dark.

They knew what the place below was, for some of them had helped to make the root cellar into a prison on the Appointed One's assumption of power in this once-paltry town.

After all, in those early days, the town had required a special place to stow miscreants, devils in human form as the Appointed One had called those certain belligerent citizens of Brimstone who had protested at the coming of the Kindred.

The ones who had escaped the long wide reach of the Acolytes rabbited to the hills, following a small group of others who had been let go, to live like feral beasts. The Acolytes now knew that had been a mistake.

But the Appointed One had promised those beast people would be hunted by the Acolytes when they had the time. But that had not really worked out that way, a disappointment to the fork-bearded brutes.

What they had been able to do, however, was deal with the ones who resisted within the town limits. They were afforded a special place to think over their sinister ways, deep in the cellar, far beneath the floor of the blessed house above, where their master dwelled.

Those who did not sufficiently embrace the ways of the Kindred were left in their cells to weaken and whimper and eventually rot away. Quick lime by the wagonload coated their still bodies.

The Acolytes hadn't been down there in several years, and yet each had sharp memories of the place, as if they had only visited the chambers but the day before, wielding their cudgels and flint-studded whips and honed chains.

They snagged hold of the big unconscious man once more and dragged him toward the hole. Face downward, his head sagged and bobbing between his shoulders, his boots clunking off each of the worn plank steps as they dragged him.

There was no light in the dank hole, so they hunted for the oil lamps they knew resided there. One was found, caked with spider webbing and cobwebs and thick with dust, but still it contained enough fuel oil to allow them to see to their task.

They spent a minute poking about the vast space, and found what they expected they might—chains pinioned to the stone walls where shelving with jars had once rested out the seasons, back when Promise was a sinner's den.

At the ends of the chains, manacles encircled arm and leg bones of those who could never bring themselves to become one with the Kindred.

Some of them had begged to do so, in fact, pleaded fealty to their last, but the Appointed One had told the Acolytes that those beggars had been deceivers, liars planted there by the disrupters who wished to introduce tricksters of the devilish sort within their midst. For this, the chained holdouts had been ignored until they ceased begging, ceased whimpering. Then, of course, they were covered over with lime.

Back to the northern wall, deep in the farthest reaches of the cellar, they knew of a last spot where a couple of chains still hung unoccupied.

They were partly correct. There had been a resident of the space, but he had died, forgotten, not even covered over. He no longer stank, and only one of his arms remained chained.

They found the rusty key and worked it in the rusty lock and were able to secure the now-stirring big man with lengths of thick, rusty chain.

They locked him there and the last one, the wide-shouldered brute who had received but a while earlier a blinding fist to the nose—in fact, he thought perhaps he had lost the sight in his right eye, time would tell—was the last of the Acolytes to straggle back to the cellar doorway.

He stood staring down at the slowly moving man. With a hard sneer he pulled back a thick leg and drove the flat of his boot heel against the big man's face.

The prisoner's head snapped to one side and he collapsed back into himself once more, sagging against the eternal strength of the chain.

CHAPTER 17

Mac dreamt he was alone on a battlefield, the sky was gray, struggling for blue, but failing. Smoke rose all about him from the bombed carcasses of horses, men, and cannon.

The stink of singed hair and seared flesh and blood, and bone shattered beyond hope of repair seeped into his deepest self. It clotted in his nose, mouth, and eyes, and pulled him inward, quivering him from within.

Hopelessness warred for dominance over him with the raw, dank tang of death. It was a foul smell, stale and . . . forgotten. As if he were not hovering above the earth in this ghost-world battlefield but beneath it, as if he had already been buried and was only now finding out this awful revelation.

Perhaps he was truly dead, for he could feel nothing, taste nothing, hear nothing, see nothing, feel nothing. So, he thought, it has finally come, Death has ridden upon me and overtaken me. How? How? The word echoed like a lone crow's call. But how could this be? How could he have died?

Then he knew, somehow he knew, with a quick and growing certainty, that he was not dead. Perhaps close to death, but not yet dead. For he had begun to feel. And what he felt was terrible.

The terribleness of overall pain. Raw, searing, throbbing, full-body pain. As if he had been pummeled by a steam locomotive on a downhill grade, then hurled from the tracks to tumble down a rock-studded slope hundreds of feet, only to be gored at the bottom by angry bison. And this almost made him smile. For it told him he was not yet dead.

And with this throb of pain came the memories, recollections of recent events. His friend, Hokum Boone, and he arriving in the town of . . . Brimstone, that was the place. And then . . . then something about good but sad men far from there here. No, not far, but high up, in the hills, yes, the men, men of the town, banished and bitter and their families left behind, but why?

Then he knew. The fat toad face of Hezekiah Creed bulged into his mind, and a crude landslide of recent memories rushed down upon Mac. He forced, with much effort, one eye to open. Then he ran his tongue tip over his teeth. One felt loose, but the others were there.

One eye, a usable mouth—he worked his jaw to be certain—that was a start. He knew from bitter, painful experience what a beating could do to a man. It was best to take it slow.

On that score, Mac was not too successful. As he grunted softly and struggled to urge life back into his humbled body, sharp close-up images filled his mind. Leering, scowling faces of the bearded Acolytes lunging close, then jerking away from him, only to dip down once more and deliver another kick or punch, their tongueless mouths wide, wet, and snapping, their teeth brown and bared. Behind them, the wagging, ragged stumps of long-gone tongues.

The fresh memories made him angry, and he growled in

the dark. After a few minutes of that, he heard a soft noise to his left. Somewhere in the dark.

He knew it was dark because he could see well enough now through the one opened eye. The other had popped open enough to form a slit through which he could see, though he made out very little of his surroundings. Thin slants of light, as if forced through thick gaps, hazed over his surroundings, enough to show him he was deep in an underground hovel, perhaps a cave.

No, perhaps a cellar. But where? Beneath that church? That cult's church! Or the leader's house. Yes, more than likely. That big foolish mansion.

He guessed long before he verified that he had been locked in a cellar of some sort. And locked was not his immediate concern. It was the fact that he was chained. Chained and there were parts of his body he could still not feel. Chief among them his legs.

What if they had broken his legs? How would he be able to help those hill men? Those women and children? The rustling drew nearer. He felt it before he saw it. Something touched his side, then his leg, he felt soft pressure, sliding, sliding and he knew it for what it was. But the fact that he felt it told him that he still had legs, at least one that could still feel something.

Mac felt relief wash through him, for he remembered from the war too many men who had suffered bullets in the spine, clubbings, or breaks that rendered them useless from the neck or the waist downward, most with no hope of ever using their legs again. This might still be the case with him, but his concerns were bigger at the moment, for whatever was now upon him was large, and kept sliding, and he knew it was a snake.

He'd seen plenty damn snakes, mostly in his travel with Hoke throughout the West's vastness. Too many thick-as-a-forearm bull rattlers with heads like fists and eyes that spewed hatred and teeth that doled out venom as easily as old men doled out lies while sitting about a potbelly stove in a mercantile on a cold winter's day.

As soon as he was able, Mac shifted his body from the awkward against what felt to be, from the unforgiving, jutting roughness against his back, a stone wall, the foundation of the place.

He'd barely moved, wasn't much able to yet, in fact. But it was enough to confirm his fear—the dry, slicing hiss and shake of a snake's rattles. Right below his sagged head, right across his thighs. And though Mac's body had been bludgeoned and all-but left for dead, he felt the weight of the beast upon him.

And he knew it was a big one, something that reigned kingly down here in the dark, dank place, something that had not yet decided what Mac was—an intruder to be vanquished or eaten, or both. But he knew if he kept moving, no matter how slight, the thing would strike. And then he would most certainly die.

Mac opened his mouth, almost giving in to a reflexive, self-preserving urge to shout, but stifled it. The thing had paused, the weight of it feeling as if it were coiling in his lap, its ample girth sagging over the outer edge of each of his thighs.

Sweat beads popped all over Mac's head, leaving an icy, itchy trail as they slid downward over his face. They stung his eyes and slid down the long length of his nose before quivering there. If a drop slipped off and struck the serpent, who knew what it might do? He knew it would not end well for him.

Hoping against hope that in the dark and near-silence of the dank hole in the ground, he wouldn't be seen or heard, he slowly raised his head, pivoting on his thick neck. The droplet of sweat at the tip of his nose continued its journey, riding the underside of his nose until it quivered at the tip, and he felt certain he was going to sneeze. Then that would surely be it. The thing in his lap would sink fang and he'd die.

Mac opened his mouth wide. With quiet and stealth, and while keeping his breathing to a minimum, he poked out his tongue, feeling the salty sting of sweat off the tips of his soaked moustaches. He had hoped somehow that droplets would stay trapped in his soup strainer. He was glad he had not yet given in to his periodic temptations to shave it off.

Then a curious thing happened—the snake in his lap shifted a little. He couldn't really see in the dark, yet he sensed that it was raising itself upward, as if it were inspecting him.

He did his best to kill his short, quick, stuttering breaths in his throat, but all that did was make him want to gasp. It wouldn't be but moments until he had to give in to a gasp.

Then the snake appeared, raising into view, such as the dimness allowed. The wide bull head, big as a small man's fist, rose before his face, a black shadow set against blackness.

Mac sensed it, smelled its dry, animalistic taint, heard it move against his clothes, felt it working its underside against his belly.

It hove closer to his face and he swore he could feel its breath. Was that even possible? He didn't know, didn't care. But he knew it was all going to be over soon, for he had to breathe.

The thing pushed closer, closer. He felt the tongue, or perhaps it was a whisper of air, touch his cheek. It swayed to his right. He had to breathe. Then he felt it settle the side of its thick spade head against his cheek. Was it trying to caress him? None of this made sense to him.

And then he could wait no longer and he allowed air to wheeze into his gasping mouth. He must have moved, for the thing began to rattle, rattle as if it were a hard, wooden cup with a few loose stones in it, being shaken by an impatient child. The snake's head backed away from him.

Here it comes, he thought, fighting to not pull lungfuls of air in, when the thing ceased rattling and slid farther along his right side. He felt it bumping along his arm, as if it were following him, taking the measure of him. He had a wicked vision of the brute stunning him but not killing him, then dragging him down some deep, dark hole. Deeper and darker than the one he was already in anyway.

Then he felt it touch his right hand, which he had already moved enough to know it was bound, pinned to the wall somehow. Mac also knew that he had at least one broken finger on that hand. It was puffed with swelling and painful to move. But he had the thought that he might somehow grab the thing, though it would have to be right behind the head. Was that madness to think such a thing? No, but to act on it might well be.

And where in the hell was Hoke, anyway? No, Mac told himself, no time to traipse down the recrimination road. He had to save his life first. Until he'd grown to rely on Boone in tight spots, and vice-versa, Mac had always made damn sure he was in control of his own life, saving it or forfeiting it.

Never put yourself in a situation you couldn't figure a way out of. At least that was the idea in life. Now, when he found himself in yet another such position, he saw the flaws in that plan. No man, as someone wise once said, is an island. But today, he had to be.

The thing flicked and slid, and though his fingers were half numb and puffed and barely working, Mac knew he had to try. Had to grab this one opportunity to save himself.

And then the snake dropped down away from his hand. It slid farther down, and he felt it move off his lap. Then he felt something behind him.

Great, the thing was circling him. Maybe it's not a rattler, he thought, doing his best to suck in air without giving in to the gasp he so longed for. Maybe the snake is a constrictor, such as he had read about, that live in tropical places and squeeze their victims to a purple, lifeless mass.

But no, this was a rattler—what else could it be? Don't let fanciful thoughts have their way with you, Mac. Daring to relax the faintest bit as the thing slid behind him, he pulled shallow breaths, aware it could flex and sink its fangs into him at any second.

But somehow, he'd been given a brief reprieve. He flexed the puffy fingers on his right hand. The left he didn't dare do more than twitch because the snake was headed in that direction. Indeed, it was likely beneath his outstretched left arm right then. And as odd as this beast was acting, it could well be staring at his hand, thinking the fingers were mice.

Then it was gone. He felt no further movement behind him, no pressure from the sliding creature. Even the feeling of sensing the snake had somehow diminished. He knew that didn't mean it had left him alone, but he didn't think he was so far gone that he'd imagined the entire encounter.

Mac was certain that if the snake had lingered a moment longer by his left hand, he would right then be experiencing the agonies of the rattler's venom pulsing through his blood.

He now realized that the notion to which he'd been committed was as foolish an idea as he'd ever had in his life. And that, to his mind, was saying something. He'd never admit it to Hokum Boone, for he'd never hear the end of it.

But Mac knew himself well and he knew that the Mac MacCoole everybody saw, while not a complete fabrication, was a bit of a shell, a show of a man, a shield behind which he might scrutinize his fellows.

He always had been a stand-offish fellow, but beneath all that lurked the very sort of man who would, at a moment's notice, dive into a fracas for the pump of excitement he knew it would bring. Or the sort of man who would try to grab a massive rattlesnake by the neck and hope—hope!—that it didn't lay him low. What had been the plan, Mac?

He smiled then in the dark, at the folly that was Keller "Mac" MacCoole. And for the first time in long, long minutes, since coming round in fact, Mac pulled in a long, deep breath, and slowly let it leak out. He repeated this thrice more, then he heard the rattles start up once again. This time, closer than before.

CHAPTER 18

"Brother Boone."

Hoke swung his gaze up from the foolish task Creed had set him to, that of sorting vegetables—the rotten from the still-edible. So far, he'd managed to find a whole lot of rotted carrot and potato and nothing he'd care to eat, thank you very much. He'd "Brother Boone" this fool, right in the middle of his fat face with a hard fist.

"What can I do ya for, Creed?"

The pudgy man winced and reddened. "Brother Boone. In future, you will refer to me as 'Oh, Chosen One,' 'Appointed One,' 'Master,' or, if you must, 'Sir,' but as long as you are intent on becoming one with the Kindred"—he smiled—"and once invited, no one has ever decided otherwise, then you will refrain from the common tongue. Indeed, you shall refrain from speaking at all unless I allow it. Is that understood?"

Rage seized Boone, and his entire body tightened and shook. It took him a moment before he could convince himself to not launch at the smug SOB, tear out his arms, and beat the man with them.

"I said, 'Is that understood?' "

Boone opened his trembling mouth, but Creed held up a fat hand. "Uh . . . a simple nod of the head will do."

Once more, Boone gave Creed the hard stare and managed one slight down-and-up movement of his head.

"Good. Now that we have come to that agreement"—Creed turned and walked inside—"Follow me."

Boone stifled a growl as he followed the waddling preacher.

Once safely back behind his big desk in his office, Creed said, "I bring news that concerns you."

Despite his bristled feathers, Boone was curious.

"Ahem. I have been in discussion with my Acolytes, and they are, as I speak, readying themselves for war."

"War?" said Boone, eyes widening.

Creed said nothing but glared at him. Boone smiled. "Old habits . . . Sir."

The religious leader simmered for a moment. "Yes, well, I thought you would find that of interest. Now, go straight to the stables and saddle up a horse. Not your old horse. That has been given to a more deserving member of the Kindred, one of the Acolytes, who has need of a decent mount."

Boone growled and thrust a long, bony finger at Creed's face, advancing as he did. He knew it was going to get him in trouble, but he didn't care. "Now you look here, Creed . . . sir. I will take a whole lot from you, but there ain't no man, no man on this earth who will take Chummy from me nor me from him. You got that?"

Despite the fact that Boone had always been treated as a menacing fellow when pressed, Creed stood his ground and gritted his teeth, his chubby face reddening. Then he snatched up a brass bell from his desk top and shook it with vigor.

Almost at once an Acolyte, one Boone didn't recall seeing before (How many of those fork-bearded, no-tongue bastards were there, anyway?), entered the office. This one looked to be a handful, but Boone thought he might be able to take him.

Then another one followed, and Boone felt nothing but weary. They hadn't fed him much, and he'd been sweating up a storm. Where was Mac, anyway? He hadn't been able to talk with him after that public viewing of that poor dead girl, but he knew his big pard was worked up about it. Enough to make a fool statement or two, not like Mac at all.

If Boone had to guess, Mac had made for the hills to tell the Outcasts not to invade, for they'd surely be slaughtered.

Well, Boone had sworn to Mac he was up to the task of infiltrating this harebrained outfit. Oh, but this was one job he wished they'd never taken. Hell, up to now, the money was but a promise. Rotten straight through, if you asked him. Like a carrot gone soft and drippy.

"Okay, okay . . . sir. But if I find one of these yahoos has hurt Chummy, I'll lay into him without cease, you hear?"

Again, to Boone's surprise, Creed actually smiled a little and nodded. Then he glanced at the glaring Acolytes and they backed off and disappeared, not without glaring at Boone themselves.

"As I was about to say, you will accompany a squad of my Acolytes into the hills to the east and south of us. You will do as the Acolytes tell you." Creed paused, as if waiting for Boone to take the bait.

Hoke wanted to, by gum, he wanted to ask how it was those tongueless freaks were going to tell him a thing, but he held his own tongue.

"All will be revealed. Go now to the stables, and you will be assigned a horse. You will be given a weapon when the time arises when you require such." Creed held up a hand, palm forward, to stop the verbal assault he suspected was soon to come from Boone.

Creed shook his head. "My word on this is final. The Acolytes will decide when and where, and if they decide you have behaved admirably and humbly as in keeping with the Kindred ways, then you will be allowed to participate in the glory of eradicating the foulness and deviltry and deceit and wickedness that is the Outcasts."

Boone shot the man one last hard look, then stumped on out of there, and once back outside, made for the stables. Had to be better than dallying with vegetables, anyway. He despised such women's work, if it wasn't related to being on the trail, that is. He didn't bother looking back, but he guessed Creed was watching him out the window the whole way. Let him watch.

He wondered if Mac might be up in the hills, helping the Outcasts. More likely he was trying to reason with them. From what Mac had told him of them, he had his work cut out for him.

"As long as he don't shoot me," said Boone in a whisper to himself. The notion of being mistakenly drilled in the head by his pard shivered him.

Long before he made it to the stable, Hoke saw the flurry of activity there. Even the Acolytes seemed excited, and not necessarily in an angry way. He resigned himself to whatever critter they would stick him on.

But he promised himself that if Chummy was being harassed by anybody, he'd drop the bastard, then hop aboard Chummy, find that blasted Mac, and make for Denver City, Kindred or no, Outcasts or no. They had all made their beds, let them sleep in them.

By the time he reached the stable, however, Boone knew he'd put up with a whole lot in order to follow through with their mission. A glance here and there showed him women, children, and a few old folks, all Kindred, all walking hangdog with nary a glance his way. Never a howdy or smile or nod, nothing. These were a sad lot, and Creed was the one to blame. He and Mac had to help them see the errors of their ways, but it seemed a big task.

The Acolytes, as he expected, glowered at him and went about their tasks of saddling horses. Boone was surprised to see how many of them there were. He counted more than a dozen, for certain, though it was tricky to land on a precise number, given that they all looked alike, with those devil-tongue beards and black togs and hats.

They moved in and out of the darkened stable to horses tied to thc corral rails outside in varying stages of being saddled.

One of them jerked his chin toward Boone then nodded toward a short, homely mule with a mothy blanket draped over its back.

Now it was Boone's turn to glare, but it didn't help. That Acolyte was a hard-looking fellow, with his right eye milky and angling downward, as if that part of his face had melted, giving him a freaky look. He also came as close as any of them Hoke had seen to laughing.

He swallowed back on the string of rank words he wanted to unleash and went inside the stable to scout up his saddle. Not only did he not find it, but he didn't see sign of Chummy anywhere.

"Hey." He looked at the same Acolyte who'd assigned him to the homely mule. The man had followed him into the stable and was half-watching Boone, and half rummaging in a stack of tack. "Where's my horse? You know, the one I rode in on. And while we're at it, where's my saddle and other gear? Huh?"

Creed didn't want him to speak, but that didn't mean he couldn't give this lout an earful.

The man shook his head and went back to his tack. Hoke took that to mean he was free to rummage and sniff around. He did that, looking out the back of the stable toward the pastures beyond. He thought maybe he saw his and Mac's horses, Chummy and Lincoln. But they were too far southwestward, and with the sun's glare to boot, he couldn't be certain it was them.

Chummy was one thing, but Mac's horse, too? Nah, couldn't be. He hoped that was not the case, for that would mean Mac hadn't gone into the hills. He visored a hand over his eyes and squinted toward the two distant shapes, but they walked away from him and he couldn't be certain.

He looked in each stall but saw no sign of Chummy nor of Mac's Lincoln, nor of his own saddle and such. Time enough for tracking it all down, right now he had to get a saddle before he was stuck without one. The Acolytes kept showing up like flies on a carcass, crawling everywhere.

Boone managed to find a sun-puckered, brown leather affair with a sorry looking collection of holes where it seemed conchos once had been. Too pretty to keep around, he thought. Got to have a life of plainness and misery. He hated this fool-worshipping group more than ever, for their sheepish ways, baah-ing and following that lying leader.

He nearly finished with the hackamore, the only usable bit of tack he could lay hands on once the swarm of Acolytes had pawed through the lot. He looked up to see the same one as before, with that lopsided eye, staring at him. He smoothed the two forks of his beard and nodded hard once, indicating Boone should hurry up.

"Don't get yer knickers in a knot, there, Happy Face. I'm almost ready." He swung up into the saddle and, with surprising ease though not much speed, he was able to urge the mule alongside the Acolyte. "He's bony, he's older than Methuselah's grandpa, and he's homelier than a stump fence. Suits me fine."

Hoke held out a hand toward the Acolyte who clearly wanted to get them moving to catch up with the mass of other riders making some distance ahead of them on up the lane away from the stable. Hoke held firm, not moving, and stared at the man. "My gun."

The man began to shake his head. Hoke said, "No sir! No sir, I ain't riding into what the big chief called a war without some sort of weapon. A . . ."

He almost let slip that he was still carrying a derringer on his person, tucked in a spot nobody but a very curious and very pretty woman would ever get him to reveal. This fool was neither. "I want a gun now and bullets. I prefer my own. Be quick about it, man!"

Boone had often found that the direct ordering of someone to do a thing usually produced results. This time he was mistaken. Droop Eye shook his head and jerked with his chin, indicating clear enough that Boone was to ride ahead of him.

So he wasn't even allowed to ride at his own pace, mule or no, let alone not allowed a single decent weapon. He didn't move, didn't urge the mule to budge one single inch. "I said I need a gun."

The Acolyte sat, too, and gave him the same stony stare he was giving. Neither moved. The day was hot, flies drifted fat and slow and lazy about them, drawn to the stink of the horses and the piles of dung peppering the dusty ground.

CHAPTER 19

"You hear that?" A young kid, Jay, cocked an ear and held the dented tin cup poised halfway to his mouth.

The rest of the men paused, trusting the youth's solid hearing.

"Aw, I don't hear a th—"

"Hush now!" whispered Toomey. Paul, his brother-in-law and the man who he'd cut off, didn't dare lip back to him.

The kid held up a hand once again and then pointed, downslope. His eyes widened and he looked to Toomey and whispered, "I heard a hoof strike a rock. And another!"

Roland nodded, stuffed his pipe in his mouth and nodded toward the small rag-tag group of men. "Okay, it might be the enemy. Get your guns. If it is, we lay them low. As many as we can. It's no more than they'd do to us. Now go."

The men didn't need to be told twice. Each man, by now, had a firearm. Most of them weren't all that much, and many were at best much-used, older weapons, still serviceable but aged. They belonged to men who had long regarded themselves as farmers first, hunters second, and blood fighters a distant third.

Then came Hezekiah Creed and his freakish tongueless, unfeeling brutes who enforced Creed's foul intentions with death-dealing tactics.

Now was their opportunity to kill, for surely that is what the Acolytes were there to do to them. But why now? Seemed a little more than coincidental that it should happen after those two newcomers arrived in town. Stranger still that one of them, MacCoole, had found the Outcast camp up in the rocks and then, promising to help them, had departed. And now the Acolytes were riding on in as if they owned the place.

No, it was all too coincidental for Roland Toomey's liking.

Jay was used to being the first chosen to do a task, especially the least pleasant. Now here he was in nearly his first gun fight. It wasn't something he wanted, but it was something he knew had been coming.

He checked for the fourth time his revolver, even though he knew those same four bullets hadn't made like rabbits and filled the two empty chambers in the past three minutes since he checked them. He wiped his palms on his ratty brown wool trousers, now more hole than cloth, as Roland had said with a sad smile.

It was something, being with these men and now being counted among them to do a man's work. The ultimate of men's work, that of killing another, evil man. Or more than one.

Jay's hatred of the Acolytes was as deep as that of the others. Their anger at those split-bearded devils who'd hacked out their own tongues to show fealty to their master,

Creed, was bone deep and would never go away until Creed and all his filth were killed.

It was hoped and frequently talked about among the men that once Creed was dead, his demonic, witchy spell over the Kindred, most of whom were all their own families, would somehow disappear.

Jay pictured the layers of lies like a skin that had been draped over the Kindred. Soon it would fall away, drying and cracking in the sun of truth once more.

He hoped for all their sakes that it happened soon, for he didn't know how much longer Roland and the rest could hold out. As for himself, well, Jay knew he was not likely to last the winter. Each of the previous three winters they'd been holed up here in the rocks, living like pack rats or snakes, was worse for him than the one before.

Even though he was younger than the others, he was one of those among them who seemed to lose ground with each season that came upon them, especially with the colder weather.

Though the valley could be a hot place much of the year, it was during the winters up in the rocky hills that wood for fuel was scarce, blankets grew thinner, clothes, too. And their boot soles showed more holes. Game was scarce, and what water they could haul pinched out quick. They had even cut their rations back and ate but one real meal a day. No, this could not stand, as Roland said.

They had not always been that way. When they'd first taken to the hills, surprised in the night, rousted from their own homes and forced to flee from their families, marked as Outcasts by Creed for not buying what he was selling, they had retreated.

But they had been many then, and in coming days, and weeks, though they worked their way daily and nightly back into their town, with the once-pretty name of Promise, now sullied as Brimstone, they were driven back, away from town.

Sometimes they were reported to the Acolytes by their own family members. Those were difficult days, maybe the hardest, because their families still seemed to miss them. Not now, though. Now they acted like they didn't know who these ratty men were, on the rare instance when one of them dared to sneak into town, into the fields to try to get the Kindred to change their minds.

Now, though, their numbers had been whittled down to a nub.

As time wore on and they were largely unsuccessful in getting back into town, they even kidnapped Kindred three different times—one old man, his ornery wife, two women, and two children, but of all of them, only the old man, oddly enough, stayed with them. His old harpy of a wife demanded to either be killed or brought back to Brimstone. She worshipped Hezekiah Creed. Those were her words, as Jay recalled. Worshipped.

The old man seemed tickled to be away from her. But he didn't last long, caught a lung ailment and died off that second winter. Then, over time, they grew hungrier and leaner and weaker. And Creed grew stronger. He brought in more Acolytes from who knew where else, and then lots of other folks came in, already members of the Kindred, with their odd clothes and no smiles or talking.

The Outcasts' numbers dwindled more. Men fled in the night. Took off for who knew where, but Jay secretly envied them. He knew because he used to enjoy reading about the big country beyond that little mountain valley. And they were going to get to see it. He had begun to doubt that he ever would.

Every time, though, that he tried to talk with Roland, who'd become a sort of uncle to him, about maybe leaving, too, giving it all up as a hopeless lost cause, he would see Roland's face, and Jay knew that Roland knew what he was going to ask him. And then Jay could never bear to ask why they were still there. He kept his mouth shut and hoped.

And now, when things looked like they could not get worse for them, that stranger came in, the big man with the nice horse. He gave Roland pipe tobacco, got him all worked up, and promised to help. Somehow, he'd figure out a plan. Give him time. Somehow, he'd help. That had been the very thing they all needed to hear.

But that man's visit also looked like it somehow made Creed once again try to wipe them out. The Acolytes had ridden into the hills three times before to try to kill them. And they'd managed to kill two Outcasts in this way over the years.

One of them had been Jay's friend, Randall, two years his senior. The rest of them had scattered out among the rocks, not having enough in the way of weapons or skills to fight the dozens of Acolytes. There must have been four dozen of the devils then.

He wondered if there were going to be that many again today. They were going to do whatever they did when uninvited folks come upon their camp. They would fire at them, scare them off. But not this time. This time it was shoot to kill.

A sharp "Pssst!" snapped Jay from his reverie. He looked toward the sound from his spot crouched behind a jut of sandstone at the high east edge. He knew Roland chose that spot for him in hopes that the action would be over before it reached him up there. But Jay swore he'd do his best to defend it.

He wondered where Paul, Roland's brother-in-law, was posted. Paul was annoying and short-fused and hot-tempered and was the single-most person Jay had wished in the quiet of the camp at night that he'd heard packing up his things and slinking out for other parts, never to be heard from again. But Paul never left.

He reckoned he wasn't the only one to feel that way, either. Paul grated everybody's nerves.

Roland pointed with his pipe downslope and westward, toward town. Then he used his hand to stroke a long beard or where one would be if his was long, and made a show to let him know it had two sides to it, two parts to the beard. A fork-tongued beard. Acolytes, for sure.

Then Roland held up his hand, fingers spread wide. He flashed his five fingers once, twice, then sort of once more. Jay tried to remember the signals they'd all agreed on, and he figured that meant there were between ten and fifteen of them. That was plenty. But why were they riding out this way in the middle of the day, bold as brass?

They waited. He heard the same sounds again. Everybody had to have been hearing them by now—hooves striking stone, saddles sliding and bunching and squawking, horses blowing.

Jay looked downslope to his right and saw a bare spot where ol' obnoxious Paul was supposed to be. He should have stayed where Roland had told him to. But Paul thought he knew better than anybody else. So he had up and moved to where he wanted to be and left that spot unguarded. And it was closer to the coming action. And a spot they daren't leave unmanned.

Jay looked upslope toward his uncle, but the man's back and shoulder were all that were visible. He was crouched, waiting, like the rest. Waiting for the Acolytes to ride upslope a little more, then they would rain hell down on them. But after that, they would have no bullets, save for the ones they gathered off of any Acolytes they might wound or kill.

They watched for a time, waiting for the Acolytes to ride on up the only true trail that led, eventually, up to the current encampment of what was left of the Outcasts. Mighty bold, was the thinking among those hidden hill fighters.

Jay, in particular, was puzzled by this calculated advancement on their stronghold, such as it was. The Acolytes, which really means Creed, he thought, must believe we are so paltry in number and weakened in mind and spirit and body that we will step before their bullets.

Jay thought this and allowed himself a rare, grim smile. For he knew what he and the men had discussed following the visit by that big man, Mac. The upshot of their long conversation about their meager fire, a mellow talk that lasted long into the night, was that though they had reached the end of their string and were played out long before these two latest strangers rode into Brimstone, it was that man's visit that showed them how truly hopeless their plight had become.

"Better," Roland had said to them that night, "that we go down to a man fighting. We've seen this mess through far longer than any of us expected. But while we still have strength and our lives, I think we ought to give it a last run. We've been fools to tolerate it this long."

"Yeah, we have," Paul had said. And for once, Roland could not bandy words with his wife's brother.

"So anybody who doesn't want to do this, let us know right now. There won't be any ill feelings. But we're going to come up with a plan tonight, a plan to attack Brimstone."

Not a man had backed out. They all talked freely then, confident they weren't being spied on, since they'd posted watch and traded that on and off as they always did. Then they'd tallied up what weapons they had—ten rifles, two shotguns, seven revolvers, an assortment of hip knives and cudgels, some of which used to be farming tools.

They'd agreed to make straight for Creed, not showing any Acolytes mercy, and certainly not Creed, come what may. The man may be powerful, they said, but there was a sense of this being a mission of higher justice. They would be answerable to themselves and to a god that they all felt certain was there for them, and not the twisted, false one Creed was hawking.

They'd decided to wait two more nights, which would give that Mac fellow the benefit of their doubts. He'd seemed decent enough to most of them, though Paul and two others voiced doubts about his trustworthiness. They decided that the majority would decide the matter. And a vote showed eleven for waiting, and three against.

Paul had grumbled, of course. Roland had expected no less from him. But he honored the vote. And the day before they were due to make their last stand, the Acolytes came riding up on them.

That was mighty suspicious. Jay didn't want to believe that the man, Mac, who he'd cautiously trusted, could turn on them so. And yet . . . riding up the trail was the proof.

Was it coincidence? Maybe so. None of it much mattered now, because instead of bringing hell to the Acolytes and Creed, it was coming up the mountain to them.

"If they want what we have to offer so bad, let's give it to them, boys."

That had been the last thing Roland had said as the men dispersed, scattering like rangy coyotes out among the rocks they were so familiar with. The rocks that had become their stony home.

They damn sure knew the terrain better than the foolish Acolytes, who thought they were nowhere near the Outcast encampment yet, otherwise why were they riding in a ragged line up the trail? Ducks on a pond couldn't be more foolish.

CHAPTER 20

The ride into the hills was uneventful for Boone, though he tried to make it otherwise. He goaded that droop-eyed Acolyte every few minutes with a backward glance, shouting, "You still there, schoolmarm? Good, thought I'd somehow lost you in all this hubbub."

The rest of the Acolytes were well ahead of them, though within sight. They were strung out and scouting, and slowed their pace, allowing Boone and Droop Eye to catch up once they rode into the rocky hills.

Boulders grew larger and trees grew scant, and soon, even the breeze that had accompanied them on the ride left them. It was turning out to be one of the hotter, clammier, fouler days Boone had spent in recent years. He could put up with a whole lot of things, but hot weather, particularly when it was the sticky, clingy sort, was something he had little tolerance for.

"Curse you all for putting me through this," he mumbled, low enough he didn't think anybody could hear him. But Droop Eye surprised him and rode up alongside at a wide spot in the trail.

The man eyed him with that hairy look all the Acolytes shared. Must have gone through a special run of training to learn that, he thought. Or maybe having your tongue yanked out and sliced off at the root did something odd to a man, odder than all the obvious things that came to mind, anyway. Maybe it made them think alike.

The next thought that came to Boone seized him as if he'd been grabbed from behind by a huge, icy hand. The feeling, despite the day's cloying heat, was not pleasant. What if that filthy, fat Hezekiah Creed was planning on having these tongueless fools hold him down and cut his very own tongue out?

"No sir, no sir, thank you very much," he said out loud. Droop Eye gave him more of that odd stare.

"If you're thinking what I am, and I ain't going to say what it is, then you can get that thought out of your crazy head right now, mister. Ain't no way anybody's going to . . ." He stopped short of finishing the sentence because he didn't want to give the rascal any ideas.

But Droop Eye spun his gaze ahead and held the rein, forcing Boone to move ahead of him once more. Boone looked ahead, too, drawn by whatever the man was seeing up there.

The only change was that the trail had narrowed until they were all forced to ride single file. He wanted to shout at them to spread out, drop back, keep their firearms at the ready. And for Pete's sake, move slower, look around more!

These sitting turkeys didn't know a thing, it seemed. He'd have bet some of them might have gone through the war, but maybe they were addled even back then by their craven devotion to whatever deity it was they worshipped. Sure wasn't the Lord he had been taught to fear as a youth.

A ruckus broke out up near the third Acolyte in line. Something had spooked his mount. The man gave an odd, throaty shout and shook his head, tugging his horse hard backward out of instinct, jerking and sawing at the reins.

That stretch of the trail looked too narrow for the horse to turn, wedged as they were between boulders and jagged outcroppings. The horse slammed hard into raw-red stone and whinnied, eyes wide and white.

"Tell that idiot to calm himself!" shouted Boone to Droop Eye. The man could not fail to hear him, but he kept on eyeing the scene ahead with a calm look, as if it would play out just fine.

Boone shook his head and slid down out of the mule's saddle and left the hangdog thing standing there. He scurried up to the left of the riders, whipping low beside them, and he passed each Acolyte in turn.

They, like Droop Eye, sat still, guns laid across their laps. One held his pistol up, eyeing the rocks beyond and above.

As Boone passed them, they regarded him with curious stares, as if he were something bizarre, a pink flower in the midst of a snowstorm. He made it up to where the man was still having trouble controlling his mount. Careful not to get trampled or pinned, Boone wormed his way up alongside the nerved-up horse. He snatched up the end of the near rein and trailed his hand up to the horse's head.

It took some doing, but he gentled the beast, even though it jerked his boots up off the gravelly slope a time or three. "Easy now, easy girl, easy. This fool don't know how to treat a lady. No, no he don't. Not all of us are the same, though I know what I'm doing. I know you deserve better than to be rode hard and jerked around like a fish on a line especially if that tongueless gob doesn't."

Boone kept up this running banter for another few moments until the horse settled and blew, flexing her quivering nostrils. Boone flashed the rider a hard look and shook his head to show his disapproval. The man, much to his surprise, almost looked as if he wanted to thank him.

He wore a gray face behind his gray-black forked beard, and his eyes were wide. He was no born horseman, likely not even one who'd put in effort to get to know the critters he rode. He probably spent most of his time walking about the town of Brimstone, scowling and terrorizing the cowed residents.

"You ought to give some thought to learning to ride, you oaf!" growled Boone, and as soon as he said it, he felt a little bad about it, because the man had at least shown a smidge of sympathy and humanity, and Boone had gone and ruined it. No ally there, he thought. But after a moment, the man didn't scowl but nodded and looked away.

"Okay, then," said Boone and trailed along the horse's neck, patting her. He looked up at the man, and in a softer voice, said, "Might be you want to not try to turn her in so narrow a space. She's spooked enough by the oddness of this place. Me, too, for that matter. And give her head a little. She'll not abuse it."

Again, the man nodded. Boone returned the gesture and walked back along the line, a little taller and a little less scowly. He couldn't be certain, but he thought maybe the others were less inclined to give him that menacing stare, too.

He mounted up and, giving Droop Eye a knowing look, he clucked the mule into a walk once more. The line of Acolytes ahead resumed its slow, winding walk upward between the rocks.

With no warning, a bullet spanged off a rock ahead of them. The line broke out into a frenzy of jumping horses and wordless, shouting men, flailing in their saddles and looking all about them.

"Give me a gun, damn you!" growled Boone to Droop Eye. He held out his hand and the man gave him a confused look.

"Now!" Boone wagged the hand again and the man parted

his cloak and tugged out a battered old revolver and handed it over, with reluctance.

"And bullets! Can't do a thing without this except club somebody. You don't make it quick, I'm liable to commence whomping on you!"

But he had no time for more ranting. For as Droop Eye sneered once more at him and tossed him a small buckskin sack, such as one might carry coins in, another shot ricocheted off another boulder, this time closer to them. And this time, from what Boone could see, it came from their right, whereas the first had buzzed in from the left.

He slid from the mule and tugged the lamentable beast after him, cursing the thing for being so blamed stiff-legged and slow. The critter was as old as dirt and twice as lazy. Sure, he didn't want the thing to get plugged by a bullet, but neither did he wish the same for himself, especially on account of this old toe-dragger.

Boone yanked it up behind a nearby boulder and gave the revolver a quick once-over while ducking low behind the nearest rocky face. Two of the six chambers bore bullets, the other four were naked. He cursed the ill-prepared fools with a "War, my sweet mother's backside!" and thumbed in fresh bullets, noting that the scrimy bastard Droop Eye had given him a cozy dozen rounds, if that, in the little satchel.

While he waited for another round, he bent low and used what he hoped was a position of relative safety between the sullen mule and the rock. He kept himself as narrow a target as possible, as he always did in such situations—and there were more in his and Mac's life than he cared to think about.

He never breathed heavily in such spots if he could help it, preferring to sip shallow breaths and save his efforts for scanning. It also made him less noisy.

By Mac's own admittance, Boone had superior eyesight, something Boone credited to his Grandpappy Muldoon on his Mammy's side. He was a corker and could shoot, as he always put it, "The nuts off a bug" at a hundred long strides in a wind, at night, during a howling rager of a storm.

Boone never tired of telling Mac that same story. To Mac's credit, for Boone knew how that must have sounded to someone not from the hills of Boone's birth, Mac never cracked a smile. Not that the big savage wasn't capable of grinding him over his origins.

Called him a backwoodsman, which Boone always took as a secret compliment. He kind of liked the name and figured if he ever set down in his dotage and wrote up a book about his exploits with and without ol' Mac, he might refer to himself as a backwoodsman.

No reason he couldn't slide in a few tales about bear wrasslin' and rescuing screaming, weeping womenfolks from raging flooded rivers, and butchering hogs with nothing but a Barlow and a smile. Yes sir, it was going to be a solid read. Not like those snoozers Mac was forever reading passages out loud from.

"But first," he muttered, "you best get your thinker on straight and find out where those Outcasts are at before one of them pops you in the head and makes this here backwoodsman deader than dead can be. And likely they will be trying, because they saw you riding on in here with ol' Droop Eye and his tongueless chums."

It was right then that Boone saw that Droop Eye himself had taken up residence close by, not but a couple of feet from him on the other side of a sharp angle in the big boulder. He and the man exchanged a glance and, for the second time in mere minutes, Boone felt a twinge of the "shameful guilts" as his Mammy would call them. The name referring to that creeping feeling in your gut you felt whenever you got caught saying something hurtful about someone and they overhear you. Didn't stop folks in his family from doing it, though.

"Eh, sorry about that, fella. Well, it's not like you give a body much chance! You don't even try to be nice to me, just glare and glower and point like I'm a wet-nose bairn! Well, I ain't!"

There, thought Boone. Spun it back on him. Give ol' Droop Eye something to think about. Then something whiskered by a dozen feet away, to his right, downslope. Hard-won instinct spun Boone toward the sight while at the same time he dropped low. The move saved him from another shot slicing in. But not Droop Eye.

CHAPTER 21

As the lead Acolyte slowly emerged from behind the rocks, clumping up the trail one jerky motion at a time, Roland eyed the length of the trail that was visible to him, enough to see that of the Acolyte riders he'd spied approaching while down on the flat below, a half-dozen of them were now likely well within the range of his men. The Outcasts were arrayed on either side of the trail.

If he waited for the last of the Acolytes, including an oddly dressed man that appeared to be riding a mule—the long ears and slow, plodding gait gave it away—then he would lose his opportunity to deal with the lead riders. No, it was time.

Roland raised the rifle to his left shoulder and smoothed back the hammer. It was a big-bore beast more suited to bringing down game on the run than a slowly plodding man on horseback, still not aware that he was closer than he thought to dying.

The clicking of his gun's hammer sounded to Roland as if it were a crashing rockslide, echoing off the boulders and down the long, narrow, winding trail. But the rider never heard it.

One last look at the Acolyte's jouncing, forked beard, black coat, and wide-brim black hat, and then Roland let memories wash over him. Hard, bitter, brittle memories, memories bristling with jagged edges that cut him to the core anew each time he called them up. And he did this each day, unable to keep from stroking them as one might a precious jewel.

He sighted on the man's chest, between the wagging forked tongue of the beard, where it split below the throat, center of the brute's breast, and Roland squeezed the trigger.

He watched the bullet, so tiny a thing, meet the man, then lift him as one might a child, shoving him backward to smack against the horse's flank before whipping to the rocky earth. That awful bearded head slammed hard against rock and stilled.

The Acolyte's rifle, released from his upflung grasp, arced in the air and dropped, disappearing in a crevice beneath a jag of stone. Roland marked the spot and resighted.

The horse whinnied and thrashed and tried to escape, but the trail was too narrow for it to do much more than flail and bruise itself, scraping rock and losing hair and skin as it bucked.

As for the Acolyte, Roland was confident of his shot and he knew the man was dead. He resettled his rifle on the chest of the man following, and even before the lead horse could bolt forward, the only direction available to it, Roland had delivered another bullet to the chest of another hated creature.

The second tongueless brute dropped much the same as the first, and a funny passing thought came to Roland—Not only did the Acolytes all look alike, but they died alike, too.

By then, his men had found their own targets and had riddled a rain of death down on the other Acolytes strung out along the cobbly trail.

That second man took his dose much the same as the first, with a grunt and a snapped-back head. This time his big black hat flew off, and in the moment before the man whipped off the back of the horse, Roland saw a bald head, red from the day's building heat, with a fringe of scraggly gray-black hair that splayed outward as he tumbled.

This one thrashed on the ground, and then again, with more vigorous flailing moves when his horse stomped him. He settled quickly and sagged, unmoving.

Roland cursed himself for losing track of where the man's revolver had got to, but they'd find it. They had to—this battle was far too young and unknown, but it had the makings of good fortune. If they could continue to lay low these tormentors, they would gain not only on that score but in adding to their meager weapons collection.

Farther downslope, rising clouds of smoke marked the locations of his men, likewise from the startled Acolytes scrambling to dismount and find cover. He sought a third victim but could not see one down the long barrel of his rifle. He'd have to find a different spot.

He was already on the move, low-walking and rock-hopping from one familiar hidey-hole to another, not certain now how many of the enemy were done for and how many were left, riled and armed and out for even more blood than they rode in for.

"Hey!" someone shouted, and Roland knew it couldn't be an Acolyte because none of them had tongues. Could be one of his own men, could be that strangely clad one riding in with the enemy.

He decided that being at the top of the trail was not necessary any longer, and he skinnied his way down the east side to check on the boy, Jay. He had vowed to himself he'd not let any harm come to him. Here, nearing the end of things, he wasn't about to let that happen if it was in his ability to do so.

He should have known better than to poke his head up at the spot he did, but he thought it might afford him a quick peek at the boy to ease his mind. A bullet sizzled as close to his head as a bullet had ever come, even through all the battles of the long war and the skirmishes since on their journey westward.

That time with the Sioux looking to make off with their crate of laying hens. If they'd only asked, he would have given them food, for they appeared quite gaunt and wanting of a decent meal. But they had not asked, they had taken, and much as he had since learned how the Indians came to regard whites for their taking ways, and much as he could not blame them, Roland was not raised to abide a thief, and a fracas had ensued.

They must have offered up some sort of signal, for soon the small wagon train, of which they were the last, their turn to ride drag as the wagon master had called it, had succumbed to an attack that lasted a full day and night.

Blood of whites and natives had stained the dust of that piss-poor country he recalled only with a sneer. Hot as an oven it was, plains country of the Dakotas somewhere. Beyond that he knew not.

In the end, they limped out of there. But in the midst of the fighting, a bullet from a brave's rifle had poked a hole through the top of Roland's hat's crown. It was a hat he replaced only some years later when it wore out from sweat and sun and toil in the fields down below in the flats by the place once known as Promise, now Brimstone.

But today a bullet left its mark on his head, blazed a trail, plowed a slight furrow as fresh as tilled earth, but this turned up not fertile soil but a slender line of red-black blood and a thin line of scalp, meat, and hair.

Roland was hatless and felt a sudden hot flood of sticky

heat streaming down the left side of his head before he knew what had happened. And when he did realize he'd been shot, he felt pure anger at the grave notion that he might die before seeing through his task. Of seeing Ruthie, and holding her once more.

CHAPTER 22

Bullets whined and rock chips flew. Boone had enough time to poke his sniffer out from behind the rock every once in a while and squeeze off a shot. He did this twice before he realized he was going to be out of ammunition quick if he kept that up.

But dang it, it wasn't right that he was all-but asked to defend himself in a gunfight with little more than a broke-down hunk of steel and a few paltry bullets. Yet all these Acolytes were cutting it up free and easy with all manner of shots, as if they were going out of business and had to get rid of their bullet supply.

"Droop Eye, you get a nick, or you out for good?"

The shots continued, from all directions, or so it felt. Boone knew that was the sort of thing that happened in a rocky place such as this—sound played tricks on a man's ears. Good thing his were near as good as his eyes.

He didn't hear a response from Droop Eye, then he remembered that the man didn't have a tongue. And even if he did, there was little chance he would choose to waste words on Boone.

The skinny, buckskin-clad man crouched lower and peered around the rock. He didn't have to look hard to see that his minder was out of the action, for good.

Droop Eye had taken a shot to the right temple and had smacked forehead first against the rock, his nose tip mushing against the unyielding surface. It looked as if Droop Eye was trying to give the hot red stone a good sniff.

The wound, facing Boone, was big enough to stick the tip of his tiny finger in. It glistened, welling fresh black-red blood, and runneled down the man's cheekbone before leaching and soaking into the odd, long beard.

Knowing it was a useless gesture, Boone went ahead and did the thing men in a firefight always do to a hit companion—he nudged the closest part of him to make certain, in case the dead man wasn't. In this case, the closest part was Droop Eye's right shoulder.

The man jostled, then his precarious purchase on the rock face let go and he slid away from Boone, the forward weight of his body pressing his face against the rock.

"Oh, Lordy," muttered Boone, wincing as Droop Eye sprawled to his side, away from Boone. He collapsed, crabbed and cramped, in a position no conscious fellow would choose.

A close-by shot, then two others ranging farther up the trail, reminded Boone of where he was, and he scooched lower. So far, the mule and the horse, and from what he could see of the other horses, were all upright and looked nerved up and properly agitated.

A couple of them jerked tight reins and Boone knew their riders had either tied them to a jag of stone or were wasting an arm's usefulness in holding the reins. He wanted to tell them to let the horses go, they were of little use up here in the rocks, anyway.

Unless the Acolytes wanted a quick escape. Sure, that was their plan. Anything for Creed, unless it came right down to their hides?

Right then Boone didn't much care what happened to any of them. He wanted to make it out of there alive. And the only sure way he saw at that moment was to shoot if he was being shot at—and not to miss.

But that would require another gun or more bullets. Thankfully Droop Eye appeared to be well armed. Boone mooched closer to the dead man and shoved the fool's tangled legs backward. He'd landed on his own gun, a revolver with walnut grips, of newer make than the little, much-used beater they'd stuck Boone with.

When he'd slumped to his side, Droop Eye's black frock coat had splayed open to reveal a fully stocked gun belt, holster, and a sheath knife, to boot.

"Sorry, Droopy, but as my old Brit friend used to say, 'Needs must.'" He unbuckled the belt and with a few hard tugs managed to get it out from beneath the dead man.

Across the trail, visible around another misshapen boulder, a black hat and an eye and half a beard beneath watched him. Boone saw the eye watching him. "Keep your eyes on the hills, fool! I'm no threat, but those hill folk are!"

The Acolyte gave him another sneer, then did as he was told, annoyed no doubt because he'd been told what to do by the unwelcome newcomer.

The shots came in from on high and all about them—save for the direct east, right behind Boone. Mac had said that these men holed up in the rocks not only lived like animals, but they likely had little in the way of ammunition. If that was the case, they wouldn't keep lobbing bullets as they had been, or they'd run out soon. Might be they did already.

As Boone strapped on the fresh gun belt, he wondered if Mac was about. He hoped his pard was among the Outcasts, and if he was, he likely hadn't seen Boone yet. Or he had and that's why Boone hadn't been shot, or even blistered close enough to worry him.

Boone kept the older revolver tucked in his belt, and the

fresher gun from Droop Eye in hand. Then he crabwalked back a few paces and skittered upslope to his left, keeping low, head tucked, and using the rocks as much as he was able. He had no solid plan, but a vague idea that if he kept on climbing, making his slow way upward, he'd be in a better position.

Might be he could get hold of one of the Outcasts and . . . and what, Boone? He asked himself. You think they're going to give you a royal audience because you ask for it? You ride in here with their sworn enemies and expect they will forgive you? He had no choice, no other plan. But that didn't mean he was going to let them shoot him. Not without a fight.

A fist-size rock caromed off a bleached-as-bone length of a long-dead tree, making a hollow thunking sound. Boone eyed in the direction of its arrival and saw the Acolyte—or maybe it was a different one, he couldn't tell them apart at a distance—who'd stared at him but minutes before.

What did that rascal want? He glared at Boone, same as the others. Reckon he thinks I'm out to save myself, he thought. He's not far wrong, but I'll be hanged if I'm going to shout to him.

The man started at him, then motioned for Boone to come to him. He kept beckoning him and Boone kept shaking his head. What did the fool think he was going to do? Wander on over there for a one-sided chat?

More than likely the man was the head of the outfit, Creed's field general, and wanted to keep Boone under close scrutiny. Boone moved upslope another couple of feet, still within sight of the man. He glanced back at the Acolyte across the trail and downslope, and saw the man had drawn on him. He was aiming to shoot him.

Once more, Boone's years of honed fighting instinct kicked in, and his left arm folded under. He dropped to his shoulder, rolled hard with a thrusting kick that helped propel him upslope and behind the nearest boulder. Just in time.

Boone growled, jerking his trailing leg tight beneath him as he crouched behind the boulder. He shook his head and vowed all manner of payback.

By gaw, he was going to hunt down the Acolytes and do for each of them. He'd had enough. A bad lot all around, thought Boone. Like their leader, maybe worse, because at least that two-faced mongrel had the sense to bed women and drink whiskey and lie about it like the rest of us. These saps follow idiots like that, believing what they say, lapping it up like kittens on a puddle of cream.

Boone was in such a fluster that he thumbed back the hammer and snaked his right hand around the downslope edge of the boulder. He gave it one quick glance, then let fly. He wanted his bullet to find a home, hopefully in the shooting arm of that weasel. Leave him alive but pained enough so he'd squirm and bleed, then Boone could find him and maybe give him another dose, up higher.

He didn't hear any yelp, but with a tongueless cur, you never knew, did you? Boone didn't wait around to find out what his bullet had done.

He kept inching upslope, roving from boulder to low, scraggly bush, keeping an eye to his right, toward the trail where the rest of the Acolytes were ranged here and there. Most of them seemed to have leapt off their mounts and taken to the western edge of the trail, such as it was. Suited him fine, as it left the east edge mostly for him.

Boone gave a look behind him and saw another broad-brim black hat, well dusted, but with a forked beard wagging beneath. The Acolyte appeared to be following his lead. As long as he kept from the man's easy sightline, Boone didn't care. He wanted to catch up to an Outcast or, preferably, Mac, and then he'd figure out his next moves.

A fresh volley of bullets rained down from above. Two winged in closer to him than he'd have liked. "Knock it off, you weasels! I'm here to help!"

His shout had no effect, and it didn't even make him feel any better. Half the words were clipped off by gunfire. He'd guessed wrong about them—they must have more ammunition than he suspected. The trick was to avoid catching any of it.

A yip and a wheezing groan reached him from below. He saw a black-clad figure, well coated in dust, roll to a stop right in the middle of the trail and lay still. Another bullet winged into the black coat, as if for good measure.

Those hill men were plenty serious. Boone decided he'd try a different approach. "Mac! Mac MacCoole! It's Hoke! Hoke Boone!"

Nothing.

"It's Hoke! Tell them to lay off!"

The shooting slowed, one more plinked into a rock and whined off into the hot, still air, then stillness. Moments passed when nothing moved save for a slow drop of sweat that rolled down Boone's forehead and traveled the length of his long nose before slipping off the end and fetching up in his lip whiskers.

He heard grunts from below and across the way, toward the west side of the trail. Presently, he heard a horse's hoof steps, shoes snicked dull on stone, scraping. A stifled whinny rose up, then the rapid thumping of a horse being heeled hard in the barrel, making for somewhere else. Another followed it.

The slope prevented Boone from seeing what it was, but he knew well enough that it was an Acolyte or two, hot-legging it on out of there, away from the fire. Then he saw the back of the horse's head, then its rider's head emerge from below the line of the ridge. He heard the same quick drumming of hooves, then saw several more horses, all with black-clad riders aboard, riding hell-for-leather back toward Brimstone.

He counted four, then a couple more. That left how many? Then, along with some of them in retreat, he spotted two, then a third riderless horse tagging along, making for home and the stables.

Boone knew that any Acolytes who were left behind were either dead, wounded, or afoot. And he was among them, though decidedly not a damned Acolyte.

"Run, you rascals," he muttered, eyeing the terrain upslope. He figured the Outcasts had seen him a time or two and likely could have popped him, too, but didn't. Was that intentional? It might mean Mac was up there, telling them to go easy on me, thought Boone. He wanted to shout out for Mac or for anybody who might be useful to him. But if on the other hand he'd merely been lucky and he was as much a target as the Acolytes, he'd only attract unwanted eyeballs by shouting.

The scratch of gravel ground beneath the sole of a boot came up on him from behind. He saw no one. Yet. Boone held tongue and his position and waited.

Nothing wrong with a man taking his time, thinking through the possibilities. He hunkered lower. The only thing he heard was his slight breath slowly rasping in and out. Droplets of sweat poured in a steady cadence down his face, tickled their way through his whiskers.

Even the far-off thunking of hoofbeats diminished, and those retreating horsemen he could still see were but wavery little lines.

"Hold there, you rascal!"

It was odd to hear a voice other than his own, and Boone couldn't help but to half-turn to see who this was.

"No, no, no, that's not how we're going to do things. I tell you what to do and you do it. Now keep your dang head still and raise those arms."

"I ain't with them," said Boone as he raised his hands slowly. He hated it when someone got the drop on him. Made him feel like a wet-nose schoolboy. Worst part was, this one could drill him right there and no one would be the wiser.

"Higher, and no fingers on triggers. I see anything I don't like, you're a dead man sooner than you will be before the day's out."

"What's that mean?"

"No, no, no talking, neither."

Boone sighed. "You sound as crazy as Creed."

"Hey!"

Boone heard boots scuffing gravel, drawing closer at a quick clip.

"I knew you were one of them. How else you know that devil's name?"

"I'm with Mac. Mac MacCoole? He's up here with you. Big fella, like a tree trunk, except with a head, moustaches, nice attitude. Rides a horse name of Lincoln."

"There's nobody up here but us Outcasts, mister. Don't know what your game is, but I am not about to join in."

"I'm telling you the truth."

"Maybe you are, maybe you aren't."

The words were followed with another one, two quick steps, then a sharp, hot pain flowered up the right side of Boone's head. The rocks, the blue sky, the blasting sun all circled into view like crazy birds, then the sky grew dark.

He felt another hot jab in nearly the same spot, and he heard a low, animalistic grunt and a groan. The voice was his, but it sounded as though it came from someone far below. He was up and away from that rocky, hilly hell. He was up, like a hawk, and circling. And then even the hazy blue light that had been the sky in which he was flying darkened, as if storm clouds had closed in.

A voice close by his head growled something . . . something like "Taste this blade . . ." Then it laughed, and then Boone heard no more.

CHAPTER 23

"Wake up, dang you!"

Boone felt a slap, then another. The blows whipped hard across his face, snapping his aching head from side to side. He tried to open his eyes but somehow there were boulders attached to ropes holding them closed. No, that couldn't be right.

His head thudded like a cannonade. If only someone would stop the battle for a moment, let him get a word out, get his eyes open, but that thudding, pounding, sounded as if it was right in his own head.

"Hey . . ." he said, but he heard it as though through water, and it sounded weak, muttered by a timid child, and muddy.

"Wake up, I say!"

Another clout. Boone gritted his teeth against the pounding in his head and he knew it for what it was now, he'd been clubbed on the bean, and he wasn't dead yet. For if he knew anything about the hereafter, he knew there wouldn't be so much headache going on. The only thing about it he had ever looked forward to was knowing he could have himself a rousing night of enjoyment with a jug of popskull, and he'd wake up feeling dandy.

He worked up all his strength and managed to crack an eye. My word, it's like shoving a dead, fat man up a hill, he thought, but he kept at it. And he got that fat man to the hilltop. It was close a few times, for the big thing threatened to roll back on him and ruin his efforts, but in the end his left eye opened, and light daggered its way in. More of the headache, but this time he used it to his advantage.

The searing pain of the sudden burst of light made him growl and snarl and grit his teeth. He heard laughter. Had to be those hill men, the Outcasts. They were the victors in that debacle he'd been forced to join in. When was that? How long had he been out of his head?

"Mac? Mac . . . thought you were here. Where you at, Mac?"

Rough hands jerked him upward, propped him up on something—his own knees. He swayed there, tried to use his hands, but they were stuck behind him, couldn't pull them around to the front. Nothing to grab. He began sliding, falling sideways. The rough hands dragged him upright once more and held him there.

He saw a shadow, then a face before him, close in. "Mac? Thought I'd find you up here. Thought you'd stop these fools before they whomped on me. That was the plan, eh? You were going to talk to those men again . . ."

"I'm not Mac."

"Huh?" Boone leaned forward. The rough hands held him from falling over.

"I'm Roland Toomey. Leader of these fools."

Boone heard those chuckles again. "Where's Mac?"

"I don't know, and I don't much care. He's not here."

"But he was here."

"Yeah, a couple of days ago."

"No, no, he said he was coming up here. That was the

plan. I was going to pretend to join up with Creed's Kindred and he was going to fetch you all . . ."

The man grunted, then moved off. Boone realized that man had stood and was walking away. "Your friend, this Mac fella. He seemed all right."

Another voice said, "Yeah, he did give us that 'baccy. Boy, wasn't that good."

Several other voices joined in, low but murmuring agreement.

"Sounds like Mac, yeah," said Boone. "My head hurts something fierce."

The man behind him said, "That'd be because I laid into your head with my gun butt."

"Well, I'd appreciate it if you didn't do that again. I'm no threat. We're here to help. I can promise you that." As he spoke, Boone worked to open his second eye, which had begun sticking with drying blood. "And undo these bonds. I can't hardly stand the pain in my arms, all jerked back like this."

"You seem to think we have come to some agreement about you," said the one who called himself Roland Toomey, "because your friend gave us some tobacco and swore he didn't find us so he could tell Creed where we were.

"But now you show up with those fork-bearded devils, right in our midst, and expect us not to believe your friend, Mac, didn't arrange all this? He's likely surrounding us right now with others, ready to lay us low. No, no, no."

The man paced and raked a hand through his beard. "You're our only chance, a chip to bargain with. What do you men think?"

Again, a murmuring rippled through the group. Boone saw now, as best he could through his teary, blood-caked eyes, that the Toomey fellow wore a dirty, blood-soaked bandage swaddling his head. That alone might account for his surly demeanor.

He also noted there were maybe a dozen of the Outcasts. And not a very solid-looking lot of men were they, either. Boone waited for their yammering to die down, then he spoke.

"That might sound reasonable to you, but I tell you true, I thought ol' Mac was here, waiting on me. It was part of the plan. He was going to get hold of you all, after he tended a few things in town.

"I was worming my way into that two-faced Creed's good graces, figure out a way to weaken him. Mac tells me the Kindred are your families. Well, you ain't got the sense God give a goose if you don't take us up on our offer of help!"

He figured that would give them something to chew on.

"You might be talking truth, you might not. All I know is you rode in here with our sworn enemy, some of the very men who took our town and our families from us. That cannot stand unpunished."

Boone's gut went cold. These men were hard. He couldn't blame them, all they'd been through, but they were short-sighted brutes all the same. None of it mattered now because they'd likely marked him for death. Had to play it out as much as he could, buy himself time . . .

"Unpunished?" he said, shouting as much as his throbbing pate would allow. "What do you think your man has done to me? Whomping on my head ain't child's play!"

Toomey paced back and forth across the dead firepit from Boone. He had an unlit pipe in his teeth. It jutted from his beard and bounced as he spoke. "Men, what say you? We'll put it to a vote. Do we let him live or do we give him"—he swung his slow gaze over to Boone—"death?"

"Ain't you fools heard a thing I said? I'm your best friend right now. All those women and children and old timers down there? They're clinging on to hope by threads."

"What do you mean?"

"I mean Creed's got them so bullied and badgered they're flat-out petrified to leave their houses for fear of stepping afoul of them Acolytes. And one little slip-up? Why, the other day, a young girl, pretty thing, she . . ."

"What? You tell us now! What happened? Who was it? What was her name?"

"No, no, I dare not. It's too awful. But I tell you that type of thing wouldn't happen if you trust me and Mac. We know what we're doing."

"Oh, you do, do you?" said the man behind him. He walked around in front of Boone and thc bound man saw him for the first time. A thin drink, like the rest, with poky whiskers and a spooked, hollow look to his dark eyes. A young man, but a man who's given up.

"That's why you're here, caught easy as a rat in a trap. You ain't much, to my way of thinking. If you was, you'd have captured us. Look who's whining for his life and look who's not, I say." The man looked at his fellows and nodded, as if he'd said something decisive.

"Might be," said Boone. "But I didn't abandon my loved ones to live like a scurvy dog up in the hills, now, did I?"

It was a low blow, but just like when he was a lippy child, his mother had always said Hoke couldn't help himself but to say what was on his mind before he could be thinking on it first.

It was true, how many times had he let loose a thought in words and seen it scurrying across the floor before he could stop it. Mama had always said it would be the death of him. Might be today she'd be proved right.

"We didn't abandon our families!" growled another of the men, a mousy fellow who looked as if it took all his abilities to stand. But Boone would give him credit—the man shook with rage.

Boone had pressed a mighty sore spot. He glanced at the leering faces surrounding him.

"Back to the vote," said Toomey in a loud voice, but he stared at Boone while he said it.

"Show a hand if you want him to live."

Boone blinked hard, tried to swivel his head around to see the men around him. There were more than he thought, as he caught sight of slight movement behind and to either side of him.

The boss man counted in silence, pointing with his pipe stem as he looked at each man. "All right, now who's for stringing him up?"

The words were spoken with a casual manner that chilled Boone's scalp. He swallowed a lump in his craw and didn't dare look around him again. He had to think of something and quick, problem was that rascal behind him had walloped him on the thinker so hard he couldn't even see straight, let alone think.

The boss man again counted, taking his time and pointing with that pipe of his. When he was done, he paused, then gingerly rubbed a hand across his bandaged head and sighed.

"Well?" said the man behind Boone.

"It's a draw," said Toomey.

"Then we'll count 'em up again!"

"We don't need to tally again. I know how to count, Paul."

"Hey," said Boone, eyeing the boss man. "You didn't vote."

The man sighed again and stuffed the pipe stem back between his teeth. "I know." Nobody said a thing. The boss man perched his work-hard hands on his hips and paced off a yard or two, then came back to his previous spot.

"Well, Roland? What's it gonna be?"

It was that fool behind Boone, the one Toomey had called Paul. Boone wanted to drive a hard set of knuckles into the fool's mouth.

The boss man must have had enough of him, too, for he pointed at the fellow and in a cold, low voice said, "You keep riding me, Paul, and you'll wish to hell you hadn't."

That must have carried some weight with the fool, because he shut his yapper. And judging from the downcast looks of many of the other men, this was a conversation they'd heard before.

While still holding his angry, thrust-jaw pointing pose, Toomey said, "Cut him loose."

Boone assumed that meant he was to live. He felt a stab of hope cut through his addled mind.

"Everybody else, take what you can from the Fork Beards. But mind there aren't others hiding, waiting us out. Can't trust them."

"What do we do with their bodies?" said a young man off to Boone's right. Under the tired look and grubby skin and clothes, Boone didn't think the kid was much more than fourteen, fifteen.

"We can use that mule he brought us." Toomey nodded at Boone. "And drag them to the east ditch. Easier to cover over with a skin of dirt. Keep the stink down. With any luck, we won't be here long enough to worry about it."

This curious remark made Boone look the retreating men over. They wore something like hope now. So they were planning a raid themselves, huh?

While the last of the men slowly trailed off, behind him Paul sliced through the coarse twine binding Boone's wrists. The young wolf leaned close to Boone's left ear and in a low whisper said, "We ain't through, mister. See how you feel once we set to scrappin'."

"Now that's a bold line of chatter, man. I wasn't trussed up, I'd take a round out of you right now. Give me some time to get my blood and you'll taste some pain, you betcha."

"Enough, you two," said Toomey. Neither man had seen him walk over to them. "You." He pointed at Boone. "We need to talk." He shifted his eyes up over the still-kneeling

Boone. "And Paul? Help the boys. We have a lot to do, and time's wasting."

"All right," said Paul. "But me and him, we aren't through."

Boone paid him little mind. He was too busy easing his sore, stiff arms back around to the front of him. In a few moments he was able to rub his raw wrists.

"When you can stand, come on over here and get some water. Then we'll figure out if you can be of use to us."

Boone took his time savoring the water. He couldn't help but notice that the dipper, a carved-gourd lashed to a length of branch, clunked with a hollow, empty sound down low in the patched nail keg that held their water.

"How's the head?" said Boone.

"A graze," said Toomey. "No worse than yours."

Boone nodded. "That all the water you men have up here?"

Toomey nodded in his slow, thoughtful manner. "It is. The spring we use off to the south of here has been pinching out of late. I expect it will give up the ghost for the season soon. We've hollowed it out and gained some days, but not many more."

"That's why you're planning a raid of your own."

"Yes, that. And other reasons."

Boone sipped. "That makes the timing of the Acolytes' raid more than a mite suspicious, then."

"Yes. Yes, it does."

"You thinking that Mac somehow squealed to Creed on you? Tipped him off?"

Toomey shrugged. "No way of knowing right now. I don't believe I or any of the men told him anything of such use. But you never know."

"I know, and I can tell you here and now that Mac MacCoole ain't one to take a man's confidence lightly. If that man says he'll do something for you, then he'll, by gaw, do it." Boone nodded in finality. Boone sipped lightly again, then said, "What do you think of me going back to Brimstone and . . ."

"And what?" said Toomey.

"Not sure, but I might be able to convince them I escaped, and then do what you thought Mac might've done. I could tip off Creed to some sort of trap. But to your advantage. I also have to find Mac. Something must have happened to him. He'd never have let this happen."

"That's none of my concern. As for you going back to town, I'll have to think on that."

Boone nodded and figured he'd let it be for a bit. This Toomey was a thoughtful fellow, he could see that. He didn't want to crowd him.

"That Paul fella, he's a mad dog, ain't he?" Boone touched his bloodied head lightly. "There was no call for him to whomp me so hard. And twice! Maybe more, I don't know. I was out of action after the second knock." Boone shook his head. "He's a hard piece of work, all right."

"He's angry."

"Who ain't?" said Boone. "You think I want to be here? I have a solid life going on back in Denver City. Get called out here and it ain't a thing like what the telegram said it was going to be. All manner of lies, mopey folks living in fear of some sort of god, or more likely of the threat of that filth, Creed. Now, you wanna know something about him?"

Boone leaned closer to Toomey and gingerly dabbed at his head with a damp rag Toomey handed him. "I snooped in that big ol' house of his, and you know what I found? Enough bottles of liquor and wine to stock a saloon. Good stuff, too. I know because I sampled some."

He could tell Toomey wasn't certain whether to believe him. "I understand your skepticism, coming from me and all, but answer me this, Roland Toomey: What if I'm not lying? And what if I told you that, in addition to that booze, I found cigars, deeds to businesses, a billiards table, and paintings of nekkid women. And all of them in the name of a fellow called Melvin Whipple."

Boone let that sink in. Toomey didn't move, didn't seem to be breathing, but his cheeks above his scraggly beard colored more with each passing moment.

"And don't get me started on his sleeping quarters."

"What?" said the man, plucking his old pipe from his mouth.

"Yeah, biggest bed I've ever seen. A fancy four-poster. And all covered in shiny bedding and pillows and whatnot. Empty bottles and big ol' dents where more than one person had been sleeping. And women's frillies, too. No sir, this Hezekiah Creed ain't the man anybody but himself thinks he is."

Toomey shook his head. "No, that's where you're wrong. I knew." He waved wide with his arm. "We knew, all the men up here. We tried, for months and months we tried. But he was good, I'll give him that. That's the only thing I will give him credit for. He was good at preaching and scaring the hell into people. Preyed on the weak minded. Lots of old folks at first. They're more prone to believing in salvation of any sort since they're closer than anybody else to dying off. Then it was the women who fell into line because they don't want their children to suffer the agonies that Creed was promising would happen if they didn't buy what he was selling."

"What about the rest?" said Boone.

"The rest? He killed off some. The ones remaining are us. The Outcasts, he calls us. That's about right. We were cast out. But only because we survived him trying to kill us first. Some of us they beat senseless then dumped outside of town. I figure they have regretted that small moment of charity. Mostly we ran, ran like scalded pups, tail tucked and whining."

"How long ago was that?"

"Three years, give or take."

"You don't mind me saying, that's a long time to hole up here in the hills. Winters must be hell."

For the first time, the man smiled. "Yeah. And I know what you're thinking. Same thing we think every minute of every day. How could our families stomach this?"

Boone shrugged.

"We never planned on living like this. Those of us who hung on, well, we're the fools, to be sure. But they're our families, all we've got. We can't give up on them, even if they've given up on us.

"I have nowhere else to go. I spent ten years of my life, happy, good years, with my wife, Ruthie, and then we raised up two children kids, our daughter, Emma"—he broke off and pulled in a deep breath, then looked away—"and there was a boy." He looked at Boone. "My son, baby Shane. Named him after my father. A good boy named after a good man. But that evil man Creed . . ."

Toomey ground his teeth as he looked northwestward toward Brimstone, not visible from where they stood. Something told Boone that Roland Toomey could see every board and nail of the place, right through the rock of the hills and across the long distance down there in the fertile valley.

"My boy's dead, that's all that need be said about that. And I want my wife back and my daughter back. And the rest of these men, they all want the same. Wives, daughters, brothers, sisters, sons, uncles, aunts, cousins, parents, grandparents. Whoever's left alive and not so far taken from us that we can't pull them back, in time. That's what we want. We have to try, anyway."

They were silent for some minutes, then Boone said, "All this time, surely one of you could have dealt a killing shot to Creed?"

"Oh, we've tried, especially early on, when we knew time was on our side. His teachings were still fresh, you see, and didn't have the power of habit behind them. But he was so cautious, still is. And our numbers have dwindled, now we don't have much. We spent most of our bullets today, so we don't even have a way to take game. We steal vegetables from the same fields we planted. Imagine that." He turned his gaze on Boone once more. "Imagine that. Thieves in our own fields, our own land."

"Nobody from outside would help you?"

"Oh, we had a few interested here and there, mostly with a promise of money. Two different lawmen poked their noses in, the first we never saw him ride on out of town again, and the second, he rode off in a red-faced huff. Creed's a powerful man with powerful friends."

"Well, me and Mac haven't a reason on earth to give up on you. Fact is, and you can buy what I'm selling or not, but this here's the sort of task we often take on. And if I say so myself, with a fair bit of success over the years. Even though this week has been a sore trial." Boone rubbed his aching head.

It took a couple of hours for Boone and Toomey to hammer out a plan to the satisfaction of each. Boone nodded and went along, offering suggestions here and there so Toomey would think he was confident about all that needed doing. Truth was, Boone was still sore in the head and more than a little worried about Mac.

He agreed with Toomey that he would ride the mule back to Brimstone, make like he'd survived a vicious ordeal, which wasn't much of a stretch, and hope Creed didn't have him shot for treason or some such. Then the real work would begin.

He'd do what he could to call Creed out in front of his followers. That meant showing proof of his lies and deceits, something real enough to convince the Kindred—not even all of them, enough to plant that seed of doubt—that Creed isn't the god they made him out to be.

This meant he had to get back in that house somehow, lay his hands on a deed, or some other bit of fancy paper that proved Creed was the rascal he was. And that he was not Creed but one Melvin Whipple. A tall order, thought Boone as he nodded to the doubtful-looking Toomey.

Boone told himself that his first order of business would be to find Mac, though he wasn't about to tell Toomey that. He was mighty concerned that something ill had happened to the big goober. And Boone was getting a serious case of the gut flutters over the matter, always a worrying sign.

As for Roland Toomey and the other Outcasts, despite their various wounds, they were shiny with confidence after what they felt was a big success driving off the Acolytes. Boone wasn't about to say otherwise, but he did argue when Toomey said he and his men were going to attack Brimstone that very night.

"Give me time, man. I need a day to get things done. You didn't give Mac the two days you promised him, did you?"

Toomey didn't respond, but he didn't say no, either.

"Okay then. A day. This time tomorrow you can sharpen your knives and load up your guns. Besides"—Boone looked at the few men still lingering about the encampment—"you and these others who took a few licks could stand with some shuteye. A tired man is not a fighting man, Roland. Trust me on that. I was in the war."

"Yeah," said Toomey. "Me, too. And a good many of the others." He nodded his head in the direction of the trail, where Boone guessed most of his men were rummaging through the dead Acolytes' bodies and gear for anything of use.

"Okay, then. Now show me to a horse and I'll be on my way."

A thin kid, looking no bigger than a boy, but with the shadow of whiskers on his chin and top lip, said, "Um, Roland?"

Toomey turned. "Jay. You okay?"

"Sure, yeah. Well . . ." The kid blushed. "It's that mule he rode here on." Jay looked at Boone.

"What of it?" said Boone, getting a creeping feeling.

"Um, it got itself shot somehow. So . . . the boys, they're cutting it up for supper."

They were silent a moment, then Boone said, "Well, if the meat is tough going, it ain't because the beast worked itself too hard."

"Go fetch one of the captured horses for Mr. Boone, Jay." Toomey looked at Boone. "He needs to get back quick. Lots to do and no time to do it, eh, Mr. Boone?"

"You ain't just whistling, Mr. Toomey."

CHAPTER 24

Creed eyed the two representatives of the Acolyte squad he sent into the hills. "You have returned earlier than I expected." He watched them closely.

"I shall assume you met with little resistance and thus, were able to render the Outcasts unto death, an eternity wandering the squalid, scorching wastes as unbelievers."

They continued to stare at their boots.

"I expect no verbal response, naturally." He emerged from behind the massive desk and approached them. "But I have been granted the ability to see the truth in all things, even in your eyes. Before the One, all is revealed. And as I am his presence here on this mortal plain, I alone possess such powers."

The wounded, bearded men still looked at their boots as if the dusty, black things were the most fascinating objects in existence.

Creed walked slowly before them, not once taking his eyes from their faces. He strode slowly behind them, then emerged before them once more and clapped a pudgy hand on the shoulder of the nearest Acolyte.

"Very well. It is an outcome I admit I have long desired, as the continued existence of the Outcasts had made life here in Brimstone a sore trial for the dear Kindred."

Creed hung his head and shook it in silent misery. "If only you Acolytes had done as I have long desired and brought me this result earlier. At least before I called in the services of those two brutes, MacCoole and Boone."

He looked the men in the eyes once more and smiled. "However, the Mac fellow is no longer a concern. He is being dealt with in a manner befitting such a non-believer. You have only to tell me that the little buckskin-wearing cretin known as Boone did not make it back to Brimstone alive and I will consider your past failures forgotten."

One Acolyte closed his eyes and nodded once, twice, thrice, and held his bowed head low in silent acquiescence to the Appointed One.

The other bowed his head but glanced over at the boss to see Creed smiling and clapping his pudgy hands together. "Most excellent. Most excellent, indeed."

Creed retreated back behind his desk and sat down with a sigh. Instinct and giddiness drove his left hand down to the big drawer there. He tugged it open. As he did so, the gentle clink of glass tapping together sounded from within. Creed looked up, eyes wide, to see the Acolytes still standing before his desk.

He'd forgotten them, so great was his relief. Their eyes were now raised and glanced from the direction of his stayed left hand to his own alarmed face. He narrowed his eyes. "You may leave. Now!"

One of the men spun and beelined for the door. The other held his gaze on Creed's for a heartbeat longer. Then he nodded once and backed to the door, exited, and slowly closed it.

Creed waited a long moment, then with a growl he snatched up the bottle of the whiskey and splashed two fingers' worth into a glass. He slugged it back and eyed the door.

Something, he thought, will have to be done about that one.

"All of them," he muttered, a smile once more forming on his fleshy face. "And soon."

CHAPTER 25

The snake seemed determined to satisfy its curiosity. Or perhaps, thought Mac, it was plain hungry and intended to eat him, bit by bit.

"Gonna be here a long time then, son," said Mac, in a soft whisper.

As soon as he did, the snake, which had been silently coiled on his lap, sent a shiver through its long body that ended at the tail tip and its quivering rattles.

As soon as Mac had whispered, he had regretted it, but he was feeling light in the head and beyond tired. It was too late to do anything about it. Let the snake do what it will.

He ached without cease, from the top of his addled pate to the very soles of his feet, somewhere deep in his boots. He would have liked little better than to have stayed in the ignorant state of unconscious, deep slumber.

By then, some hours into his reluctant wakefulness, he had recalled all of the events leading up to his current predicament. All, save for the actual moment when he'd been overwhelmed by the savage, tongueless Acolytes.

They had come from nowhere and everywhere, a black-clad swarm. There had seemed, in his recollection, to be more of them than he and Boone had seen in town. Where had they been keeping themselves? He recalled perhaps a dozen of them at once.

It was rare that Keller "Mac" MacCoole had ever been bested in a fight, be it a flat-out two-man brawl or a stacked battle of multiple men, odds be damned. But he'd been ambushed, he now recalled, by a hard blow to his head.

Something that had buzzed in from behind—a split of firewood? A rock? Whatever it had been had done the job. It had brought him to his knees in the midst of the swarm of Acolytes. From there, it had been easy work for them to set upon him as starved range dogs will on a tendon-snapped deer.

They rained fist blows and kicks with eager precision, offering little more than grunts and odd, wet, leering sounds as they pounded him. He didn't collapse quietly, despite the smack to the head that had dizzied him and tricked his eyes into seeing double of everything.

There in the dank, dark of the hole in which he found himself chained, Mac wondered if maybe there hadn't been as many of what Boone had been calling the "tongueless dogs" after all. Perhaps they'd been doubled in number by his deranged eyesight.

Then his thoughts turned to Boone. Where was his pard? He was supposed to be doing his best to convince Creed he was interested in becoming a member of the Kindred, but Creed was a shrewd operator and would likely see through the ruse. Still, Boone could be mighty convincing, especially when there was a big payday in the offing. Or when he sniffed a righteous injustice.

Mac wished Boone had accompanied him up into the hills to talk with the Outcasts. They'd been a surprising lot, worn to a nub and yet, not entirely without hope. He reckoned having loved ones so close yet so far in so many other ways could keep a fellow hoping. But in his experience, hope only carried a man so far. If his body didn't have nourishment, hope would die away along with his muscles and bones.

Is that what would happen to him? Mac tried to rouse himself with a quick shake of his head, which set off a throbbing somewhere between his ears that felt like hammer blows from a muscled smithy. And worse still, something in his lap rattled and moved. Ah yes, the snake. Mustn't forget the snake . . .

CHAPTER 26

Boone had been trying to get somebody to talk with him, anybody, about Mac, since he returned to town from the hills.

Not a soul had seemed to care that he'd returned alive. He got one quick glance from a Kindred man tending some infernal plants on his way back to town, then nothing.

"I'm even sporting a bandage on my pate!" His comment reached no one but the horse on which he rode. He thought Creed for certain would haul him into his office and chew on him a while about how he was in league with the Outcasts or some such. But no, he was as if a ghost in town.

He shrugged, and he and the horse plodded to the stable. Once he got the beast righted around, he scouted for Mac, keeping an eye on his backtrail lest one of those Acolyte goobers be stalking him. But on that count, he had little to fear.

He searched for Mac in the pasture beyond the stable where he was relieved to see both Lincoln and Chummy grazing together, somewhat close by, and looking well-tended. But seeing Mac's mount only fevered his desire to find the man. His gut was roiling something fierce, along with his aching head, and telling him Mac was in some sort of fix.

He had no weapons and had recalled he might be able to scare up such in the stables. He was about to dart back and rummage in the hay and feed bins and tack when he spied an Acolyte near the back of the big house. Boone figured he had little to lose, so he marched over to the dour-looking brute.

They recognized each other at once. Boone saw the man whose mount he had gentled up in the rocks, the very Acolyte he'd ridiculed for his lack of horsemanship. But the man had shown the slightest nub of humanity any of his ilk had shown him—he'd nodded and had seemed to take Boone's criticism how it had been intended, an anger-wrapped kindness by Boone.

"I know you," said Boone, nodding.

Again, the Acolyte nodded, his perpetual scowl lessened by the action.

"I'm looking for my pard, Mac MacCoole. You know, the big goober I ride with? He's missing, and I'm afeared harm has befallen him. You ain't seen him, have you?"

For the merest moment, Boone swore he saw something in those dark eyes flash. They widened and he looked away for a moment.

"You know!" said Boone in a low voice. "You know something. Mister, do you know where I can find my pard?"

The Acolyte looked at him again.

"Where is he?" said Boone in a low voice, moving closer to the man by a half step.

The Acolyte looked toward the house, thirty feet away, then back to Boone. He nodded once and jerked his head toward the back of the house.

"In the house? What, is Creed entertaining him?" Boone smiled, but the Acolyte shook his head not once, quickly, then nodded again in the direction of the house, but behind it.

Boone's eyes followed and he saw many boot prints, and what looked to be drag marks in the earth. Boone's gaze trailed along them to a shadowed area at the base of the wall, tight to the foundation. It was built out, jutting from the house, a dark construction of stones topped with black wooden doors.

"He's in there?" said Boone, his voice almost a whisper. He looked back to the Acolyte, but the man was moving away. Boone made to grab him, but the man angled quickly, and as the man strode quickly away, Boone heard a soft metal clinking. He looked down and where the man had been standing, a rusted steel ring and two sizable and equally rusted steel skeleton keys lay in the dirt.

He scooped them up and, with one backward glance at the retreating Acolyte, he glanced around him. Nobody else was in sight. The house was nearly windowless back here, odd for its mass, but it suited his purposes.

Boone scuttled to the mysterious black doors, similar to others he'd seen that led to root cellars. Along his path he noted the drag marks surrounded with other boot prints. Many others.

So Mac had been ganged up on, man handled, and what? Chucked down here? Was he dead? Chill thoughts shivered through Boone, and he shook his head to dispel them. No, don't think like that, man, he told himself.

He grasped a wooden handle, and hefted the top door. It budged, then swung upward.

Stale, musty air wafted upward, clouding his face. It stank of must and dry-bone death. He raised the door all the way and laid it back fully, where it flopped to the dry earth. He did the same with its companion and hoped that would give him some light down there.

The steps down, a dozen of them, creaked and popped under his scant weight. He patted his tunic for his small possibles bag and felt its reassuring shape. It contained fire-making supplies, and a goodly handful of matches.

He was about to strike one to see what sort of gloomy den he'd descended into when he saw a lantern hanging on a peg in a beam before him. He lifted it down and sloshed it—still had oil in it, too. He raised the sooty glove and struck a match, then lit the wick.

He couldn't be certain but the lantern looked to have been used recently. If Mac were down there, likely it was that day.

"Okay, then," whispered Boone. "Time to see what we can see."

He raised the lantern and peered all about him. The darkness was not quite complete, due to the light shafting in behind him from the doorway above. He hoped again that nobody came along and decided to be a good person and close those cellar doors.

"If I were a big goober, where would I be?" Boone walked forward, his steps slow and measured. He cursed himself for not trying to find a weapon. Those blasted Outcasts had cleaned him out.

They'd filched the revolvers he'd ended up with in the fracas and then when he'd been unconscious, one of them, likely that brute who'd clubbed him, had lifted the hide-out gun from his tunic.

Boone vowed that if he got through this, he'd make the chance to trail that fellow. Toomey said his name was Paul and seemed defensive of him. Boone guessed he would be, as the ornery cuss was Toomey's kin by marriage.

"If I had kin like that, I'd have drowned him in the creek when he was a wriggling pup," he whispered, mostly to have something to keep him company in the dour, musty hole in the ground. Then Boone recalled that he did, indeed, have kin like that. A whole passel of them. Generations of them. But that was different, he guessed. Not certain how, but it was.

Time to get Mac and get out of here. He kept telling himself that his pard was alive, that he was unlucky enough to end up stuffed down here for some odd reason.

The more Boone walked in the gloom, the more impressed he was by its vastness. Somehow it seemed bigger than the size of the house itself.

Thin orange light shone on something powdery by his right foot. He lowered the lantern and scrutinized it. Looked to be a long mound of gray, sandy powder. And there, jutting from it . . . the rounded tea-colored end of a bone. And beyond it, the larger round dome of a skull.

He reached for it and rushed away some of the gray sand. A dark hole appeared. An eye hole. It was a human skull, likely a human bone, and likely this whole thing was a human grave.

Boone's breath hitched in his throat and he stood not breathing and shook his head, not daring to let his thoughts go where they wanted to. Mac had to be okay. Had to.

"Mac?" he said, not wanting to raise his voice too loud, in case he was under some part of the house where dwelt a person crazy enough to live smack above his dead enemies. A crazy person who went by the name of Hezekiah Creed.

Thinking of the name set his teeth tight together. Then he thought he heard a slight noise ahead, sort of a slidey, soft, rattly sound. "Mac? That you?"

CHAPTER 27

"Boone, good to see you . . ."

"God-a-mighty, Mac! I hope that ain't what I know it is . . ." Boone swallowed, his eyes as wide as beer-glass bottoms and his Adam's apple working in his throat like a pump handle.

Mac squinted in the glare of the lantern. He looked down at his lap to where Boone stared. Across his body, stretching from his gut to his knees, in a ragged ghostly line lay a ribbed, papery thing.

"What is it?" said Mac, hearing his voice as if through water.

Boone looked at him, held the lantern up and looked at his face closely once more. "You took a nasty knock, no doubt, elsewise you'd know a snake skin when you see one. Only I ain't never seen one so . . . big."

Boone gulped audibly again and said, "We have to get on out of here."

"Can't," said Mac, and tugged his arms, the chains binding him to the wall making a faint clinking sound.

"Yeah, I saw them." Boone smiled. "I think I can help you out there, pard."

"Not unless you have keys. Or a mighty strong grip."

"Well now, as to the grip, you bet I'm plenty strong enough to deal with these here paltry chains of yours. But why show off when I can use these?" He held up something and rattled it, dull metal clinked against dull metal.

"Keys?" said Mac, straining to see them. "How . . . ?"

"Aww." Boone set the lantern on the floor beside Mac and felt along the big man's arm until he reached the manacle. "I could lie and tell you how I bested a dozen of those tongueless freaks, but my sainted mama never could abide a liar."

Mac snorted and in the near dark beside him, Boone smiled as he fumbled with the keys and the lock, both of which were rusty and thick and stiff.

"I will allow as how you are in a worse-off way than I am, and so your mind may well be addled beyond compare. Elsewise, I'd be obliged to take a round or two out of you for calling me a liar."

"I did not."

"Nearly so. What a fella doesn't say in life is almost as important as what he does say."

The manacle encircling Mac's right wrist loosened with a dull pop, and he sighed. "Hoke, you could say any darn thing you like, and I'd not argue. I've never been so glad to see anyone in my life. Now get over here and free up my left arm, will you?"

Boone didn't move.

"Hey," said Mac, jiggling his left arm slightly, feeling invigorated with the notion of being freed in the offing. "What's wrong with you?"

"It's there," said Boone in a whisper.

"What is?"

"Snake. Big, big snake."

Mac seized in place. "Oh."

"Yah. Right under your left arm."

Mac swallowed. "You still have your hide-out gun?"

"Those cursed Outcasts filched it off me when I was knocked out."

"Oh. Well, how about your knife?"

"Just the Barlow folder." Boone's voice was barely audible.

Better than the one I don't have, thought Mac. "Get it out and . . ."

"And what?"

"Kill it."

"Oh." Boone slowly reached with his right hand into the inner pocket of his buckskin tunic. He kept his eyes on the dimly lit region on Mac's left side.

"It moving?" said Mac, his voice little more than a breath.

"No. Seems like it's sleeping."

Mac flexed his right hand and arm. Hot pains lanced up and down it, but he welcomed them. The needle-like prickling pains in his swollen fingers were abating. He felt along the dirt floor for something, anything, to grab. His clumsy knuckles nudged the lantern. The bail clinked, and the light wavered.

A soft rattling sounded from Mac's left side.

Boone's breath hitched in his throat. "It ain't sleepy now."

Mac didn't dare turn his head to look, but kept groping for a rock with his right hand. His knuckles nudged something else. It was round, his hand closed over it and he made to lift it. For a rock it lifted with ease. Must be his arm was tricked somehow strengthwise . . .

It was not a rock, he saw, but a leering, hollow-eyed

skull. Still, it would have to do. Mac would lob it to distract the brute snake long enough for Boone to lunge with his folding knife's single blade.

As with all his gear, Boone kept his Barlow in top shape. This meant his blades were honed to a keen, hair-splitting edge. And it was this habit that saved them, for while a dulled knife would barely gouge the thick, scaled girth of the meaty serpent, Boone's aim was usually true, and Mac knew his pard's honed blade would slice clean into the snake's meat.

So as Mac scrounged in the dirt with his freed-up right hand, Boone tugged free his bone-handled Barlow and as slow as he dared, though not too slow, he hooked a thumb nail in the little groove at the back of the blade and pulled it upward. It clicked open and the faintest tang of bear grease tickled his nostrils, as it did each time he opened the knife, often a dozen times a day.

The folder was as vital to a working man's daily life as drawing breath or admiring the shape of a woman's body, even hidden as they usually were under layers on foolish layers of cloth. A good pocket knife could help a man survive, by splitting and fuzzing up sticks for the fire, by slicing meat from bone, by all manner of such tasks.

And in this instance, it proved most useful in defending a couple of fellows from the toothy intentions of a bull-rattler of significant size. It was this last that caused Boone to get over his reticence to kill the creature. No doubt it had gained its tremendous size by being well fed and long lived.

He struck the wide, pale underside of the snake as it went for the whitish rock Mac lobbed past it.

The blade sunk in and as soon as the meaty girth of the body began parting beneath the slice, the snake whipped back on itself, fanged-up and lunging at its unexpected attacker. Boone yanked his arm back as the snake's broad dagger of a head slammed back at them. It drove straight at

Mac, still chained and unable to jerk away fast enough. But Boone was quicker.

He drove a big-knuckled fist straight at the lurching, nearly severed snake head. The slice, a hand's length behind the head, was a deep one, and the brute, still driven by blind, defensive rage, was unable to carry through with its dwindling intent. Its jaws parted wide, gleaming white teeth, curved like scimitars, snapped on stale air, nothing more.

Boone's fist slammed the speeding head behind the snapping jaws. The impact drove the head whipping backward on itself. The visible stump flailed and welled with dark liquid, as if a bottle of India ink had upended and sprayed its contents.

Mac jerked as far to his right as he was able, which, owing to the chain binding his left arm to the wall, was but mere inches. Still, he rolled his body, jerking his long legs up and to the right as Boone lurched to his own right. The Barlow's blade drove in again, the dull glint of blood on its diminutive length glinting in the low lamp light.

As with every killing, no matter if it be a mouse gnawing holes in a grain sack or a grizzly on the rampage, or the thousands of game beasts killed to sustain a body on the trail, Boone knew he would feel regret and not a little sorrow at the serpent's death.

He'd spent time with a Seminole family years before and, among the many nuggets of wisdom they imparted to him was the notion that we are all connected by threads of life. No living creature can survive without another. And each time we lay one low, we do so at our own peril.

Boone found some of what they told him tricky to understand, but all in all, it made sense. He'd always been of a mind that he was no better, no more worthy, than a rat or an eagle or a trout. It was pure luck and cunning that allowed us to live to whatever end we each found.

And on that day, in the dusty, hellish cellar in Brimstone,

that big ol' snake, mighty and impressive as he was, found his—or her—end. One day Boone knew, he would be the one laid low. But it was not going to be that day. And if he could help it, ol' Mac wasn't going to meet his end quite yet, either. Then the thing thrashed wilder than before.

Both men knew that a wounded snake was not only not dead, but also very much an angry snake. And, as with men, rage fueled by the fact that a critter had nothing left to lose went a long way in keeping a nearly dead beast dangerous beyond measure.

Even then, a snake's head will snap and bite with force out of pure reflexive rage. And the rest of its length will coil and flail and whip until it seems as if it will never give up its ghost.

Such was the way with this viperous lord of the dark. Boone lurched to the left of the cellar dweller's whipping length. Denying his innate nature to avoid danger, he hopped over Mac's fast-sliding legs and bent low, dancing a jig as the snake, the head of which was still not fully severed, lunged and snapped at the two big intruding creatures who had brought the ultimate pain with them.

Boone stomped as if he were trying to smack out errant, wind-blown sparks from a campfire, in turns avoiding the biting head of the snake and trying to stomp behind the shovel-headed thing, while transferring the knife to his left hand. This freed his right to fend off the slamming body of the snake.

In all his years roving the wilds, and among all the snakes he'd seen—and shot and eaten—he'd never seen the equal of this beast. Finally, the log-like girth of it smacked him upright along his chest and head and he wrapped his right arm around it, hugging it close while with his left he lunged downward. He kept his white, tight-knuckled hand grasping firmly about the Barlow and away from those snapping jaws. In the lamp light, he saw the fangs, three inches long and curved, dripping with their death juice.

He finally managed to land a heel, with a solid stomp, that pinned the flailing head to the earth. Crouching, he shifted all his weight to that left boot while the head wriggled beneath his boot. He let it up enough to sink the knife blade into a pale patch on the underside of the vicious jaws.

Not one to waste an opportunity, he slashed once, twice, opening the gawping thing's throat. It barely slowed the snapping jaws.

"Lordy," gasped Boone as he struggled with the wriggling, flailing snake body with his right hand, while the thing still bucked beneath his left boot like a booze-fueled brawler.

Mac jerked his legs around and managed to gain his knees, his head thudding like gun volleys in battle. "Where's the key?" he growled.

"Dropped . . . it." Boone shoved the big body off and away from him, but kept the snapping head held firm beneath his left boot. He thought it might be weakening.

With his free right hand, Mac patted the dusty floor until he felt things beneath his still-numb palm that were not steel keys, but weren't dirt floor, either. They were sticks of some sort. And as he continued feeling for the tell-tale heavy stiffness of the knobby steel of rusty keys, a thought came to him that perhaps the space had been used to store wood for fires.

Unlikely, but then again, he had no idea where he was. Hadn't Boone said something about a root cellar? It all felt muddled. Everything in his head had become a thudding scramble.

Then he found them. "Hurry up," said Boone nearby. "I'm holding this thing so it don't lash out with you still bound and nowhere to go."

"Got them." Mac swung his right arm around, accidentally hit Boone on the left shoulder.

"Hey, mister . . ."

"Sorry, didn't see you."

"That's cause the lantern's losing flame," said Boone. "Hurry before we're blind all over again. Then we'll never get out of this hell hole."

Mac's fingers were prickly, numb, as if he'd slept on his hand and it was still slumbering. With his fingertips, the least-numb part of the hand, he groped the left manacle and found what could well be a key hole.

Boone said, "There's two keys on that ring. Try the one that works."

Mac growled and found luck with the first key. He felt a click close by the nub bone of his wrist, almost as if his bones were popping. He wrenched the key once, twice, in a circle and another click, then a pop, and, with a small grating squeak, the manacle parted and his arm dropped.

"Easy there!" Boone scooched the snake head farther away, still keeping it shoved tight to the floor. "This thing can still bite and kill!"

Mac didn't seem able to control the arm or hand very well, but freed now of the chain, he dragged the limb away, sidestepping on his knees to his left. He palmed the rough rock wall to his back and used it to help him get one foot, then the other beneath him. He leaned over, right hand on his knee and shook the left arm slowly back and forth by swaying his torso. "Come on, come on!" he growled at the cursed lifeless arm.

Soon, a stinging sensation prickled through his thumb, then spread to the other fingers.

Boone shoved the snake back into the darkness of what seemed like a corner and backed away from it, crouched low and waving his Barlow before him, ready to strike lest the thing spring afresh at him from the shadows.

His right boot clunked against something hollow and it rolled backward, nudging Mac's left boot.

The lamp sat before him and lit the thing Boone had knocked. Mac looked at it, dull yellow and . . . grinning up at him. "It's a skull," he whispered.

Boone looked down at it. "Oh, no, no, no. We have to get gone from here or that'll be us." He looked at Mac. "Who knows how big that brute's family is."

That was a thought neither man had had before that moment. And it was one neither wanted to dwell on. "Lead the way," said Mac. He bent to lift the bail of the lantern, but Boone beat him to it. "Careful. We need this thing, paltry as its light is, at least until we get out of here."

They shuffled slowly forward, and away from where Mac had been. "Someone up there would have heard us slamming around down here by now."

"Maybe, maybe not, pard," said Boone. "Way I figure it, there's a whole lot of house above us. Place is big. Near as I can figure, this is a root cellar dug into the earth and boarded up and over and around, layered with planks and logs and dirt and rocks and what-all-else, I don't know. For that matter, I'm not so sure we're even under the house over here."

Mac paused and leaned over, resting his palms on his knees, then straightened to half height. "Remind me to never have you build me a house."

"No worries there. That's a profession I am not suited to. Now, you take my uncle Jarvis, twice back in my mammy's side. He was a builder, oh yes. I ever tell you about him? He had hands the size of wash tubs, no lie, could lift rocks and logs with ease.

"Had himself a natural ability to stack them atop one another until, before you knew it, you had yourself a chicken shack or a hog pen or a cabin or a smoke shed. Yep, he was talented that-a-way.

"Had to have help, though, on account of him being no

taller than a decent-size child. Full grown man, but the runtiest legs you ever come across. And sort of bowed, like he spent his childhood years tied around a log or some such. Odd, sure, but the man could build things."

Boone whistled. "We can't spend all day jawin' in here, we have to get cracking. Lots to do. You with me, pard?" He leaned over to look at the bent-over Mac's face.

Mac had paused and was bent over, shaking his head.

"Too much pain? Lean on me. I reckon together we got enough gumption as one good man."

"Boone?"

"Yeah, Mac?"

"I had no idea I'd miss hearing your windy tales."

"Windy tales? You think I'm making up such things? A man ain't a man who'll lie about his kin, Keller MacCoole! And anyway, this hole we're in is deep and solid. We best get out of here. Giving myself the creeping willies."

CHAPTER 28

"Well, well, well."

Mac and Boone looked up, blinking in the day's waning light, to see Hezekiah Creed flanked by six Acolytes, several of them sporting bandaged heads, swollen noses, and purpled eyes.

"To my knowledge," said Creed, smiling down at them. "This has never happened."

"What's that?" said Mac, trying to decide which of the three Creeds offered to him by his fouled vision was the correct one. He'd have to hold off on a lunge at the madman until he knew for certain.

"Why," said Creed. "That no one has ever emerged from the root cellar alive. At least not someone who has been chained down there."

"Then you admit to keeping prisoners down there," said Boone, pointing at the black maw of a hole they'd emerged from.

"I admit to nothing. The Holy One sees all, hears all, and has made it as such."

"That clears it up," said Boone, sideways, to Mac.

"It seems to me that you two have become far more trouble than I ever anticipated you might be. I hired you to rid me of my biggest problem and instead you make more trouble for me.

"I have no clear idea how you were able to survive the attack on the Outcast camp. Yet here you are, alive when so many of my Acolytes were murdered. Curious. Ah well, no matter. I have other plans for you."

"That's funny, because we were about to say the same thing to you." Mac did his best to stand up tall and look menacing. He felt anything but that. And from Creed's reaction, he wasn't too successful.

"It's a shame I didn't know you were to prove so ineffective to our cause, gentlemen. But there is a last thing you can, and will, do. You will help us, the obedient denizens of Brimstone, to usher in a new age. For tonight we celebrate, in the most humble of ways, naturally, the defeat and demise of that freakish clan of hill rats, the Outcasts by my trusted Acolytes. At the same time, I will rid myself of the usurpers, the last of the plague-carriers in our midst."

"That mean you're leaving town, Creed?" Boone sneered at the fat man.

"On the contrary, Mr. Boone. It means you will be leaving Brimstone. For good." Creed nodded to the Acolytes and walked ahead of them toward the stables.

Mac and Boone traded glances. Did that mean he was going to free them and turn them loose?

Though each was uncertain of how he felt about that, they shared a thought—they could ride to the hills and intercept the Outcasts before they descended on what would surely become a suicide attack.

Ahead, Creed rounded the corner of the house, and then the Acolytes behind them forced them to do the same. As they walked toward the front of the house and the street beyond, and farther from the stables, they exchanged glances.

"Well," said Boone in a low voice. "At least we got out of the frying pan."

"Yeah," said Mac. "But we landed square in the . . ." He didn't need to finish the thought, because the scene before them did it.

In the center of what had once been the village common sat a huge pile of firewood. It was arrayed in a rough mound half as tall as a man and fifteen to twenty feet across. Emerging from it, two poles jutted skyward. A funeral pyre.

Two older men and several women, Kindred all, and all pinch-faced and grim, were busy arranging the wood. Another man, also a member of the Kindred, arrived at the pile pushing a wooden wheelbarrow laden with yet more wood. From a storehouse to the north of the mansion three women carried wicker-basketed glass jugs, two each on shoulder yokes. They were obviously heavy loads and Mac and Boone knew what was in the jugs. Lamp oil.

"Yes, gentlemen. Sort of makes you miss the cozy confines of the root cellar, no?"

Mac pulled in a deep breath and stood full height. He fixed his gaze on Creed. "And what is it you are planning to do here, Creed?"

Despite the fact that the six members of his Acolyte squad had their guns drawn and cocked and aimed at the two strangers to Brimstone, Creed stepped backward, so very large and menacing did Mac MacCoole seem at that moment.

The pudgy man regained his composure and smiled once more. "I should think that was obvious, MacCoole."

He stepped between the Acolytes and walked farther around the pyre, then climbed three steps to stand atop a small, newly built dais with a waist-high front rail. He puffed up his own chest and thumbed his black frock coat's lapels and surveyed the crowd until everyone settled.

Then Creed leaned forward and raised his arms and

shouted, "MacCoole and Boone! You have proven yourselves unfit to dwell among the Kindred! You carry a taint far worse than that of the Outcasts! The only remedy is to purge you from this place! And in so doing, so we shall all be purged by the flames of righteous truth!"

Dozens of Kindred, older men and women, some younger, working-age men, and a number of women and children, had been making their way to the town center, drawn in pairs, singly, and in small groups. They emerged from all directions, walking toward the unlit bonfire in the midst of their town as if they were called to prayer.

"Yes!" shouted Creed. "Yes! It is here we shall cleanse the very soul of Brimstone while we conduct this most-special prayer meeting. It is the will of The One. It was foretold to me in a vision! And so it shall be!"

The phrase was murmured, echoed by the Kindred as they straggled closer and closer in a shambling walk, their faces drawn and grim, mouths unsmiling, their eyes downcast. "And so it shall be . . . And so it shall be . . ."

"Well, pard," said Boone in a low voice, "got any ideas?"

"Sure, always. Just so happens that none of them are worth mentioning at the moment."

"Well, let me know when a good one comes up, okay? Meantime, I have one myself."

And before Mac could reply, Boone shoved forward, covering the dozen or so feet between him and Creed. He held his hands up where the armed Acolytes could see them, and despite their hustling to cut him off, he made it to Creed's dais before they did.

"Creed! Creed, you gotta help me here," he said. "I'm telling you, I didn't escape from the clutches of those foul Outcasts to burn up here in town! Why, I can help you . . . oh Appointed One!"

That was all he was able to spit out before the Acolyte in

the lead raised an arm to strike him across the head with the butt of his revolver.

Boone ducked. "No way, man! Not again! I'm trying to have a conversation with Mr. Chosen Creed, dang you!"

"Language of the foul sort will not be tolerated, Mr. Boone. But I am intrigued by your . . . begging." Creed crossed his arms. "How is it you can claim to help me? What is it you have in mind?"

"See, I only saved him from the cellar because—"

"How did you know he was down there, anyway?"

"Well, I'm a natural-born tracker, get it from my Pa's side, but that ain't important right now. I'm here to tell you I have figured out a way for you to have your cake and eat it, too!"

"Cake is a confection, and as such is sinful."

"You bet it is, yes sir. What I meant to say was . . . I can make you, that is to say your church and all, richer than you have ever thought of being."

Creed's narrowed eyes regarded the rangy, haggard, blood-crusted face of Hokum Boone. "There is no reason on earth I should believe you, especially considering you are begging for time to save your sorry, pitiful soul. But . . ."

"But?" said Boone, eyes wide, leaning forward in anticipation.

"But I am intrigued. Not, however"—Creed held up a finger pointed toward the sky—"for the promise of the devil's own filthy lucre! No, no!"

The gathered Kindred, all craning their heads forward, taking in the odd scene before them with wide eyes, chanted, "No, no, no!"

Boone shook his head and repeated, "No, no, no, course not, no, no . . ."

"But because should your likely foolish notions have even the remotest whiff of bearing fruit about them, I certainly can spare you several extra minutes before I burn your filthy soul beside that of your friend there."

"Well, Mr. Chosen, that's good. That's mighty big of you. Appreciate it, I do, I surely do."

"I'm waiting."

"Yes, I see that. Well, sir, truth is, my notion, my idea, my plan is fairly elaborate. It involves some of what the big finance folks call capital outlay at the outset. That'd be first, see. Like the man says, you got to spend a dime to make a dollar. You see where I'm headed with this?"

"Not really, but go on."

"Well . . ."

"And hurry up. One more attempt at stalling and I shall snap my fingers. And when I do, the Acolytes will march you to the pyre and I will personally begin the ceremony early. Do you understand?"

"You bet I do, yes sir. So here's what I'm thinking." Boone hunkered down and began sketching a large rectangle in the loose dirt at their feet. He gridded it off and began labelling each square with a number.

"What are you doing?" Creed's color rose, and his face took on a red hue that darkened the longer he watched Boone.

"I am . . ." Boone scratched a bit more.

From Mac's vantage point, it looked as if Boone was looking for a dropped penny. He looked to either side, trying to find the weakest Acolyte to barrel into. He needed a weapon. It was their only hope.

"Mr. Boone, you are done. You have brayed your last, humiliated yourself for the last time on this sinful earth." Creed clapped his hands and nodded. Two Acolytes strode forward and snatched the flailing, squawking Boone, dragging him backward between them.

Then he howled. "But I wanna be a Kindred! Got to be! It's the only thing ever made sense in my whole pitiful life!"

The gathered Kindred set up a loud moaning that built into a chorus of sound.

Creed looked at the crowd, his crowd, his creation, and his eyes widened. He held up his hands and quieted them. Then he turned to face the still-struggling Boone. "There is one way you can win yourself back into my good graces."

"Oh? How? How's that? Anything!"

"You can be the one to put that verminous heathen"—Creed nodded toward the surrounded Mac—"out of his pitiful misery, once and for all!"

The Kindred roared in approval.

Creed offered a solemn nod of commiseration. "If you show me you can do that, I will have no need ever of doubting your sincerity to me!"

"Why . . . me?"

"Because I suspect I will have need of a fellow such as yourself, one who not only has shown that he has the intelligence to recognize the need for the presence of The One in his life, in all our lives . . ."

He paused and the Kindred filled the silence with shouts of approval.

Creed nodded. "But who also has the ability to evade capture by the heathens who would do us harm."

"What, you mean the Outcasts?"

"Yes, indeed. How you managed to escape from their clutches when so many noble Acolytes fell . . ." He looked downward as if in deep sorrow. The Kindred all moaned.

The way Creed said it made Boone think that Creed didn't buy what he was selling, not for a moment. But Creed had given him what he was sniffing for—a few extra minutes. Each man knew what the other was willing to get up to, but neither was willing to admit such to each other.

Boone, half facing the crowd, said, "I hear you, oh great Creed. Uh, Appointed One. It was rough, I tell you. But when the time comes, I'll be your man! No worries there!

Don't mean I have to like it. But I am here for the everlasting glory of salvation, after all!"

The Kindred pressed closer, curious to hear what this odd stranger was saying.

Creed growled low and held up his hands. "What did you say, Mr. Boone?"

"Uh, that if we are fortunate enough to get there, at the end, I mean, then there will be some sort of big feast or fancy place . . . Ain't that what you and the Kindred here believe?"

"No! You are a fool! We are here to do the bidding of The One, no more, no less. The most we can hope for at our body's end is for a slow demise filled with pain and suffering, then an eternity spent shrieking and howling in blindness and pain. That is how we may best serve The One."

A loud ripple of murmuring questioning looks spread through the crowd of Kindred. They looked from Boone to Creed. What the Appointed One said was not what they had been led to believe.

Boone looked to the crowd, then up to Creed. His eyebrows rose until they disappeared beneath the ragged, blood-smudged bandage swaddling his head. On his journey back to town, he'd tended his head using a bandanna he kept in his tunic's poacher's pocket. "How's that, Creed? Sounds awful, if you ask me."

"Nobody has asked you. And if you balk now, Mr. Boone, you shall lose the privilege of a place in line of service to The One."

"Oh, yes, well." Boone cleared his throat and glanced up Brimstone's long main street, toward the east, and squinted into the day's waning light. "Okay, then, now about that fire . . ."

He had nearly turned back when his head spun once more and he squinted harder. It was enough to attract the attention of Creed and several Acolytes, as well as Mac.

"Is there a problem, Mr. Boone?" said Creed, looking narrow-eyed up the lane.

"Huh? Oh, no, no, ol' Chosen One. I . . . I thought I spied a bear is all. No lie, I've seen a passel of them in my time and that had all the looks of one. Then I realized it was a shadow." He forced a laugh and shook his head as if he had indulged in a flight of fancy.

"Enough!" shouted Creed, his face red, his eyes round, his mouth pulled wide as if he sorely wanted to smile.

The bellowed word took everyone by surprise. Creed puffed up as he pointed a fat finger at Boone. "Seize him and drag them onto the pyre! Tie him beside his fool of a friend! They shall scream their last together!"

Mac had attempted a lunge to his right, but his vision was still addled enough that he ended up half a foot away from his target, the loosely holstered revolver of the Acolyte beside him. The split-beard grunted and flailed as he toppled.

Mac rolled with him, determined to fight like a cornered wolverine, to the last.

The other Acolytes moved in on Boone, the sneering grins above those wagging split beards showing their approval of the situation. Finally, their faces seemed to say, the Appointed One has come to his senses.

"Seize them now!" screeched Creed.

A couple of dozen Kindred had formed a semi-circle about the far side of the pyre. The closest of the group stood to Boone's left and right by a dozen feet. Nab one as a hostage? His mind riffled through possibilities, each more absurd than the one before. He fumbled backward farther, and his legs hit the jags poking from the massive jumble of wood.

"Any ideas, Mac?" he shouted.

But his pard, though offering a hell of a bucking struggle, was held fast by four Acolytes. He looked as tall as ever to

Boone but he kept blinking his eyes and giving his head a slight shake as if to dispel an irksome bee.

He looked to Boone to still be half coherent and no help. All Boone needed, though, was a little more time. Maybe even less than a minute. But as he well knew, a whole lot of damage could be rendered unto a man in less time. Far less time.

The first of the advancing Acolytes reached Boone. The tongueless savage uttered a guttural, choking sound as he pulled back his rifle and lurched forward, swinging. Boone didn't wait for the blow, but dodged, snagging his trousers on a jutting branch.

It was dry enough and wedged tight enough at its far end to snap as he bulled his way to his right. It gave him time to strike with his one weapon, the feeble Barlow. He crouched low, then sprang upward, the swinging rifle glancing his topknot, damaging little more than Boone's wiry thatch of sandy hair.

It didn't slow his momentum, though, and he shoved upward with his knees, the blade thrust forward like an accusing finger. Momentum forced the Acolyte to follow through with his attack. His black frock coat and his split beard both parted as he swung the rifle. The movement bared his gut in full, and his wide, white eyes knew it.

Boone knew he had mere seconds before the others were on him. He weaved to his left, and with his right hand shoved that blade into the man's gut. It sank deep, tickling backbone. The brute shrieked, sagging and jerking. His sudden spasming caused the blade to carve a wide wound. As Boone jerked away, the man's falling body seemed to follow him, keeping the blade within his belly.

Boone felt the hot gush of gut and life juices, and shirt and vest fabric all slopping down over his hand. The knife ground into something deep within and lodged there long enough that Boone's right leg was trapped beneath the Acolyte as he dropped, face down, to the dirt, still jerking.

With his right arm and right leg trapped, Boone clawed with savage effort to free himself in the dusty gravel of the street. Then the others set upon him. Trapped as he was by the dying man, they had a tricky time in gaining a solid angle on his head, their prize.

They rained one, two awkward blows on him as he kept their fellow Acolyte's body angled over his head. He kept jerking that trapped arm. He was reluctant to lose his knife, his only weapon save his own fists and mouth. Finally, with a last, quick pull, the Barlow was free.

From between the gutted Acolyte's unmoving shoulder and the earth, Boone saw Mac, now only held by two split beards, thrashing and, right before Boone's eyes, turning back into his old self, a massive, seething man with fists like river rocks.

Mac managed to evade the seeking snout of a revolver from one while slamming the head of another to the ground.

With that one momentarily immobilized, Mac snatched the revolver's barrel and jerked it around, not quite freeing it from its owner's grasp, but he didn't need to. He shoved in close as if he were about to dance with the man, and then Boone heard a shot.

Both Mac and the Acolyte staggered, the split beard backward, with Mac, losing his footing, falling forward on the man. But only Mac rolled away. The Acolyte had taken the bullet Mac had triggered low in the chest.

The brute lay still, and Mac spun, the revolver in his hand. Just in time, as the one he'd slammed to the earth had regained his senses and dove at the big man, slamming into him at the knees.

A woman's shriek from the crowd stilled the tussles long enough to draw most folks' attention to the far end of the street.

A handful of strangers, spread out wide, and wielding an assortment of odd weapons, strode forward toward them all, not quite at a run, but showing no sign of slowing.

And then they ran straight for the townsfolk. The Kindred stood in the street like a flock of sheep seeing something in the distance that, too late, turns out to be wolves bolting toward them. Then the sheeplike Kindred began bleating and running in all directions.

Behind him, Hezekiah Creed bellowed and raged atop his dais, shaking his fists and screaming, "Kill, Kindred, kill! Tear asunder the evils that descend upon Brimstone!"

Boone had no time to concern himself with Creed's ranting. With any luck, he'd deal with that porky bastard later. Right now, the thing he had planned for, but had secretly doubted would happen, was indeed taking place.

Vengeance had thundered down on Brimstone, vengeance from on high. The Outcasts had arrived.

CHAPTER 29

Roland Toomey let Paul lead the charge, or, as he thought of it, the reclamation. Roland kept the kid, Jay, by his side, and Paul, along with two other men, took the lead, soon leaving the other Outcasts behind.

If he thought they could slink into town and stick to the shadows, as was his intention, Toomey saw that idea was not a possibility within seconds of spying Acolytes at the far end of the street. It looked to him as if the entire town had turned out for some sort of meeting, and everyone's backs were to the Outcasts, to a person. This, thought Toomey, could work to their advantage.

But then they saw the pyre and the torches about it, even though the day's light was still with them and would be for the better part of an hour. They saw enough to know bad events were in the offing. And then two of the Acolytes and several Kindred moved, shuffling positions for their own better view of some proceeding in the midst of the crowd. In doing so, they revealed a scene that stopped

Toomey cold. He held out an arm to hold back the boy from advancing.

"Is that . . . ?" whispered Jay.

Roland nodded. "Yes, it is. We can't let that happen."

His brother-in-law had stopped and looked from the scene unfolding ahead back to Toomey. He hurried back, and in the hushed tone they had all adopted since entering town, he said, "That is none of our affair! Those men knew the risks and still they stuck it out. No, I say. We go ahead with our plan, come what may!"

Toomey looked on his brother-in-law as if for the first time. "You can stand there and tell me you'd abandon those men, though they be strangers to us, who have risked their lives to help us?"

"Yes. All day I say yes. You said it yourself, they are strangers to us, nothing more." The men crowding around Paul all nodded in agreement. Only Roland and the boy, it seemed, were not nodding. He looked at the boy, but Jay was looking at his feet. Ashamed of who, thought Roland, him or Paul? Or himself?

And so, Roland realized he was alone on this quest. They all wanted the same result, to have their families back, their town back, their old lives back. But the rest of them, he now saw, would go about it in a different way than he.

Roland looked at the kid, who had raised his eyes and now looked at him.

"Jay, you are old enough to make your own choices. I won't hold your decision against you. As for myself," said Roland, "I will not live well in my own skin knowing those two strangers sought to help me and I let them die on my behalf. That will not stand with me." He looked at them all once again, not letting his eyes linger on the boy. He did not want Jay to feel burdened with guilt or the weight of indecision.

"If you live, brother," said Paul.

Roland did not look at Ruthie's brother again. Let it be, he told himself. Let it be.

Roland Toomey turned and walked deeper into the shadows in which they were all crowded. He angled back behind the building to his left. He didn't know which structure this was anymore. Old McGuire's place? The seed drying shed? He had no idea. Nor, he thought, does it matter. I am alone, and I will find my Ruthie and my child, and then we shall see.

But before that, he must make haste toward that pyre to help those men. As he rushed behind the row of houses, skirting water barrels and fences, chopping blocks, outhouses, and chicken sheds, Roland kept whispering, heard only by himself, "Come what may, we shall see. We shall see, come what may . . ."

Back on the street, the group of men, his men, dithered in the shadows, awaiting guidance from Paul, now their unspoken leader. Only Jay looked elsewhere. He looked toward the shadows where Roland had disappeared.

As Paul finally spoke, in a voice dangerously louder than the hushed tones they had been told to speak in by Jay, the kid, already well hidden from the rest, from the world itself, it seemed, took one, two steps backward. Gripping the rifle Roland had allowed him to keep after the battle with the Acolytes, the kid catfooted into the darkened, shadow-filled side of the building to his right. He had made his choice, and it was, as Roland had often told him about life's choices, one he would have to be satisfied with in life, come what may.

If the men Roland left behind—most of them good men who had been kind to him these past few years, all save perhaps for Paul—noticed he was not among them, none of them whispered or whistled or gave chase.

The kid wished it was darker, but then again, he had little memory of the layout of the town, and especially not now. All he knew was that he'd never felt so nerved up in all his life. Not even when he'd shot that Acolyte in the hills.

The only thing he wanted tonight was to do that again. He'd do about anything to have Roland proud of him once more.

CHAPTER 30

Night had begun to descend without Mac noticing. One moment he was lashing out with the rescued revolver and his fists, fighting lessening waves of dizziness and snatching at the swinging coats and flailing arms and beards of Acolytes, the next it seemed more difficult to see them. He also realized this bit of camouflage worked both ways.

The revolver had turned out to be empty, and thus, useless to him. He tossed it aside and, hearing gravel crunching beneath fast-approaching boots, he spun, dropping low. He did so out of instinct and a fighter's knowledge, born of long experience.

An Acolyte, nearly as tall as Mac, but sloppy and narrow at the shoulder, barreled toward him, not but a few yards away. The man held a rifle out before him like a pointing finger. Though it was darkening, Mac saw pig-eyed rage contorting the man's face.

Mac let him have one more running stride, then, springing from his knees, Mac reached up with his left arm and sidestepped as the man reached him. He jerked downward hard, wrapping his arm about the rifle and jerking it to his left.

Mac followed with a sidestep and drove a hard, ramming blow of his ham-size fist to the man's throat, barely exposed between the flailing, parted halves of his long beard.

Mac felt the small bump of the man's Adam's apple collapse beneath his knuckles as his driving fist met with the man's lurching bulk. The man's neck collapsed. Mac felt the cartilage and spongy flesh smear against bone.

The Acolyte's chin snapped down hard on Mac's fist, then bounced backward as if jerked by a hidden string. At the same time, a harsh, gagging sound frothed up out of the man's gasping mouth. The split-beard sagged and slid from Mac's fist, collapsing to the earth.

The Acolyte was now little more than a sack of jerking muscle and bone. Mac ignored it and once more dropped low, pivoting on his right boot, sweeping with the same bleeding, death-dealing fist, in case anyone should have thought it a good idea to attack the big man from behind.

No one was close enough to pose an immediate threat, but that didn't mean a barrel wasn't trained on him. He reached back and snatched up the dead man's rifle. He didn't have time to search the tongueless freak for other, more useful weapons in a close-in fight.

And still Hezekiah Creed howled and raged on, bellowing of the evils of outsiders, of the desperation and soul-killing filth that the newcomers had brought upon them. As the words spat from Creed's fleshy face, a gang of Kindred spun on Mac in the dusty near-dark street.

The closest were still a dozen yards away, but closing in fast, waving cudgels and pitchforks. He saw at least one man toting a revolver, though he either did not want to shoot the thing, or had forgotten he held a gun. But Mac recognized it as something useful.

He had only to cut through the charging horde, then snatch the gun. Simple. As they closed in on him, Creed's unmistakable shouts rose to a frenzy, exhorting his Kindred to attack, to drag Mac to the fire, to set him ablaze to appease the angered Appointed One.

"I'll be damned if I end up as firewood for your blaze, Creed!" growled Mac, though in the atmosphere of cacophonous high dudgeon, his words were lost. No matter, giving vent to his raw anger with that repugnant preacher man felt good.

His glee was further heightened by the pure animal energy of the moment, all too rare in his life since the war. Fights seemed to be the only times when he felt as if he were truly alive, as if the fleeting moments of danger and intensity justified his waking each morning.

The horde closed in. The nearest were but a few yards away. As far as Mac knew, there were no Acolytes to his back, so he concentrated his attention on the foolish sheep before him.

Their glazed stares reflected the base-level affrontery all blind followers show when their deity has been harried. Their raised voices were little more than unintelligible shouts, howls of anger and seething with blood lust gone over the edge of reason. Again, Mac smiled.

Part of him wanted an excuse to squeeze the trigger of the rifle he'd freed from his last attacker, but he knew many of these people were the family and friends of the Outcasts. He could not heap more pain on the pile of grief those hill men had already felt.

Though if they set upon him with their weapons, he'd give them a taste of the walnut stock of the gun. No sooner had he shifted his hands to bring the weapon into play as a club than the first of the Kindred set upon him.

The man, older than Mac by at least twenty years, led his

private crusade against this big infidel with a three-tine steel pitchfork. Those stingers would lead Mac to a slow, oozing death.

"No, thank you!" he shouted as he feinted a dodge to the man's left, then leaned back in and snatched the fork's shaft and pulled the man close.

For a moment, they were eye to eye, and Mac bellowed, "Knock it off!" at the man's bearded face, his eyelids twitching with a blend of surprise and rage. The old timer sneered and bared stained teeth nested in his voluminous beard.

In that moment, he looked to Mac as less man and more starved range dog. Mac laughed in his face and, while holding the pitchfork's long wooden handle in his big left hand, he swung the rifle as if it were a split of stove wood in his right. He slammed the old fool on the side of the head.

The sturdy fellow stiffened, his eyes snapped open wider, and a low, wheezing groan leaked from his mouth. Then his eyes spun back in their sockets, his lids fluttered, and he slopped to the earth at Mac's feet.

Dropping the old knot head, the outlier of the bunch, in his tracks, had the momentary effect of halting the seething clot of Kindred but a couple of yards from him. It was as if they simply could not believe that anyone could have bested one of their own in such short order.

The moment of stunned disbelief was short-lived.

Creed's surprisingly resonant, bellowing voice cracked the moment apart, thundering all about them from where he stood, spraddle-legged, exhorting his followers from atop the dais.

The Kindred closed in on Mac, and he stepped over the fallen man, offering a quick thought of hopefulness for the old fool. He didn't hit him hard enough to kill, but you never knew when a person's skull was involved.

That was all the time he had for such thinking, because a squat woman wearing a black bonnet that sat canted atop her head launched herself at him as if she'd been thrown. It wasn't the clawing, animal-like fingers on her left hand, extended before her like a guide, that worried Mac. His concern was for the sheep shears in her right hand that she snicked in a frenzied rhythm, their gleaming, honed blades sliding across each other as if they had grown weary of wool and now thirsted for blood.

And Mac knew it would be his blood they would drink if he didn't act with haste. But he hesitated a beat too long, for she was on him, gnashing at him with her choppers, much as the older man had seemed inclined at the last moment to do. Her momentum knocked Mac to one knee and he jammed the rifle behind him for support.

With his left hand open, he swatted at her, knocking that foolish bonnet further askew. His hand didn't stop there, though, and he snatched at her right arm wielding the shears. But not before the tip of one blade sliced his ragged left sleeve and dug into his flesh. He felt the cut, sensed the blood welling, but doubted it was a deep wound.

It did serve to tighten his senses. In response to her vicious, sloppy little attack, Mac whipped his big knuckled hand hard across the front of the flopped bonnet. He'd smacked a lady across the face, something he'd never done before. He guessed he should feel regretful about it, but the little demon had it coming.

Before she'd crumpled to the earth at his feet, two more Kindred were on him, one a child no older than ten years, a boy whose face showed fear and young rage, though he wielded a cudgel with menace. How could he fight a child? This is madness, thought Mac as he shoved the kid away from him. The kid staggered and fell on his backside, then spun and knee-walked back toward his group, wide-eyed and frightened.

Mac turned to see three Acolytes searching the street. He made eye contact with one, then a second, who shoved a third on the shoulder to gain his attention. Soon, all three were bolting for Mac, shoving the Kindred away from them as water parts off the bow of a ship.

Mac saw no point in continuing to fight the townspeople, the Kindred themselves, even though they all wanted to fight and presumably kill him. He needed to get to the beating, if withered, heart of this outfit. And that was Creed.

To do that he had to lay waste to the Acolytes, one by one. Those three were coming for him at a tight clip, but he needed a better, more useful weapon for close-in work. He wanted a revolver and that old man who had one had disappeared. Mac hadn't had time to snatch it from the man before the crazy woman attacked him.

He looked quickly for him, but with the black suits, hats, and beards, the Kindred men looked as similar to each other as did the women among themselves in their black dresses and bonnets.

". . . war against the non-believers! Crush the throats of those who would defy me!"

Creed's patter was as loud as ever, but the Kindred, despite their leader's commands, were looking less convinced of their righteousness and more confused. The snatches of Creed's shouts Mac heard, floating over and cutting down through the din in the street sounded tired, used, repetitive. They were the same thing he'd heard before a hundred times over, in side-street revivals all over the country.

He'd seen plenty such acts, most folks had, for preachers, honest and earnest ones as well as the foul, self-serving kind, were a roving lot and shared many similarities. Top among them was the ability to stir a crowd. In Mac's scant experience, Creed was one of the best he'd come across.

As the shouting and urging from him carried on, Mac knew he had but moments before the Acolytes came within range. They would have revolvers, and they would not hesitate to use them. Nor would they hesitate to club or shoot any Kindred between them and their prize.

His two recent attackers had resumed their assaults. He shoved and kicked at the old woman and sent her sprawling while the kid flailed that cudgel at Mac's left hip. It hurt like the blazes but he could only kick in one direction at a time.

He saw the Acolytes shoving through the crowd and he, too, shoved, sending the kid hurtling backward once more, this time far enough away that it would take him a few precious moments to return and renew his thumping attack on Mac's already bruise-covered body.

The big man finally had a few precious seconds unhindered, and he didn't intend to squander them. He dropped to his knee and raised the rifle, sighting it at the first Acolyte. The man saw this and jerked to his right, leaving the Acolyte behind him in Mac's full view. Mac did not waste the moment, as he'd learned long ago on the battlefield. When the thing you wish to hit with your bullet appears where you want it at the end of the barrel, you're already too late, but squeeze the damned trigger anyway. This he did.

His bullet smacked into the running man high in the breadbasket, catching him in mid-stride. The oaf looked as if he had been snagged backward by the back of the neck.

The split-beard was close enough that Mac heard him make a squealing, piggy sound as he thrashed and bucked on the earth.

The others, only a few strides away, leapt over their fallen fellow and dove at Mac. He had time enough to load another round in and squeeze the trigger before they were on him. The moment the shell was in and the gun cocked, Mac pulled the trigger.

Nothing happened.

He squeezed it again and it still did nothing more than click. One glance at it told Mac it was now useless as the gun, perhaps empty. He whipped it up, stood crouched before them, and the other two tongueless dogs barreled into him.

As the black frock coat of one parted, Mac saw something he wanted and snatched at it even as the slop-gutted Acolyte slammed into him. Mac had bent lower in his crouch, and as they went over, Mac backward, he guided the Acolyte over his right shoulder.

They collapsed in a breathless heap in the dust. Mac scrambled to his feet faster than the Acolyte and he held in his hand a hip knife that put him in mind of his own favored blade. He wondered who had it now. Maybe he'd find the thief before this foolishness was over.

In the meantime, he made quick use of this new blade. Without waiting to size up his foe, for he knew the man had a revolver, he slashed, the knife gripped in his right hand, the blade finding meat and blood within a heartbeat of time. And heartbeats were something the Acolyte was now short of.

The Acolyte had risen to his knees, and his revolver dropped from his right fingertips as he looked down at himself. His belly wore a wide smile. From that newly carved mouth slipped wet, red ropes of gleaming gut. His bushy eyebrows arched high and his mouth formed a big O in the depths of his crazed beard.

He'd lost his hat in the tumble, and his hair, near shoulder length, was a sweated, tendrilled mess splayed in all directions. The man moved both his hands slowly up to contain the contents of his body. It was far too late a gesture to do anything more than grip the squishy, bloody mess in his shaking, claw-like hands.

He looked at Mac with innocent, bald fear in his eyes. Mac, kneeling but a few feet before the man, said, "I'm sorry, mister . . ."

If he heard him or understood, Mac never knew, for a

big, pink bubble formed on the lips of the gutted Acolyte. It grew with his last, slow, wheezing breath. The man pitched forward, eyes still wide, and as he collapsed face-first in the gravel and dried dung of the street, the blood bubble popped.

Then, from behind, Mac heard high-pitched shouts and shrieks.

CHAPTER 31

Hokum Boone giggled, despite the situation in which he found himself—surrounded by craze-eyed women, youngsters, and old folks. He hadn't seen so many loopy-eyed people since the squawky revivals of his youth back in the blessed hill country of far away and long ago.

Back then, the roving preacher man would spend all day, sometimes two or three days, working himself up into a righteous lather, starting off innocently enough by pacing back and forth at the front of the crowd, usually up on a wagon someone had loaned for the event.

For some reason that would get the normal folks Hoke knew, their neighbors, the shopkeepers, even the pinch-lipped old biddies, all worked up and moaning and tearing at their clothes and rolling their eyes. From high up in a tree, he and Merd had had a heck of a time taking it all in.

After it ended, Hoke had asked Pa why folks acted that way. Pa had told him it was because they were weak in the head and let others in there to rearrange the furniture. Made them all nutty for a spell, sometimes longer. Pa had also told him not to let folks into his head. Hoke told Pa he'd reckoned he'd keep his furniture right where it was, thank you.

All those years later, Hoke reckoned he was more like Pa than he ever knew. For he never had seen the point in all that yowling and thumping. But he saw that twitchy behavior and bulgy, wide-eye looks and jerky, shaking faces in the Kindred folks swarming at him. Heck, some of them were even drooling.

It was as if they were under some powerful bewitchment. And then it came to him that yes, indeed, they were. It was something stronger than any whiskey he'd ever had, and that was saying something. It was the power someone else has over you when you let them into your mind. Pa was right.

Something told Boone to turn around, so he did, in time to see the first of a batch of Kindred coming his way, a burly woman swinging a stout wooden spoon the size of a child's leg. It was sailing smack toward his face and would have raised a significant welt—at best—if he'd not spun in time.

As with Mac, he'd gone into this fracas with the intention of not hurting any of the Kindred, namely because they were mostly women and girls and children, not to mention the old timers. But by gum if they weren't making him rethink that promise to himself.

"Look, you old bird!" he shouted, dodging another swing. He spied over her shoulder that only one other Kindred was close enough to bother with, a rail-thin, tall young girl in a black frock. She was dithering, holding a broom, uncertain what she should be doing. Good. Let her keep it that way.

The rest of the mass of Kindred that had been behind her had become distracted by folks who didn't look, even in the gloom of the slowly setting sun, to be Kindred. But Boone knew who they were, the Outcasts, dressed in their rag-tag clothes, and doing their best to not whomp on their loved ones. Still, he reasoned, it had to be a mighty temptation not to dole out a few knuckle bumps to those Kindred rascals for putting them through all this madness.

Of course, according to Roland Toomey, many of the Kindred were not related to them, but had come later, from some other place where the fools were plentiful. So that might leave enough to lay into without guilt.

Toomey had assumed they'd been summoned by Creed to help populate Brimstone and outnumber the original settlers, even if they, too, were under his devilish sway.

If he weren't about to tussle with this burly woman, Boone would have liked to see how the Outcasts were going to deal with the Kindred. As much as none of the hill men would like to believe so, even those Kindred who were their friends and family members were not going to be inclined to treat them with kindness. Instead, Boone wagered that the Kindred were going to attack their Outcast kin, much as they were plaguing him.

He dodged another swing of that stout spoon. "Hey now! What'd I ever do to you, lady?" The sound of his voice only seemed to anger her, for she growled and spittle flew from her mouth. From behind her clenched teeth, she seethed an impressive amount of rage.

He wanted to ask her just what it was she was playing at, or better yet what was it about Creed that got her so all-fired feverish. But he didn't get the chance, for she surprised him and lowered her head like a charging bull, then made for him.

Of course, he sidestepped and she whistled right on by. Her momentum kept her going, and she ploughed straight into a post anchoring the end of the mid-street watering trough.

He even heard the thump as her head met the upright, and that post did Boone's job for him, because she sagged in front of it and, as if time slowed for a moment or two, she flopped to her side and lay there as if she were taking a quick nap.

Boone ran to her and snatched up the spoon, which as he spun he noted had taken on a dark stained appearance from years of use in a hot stewpot, most likely. He swung it like a sword, testing it. Good heft, nice weight to the spoon end. It was a well-carved utensil.

He admired a solid item such as a wooden spoon, something he'd often carved on the trail. His were often cobby little affairs that barely did the job of getting his beans to his mouth, however. In the end, he usually upended his tin dish and licked 'er clean.

"Better than nothing!" he shouted, grinning and dashing at the skinny young woman with the broom, still looking as if she hadn't decided if the street needed a good sweep or not.

Turns out she decided it could stay as it was, much to Boone's relief. He wasn't certain what he was going to do if she'd stood her ground and put up a fight. Letting a fat, ornery thing like the spoon woman crack her own head was one thing, but to whomp on a young lady?

"No, no," said Boone, to himself, keeping low and taking advantage of the momentary lack of interest in him to scout for the head of the snake.

"Creed!" he growled, spying the porky rascal on the far side of his dais. He'd left off with the shouting for the time being, and appeared to be watching the various scuffles, maybe seeking someone. Boone made for the dais, wishing he had a gun, anything more than the pocketknife and that hag's spoon.

The dais raised the fat preacher about four feet higher than the shoulders of the Acolytes below him, protecting him, but it was high enough to give him the advantage of sight of much of the street.

Creed visored his eyes and eyed the scene below him. Two torches nearest him licked the darkening air with bold tongues, throwing eerie shadows on the ready-to-burn pyre, and on Creed's thick, red, sweating face. He turned his head slowly and stopped as he laid eyes on Boone.

"There!" he bellowed, pointing at Hoke with a fat, trembling hand.

"Uh oh," said Boone, who had hoped to cover more ground between him and Creed before being seen, namely because there were still a half-dozen Acolytes gathered around their boss's rickety dais.

Three of the Acolytes bolted for him, but Creed shouted and said something Boone couldn't make out. One of them kept on, and the others stuck close to Creed. Maybe that meant Mac was nearby, maybe on the far side of the street? Boone was worried for his pard, not because the man couldn't handle himself, but because he had been addled when they had climbed on out of that snaky hole beneath the mansion.

Still, as that tongueless brute was halfway to him, and Boone was for the moment not plagued by crazy women or old timers with hoes or pitchforks, he set himself for the attack. The Acolyte, thankfully, didn't seem about to draw a gun, but looked intent to maul him by hand instead of by bullet.

Fine by me, thought Boone. He swung that spoon and charged the split beard. Thinking that if he were to ram the beast head-on he'd come out the worst in the collision. An image of the stout spoon woman came to him, of her flopped on her side, and he smiled and covered the last twenty feet between the two of them.

Before they met, he jerked himself down to his right, hard, losing balance and feeling a hot, sharp, corkscrewing pain in his ankle bone. "Dammit!" he howled, rolling with the move and doing his best to ignore the pain.

If it was somehow broken, that meant he was not as fit as

he thought, to let a little maneuver like that crack a bone. Nah, had to be a wrenching. Even if it did hurt like Ol' Scratch himself was poking it with a grimy, glowing fingernail.

The split beard lumbered by but was quicker at his recovery than the stout woman had been. Boone wasn't quite ready for him, but he spun to face the brute anyway, wielding that long, hardwood spoon with menace.

It sported a leather thong looped through a hole at the top of the handle, which he'd slipped over his hand. It enabled him to swing it in tight, vicious arcs, and in this manner he was able to lay the scoop end of the spoon right alongside that Acolyte's large, long nose.

He heard a snap and thought for a moment that his new handy weapon had suffered an injury against the man's knotty head. But no, he soon learned something quite different. The Acolyte halted and bent forward, his big hands, which moments before had been grasping for Boone, no doubt to choke the last breath out of him, now grasped at his own face.

And between his fingers leached blood. Boone had busted the jackass's nose! He grinned and was about to deliver another round, but glanced behind him quickly to see everyone else, including Creed's remaining Acolytes, engaged in lively fighting with the Outcasts. Boone looked at his foe, who was still holding his head and making a god-awful simpering sound, part gagging, part mewling.

He circled around behind the man as quick as he could and, while the brute was still bent over, Boone leapt aboard, high up on the man's back. Before the beast could bring his arms around, away from his face, to grab at him, Boone grasped an end of his spoon in each hand and brought it around in front of the man's face, pinning his hands to his mashed, cracked nose. Now the man couldn't grab at him, at least not for a few seconds.

The Acolyte wasn't so incapacitated by his injury that he didn't straighten and shake and spin, bucking and making louder but still awful sounds. Boone howled along in laughter, riding the thing as if it were a green mustang. "I guess those pitiful animal noises come with the territory when you hack out your tongue!"

As the Acolyte jerked and tried to free his arms, Boone rammed the spoon backward harder, harder, pinning the wrists down below the jaw and giving Boone even more of a chance to do some damage. He didn't waste the moment and felt his muscles straining beneath his buckskin tunic. Sweat beads popped on his forehead, rolled down his face. He held his breath, his mouth bulged like a bullfrog's. The Acolyte was weakening, staggering now, and Boone doubled his efforts, jerking backward harder than ever.

The pitiful brute offered up a last gagging, slobbery sound and pitched forward.

Boone rode the heathen down, and as the Acolyte slammed face-first to the ground, Boone jumped free. But he forgot that his right wrist still wore the spoon's leather thong.

Try as he might, he wasn't able to free his arm from beneath the slopped man, as the thong was snagged somehow on a button or some such. It was also pinched tight and cutting off the blood flow to his hand. Boone tugged and jerked, and succeeded in revealing an inch or so of the leather strap. He tugged free his Barlow and sawed it loose.

He glanced around to see if anyone was drawing down on him, but so far he was lucky and free of unwanted attention. He tried again to drag that spoon out from beneath the man, as he had a mind to keep on using the useful utensil, thinking it had brought him a dose of good fortune. But he heard voices and saw some of those fool Kindred eyeing him, so with great reluctance, Boone gave up the fight for the spoon.

CHAPTER 32

Mac glanced up in time to see he was about to be pummeled by what looked to be a gaggle of shrieking schoolchildren. And indeed it was, all clad in black, their faces red with frenzy, their hands filled with all manner of small implements, from fireplace pokers to wooden clubs no fancier than splits of firewood. One little girl even wielded what appeared to be a spare apron, lashing at him with it as if it were a whip.

The strangest bit of it was their voices had settled into a cadence all roughly the same pitch as they approached and surrounded him. It took him a moment to realize they were chanting some sort of words, not unlike a prayer.

Seeing their anger and hearing their voices struck him as one of the most horrific of all the mad things he'd witnessed on this insane trip. Children hoodwinked into this foolish attack. It was beginning to feel like a bad, bad dream with no end.

"Get back, you little heathens!" Mac growled the words, standing spraddle-legged and with arms wide. He tried to look menacing, which, according to a good many wrongdoers in the past, he was quite capable of. Apparently, this gaggle of children, none of them older than ten, had been born without a bone of fear in their bodies, for they continued raging and seething as only children can—their voices burbling a quick murmuration of prayer, reciting undecipherable words by rote.

Mac had no intention of hurting children, nor of letting them hurt him, if at all possible. Their parents, however, were another matter. Now that they had reached him and were wailing on his tree-like legs and torso with their diminutive weapons, he did the only thing he could do—he shoved them away and bolted from them.

For the moment, his path was clear. Daylight had nearly pinched out. The most reliable light source was the ring of flickering, smoke-drifting torches standing upright about the pyre.

The great clutter of wood lay off to his right. To reach Creed he would have to maneuver through two throngs of adult Kindred of roughly a half-dozen people in each. And though Mac couldn't be certain, he thought he spied at least two Acolytes among them. Both appeared to be armed with rifles held across their chests, ready to bring to bear on him should he barrel straight for them.

They had not yet seen him, he reasoned, otherwise he would not be standing here dithering, but would be dodging bullets.

As if his thoughts were bent on betraying him, Mac saw one of the Acolytes stiffen, then crane his head forward. He reached to his right and cuffed the other on the shoulder, then pointed at Mac, a quick gesture that preceded his jerking the rifle stock to his cheek and sighting on Mac.

The big man had enough time to dive to his left toward . . . nothing. He hit the dirt already contracting, hoping to spring into a roll. He landed hard on his left knee, the same knee that had through the years given him trouble on occasion.

All because of that green kid from Maine, the drummer who'd panicked in the night and begun swinging his rifle by the barrel at a perceived enemy spy cutting through the perimeter of their camp in Tucker, Virginia.

The spy had been Mac and he'd been checking on the green kids himself throughout the long watch in the small hours. Not only had the kid not been at his post—he'd ducked back to his bedroll to retrieve a bundle of letters from his mama, never mind that he wouldn't be able to reread them again until daylight dawned—but he'd screamed like a startled chicken and it took four men to shut him up.

The next morning, limping from the surprisingly painful crack to the kneecap he'd taken from the riled kid, Mac had sought out the still-trembling drummer. The fool kid wasn't any older than fifteen. Hell, thought Mac on seeing the youth, he wasn't even certain a razor had ever touched the boy's peach-fuzzy face.

"What are you doing here, son?" he'd said, feeling a little odd using that word, but knowing somehow it was the right one.

"They . . . they told me to stay put."

"No, I mean in the army, in the war. You look too young yet to have joined up."

For the first time, the trembling in the kid's shoulders and the nervous tic on his cheek ceased. He gave Mac the hard eye. "The war took my daddy, sir. I figured I was next to go. Somebody has to defend Mother and Sissy from the Reb Menace . . . sir."

Mac didn't know whether to laugh or sigh. He chose the middle road and gave the kid a wry grin. "You would be of more use to them if you'd stayed on the farm."

"Sawmill," said the kid. "Sir."

"Sawmill, then. Do us all a favor and go back there, will you?" Mac turned to limp away. He knew it was a harsh thing to say to the kid, but he was tired, bone tired, and he didn't want to see any more children like him hurt or killed in a fight that wasn't theirs to begin with, no matter what the politicians and newspapers told them. The possibility of a Rebel Menace sweeping through every little backwoods hamlet in Maine was all-but zero.

"You're him, aren't you?"

Mac paused, turned and looked at the kid. "Who?"

The kid was back to being red-faced and shaky. "The one I hit in the leg with my gun, sir. I am heartily sorry for that."

Mac sighed. "I know." He regarded the kid a moment. "You had anything to eat yet?"

"No sir."

"Well, come on then. If you're half as hungry as me, you could eat a dozen chickens, the coop, and all."

"We'll likely have to settle for corn mush, sir."

Mac smiled as they walked, he limping and trying not to. "Better than sawdust," said Mac.

He thought he heard the kid say, "Barely."

He'd thought of the kid more times since that day than most folks recall strangers in their lives. Mostly because every time that knee pained him, he cursed the kid and the army for taking on a kid and the entire messy affair of war.

And it always left him feeling bitter and cold, because he'd then recall that the kid, who he came to learn was named Chilton Swannick, the drummer from Maine, had been only fourteen years old. He never saw fifteen, for he took a bullet in his right eye and bled away his young, promising life barely a week after he'd clubbed Mac's knee with his rifle stock.

When Mac had inquired about the kid's letters from his mother, he'd been told nobody had found them. Then he found out later someone had filched them to start a campfire. War. And now here he was, all these years later, still being shot at by someone who bought what a snake-oil salesman was selling. A different sort of war but still a war. Nothing more.

Mac rolled with the scant momentum of his leap, wincing from the pain, and came to rest against a stack of heavy barrels. Another shot bored its way into a barrel stay a couple of inches above his head. He hustled his efforts, digging his elbows into the earth and ignoring the various throbbings in his head and all over his body.

He hoped Boone was having a better time of it than he was. To go from a dank cellar menaced by a massive snake to being stalked and shot at in the dusky dusty street by a tongueless man and then thrashed by a gaggle of mindless children left Mac doubting with increasing seriousness the notion that he was indeed awake.

"Has to be a damn dream," he grunted, pawing the dirt and dragging himself behind the barrels. Just in time, for another bullet furrowed where his trailing boot had been a second before.

What he wouldn't give for a rifle right then. And speaking of guns, where were those damned Outcasts, anyway? They'd appeared when Boone was trying to keep him from burning alive, but he'd not seen them amount to much since then.

Cowering behind barrels wasn't much of a way to live, and even less of a way to die. Mac bent low, and with his right cheek to the earth, he inched his head around the farthest barrel. The Acolyte was striding with caution toward him, rifle held out, at gut height.

Mac pulled his head back in slowly, aware that quick movement attracted attention. He heard the shouts of the Kindred beyond, heard Creed's resumed ranting, something about "heathens who must be vanquished" and "putting Brimstone in eternal peril."

Closer by, he heard the high-pitched murmurings of the

gaggle of Kindred children, whip smart, no doubt, from the threat of the Acolyte presence always in their lives.

Behind him, Mac had seen the dark, looming presence of a building—the granary, if he remembered correctly. He also knew none of the doors in town were locked. Easier for the Acolytes to barge in on folks, he reckoned. All on Creed's orders, of course.

It would be risky to bolt for the door, but even riskier the longer he waited. The Acolyte stalking him must have been less than a dozen yards away.

Using the stack of barrels—six large at the base, with demi-barrels arranged atop, they would provide adequate cover for the next few moments, but no longer.

As he righted himself, working to get his legs beneath him and ready to dash for the granary door behind him, one of the smaller barrels atop, and close by his shoulders and head, jostled. It was empty. Perhaps all of them were. He added a quick bit of complexity to his meager plan, and, as he had trained himself to do once he'd settled on a notion, Mac tensed and launched into action.

Keeping low, he spun, snatching around its base the smaller barrel that had jostled. Though nearly empty of whatever its contents might have been, it nonetheless offered reassuring heft. The next moments would be the trickiest. Keeping as hidden as he could behind the barrels, Mac grasped the small barrel with one big hand at each end, his grip firm on the rims, and yanked it backward.

A rifle shot blazed and thunked into the barrel he now crouched behind.

He didn't wait to see if it had found its way through the barrel and into him, but he sent that barrel in a low arc straight at the black mass of a man dashing toward him.

Emboldened by the darkness and rifle clutched in his hands, the Acolyte had not expected something so solid and large to fly at him out of the night air. It collided with the man, but Mac was already making for the granary door behind him, doubtful that the small barrel would incapacitate the Acolyte enough to allow him to dart over, grab the rifle, and shoot the tongueless fool.

He was proven correct when a shot shattered the granary's front window to his left. Mac pulled his head even lower and jerked open the door, relieved that it was, indeed, unlocked. With the way his day's luck had been running, it would not have shocked him to discover the door locked, barred, and bolted.

He now had a slight advantage. If the Acolyte were dumb enough to follow him in, he could ambush him. Simple.

Mac half-smiled in the still, darkness of the floury-smelling room. Boone was always spouting some hare-brained scheme, then smacking his bony hands together and saying, "Simple."

"Hope you're having a better time of it than I am, Boone," Mac whispered, pricking his ears for the tell-tale crunch of boots on gravel out front. He didn't have long to wait.

CHAPTER 33

Paul nodded up the street, and the Outcasts under his charge parted to let him pass. The rag-tag dozen spread out in the half-cover of near dark. The street down which they walked was still familiar, though to a man they felt as strangers there. Each experienced odd, haunting thoughts of family and friends and the changes wrought on their lives by the coming of Creed.

They walked up the street, toward the gathering of Kindred thronging and shouting about something hidden as yet from their sight before the torch-lit, massive pyre waiting to be touched off.

Beyond it, lit by the multitude of flickering torches and the day's setting sunlight, the Outcasts saw Acolytes loosely gathered, their backs to a raised platform of some sort. And it was on that which stood Hezekiah Creed, the source of all their collective misery and earner of their enmity.

Paul walked directly at that one raised, fat figure. Before his chest he held a rifle, one that had belonged to one of the fallen Acolytes from the scuffle in the hills. He needed only to get close enough to halt, raised the rifle to his shoulder, the stock to his cheek, his left eye to sight down the long barrel, and then squeeze that trigger. That would send that hell-hound barking and wailing in a death agony back to whatever foul pit he had crawled out of years before.

"That's all I need," he muttered as he walked faster, all thoughts of his fellow Outcasts gone, his own safety forgotten as well, lost as he was in his burning need to kill Creed.

The man had taken all from them, and had robbed from Paul a future with a woman he'd come to love dearly, the schoolmistress, Demelza Schmidt. He'd learned she'd taken her own life two years before, though how and why remained a mystery to him. But he bet Creed knew.

Paul did not hear his fellows hissing and whispering to him to stick to the sides of the street where the shadows were long and would provide cover. He did not let his thoughts turn again to the woman he had loved, the one he had intended to marry and raise children with. His beautiful Demelza. No, he had dwelt far too long on thoughts of her.

Paul also did not notice that a number of the Acolytes had begun to spread apart, melting to the left and right into the coming night, moving swift and sure along their street to render dead the gaggle of freshly spied Outcasts making for the Appointed One.

Paul did not see them. He only had eyes for Creed, still too far ahead to get a clear shot at. And Hezekiah Creed was the last thing Paul saw as a bullet from an Acolyte's rifle drove, like a raging bee, into his right temple, and burrowed out again through his left temple. He stood but a moment longer, his look of certainty slowly replaced with the disappointment of defeat, before the cloudiness of death dropped him where he stood.

The shot parted the heavy, pressing night air of main street, Brimstone. And for a moment, all the Kindred turned to see what this had been that dared interrupt the preaching of the Appointed One.

What the startled Kindred saw was a man swaying, then toppling to his side to lay, unmoving, in the street.

Ragged shouts of "No!" rose out of the dark along the street.

Several of the Kindred men made to move toward this sight, but Creed's voice cut through the murmuring. "Leave the filth where it lay! It carries a taint far worse than mere death! It is the taint of the non-believer! To touch it is to lose all hope of the eternal!"

"Yes, yes!" chorused the Kindred, turning back to face their leader.

From the south side of the street, peering between two buildings long unfamiliar to him, Roland Toomey fought back the urge to dash into the street. Surely Paul was still alive—after all this time, surely it could not end this way for the young man, his brother-in-law, Ruthie's younger brother, the young man who'd accompanied them westward . . .

Roland gave over to his urge and bolted, emerging from the shadows. But strong hands grasped him, jerking him backward. He landed in a pile atop his attacker and struggled to right himself, to kill this fiend who would dare stop him.

Roland flailed, groped to rise to his knees, and scrabbled for his rifle, which he'd dropped when attacked. Then he saw a face below him on the street, felt the man also thrashing, but pinned for the moment by Toomey's pressing left knee, the weight of him holding the attacker at bay.

He pulled his right fist back and drove it downward at the face, even as the attacker shouted, "Roland, no! It's me!"

The attacker jerked his head to one side, and Roland's fist slammed the cheekbone and glanced off the man's ear before hitting the earth. The attacker didn't wait, but bucked and wriggled enough from beneath Roland's pinning strength to land a hit himself. The blow, to the left side of

Toomey's face, set off a carillon of bells in his head, stunning him for but a moment.

"Roland, dammit! Knock it off!"

The voice was close and . . . familiar. Then he knew who it was. "Jay?"

"Yes! What are you doing?"

"Jay, boy . . ." Roland looked over his shoulder toward the street. "He's out there, I have to help him."

"Paul's gone, Roland. Paul is dead. What good are you going to be to Ruth and the rest if you get shot dead in the street, too? Huh?"

Roland stared at the barely visible face of the kid for a few moments, then shook his head. "I thought you were sticking with the others." He slumped backward to sit on his rump, leaning against a building.

The kid shrugged. "I don't know. You left, didn't give me much of a chance."

"Okay then," said Roland, pulling in a deep breath. "What next . . ."

The kid knew it wasn't so much a question directed to him as it was Roland thinking out loud, as he often said of himself. But the kid was ready with an answer. "We need to help those men, the strangers who vowed to help us."

Roland looked at the kid, then nodded. "Yes, yes, that's right." He turned around, laid a hand on his rifle. "And then?" again, speaking as if to himself.

"And then," said the kid. "We track down Creed and make him pay for . . . everything."

With no more words necessary between them, Roland led the way out of the mouth of the gap between buildings. The way lay shadowed, and the two figures stole westward up the street toward the commotion.

Back along the street, to both sides, the rest of the Outcasts, for the moment too stunned to move forward at seeing

Paul killed before them, stayed unmoving, half in shadow, too much revealed. Acolytes, emboldened by the quick kill, and familiar with every footfall the street required, stole with solid purpose, armed and moving, toward these intruders who would do harm to their Leader.

It was Zeb, the oldest of the rest of the Outcasts, who saw the foolishness of their position for what it was and, ducking low, scuttled back to his right, deeper into shadow, barking a barely whispered oath at the others to do the same.

They heeded, but not before they were seen from across the street by a menacing figure in black, a split-beard who they saw as a fleeting movement ducking behind a stack of pine planks, blocked and drying.

"He's there," said Zeb. "I seen him."

"Yeah, well, what good's that to us? We need to get up to that end of the street and quick, otherwise Creed will scuttle back into his big house and we'll have a devil of a time rousting him out again."

"Naw, we won't neither," said a bony, grim-faced man named Merle. He used to be the town sign painter and all-around handyman. It had been generally known in Promise that there wasn't a thing ol' Merle couldn't put right if he had enough time to "mull on it," as he liked to say.

He scratched at his beard and wished he had a quid of chaw. Times like these a wad of 'baccy did a man's thinker some good. "Tell you what, boys. I'll follow him on in there, and damn the consequences. The rest of you, take to the street and move like hell on the crowd. Looks to me like we outnumber the Acolytes, anyway. Do it, do it now!" And with that, Merle bolted for the shadowy figure.

The rest hesitated a moment, then Zeb, in a loud voice, said, "Let's go!" And he led the charge. The Outcasts rampaged right up the main street of Brimstone, spread out and howling for vengeance.

Back in the shadows, Roland and Jay had continued to make their way up the street, but half hidden as they hugged the buildings on the south side of the street. Soon, they were almost parallel to the pyre. Clusters of Kindred were facing the oncoming straggle of Outcasts. Others were behind, tending to the building of the fire.

And then Roland saw her, his Ruth, struggling under an armload of wood. She neared the pyre, with her face revealed beneath a black bonnet tugged back as much as a woman in the Kindred felt on such a hot night that she could get away with.

Her cheeks were red and slick with a sheen of sweat. The firelight danced in her eyes. Even across the couple of dozen yards that separated them, Roland recognized her as the same beautiful woman he'd married, and still loved. And at that moment, teams of horses would be unable to drag him from running to her.

He was halfway across the street, shouting her name, "Ruthie! Ruthie!" when he was descended on from two sides by Kindred and by an Acolyte.

It all happened so quickly, Jay had little time to react, and no time to grab for this man who had become very much a father to him. He chased after Roland, but jerked short but a few strides into the street. Roland was swarmed, and Jay would be next. He could only help the man if he was free. But what to do?

He stepped back into the shadows even as Roland shouted his wife's name, and lashed out at the hands grasping him, pummeling him, dragging him toward the pile of wood.

CHAPTER 34

Mac waited inside, behind the parted door of the granary. Long moments passed before he heard more gravel, then boots on boards. Then he did—a slight, scuffing sound, but it was there. Then a shadow darker than the others moved slowly into the room. Mac tensed, waited, waited . . . and the Acolyte shoved the door hard with an arm, spinning at the same time.

It was a gamble on the brute's part to assume Mac was behind the door, but a solid guess. But Mac was ahead of him and had slid along the wall as the Acolyte spun. He brought his locked hands down like a sledge, landing a solid blow to the split-beard's neck.

It wasn't enough of a hit to knock out the man, but it did drop him to his knees and send an odd, grunting sound out of the man as he crashed to the floor. Mac straddled the collapsed form. As the Acolyte rose with awkward moves, still clutching his rifle, Mac palmed the back of the man's head with his right hand and with his left, grasped the beard-covered chin. He brought all his considerable arm muscles into play as he jerked upward with the man's chin.

The sound he hoped to hear, one he had forced from men in the past in other such situations, filled the otherwise still air of the granary—a dull snapping, as a snapped carrot makes when cracked in two.

A wheeze leaked out of the man's mouth and he sagged, face down, to the floor. Mac let go, snatched up the rifle, and felt his way in the near-dark to the shop's back door.

He made it out and around to the shadows out front once more, when a man's frenzied shout directed his roving eyes to the cluster of people about the pyre.

He looked behind him toward the loose smatter of people in the street and saw flames, not only from the torches but down lower, beginning to lick around the base of the pyre, to curl upward like gasping claws. Someone had touched off the blaze, but with what intent?

Then Mac saw the reason, and it was the source of the man's increased frenzied yelling. At the edge of the pyre facing Creed's mansion, the flames had not yet worked their way around fully. Four Kindred men and three Kindred women were carrying a struggling man, the one yelling, and mounting the pile in a clumsy manner.

The group shifted, and the members looked down briefly, searching for a next foothold, but Mac was unable to get a glimpse of who it was they were hauling to his death.

For a brief moment he thought that this surely must be a poor joke, perhaps a way to frighten the poor fool into leaving them alone. But he pounded forward, knowing this was not a joke. Whoever it was, he didn't deserve to burn.

Mac failed to see the figure rising out of the darkness to his right.

The figure closed in on him, but Mac caught sight of it too late to do much more than break his stride and fling up his right arm. It was no Acolyte attacking him but a smaller, beardless young man, likely another of the damnable Kindred. But this one wasn't trying to bite him or kick him.

"Mister!" growled the young man. "Help—you gotta help! It's Roland!"

Mac gripped the youth by the shoulders and held him at arms' length. He recognized him now as the young, quiet kid who hung on Roland Toomey's every word.

"What?" he said, then catching on to what the kid was saying.

"Yeah, they got Roland. Knocked him clean out and now they're going to burn him alive! I need help, oh I need help. It never was supposed to be this way!" The kid began to sag in Mac's big hands. Mac jerked the kid hard upright and delivered a quick slap across the kid's maw. It worked—the kid stiffened and stared at Mac.

"You're sure that's Roland?" he said, pointing at the struggling forms mounting the pyre, though it didn't matter who it was.

Mac saw now they were struggling but only because their footing was awkward as they mounted the jumble of logs and branches and scrap planking, ascending to one of the raised center poles.

"This cannot stand," growled Mac, and, shoving the kid to one side, dashed forward, heedless of the danger of Acolytes and Kindred who wished to see him dead.

It didn't take long to attract their attention. But he had a secret weapon in the kid, who showed no hesitation in helping him. They fought through the teeming mass of enraged Kindred, side by side, with the kid using his rifle as a butting, battering tool, as they were fighting too close in to be able to shoot without injuring one of the Kindred.

Mac smelled the smoke, heard the crackle of wood succumbing to flame, and heard shouts of praise from Creed far to his left. He assumed the little freak was still atop his dais, whipping up the Kindred into greater heights of fervor.

The voices of the Kindred rose in pitch and intensity, but there was something else there, too, something odd—breaks in the shouting, as if some of them were dropping out. He saw some covering their mouths, though he was too busy driving his fist into the faces of anyone barring his way.

He thought at one point that he punched a gaunt, whiskered fellow in the face. It was only a moment later when he was busy shoving three black-dressed women aside that the face of the man he'd punched came back to him. He was an Outcast.

So the kid and Toomey weren't alone. Good. They'd need all the help available. He didn't look around to see much more, aware that there were likely Acolytes closing in, aware that a bullet could end everything for him at any moment. But Toomey was up there, atop the pyre, not more than a few yards from him now.

"Go!" shouted the kid, closer by his right side than Mac had thought.

"You okay?"

"You bet!" shouted the kid, swinging the rifle like he was racing the clock as he scythed a wheat patch.

Mac kept low, which for him was tricky, and shoved a last, grasping Kindred out of his way—an old woman with fire reflected in her wide eyes and hate pulling her mouth wide in a rictus of rage. He sent the old bird sprawling backward in the dirt and not for the last time wondered where the Acolytes had gone. Don't think about it, Mac, he told himself. It's a gift.

Up he jumped between two spires of flame. Already the fire had spread beneath the mass of wood, a broad jumble twenty feet across wreathing the raised poles in the center.

The heat built, and he cursed as he leapt from one solid-looking spot to another. One of them wasn't that solid, however, and his right leg jammed through and disappeared into the fiery mass below. He felt the canvas of his trousers pucker, tighten, and burn, the heat blistering his leg beneath.

"Gah!" he growled, yanking his leg back up above the wood. He'd lost his balance so he had to grab at whatever he could to hoist himself to his feet again. It was an awkward scramble, but what he saw still ten feet above and before him made him double his efforts.

Roland Toomey was awake, fully, and though a rag had been wrapped tight about his mouth and tied behind his head, his eyes bulged and he thrashed and screamed, his moaning, wordless voice sounding oddly like those of the tongueless Acolytes.

Toomey was bound by ropes that would serve to hold him upright to the post long before they burned through themselves, and long after Roland succumbed to the killing heat and flame.

Beyond Roland, a curtain of shimmering heat and flame showed the shapes of the Kindred as wavery, ghostly forms.

"Help us!" shouted Mac, as he scrambled and lurched toward Roland. He had to free the man, or they'd both die atop this hellish mound.

One shape broke from the others and moved toward the fire, shoving with a pole. It looked to Mac like a broom or pitchfork. The person used the pole to attack the logs, parting the fire, while others followed.

Mac didn't waste time seeing how many Kindred were coming for them, but he was amazed that they'd risk the fire to get at them, so freakish was their devotion to Creed.

He reached Toomey, and his presence seemed to snap the man out of his wriggling frenzy, if but for a moment. His attackers had tied the gag around the pole so that Roland's head would stay upright as he burned.

"Devils!" cursed Mac as he dug at the knot with his numb, hot fingers.

Roland jerked and twitched and writhed as much as the tight ropes would allow. Mac, half blinded by intermittent washes of rising smoke, coughed and spat, yelling what he hoped were encouraging words in Roland's ear, all the while struggling with the knots.

"Knife!" he growled, knowing merely saying the word wouldn't conjure one.

He usually carried a Barlow folder, something he and Boone had in common. It had been a gift from Boone, in fact, many years before. But it had been lost somewhere in one of the many scraps he'd been treated to in the last day or so.

Roland kept jerking his head toward him and bugging his eyes down as if . . . pointing?

Mac looked down, patted Toomey's right side and felt a tell-tale shape in his pocket. He reached in and pulled out a knife, tugging up a blade, all in a swift motion. He touched it to the rope, sawing with speed, not caring much if he cut the man—skin could heal from a cut, but not from a full-body burning.

Though Roland was lashed to the pole with what seemed a mile of rope, the coils began to fall away and Mac slashed hard at them once, twice, thrice.

It was then that the first Kindred, the figure Mac had seen shoving at the fire, parting it with a long tool, came into view, dancing, stumbling between the flames. It was a woman in a long, black dress, and the dress was on fire in two spots. But she didn't slow.

She looked up and, in a moment of clarity, when the acrid thick smoke parted, as a cloud will drift to reveal blue sky, Mac saw something on her face, in her eyes, that he did not expect—he saw the clash of fear, doubt, and desperation in equal measures in her reddened, tearing eyes.

"Ruthie, no!" shouted Roland, trying to reach the woman, but the coils of rope were still wrapped about his boots and he pitched forward.

Mac dove for the fallen man, whose arms had shoved through the many flame-filled gaps in the pile.

Mac smelled hair burning and the stink of charring clothes and blistering flesh coming from either him, Roland, or this Kindred woman, apparently Toomey's estranged wife.

Had she risked her neck to ensure the man burned alive or was she snapping out of her zealous stupor and risking her neck to save him?

No matter, all three were stumbling and flopping about on the crackling pile of flame and wood. Mac was the first of the three to gain his footing and, straddling Toomey, dragged him toward the edge, the path the woman had taken. Her tool, he now saw, was a long-handled wooden hay fork that stood jammed and leaning in the big snag of burning wood. She was alternately patting Roland's smoking hair and jerking the bottom of her body, trying to keep the flaming dress from burning her legs beneath.

Beyond her, other faces appeared, more Kindred. Mac figured he could bull through them, knocking them away, back toward the edge of the pyre and, hopefully, to safety as he dragged Roland away from the center.

Mac pulled and pulled, growling and making awful guttural sounds when the man finally came free. As he dragged him away, nearly stomping on the woman who had regained her own feet, Mac saw that he'd pulled the man clean out of his boots. They were still wrapped in ropes and curling and puckering, the shafts transmitting smoke and small tongues of flame upward like two chimneys.

Mac coughed without let-up, and could not call up any of the handfuls of black tar he was certain were lodged and clogging in his throat.

Still, he kept dragging, with Roland wrapped under his left arm, and the woman, her head facing the fire and her backside facing forward, under his right.

The Kindred before him fell back, in part because he bowled into them. They dropped, fell, staggered, and sprawled in the dirt, away from the fire, and he did the same staggering and dropping square on his bum knee.

He wasn't certain which pain was worse, the stabs of lightning-bolt pain in that knee shooting up and down his body or the fire in his chest from the smoke and heat he'd staggered away from.

He let go of his two charges and fell face first on the street, the gravel feeling oddly cool against his burning, blistered cheek.

In a moment, sensing commotion, he forced his eyes open and tried to raise himself up, using his hands to push himself upright. He felt wetness and knew his blistered hands were oozing pus. He looked through watery eyes and gritted his teeth. Kindred surrounded him.

So now they were moving in for the final blow, was that it? Hell, he thought. Out of the fire, into the pit of eternal damnation?

CHAPTER 35

Through gradual attrition caused by days and now the beginnings of a night of sporadic attacks by Mac, Boone, and the Outcasts, the Acolyte numbers began to diminish. As Boone drew closer to Creed, still atop his dais—waving his arms and cursing his followers, looking sweatier and stranger, dare Boone think more desperate?—Boone noticed for the first time that there were no Acolytes ringing Creed. This was an opportunity he could not ignore.

He altered his zig-zag course and made straight for the man's platform and climbed the four steps at the back, which faced the mansion about one hundred feet away. He was halfway up the steps when Creed must have felt the rickety platform shifting under Boone's slight weight.

Creed turned to look behind him. He was in mid-shout, barking something about a lost eternity spent in fire, if Boone heard him right. In the flickering glow of the pyre's flames, Boone saw spittle flecking from the man's wet, angry lips.

The word "devils" snagged in his mouth and he and Boone exchanged a glance. Uncertain what he was going to do, Boone knew it was time to act, even if it meant sacrificing himself to the crowd. Creed looked like he wanted to be back in his mansion, a guzzle of whiskey at hand, and a woman at the other.

Boone recognized the allure of those thoughts, too, but pushed them away. No time for frippery.

"You!" growled Creed, shoving a boot at Boone. The wiry man grabbed it by the heel and yanked, upending Creed. The chunky man crashed to the floor, swaying the dais once more.

Nearby voices shouted, and Boone knew the Kindred, and likely a few Acolytes, too, would be on them, and quick. The commotion at the pyre, most of which Boone hadn't seen because it had been too smoky and he'd been too busy, was enough of a distraction that it had until that moment, prevented him from being seen attacking Creed. Now, though, he expected he'd be attacked.

And then Creed did something for which Boone was unprepared—the fat preacher man rolled at Boone, half-rising to his left knee, and shoved Boone backward. Boone hadn't made it all the way up to the top of the dais, and his balance was off-kilter. Flailing, his right hand grabbed whatever was available, which happened to be Creed's trouser leg.

Then Boone saw that the voices he'd heard were not solely of the Kindred—he spied Outcasts closing in on the clot of Kindred, herding them toward the pyre. What were they going to do to them? Surely not harm them, many were family and friends.

The fat man had once more lost his own balance and had flopped to his backside. Boone's left arm windmilled, but he kept a firm grip on Creed's trousers with his right. It wasn't enough to stop him from toppling, and his momentum, coupled with Creed's own flailing movement toward him, pitched them both backward.

Boone landed hard, with Creed atop him. Boone's breath

whooshed from him and left him unable to do much more than flail and gasp.

Creed fared better, and shoved off and away from Boone. He squealed and struggled to gain his feet.

As a trickle of breath rushed into his lungs, Boone watched as Creed bolted not for the steps of his dais once again, but this time through the dark toward the front steps of his mansion as fast as a fat man's legs will carry him. As he hustled, Hezekiah Creed bellowed words that, to Boone, sure as heck didn't sound like anything a God-loving man would utter, especially not in the presence of so many ladies and children and old timers.

Boone struggled to pull in breath, whistling air into his lungs as he shoved to his feet. Shaky at first, and still fighting to breathe, he ambled after Creed. He glanced back once, but the crowd hadn't moved much toward the dais.

Nobody seemed to notice that their leader wasn't still screeching at them, no Acolytes were in sight. What was going on at the pyre? He glanced back and saw building flames slowly flicking skyward, with hordes of black-clothed folks, the Kindred, moving about in a commotion.

Good, let the fools bother with themselves. He had a snake to catch—again.

Cursing himself for his ham-fisted waste of a good opportunity to knock cold Creed, Boone loped toward the mansion. He'd corner the rascal in there. Then he had a quick thought. It would be even more effective if he could get a little help.

And that one thought did two things—it brought a smile to Boone's face and it altered his course. Instead of making for the front steps to the mansion, he angled left, toward the stables.

The morning before, he'd been play-acting being a part of Creed's foolish following. All that was a thing of the past now, he intended to end this mess before the night was through. First, though, he needed a little help. And he knew where he might find it.

"If a little luck is with me," he whispered, as he bolted through the night for the stable.

He reached the double doors, one of which was closed, and he bent low and peered in, uncertain what he might see. The inside was darker than the outside. He heard a horse whicker, sensing his presence. Boone pulled his head back and clawed up a handful of gravel and tossed it in through the open door. He heard the pebbles scatter and bounce along the straw and dirt. No shots bloomed in the night, no footsteps of humans within sounded.

Heck with it, he thought, knowing that attitude had gotten him in trouble in the past, plus earned him a knife scar and a few holes in his hat. He missed his hat and wondered where he'd lost that favorite green topper, anyway.

Hunching low and catfooting forward, Boone rounded the closed door's edge and made his way fast into the dark inside the stable. The warm, earthy smells of hay and horse and dung and grains wrapped about him, and he felt better than he had all day.

Funny how something familiar can calm a man, he thought. And the other thing that would calm him would be if his gear, which he'd spied that morning tossed in a corner like it was worthless junk, was still there.

He remembered the general direction, but in the dark, he wasn't certain where the stall dividers were located. He felt ahead of himself in the dark, waving an arm back and forth. Presently, his knuckles backhanded a wooden pole as thick around as a man's head. It smarted and made a sudden noise in the otherwise silent space.

Far beyond, outside, on Main Street, sounds of raised voices reached him. The Kindred, though, sounded far off. Still occupied with their fool fire, he thought. He dropped to his hands and knees and patted the space before him, half worried he'd unknowingly crawl beneath a big ol' plow horse and get a big steel shoe to the forehead for his worries.

But no, the stall into which he'd crawled was empty of beasts of burden. And it felt like the right one, the one he'd seen that held his gear.

He patted and raked at the hay with his fingers. Nothing for long moments and then a lump, and he felt something solid beneath hay. He pulled the loose, dry grasses back and was rewarded with the feel of leather beneath his palm. His old saddlebags—he wanted to hug them.

If the smells of the stable were comforting to him, the feel of that leather satchel that had ridden tied down behind his saddle's cantle atop Chummy all these last years was the reacquaintance of an old friend.

Next, he had to find Mac and then their horses, then they could get out of the madness that was Brimstone.

But first, he had a house call to make.

Boone rummaged in his bag and pulled out several items, then, reluctant for the moment to set it back down in the hay once more, he finally covered it over. "No time," he whispered, hearing his voice quaver, not something he usually noticed about himself. He was usually cool and calm in a situation such as this, and he and Mac had been in enough of them in the past few years.

But this time, something was different. Not only were there a whole lot of lives at stake, but most of those people didn't really want to be helped. Heck, for that matter, the Outcasts hadn't been all that keen on having their help, either.

What are we doing here? he thought, not for the first time on this venture.

But Boone knew the truth. Neither he nor Mac could be pulled away by a rogue team of horses when there was a situation such as this—one in which a bullying brute was making lives miserable and costing lives in the process.

Boone crept to the door once again and peered out. It was lighter outside than it had been in the belly-dark barn, and in the distance to his right he could see the glow of the fire beyond the corner of the big house.

He mulled over Creed's far-reaching powers as he dashed to the house. According to the deeds and other paperwork Boone had glimpsed in the man's secret, inner office, Creed had vast business holdings far from Brimstone. And from what Toomey had told both him and Mac, Brimstone was not the first town Creed had infiltrated, taken over, and altered.

But it was, Boone guessed, the first that was so perfect in so many ways. The climate for growing food and the proximity to large quantities of timber to sell for lumber. It was also a desirable location for a train depot. Why, Boone thought, he didn't doubt that Creed had already sent out scouting teams into the surrounding hills to search for valuable ore, too.

Boone made it, low-walking at a quick clip, to the near corner of the big house.

If Creed had his way, the region would soon become a godawful city with all the noise of any other place filled with more people than sense. Then why not have booze and cards and women? Why no bars or brothels yet? Because it didn't fit the false religion he'd devised. He couldn't sell that to the dullards of the world while allowing them access to all manner of vices.

That notion gave Boone pause for a moment. He crossed behind the back of the house, hugging the wall. It was such an odd, big place, he hadn't known when he was inside where he was in relation to the out-of-doors.

It hadn't helped that Creed's inner chambers hadn't had any windows to speak of, which gave his office and game room with the billiards table and booze bottles and naked lady paintings and his odd bed chamber a certain secretive mysterious air.

And now here he was, looking once more for a way into this oppressive pile of bricks, boards, and ill will. "And what will you do if you do get in, huh, Boone?" he asked himself. He had no plan, save for trying to halt the vicious little wind bag.

He mounted the short run of steps that led to the kitchen. The route had worked last time, why not again? No roaring blast of a shotgun greeted him as he poked his nose into the kitchen and took a look around. The room, as before, was somewhat shadowed. He held still a moment, listening. Hearing nothing, he proceeded in a creep toward the far end of the room.

Once he gained the far end of the kitchen, he nudged open the door and looked into the hallway beyond. It sat in darkness, as did the entire place, but that didn't mean Creed or someone else wasn't in there. Somewhere ahead, off to his left, he heard a noise, a slamming, then crashing, as if someone were shoving things to the floor, or throwing them around. Had to be Creed.

Not wanting to waste more precious time, Boone made straight for the noises, come what may. As he walked, a paltry plan formed in his mind. He clunked his bony knees twice against things, one was a chair that scraped and squawked against the floor. He held still, wincing at the brief throb of pain, and held his breath, but the sounds ahead continued.

Creed's voice was closer, a murmuring that sounded hurried, rising at times as if frantic.

Another doorway and he'd be one door away from Creed's inner chamber. Boone went over his meager plan again: Confront the man with his trusty revolver, then hold Creed hostage. He'd march the fraud right outside and make him confess, at gunpoint, to everything he'd been doing in secret, in private, like a sneaky child who'd filched cookies and then lied about it. Those people deserved to know what sort of a man they had been revering.

He'd much prefer to cut the head off the snake by killing Creed and be done with it. But if that happened, the entire town would think Creed was a hero, a martyr, and nothing would change. Likely it would only get worse.

The sounds ahead receded, and he figured Creed was back in his freaky bedchamber. Boone hurried and opened the door before him. The man's secret office was in there, but it looked to Boone as if it had been attacked by a swarm of crazy monkeys.

He saw all this because Creed had left an oil lamp burning on his desk. The room was a mess of papers, books had been dragged off shelves and strewn about the floor, and papers had been swept off the desktop and lay on all surfaces, as if they had been thrown into the air.

A chair lay on its side, and a steel safe, waist high and lodged behind a secret panel in a bookcase behind the desk, sat open, its great, heavy mouth wide and spilling coins and paper money, folded papers, and documents with scrolly writing.

A crash deep in the next room jerked Boone out of his brief moment of scrutiny.

Then the door in the far wall, the one that he knew led to the bedchamber, opened quickly and there was Creed, a bulging carpetbag in each hand, and rolls of documents and other papers were wedged under his arms.

"Where is that other bag? Dammit, man!" He cursed himself in a growly voice that soon gave vent to a flurry of blue words spat in frustration, words Boone wouldn't even utter after a long night filled with booze and losses at the poker table.

"Naughty tongue you got there for a preacher man, Creed."

The Appointed One froze, a look of utter shock pulling his round, sweating face into a long frown. "What . . . what are you doing in here? You don't have the right!"

The words were meant to sound menacing, but to Boone they were as weak as old tea water.

Boone brought the revolver up to bear on Creed, who stood a few feet into the room, the bedchamber's open door behind him. Another lamp glowed low in the room beyond.

"No . . . no!" Creed shook his head, his anger coloring his fat face once more. He gritted his teeth. "Get out of here, Mr. Boone! You . . . you're fired!"

Boone laughed at the absurdity of Creed's words. "You can't fire me, Creed. I quit. Me and Mac both. Now"—he wagged the pistol—"you set those bags down and march on over here, nice and slow, them hands high in the air. I want to see you try to tickle the ceiling, you got me . . . oh, Chosen One?"

A long moment passed. Boone watched a smear of emotions pass over the man's face, then Creed shouted, "Bah!" and spinning, bolted through the door behind him.

Boone recalled there was that narrow passageway, a little hallway that led from that room out into the front hallway. He guessed Creed was hoping to make a run for it, that he wasn't quite through gathering all his desired goods, but maybe he'd gotten enough of the choicest ones that he could afford to skedaddle. That means he would be making for the stable.

Boone couldn't picture Creed atop a horse, but then again, this week had been nothing but a series of experiences Boone had never even given thought to before.

Boone bolted after him, then he slipped into the bedroom and had a delicious idea. He tugged out from beneath his tunic one of the items he'd found in his saddlebags. One of his own specialty "widowmakers," a dandy, slim, smooth stick of dynamite. He grinned and, acting as quickly as he could, he scratched a match alight with his thumbnail and set fire to the six-inch curling wick.

"Do your best," he whispered to the sizzling, smoking little thing in his hand, and tossed it toward Creed's massive desk. It over-ended and landed atop the big wooden beast with a clunk, then rolled off.

Boone didn't wait. He'd lobbed enough of these in his day to know it would all end as he hoped. He slipped into the bedroom and slammed the door behind him, diving for the wall where he saw the other door, the one that led to the little corridor and thus, to the rest of the house.

He had almost reached it when the stick did its trick. The explosion behind him felt as if it had happened within him. As the room was dark, he had only seen the darkened space where the door stood.

Now that the explosion behind him had lifted him off his boots and carried him, in non-too-gentle hands, forward, he was relieved to see the door had been left flung open by Creed. Boone sailed right through it, only hitting the floor—and one wall with his right shoulder—when he was halfway down the corridor.

It wasn't a landing he could be proud of, but it did the trick. He regained his feet quickly and patted himself for everything he'd been carrying, and found it all to be intact, notably his body, save for that right shoulder, which felt as though Mac had slugged him.

Thinking of him, he hoped his pard was faring okay with those tongueless devils and the freakish madness of the Kindred.

Boone staggered down the rest of the hallway, owing as much to the ringing in his head as to the fact that there was no light any more. He also thought maybe he smelled smoke. He looked behind him once, but saw no light of flame. Still, it would stand to reason that those lit oil lamps back there would have been upended and eager for fuel.

"Where you at, you fat devil?" shouted Boone, cackling as he lurched through the gloom of the suddenly living mansion. It was an odd thought, but the place felt as though it were beginning to awaken around him somehow.

He reached the end of the corridor and at the far end of the room facing him, a faint, flickering orange glow told him this was the front of the house, and the glow was that of the pyre. Boone paused and looked back again. He still had one more stick to make things go boom, but this was a big ol' house. Had to place it just right. For maximum charge, as his old boss used to say.

Tickles Johnson, the munitions man in their company back in the war, had been the leader of the munitions men, which included himself, Boone, and two other fellows. On one particular day, a day Boone would never forget, he had gone on a supply run while the others had gone with Tickles on a risky raid to set charges on a railroad trestle crossing a deep wash in the blue hills of the Carolinas. None had returned.

Boone found out later that though they had succeeded in blowing the trestle, Tickles, who always had a taste for corn mash, had overdone it on the mash and on the load. He'd blown it hot, taking all three men with it, who rained down in various pieces and parts for a quarter mile around.

That had left Boone to smarten up fast to the ways of explosives. And he had. And now look at me, he thought, resuming his run across the big room. There was movement ahead, then as his own bootsteps echoed in the great room, the thing moving ahead of him stopped and screamed.

Creed.

"You! What have you done? My house! My house!" Creed ran back and forth in the big entrance hall.

"What's it to you, Creed? Looks to me like you was heading on out yourself. I figured it was only right to send this old buzzard off with you!"

The fat preacher man howled again, his arms still laden with all manner of paper scrolls and stacks of documents that had begun to slide from his grasp without his seeming to notice. The two bulging carpetbags in his hands, their mouths agape, the contents brimming up and out—more paper, open-topped sacks of coins, a couple of booze bottle necks poked up, and more. The weight on his arms looked significant.

"That door in front of you is the only way out, Creed. You're gonna have to get by me to make it to the back door through the kitchen. You hear me, Creed?"

Boone cackled, then said, "Huh, that reminds me, and he thumbed alight another match and held it up before his face, taking one step toward Creed, the match flaring, the stick of dynamite in the same hand, its wick wagging like a parched tongue.

"What's the matter, Creed? Don't have the gumption to go out the front? Into the waiting arms of your beloved Kindred? And their newfound loved ones from up in the hills?"

Boone took a step forward toward the sweating, chest-heaving fat man and his laden arms.

"Where are those Acolytes of yours now, huh, Creed?"

"You!"

"Yes, you already said that. Now, I suggest you drop those sacks . . . no, no, better yet, I suggest you waddle on out that door there and hold on tight to all that baggage you're lugging. You're going to need it."

"I . . . I am?"

Even in the low light, Boone saw a look spread on Creed's face that was by now too familiar. It was the smug, greedy look men get when they are doted on and given whatever they whine for. What Boone had expected to see.

"Yep, you see, I have a plan that involves you, me, and all that loot of yours."

"What?" Creed tightened his grip on his satchels, his

eyes narrowing. A fresh round of cracking timbers and crackling flames from the glowing heart of the mansion, far behind Boone in the darkness.

"You heard me, Creed. Easiest thing to do right now would be to shoot you and take your loot, but my sainted mama never did raise any of her offspring to behave in such an uncharitable manner. Another thing that tells me you and me ain't related. Anyway, I could get over that and take to shooting you. Elsewise you could march on out that front door. Up to you."

"But . . . they'll . . ."

"Your people? The Kindred? No, don't sell them short, Creed. Those deluded fools love you to pieces."

As Boone spoke, Creed's eyes cut to his left, toward the kitchen. Boone had expected this and knew the piglet was thinking of bolting for the freedom that lay beyond, in the form of a fast horse.

Creed went for it, but Boone, closer to the kitchen door, stepped over to his right quickly and cut off Creed's exit. He thumbed alight the match he'd been holding and Creed, closer to him before, said, "You wouldn't dare!"

"Oh no?" Boone held the match an inch from the end of the wick.

"Wait, wait, wait! I . . ." Creed made an effort to heft the two laden satchels. "I have money, more than enough for the two of us to share. I'll cut you in. We can ride on out of here. Help me and we're as good as gone from these rubes."

Boone held the flickering match close to the wick. It was going to burn his fingertip any second. He pooched his lips and looked at the ceiling. "Nah, I don't think so." He lit the fuse and held the stick in front of Creed, the sizzling wick a dancing, vicious thing between them.

"No!" screamed Creed, his eyes wide and white with the horror of his impending doom.

"Get on out that front door now." Boone stepped closer. "Or I'll stick this thing down your throat."

Creed gulped and bustled to the front door. He toed it open and squeezed through, with Boone on his heels. At the last second, Boone whipped the stick back into the entryway. It landed halfway up the long staircase and clunked down one, two steps, then rested halfway up.

"What have you done?" screamed Creed.

"Something those fools should have done years ago!" Boone shoved the sweaty fat man, who stood atop the steps looking down at a crowd that had gathered before the heaving building.

Confusion and pain and anger were writ large on the faces of Kindred and Outcast alike. Mostly anger.

CHAPTER 36

Mac arose with a helping hand from the kid and walked backward away from the gathered horde, who all still stared at him with eyes wide. What he couldn't read were the looks on those faces. They seemed confused, not filled with their irate, seething rage as before.

He also noted that Creed's voice was no longer haranguing the crowd. Instead, the sight of Roland Toomey about to be burned alive by their very hands, their once-friend and neighbor, founder of their town, had captured the crowd's attention.

Seeing this and hearing the shrieks of the man's wife seemed to have snapped them out of their foolish stupor. For how long, Mac knew not and didn't care.

Maybe they were collecting themselves for another go at him. Either way, he didn't intend to wait around to find out. He backed away, feeling his strength returning to his sore limbs, his only real pain pulsing from the burns he suffered, though none so bad he couldn't function.

"You okay, mister?"

Mac looked to his right. The kid was there, looking at him with narrowed eyes.

"Yeah," he said. "Thirsty and sore, but I'll live. You're bleeding," he said, nodding at the kid.

The kid touched fingertips to the side of his head. "Somebody whomped me right as he was taken."

"Just as well, then. You would have been up there with him."

"That's where I should have been."

"No," said Mac. "You need to stay alive. The others are going to need some help getting through to the Kindred. Speaking of help, have you seen my friend?"

"Yeah." The kid nodded. "I saw him take off for the big house after Creed."

Mac looked to the front of the big house.

The kid shrugged. "He was making for it, anyway."

As Mac and the kid watched, Mac spied two big, burly forms that looked a whole lot like Acolytes, creeping around the left side of the house. If Hoke is in there, he thought, those two aren't going to do him any good.

He laid a big hand on the kid's shoulder. "Thanks for your help. And keep your eyes open." Mac looked at the crowd, some of whom still stared at him, moon-faced and subdued. "I wouldn't trust any of them yet."

The rest had gathered about the stretched-out form of Roland Toomey, who was attempting to sit up. Mac liked the fellow and hoped he was going to be okay. But right now, he had a friend to help.

"Yeah," said the kid. "Got to at some point, though, right? I mean, isn't this what we've been waiting for, after all?"

Mac could only smile and nod. "Indeed, Jay. Indeed."

He made for the dark left side of the house, on the trail of those two Acolytes, hoping that if Boone was in there, that he could get to those two split beards before they got to Hoke.

"Here!" the kid shouted as Mac loped away from him. The big man stopped and the kid caught up and handed him his revolver. "It's full up."

"No, no, you might need that, Jay."

"He'll not need it," said a thin, old man in scruffy clothes. Mac recognized him as Zeb, one of the Outcasts. Zeb toted a rifle and a revolver. Mac nodded and took the gun from the kid. "Thanks. Hope I won't need it."

The thin man said, "If it's the split beards you're after, don't count on it. They're down in number and they only get meaner, crazier when they're cornered." He glanced about at the night beyond the blaze. "There's still some lurking about."

Mac nodded thanks for the advice he already knew. Still, hearing it sped him along his way to the house. He cornered, and glanced to his left, toward the black hulk of the stable in the night. He suspected that some of their gear was still in there, but did he have time to go rummage? Did it matter? He had the revolver, and the kid had said he'd loaded it. No time to waste on a fool's errand. Time to hunt some split beards.

He low-walked around the rear of the place, sensing rather than seeing the spot where the Acolytes had pummeled him and dragged him down into the musty pit of a cellar.

He shook off the sickening feeling that rose like bile in his gorge at the memory of the place and that beast of a snake. Had it even happened? Perhaps they had drugged him somehow.

The town, the people, the religion they had going on, all of it was odd enough that he didn't doubt that anything was possible. For the first time ever on one of their jobs, he felt they had done enough. More than enough. They had almost died.

He had to get Boone and, as his pard was wont to say, "Git gone."

The back door of the kitchen stood ajar, the angles of the frame and the shadows therein barely visible in the night. Mac thumbed back the hammer and stepped into the room, keeping hunched and angling sideways, leading with his gun hand. Nothing moved.

He paused, heard nothing in that first moment, then, as his training taught him, he waited a few heartbeats longer.

There . . . slow, cautious bootsteps sounded within the building, beyond the kitchen. He didn't think the Acolytes would suspect they'd been followed. They were going in for the sneak attack themselves, from the rear, so he would be on their tail. If luck was with him.

Fortunately, as he'd said to Hoke in the past, he didn't believe in any luck he didn't make for himself.

Thin fire light, waning after traveling halfway around the house, shone a dull glow through the one window in the gloomy room. He stepped in silence through the stillness of the kitchen and nosed the revolver through the half-open door leading beyond.

He was unfamiliar with all this bit of the house, save for Hoke's descriptions. Fortunately, Boone was a storyteller and, though guilty of knitting colorful patches in his tales, he usually got the facts about right.

If that were so, to his left would be another door leading to a room that then led to Creed's inner office, the "secret rooms," as Hoke had called them.

In the next moment, none of that mattered because to his right he heard a whisper of cloth, as if a sleeve brushed against a jacket. Instinct drove Mac to his right knee as he swung around the revolver. His hand and the gun slammed into a man's arm and belt.

Mac saw the leering face of an Acolyte—sooty, bloodied, gritted teeth showing behind the tangled split beard, below eyes that seemed to glow in the dimly lit room.

Mac ducked his head as the silent, seething, tongueless man brought an arm down in a fist toward Mac's neck. Mac had shifted enough to his left that the blow thudded his right shoulder, knocking him off his knee's balance.

The Acolyte tried to grab Mac's gun arm above the wrist, but Mac twisted out of it and had no time before the Acolyte shoved forward into him. It flicked through Mac's mind that the man must be unarmed if he hadn't shot or gutted him by now. But he didn't count on it.

The Acolyte swung a hard fist that Mac sensed coming at the right side of his head. He ducked from the blow, but ended up moving straight into the punch. It slammed into his head, mashing the top of his right ear and setting a chorus of bells clanging in his skull as if a bell ringer had gone mad in there.

The blow spun him and jerked his gun hand in reflex. His finger pulled the trigger, and the snap of the shot was a muffled thing, though something even Mac could discern in his addled state. Then the large and heavy Acolyte fell over on top of him, slamming him backward to the floor and sagged over him as he flailed, pinned.

Mac managed to shove the mass of dead weight from him and suspected the shot had drilled straight through the brute's heart.

"I'll not weep for you, you sad, misguided fool. But I do feel bad for you." He whispered this as he made for the door to his left where dim lamp light leaked out along the bottom.

The sound of the shot, muffled though it had been by the man's body, would likely attract the other Acolyte. Because the kid saw two making for the house didn't mean there weren't more lurking in the shadows.

The thought brought a sneer to Mac's lips. He bent once more and crept forward, toward the door leaking light. There was something familiar about this place, though what it was, he knew not.

He reached it and set a hand to the knob, cautiously opened it inward. It squeaked and a faint, rustling sound, not unlike that made by his previous combatant, rose up to meet him.

Mac let go of the knob and waited, the door to the hallway open enough to allow him to pass inside. The low lamp glow showed him the reason it had seemed familiar—this was not the office Hoke had told him of, the hidden inner office with all the illicit goods piled high, long, and deep. It was the office Mac had already been in. Something was off.

He peered in, lower than he normally would, and was rewarded with a shot to the doorframe from a gun in the depths of the dim room. He saw the flash of the barrel and almost sent his own return shot but held back—what if it was Hoke?

A moment later he heard something that told him Hoke was likely well. A tremendous cracking sound followed with a *whoom,* and the entire building shuddered about him. Part of the wall inside the room to the right of the door looked as if it were a person's chest, the lungs working in and out.

It bulged inward, into the room, breathing, then pulled back before shedding some of its ornamentation—paintings flew away as if thrown, and a wall sconce shattered, sending a spray of glass clouding outward.

He heard a guttural moan, and then sloppy, heavy bootsteps thundered toward him. He doubted it was Hoke. He saw a dim shape through the smoke and floating debris. His pard was not that big, and even dazed was light on his feet, more catlike than this approaching shape.

Besides, Mac knew how that explosion came about. Hoke was somewhere beyond, deeper in the house. But why explode the thing inside when you were still in there? Unless he wasn't in there and that was the first of the two charges Hoke always liked to touch off. Uh oh. . . .

Mac had no more time for that thought, because the crashing form whipped the door away from him and slammed it inward before barreling through and past Mac as if it hadn't seen him. But Mac caught enough of a glimpse to see it was an Acolyte. And one who looked a whole lot worse for the wear.

The black-clad brute was smoking from head to foot, though Mac didn't see any flame or spark dancing on the madman. He appeared to know where he was headed, toward the front door of the house. From the rumbling behind him, Mac figured he ought to follow suit, but . . . what if Hoke was in there?

"Dammit," he muttered, tugging the top of his battered shirt up over his mouth and nose. Squinting into the dusty gloom, he dashed in, making for the doorway he hoped was there, far down the right-hand wall.

The room, as he dashed through, was a welter of debris, but still recognizable as Creed's office. There was no door where he had thought it might be, but there was a gaping, ragged hole in the wall. Smoke boiled out and upward toward the tall ceiling. He ducked low beneath it and peered beyond into another room.

A dozen small fires licked and curled at anything that might provide them sustenance. Several had already found toothsome wall hangings and sent crackling racers along ceiling beams. He doubted the entire place would last the night.

A couple of large paintings of nude women popped his eyes wide for a moment. Even sooted and slashed by debris from the blast, they were impressive in detail and size. Bottles lay strewn about the floor, some smashed.

"Hoke!" shouted Mac, grasping a bottle nearby and popping the cork. He sniffed it and the harsh, yet welcoming tang of whiskey fumes greeted his nostrils. He upended it and slugged back one, two, three long pulls, then set down the bottle and let the liquid fire blaze a trail down his gullet.

"Hoke Boone!" This he shouted louder, glancing about him in case anybody he didn't want to see was about to draw down on him. Nothing.

He ventured deeper, the smoke building thicker above his head, so he crouched and skirted a billiards table. There beyond it stood another open doorway. He low-walked to it and looked in to see another room, equally as smokey but with more flames already devouring what appeared to be a big four-poster bed.

"Hoke! Hoke Boone!"

Nothing.

The smoke was too much, and Mac knew if he didn't get to fresh air soon, he'd be a cooked goose. He held his shirt tighter to his face, coughing into it with a harshness that nearly stopped him. His eyes watered something fierce, so he dragged the back of his gun hand across them and squinted hard.

It helped clear the sweat and tears long enough to reveal yet another door, this time in the far wall, narrow and leading to what looked to be a dark passage beyond. Could be anything there, but it beat being stuck in a fire-riddled room.

He made for it and nearly tripped in yet another rupture in the wooden floor. The ceilings, walls, and floors in each room so far had all sustained damage, with the spot between the bedroom and the billiards room the worst of all. It was past him now, and he shuttled along what proved to be a dark, narrow corridor, but with a glow of light ahead. Another fire?

"Hoke Boone!" he shouted, his voice hoarse and more of a wheeze than a shout.

Then he emerged into a tall-ceilinged room already filling with smoke from behind, bubbling up and out of the passage from which he'd emerged. There, more light ahead!

He made for it, disregarding any more floor damage that might trip him up. This room didn't appear to have been blown apart, yet. If he lived through this, he was going to have a talk with Hoke, something along the lines of making damn certain he knew where Mac was before touching off his cursed widowmakers.

To his left something tall loomed, and he recognized it after a moment as the central staircase that led to the upper floors. Just then he heard a voice before him. The smoke was thinner here, but filling up.

Ahead stood the big, double front doors, and through them he made out the flickering, snapping glow of the pyre fire and its surrounding torches. But closer in, at the top of the steps, he saw a familiar figure. It might be Hoke . . .

Another unexpected jag of coughing nearly jerked Mac to his knees, so violent was it. Then the voice, and another nearby, also from outside the big doors ahead, raised up in a shouting match. Mac thought he saw something whip by to his right, some feet in the air.

It looked like a bird flying in. It hit the stairs and even in the smokey gloom Mac saw the hissing, dancing line of sparks where the thing thudded, dropped down a step, then came to a standstill.

"Hoke, you bastard!" Mac gave up on the coughing and

bolted for the door, smashing the one that was half-open back on its hinges so hard the glass in both shattered from the impact. He piled into somebody and then another person, and they all ended up in a heap at the top of the stairs.

At that moment, the tossed dynamite stick gave its all and shoved what felt to Mac like half the house's lumber at them.

The doors he'd piled through had spasmed back inward enough to take the brunt of the first push and gush of debris—missiles of wood, shards of glass, tiles, furniture, lamps, and hardware shot out like a cannonade.

For a brief moment, Mac and Boone each were transported back to battlefields in the war of futility. Once more they were surrounded by the blood and screams and mewling of death and death soon to be.

Then they were yanked back to the present, still accompanied by screams of surprise, but these were from the people gathered below, at the bottom of the steps.

"Mac? That you?"

"Yeah, still here."

"Oh boy. You look awful, pard."

Mac cracked a smile. His teeth shone white through the soot covering his face. "Why, thank you, Hoke. Normally, I'd resent such a remark, but considering all that's happened, I'll take it as a compliment."

Boone shrugged. "Suit yourself. Didn't mean it as such."

"Hoke," said Mac, looking over his shoulder at the smoking mess behind them. "You think maybe you set that charge a little hot?"

"Aww, maybe so, maybe so. But dang-it, Mac! It's so durn pretty when everything goes boom!" He cackled and then prodded Creed with the revolver. "Could use your thinker right about now. Not sure of the best next step here."

"I see that," said Mac, then raised his voice. "Not much for us to do here but tell these fine people"—he waved his arms at the crowd—"just what we saw in that house back there!" He gestured with a thumb behind him.

"Oh, you mean that big, old, burning mansion?"

"That's the one, yep."

Boone prodded Creed in the back once again and the chunky preacher man saw he had nowhere now to run. He was hemmed in on all sides by people either prodding him or staring him down. Their haggard faces showed confusion, distrust, and outright anger.

"You . . . you people need to back away now!" Creed shouted, desperation rimming his shaky words.

"What say we show these folks what you're lugging, oh Appointed, Chosen, Fancy One?" Boone nudged the man in the back again.

"Stop that!"

"I will as soon as you show them . . ."

The crowd closed in. Among them, Mac saw familiar faces, some of the old women with their dour, pinched mouths looked worried. The younger women and older men looked suspicious, and pressed in, holding torches aloft for light. Several held lanterns.

"Show us, Leader!" shouted one tall man, angling through and thrusting a lantern close to Creed's satchels. The light revealed the two bulging carpetbags.

Creed stood still, his soft jaw thrust out, his eyes narrowed. "How dare you address me in such a manner!"

For a brief moment the man's words chilled the assemblage, but his power over them had dissipated.

"I for one dare you, by gaw!" Boone shoved his revolver into Mac's hands and stepped around Creed, pawing one of the bags open wider. It, as with the other, were still held by their long loop handles in Creed's trembling arms. The weight of them was obvious, and it wouldn't be much longer before he dropped them out of exhaustion.

"What have we here, Creed? Or can I call you . . . Hezekiah?"

The fallen leader sneered at him.

"Oh, maybe you prefer Melvin Whipple?"

Creed's eyes widened, but he said nothing. He didn't need to, for the look of a man whose lies had been found out was stamped all over his fleshy, oily features. Sweat dripped off his nose.

Boone reached into the near bag and tugged out a box of cigars. "Oh, now, that's nice. You have good taste, mister. Hope you don't mind if I sample one." He thrust it in his mouth. "Nah, maybe later. It's a little smokey out here now."

He stuffed it in his pocket, then did the same with a second. "That's for my pard, Mac, there. He has awful taste in ceegars, and I think this might help convince him there's more to life than them little sinkers he chokes on."

He rummaged deeper in the satchel and tugged out a bottle of whiskey. "Oh, yes, now this will go down dandy." He winked theatrically to Creed, then shouted, "You won't mind, will you? After all, you got a few in here, and plenty more back in the house, in that room full of liquor and fancy paintings of the nekkid ladies and a pool table and all. And don't get me started on that fancy bedchamber! I never saw the like. If I didn't know better, I'd say you were a king or a sultan or some such. What do you think, Mac?"

"Seems to be the case, yep." Mac let Boone have the floor. He was keeping his eye on the crowd, wondering where the rest of the Acolytes had gotten to. He had no idea how many there were left alive or conscious. He suspected some of the Outcasts had captured them or had done so with the help of the Kindred. For now, he'd keep his finger done, so on the revolver's trigger.

"Strikes me as lazy housekeeping, Creed, to forget all that fancy stuff of yours in your secret offices and gambling den and that bar of yours. But it's none of my business."

Creed made to shout, but Mac prodded him with the pistol's barrel. The fat man shut his mouth and scowled at the ground. His attempt at anger was not convincing, overruled as it was by his twitching mouth, fast breathing, and sweaty face.

Boone kept right on tugging out items from the sack. "Oh, these papers here, they look like deeds. Must have come from that fancy safe you had behind your desk, huh?"

"They're for the business of running the town!" shouted Creed. "Who else do you think has made Brimstone into such a . . . it's all due to my hard work . . ." His words grew quieter, then pinched out as the crowd pressed in closer, any fear or doubt now gone from their faces.

"Oh, look at all this cash money!" Boone held up wads of paper money and then a pendulous sack that must have contained coins. He tossed it on the ground and gold coins spilled out.

Creed whimpered.

Boone kept on tugging out items from the satchel, then moved on to the second bag.

He pulled out all manner of folded papers and small, tied scrolls, giving them a quick look before tossing them into the crowd. "Deeds, deeds, stock certificates, boring stuff, or my name ain't Hokum Boone."

Then he tugged out a large scroll of paper that had been bent in half and jammed into the bag. He unrolled it and scrutinized it, looking at the crowd, then as if beyond them, over their heads. "Oh yeah, I see it now, Creed. Very impressive, mister."

He looked at the faces before him. "Oh, you want to

know what the man's plans were, eh?" He turned the paper around, and across the top written in letters large enough for the first row of folks to read it said, "Master Plans for Creedville."

"This is nothing new for you, is it, Creed?" said Mac, shaking his head. "You've done this before, in other towns, to other people, but not on as grand a scale, am I right?"

Nobody said a thing, Creed fumed and glanced about, considering a run, perhaps.

"Creedville, eh?" said Mac. "Doesn't have much of a ring to it. What do you think, Hoke?"

"I have to agree with you there, Mac. But then again, I'm not the best judge of such matters. But look at this here, folks!" He tapped the wagging paper. "That's a railroad line, looks to be running straight through this little valley. Not much room left for crops after you get all these buildings built. And that river, well, that looks like this plan will tidy that up, too. Diverted right there, mostly to make room for, what's that say? A granite mansion? Huh. And statues lining that space there. Somewhere about where we're standing, I think."

Boone shrugged and tossed the scroll into the crowd.

It was as if he'd lobbed fresh-cut steaks into a wolf den. The Kindred, with a few Outcasts mixed in among them, swarmed the portly preacher. Mac and Boone exchanged glances and then backed away, scooting off to the side as the townsfolk roared and howled and attacked. Raised fists drove downward. The contents of the carpetbags—cash, cigars, bottles, deeds—flew up and over the frenzied crowd, no one paying the items any interest. They all wanted a piece of Creed's hide.

"You think we went too far?" said Boone.

Mac gestured to him with a jerk of his head and they

moved farther away. Mac still held the gun trained before them. "Not our affair, Hoke. He's reaping what he sowed. I'd rather they reasoned all this out, but . . ."

"I don't think that's going to happen. At least not tonight," said Boone.

That's when Mac saw what must have been the Acolyte who'd run by him after the first explosion. The man was covered with debris and soot, his hair and beard were frazzled and singed and his eyes were wide and bloodshot.

He was flanked by two men, one an Outcast and the other a Kindred, both held an arm of the Acolyte, though his hands were bound tight before him.

Mac spied two more Acolytes, both also bound and guarded. All three were moved toward the front of the crowd, where they watched the roiling, angry mob. The palpable fear and anger kept them from bolting forward to try to save their beloved leader.

The seething crowd moved down the street toward the smoldering pyre. Others ran ahead and lobbed fresh wood, renewing the mighty blaze.

In their center of the crowd flailed the weakening, chubby form of Hezekiah Creed, his face already swelling from the thumping they'd been delivering unto him. He faced backward, toward Mac and Boone, toward his cherished mansion, now a flaming mess.

A series of softer explosions cracked deep inside the building.

Creed howled, his eyes wide as he and the entire town watched his mansion swell in the middle, as if it were pulling in a big draught of air before it exhaled. The roof had been breached and like a volcano emitting sparks and fire and ash and lava, the mansion belched brick and timber and raw, ragged debris skyward. Most of it dropped straight back down, and the great pile of a structure began a slow collapse in on itself.

"Aww," said Boone in awe of the scene. "Imagine what I could have done with a half-dozen more sticks!"

Creed howled and screeched, and then a single gunshot cracked the scene open wider, stilling the grim proceedings for but a moment. They saw Creed stiffen, his howls ended. He collapsed backward and the crowd stared down at him for a long, silent moment.

The only sounds heard were the crackling of wood from the smoking pile of the mansion and the pyre behind them, building in intensity.

Then the crowd as if sharing a single thought, shouted again, a buzzing, growling, angry sound, loud in liberation. They seized Creed's burly, flopping body and surged toward the pyre.

Mac said, "Oh no . . ." But already it was too late, and there was no way for them to stop the fright the scene had become.

"Let's hope he's truly dead," said Boone. "I wouldn't wish burning alive on anybody, even that lying sack of dung."

The body of Creed was hoisted high and shoved, then tossed, into the midst of the now-roiling, blazing pyre. The three remaining Acolytes, as if on cue, ripped themselves free of their captors and clambered up onto the pyre, their progress awkward and messy.

They met in the center, around the sagged form of their beloved leader, the Appointed One. Already the flames surrounded them, consuming their clothing, their hair. They knelt about their master in the midst of the quick, hot fire, their arms raised high, wavering like huge flames themselves, their tongueless mouths shrieking as the merciless flames consumed them.

Mac and Boone, along with the rest of the people there, stared at what they were seeing. Soon the last, wordless shrieks were defeated by the crackling, raging conflagration smack dab in the midst of Brimstone.

One at a time, the Kindred seemed to awaken as if from a long, horrible dream. They wept, they shook, they fell to their knees, they hugged and were hugged by other Kindred, by the Outcasts, all now nothing more or less than their neighbors, their friends, their families.

There were others in the street, Kindred still marked by their dress, clad in black, who hung back, a sizable number of them, looking more uncertain than anyone else.

They were, Mac surmised, Kindred to whom devotion had been—and likely still was—a blind obedience, unwavering as time. They would find another false deity to worship. He hoped it wasn't here.

He guessed that those of this other group of Creed's followers were not originally of the town. They were those who had been his blind followers from elsewhere, as Toomey had told him. These others had come from other towns where Creed had already burned his mark. They had then ventured here, to Brimstone, beckoned by their master, only too willing, ecstatic even, to heed his call.

Already they were getting looks of suspicion from the Outcasts, who were armed with more guns than Mac had suspected they'd carried into town. He guessed they had liberated other firearms from fallen Acolytes, as well as from their families and neighbors.

If he were a betting man, and he'd still rather leave that foolish pursuit up to Hoke, Mac would lay odds that the stranger Kindred folk would be sent packing to wherever it was they cared to go, as long as it was not in Brimstone—or whatever name they chose to rechristen the town with.

The town was still worth saving, still worth working for, still filled with promise, if only for its location, let alone for all the other things they'd established there. But would they make it work again?

It would never be the same, that much was certain. Different, yes, and often in Mac's experience different proved to be as good as or better. But sometimes, too, it proved to be a failed attempt at change.

Mac sighed, and Hoke, not but a dozen feet away, sighed at the same time, as two people who spend a whole lot of time together are wont to do.

Hoke unfolded his arms. "You had enough of your surmising and speculating, MacCoole? I got me a hankering to get the hell out of here. I've had more than my fill of crazies. Let them sort out the rest of their messy lives themselves."

Mac smiled, feeling the burned, puckered skin of his face stretch. That would take some time healing. "Truer words have rarely been spoken, Hokum Boone."

Boone nodded toward the east. "Here comes another day."

Mac looked to see the first pulse of purple in the sky. "About time," he said, rubbing his sooty face.

"Yep. Let's get the hell gone from this nest of loons before they ask us to help them clean up their mess."

"You made the biggest mess of all of them," said Mac, nodding at the smoldering wreckage of the mansion as they walked toward the stable.

Boone looked over his shoulder, eyes wide. "Hush up, will you? They don't need to know that!"

Mac chuckled. "Okay, let's skedaddle."

"Hey," said Hoke, already making for the stable, and the corral out back, where Lincoln and Chummy awaited them. "That there word's mine."

"You can't lay claim to a word, Hoke."

"Oh no? I ever tell you about my great-uncle Crawfish, on Pa's side of the patch? He was a great one for making up words. Why, I don't doubt he might have gone on to proper schooling instead of taking to the woods to live in that big, hollow tree that felled a number of years before he was even born. But that's another story. Yes, I dare say he might have made a name for himself as a maker of books and such."

"You mean an author?"

"No! In fact, smarty pants, I mean a writer."

"Oh. Say, Hoke?"

"Yeah?"

They finished cinching their saddles and gear, then, without a glance back toward the smoking wreck that was main street, Brimstone, they began their ride that would cut wide northward, then finally east toward home.

"Whatever you do, make sure you keep on being Hokum Boone."

"Well." Hoke ran his hat—which he'd found hanging on a nail in the stable, oddly enough—back and forth over his head. "That's about the oddest thing you ever said, Mac. And you've said a pile of oddness, I don't mind telling you."

Mac smiled and shook his head, and they rode on out of that crazy town. It wasn't until daylight had shown itself in full that either man spoke again.

Mac said, "I wonder how long it'll be before somebody else with fanciful ideas rides in and takes advantage of them once again."

In reply, Boone merely shrugged.

Mac sighed. "Well, I guess we can take small, cold comfort in knowing we ultimately did a good thing. It was a messy job, though."

Boone grinned and tugged a leather sack from inside his tunic. "You go ahead and enjoy that cold comfort stew you got on the boil. Me, I'll take this here bundle of gold coins I liberated from the safe in ol' Melvin Whipple's secret office."

"Then we didn't do this for nothing?"

"I thought you said we did some good."

"Yeah," said Mac. "For them. But for us, I was hoping for something to buy pie with."

"Pie! My word. Think of the fun to be had with your share of this, mister! Why, I know a half-dozen doves at Manny's who would club each other to get to you for a night or three!"

Mac chuckled. "That's all right, Hoke. I'll leave them for you. Me, I am looking forward to a nice, hot bath and an even hotter meal at Marta Mae's."

"Bah on both counts," said Hoke. "I'll take a warm girl and a cold beer and a hot game of stud."

"Then let's get home."

"You bet, pard."

CHAPTER 37

The midst of their third day out found them still riding eastward for their home base of Denver City. They had entered hill country the day before, but were in little hurry as they had meat and what other supplies they'd brought with them at the outset of their trip.

Neither man had spoken a word since they broke camp that morning, and Mac, for one, was pleased to hear nothing but the wind through the trees, perhaps the occasional piercing scream of a high-up hawk.

He was thinking that, of all the things he'd lost in that week, not a one of them was anywhere close to what those folks had lost, either the Kindred or the Outcasts. Things in their lives they could never regain—children, good times, smiles, meals shared.

He hoped they would be able to regain some of those simple but vital things in their lives. As for himself, he'd lost his hat and his rifle, but he found his Colt Dragoon and his custom hip knife. And he and Hoke had come through that mess with their lives. That was more than enough to be thankful for.

Yes sir, the quiet of the day's ride was lovely. But he knew it couldn't last.

"You know." Hoke scratched his chin hairs. "I hate to say it, but I do believe I have one thing in common with that dirty rascal Hezekiah Creed."

"Oh, what's that?" said Mac, setting fire to a smelly cigarillo and trying and not succeeding to think about hot coffee and an ample wedge of Marta Mae's pecan pie, topped with a fist-size dollop of whipped cream.

"It's what you call that something about a fella that he can't help."

"Oh, well, it can't be that musky smell your buckskins give off on a sunny day, then."

"I heard that, MacCoole. No, I'm talking about a pure animal instinct sort of thing. Lions got it. And eagles, too. Only the males, though, and not all of them. It's one of them things you can't quite put a finger on, but when a fella has it, you know."

"And Creed had this thing, eh?"

"Sure, he did. Why else would all them women go so nutty about him?"

"And you have it, too?"

"Sure enough I do, you bet." Boone nodded. "Yep. How else you gonna explain why Trissy always flutters around me like a moth to a candle whenever I'm in town?"

"You don't think it has anything to do with the fact that you are usually flush with cash and looking for a good time, do you?"

"No, no, I don't think that's it. No. But don't think I don't know what you're driving at, mister!" Boone pointed a bony finger at his pard.

Mac held up his hands as if it were a stick-up. "Me? I'm not up to anything."

"Darn right, you're not. It's because you don't have the thing! I'm sorry to have to tell you like that, but there it is."

Mac leaned over, his saddle creaking. He pulled a long, theatrical sniff in Boone's direction. "If that's the thing you're talking about, then I thank the Lord above I'm bereft of it."

Mac had enough time to heel Lincoln into a run before Hoke's fist found purchase on his sniffer.

The pair raced across the long flat eastward, back to Denver City, sore and battered, but lucky to be alive, where they would rest up, heal up, and wait for another telegram.

Mac rode in the lead, laughing long and low, with Hokum Boone trailing in high dudgeon, shouting and shaking his fist.

Turn the page for an exciting preview!

JOHNSTONE COUNTRY. THE BULLET STOPS HERE.

No one knows better than the American masters of epic Western fiction that forging a new life on the frontier takes hope, drive, and plenty of ammunition.

The war is over. But a new battle is on the horizon. Based on true events.

It's 1852. The wounds of the Mexican War are healing. Regis Royle, co-owner of a steamship fleet, has made it out alive, relatively unscarred and with enough profit and foolhardy ambition to envision a new life in south Texas. With the help of his crack-shot kid brother Shepley, his glad-handing riverboat partner Cormac Delany, and his old friend, raw-edged former Texas Ranger Jarvis "Bone" McGraw, Regis is laying claim to the prime jewel in a magnificent rolling prairie: the Santa Calina range teeming with wild mustangs, cattle, and eighteen-thousand acres of lush promise.

But all dreams have a price. For Regis, it's hell to pay—and the fire is coming at him from all directions. On one side of the border, it's *banditos.* On the other side, the Apaches, slave traders, and outlaws have Santa Calina in their sights. And none of them are going to walk away from the bloody battle.

The brothers Royle and their partners have the most to lose—including their lives. They made a pledge to themselves to build the greatest ranch in America. To see it through to the end, they'll have to ride hard and learn the bitter necessity of violence and bloodshed.

National Bestselling Authors
William W. Johnstone and J.A. Johnstone

FOREVER TEXAS
A Novel of the American Frontier

Live Free. Read Hard. www.williamjohnstone.net

Coming in March 2023, wherever Pinnacle Books are sold.

Visit us at www.kensingtonbooks.com

CHAPTER 1

The first shot pinwheeled the tall man's hat off his head. The second sent him diving for cover, and the third spooked his mount and sent it crow-hopping and snorting into the puckerbrush.

He heard a harsh, barking laugh followed with shouts of "Die, gringo!" . . . then shots volleyed at him from all sides.

The tall man managed to crank off a shot of his own. He heard a groan and a curse drift up on the still, hot air as the gunfire echoed and tapered off. Regis Royle had enough time to suck in a sharp breath between his tight-set teeth before a fresh fusillade pinned him tight in a wedge of sun-warmed sandstone.

He counted what he thought might be several guns still blazing, or someone was good at reloading. He trailed his fingers to his gun belt and felt his sheathed knife. He had three shots left in his gun. Fresh ammunition rested snugly in his saddlebags on the ass end of the horse he'd likely never see again.

"What you want here, gringo?"

Regis Royle spun his gaze toward the voice and closed his hand tighter on the walnut grips of his revolver. He saw nothing save for an anaqua tree. In the blue sky far beyond, a lone gray cloud teased apart on a breeze. A meadowlark bobbed on a spiny jag and warbled its morning song.

"Who's asking?"

Ragged laughter echoed off the slabs of sandstone chiseled by wind and time.

Not a man prone to twitching at imagined spooks, Royle nonetheless felt a shiver of ice ripple his backbone. He hunkered lower and eyed around the boulder, looking longingly toward the receding view of his squirrel-headed, bucking mount, and with it his shiny new rifle.

He held the pose as if he were part of the warming stone. The meadowlark rose into the air, trailing dewy notes, and in a series of short swoops landed on a jut of gnarled mesquite some distance to the west—two hundred, three hundred feet.

Could be the bird was a friendly sort. Could be if Regis were a betting man, and at times he was, that bird was looking for a handout, a morsel from a kindly stranger. Could be that bird found the curious laughing man for him. Could be now was the time to place a bet.

Regis almost shrugged, almost smiled at his fanciful notion. Then he didn't smile, for he noted a shifting of light, less than a shadow's worth, in a darkened gap in the stony declivity beyond and below the twitchy, curious little yellow-and-brown bird.

"Thanks, bird friend," he whispered, and licked away a slow drop of sweat from the corner of his mouth, unseen beneath his thick black moustache. Too early by half for this sort of tomfoolery. He had land to check on, friends to catch up with, and an appointment in Brownsville to keep.

Now he was more annoyed than afraid for himself. He'd

known, of course, of the danger of brigands out here, and had even been reminded of the cautions he should take when friends at the docks learned he was riding inland alone, on his way to Corpus Christi to visit other friends.

"Why you want to do a thing like that, Cap?" Lockjaw Hames had said. "No sir, if I was you I'd stick to the water. Safer around here. No injuns or Mexicans out to lay a man low, steal his boots and his hair, then pillage what's left out of his middle."

Lockjaw, who earned the odd moniker because his lips rarely seemed to move when he spoke, a task he was unafraid to undertake, had shuddered then as if he'd had a vision of something horrific happening that was fated.

Lockjaw was as solid a seaman as they'd come. Reputedly a former slave and now self-proclaimed free man, he was also the biggest man Regis had ever met, and that was saying something, as Regis himself was north of six feet tall by several inches.

Lockjaw was a steady presence on the steamers and riverboats, turning his hand to whatever task Regis or his partner in the shipping trade, Cormac Delany, asked of him.

Didn't mean Regis was about to take his advice to heart. He'd chuckled and said, "I appreciate your concern on my behalf, Mr. Hames, and I will endeavor to remain on the good side of the soil with breath in my lungs."

The big black man had paused, sacks of quicklime balanced on each shoulder, his bulging arms steadying them, and said, "Ain't no call to get uppity about it, boss. But you don't come crawling back to the safety of the docks saying how come ol' Lockjaw didn't warn you!" He'd stomped off, loading the hold of the *Missy B.*, a recently acquired craft Cormac had christened after a younger sister long dead, or as Cormac had said, "called to her glory."

And now here Regis was, pinned down in the rocks and grasses of this pretty river valley by an outlaw, no doubt. "Looks like you were right, Lockjaw," Regis mumbled.

Another shot, this time slicing in from east of him, scored a fresh groove in the dusty rock above his head. "Okay, at least two outlaws."

As if in response to his thought, a third, then a fourth shot, each from different directions, pinged and whined in ricochet harmlessly above him. For the moment he was safe, but if they—by his best guess that would make at least four scurvy-addled curs out for his blood—decided to close in, he'd be a dozing fawn to their pouncing lion.

His ire with himself almost outweighed any animosity he felt toward the would-be thieves. Almost. He'd save his full steam for dealing with the prairie scum. And he knew he would, in part because Regis Royle was a man who never failed at anything he attempted.

He had fought his way to his position as partner in a shipping business, co-owner of a growing fleet of riverboats plying the waters of the Rio Grande and up and down the coast. He and Cormac had worked like demons during the Mexican War, the wounds of which were slowly healing, though still bleeding aplenty, since 1846.

Here it was 1852 and he was still scrapping his way through life. He sighed and carefully extended a long leg and flexed it, massaging his knee. A bullet pinged a few inches below the heel of his stovepipe boot. He yanked it back and sucked in air through his teeth.

He needed a plan, because sitting here wasn't getting a damn thing done. What sort of plan could he hope for? Stand up and shout, "Hey, gents, how about we talk this over?" He grunted at the folly of his thoughts. No, best wait them out, keep alert, and take advantage of the relative safety of this rocky hidey-hole he'd managed to wedge himself into.

Then another thought came to him: What if he weren't the only critter in this hole? If it got cold at night, which it would surely do, would a pesky rattler slide out of that crevice behind him and try to get cozy with whatever warmth might exude from his cramped body?

The idea didn't do much for his mood. Regis cursed his horse again, a feather-headed thing with a balky streak a mile wide. When he got back to Brownsville, he was going to buy it from the hostler he'd rented it from and either train it right or shoot it in the head and start with a fresh beast.

A smile tugged a corner of his moustache upward. He was thinking of the very reason he'd ventured out on this fine jaunt in the first place. It had been three days since he'd left Brownsville and ridden northward to Corpus Christi. He'd intended to pay a call on friends who'd moved there, attend a fair he'd heard was to take place in that bustling town.

Really, it was little more than a convenient excuse to get away from his beloved steamers. He still enjoyed the work, but he'd been at it for years without letup. He was still a young man, but sometimes he felt like he was ninety and ready for a rocking chair by a fireplace.

He knew the itch, for it had never really left him. He wanted to—no, he needed to venture beyond the waterways. And a trip on horseback, even if only for a few days, would help scratch that pesky, restless feeling.

But a funny thing happened on his way north. He'd cut inland a bit, in a northwesterly fashion, and he'd found a distraction he'd not even known he had been seeking. In fact, it up and smacked him in the head before he knew what was happening.

Actually, it had been more of a slow saturation of his senses. The day had been hot, as were most days in April in southern Texas, and he found himself riding without care or hurry. In light of his current situation, he knew he'd been lucky to make the journey unmolested.

Even the balky buckskin had seemed lulled into peacefulness by the green rolling prairie Regis found himself in. The wind played over an ocean of long floss-tipped grass stems, as if they were the surface of an endless sea. A little farther on and the land sloped gently to his left. Soon he smelled it, the earthy richness of flowing water. And then he saw it at the same time he heard it.

Or rather, he heard a splash. His horse's ears perked, and he reined up and watched something he'd never before witnessed. The scene fascinated him and hooked him in all at once. A herd of wild mustangs, perhaps half a hundred, were wading into the river to his left, dipping their muzzles and sipping long of the cooling flow.

All of them, that is, but a magnificent dappled brute of a stallion with wide flexing nostrils and a near-black mane and tail. His gaze scanned the far bank and raked across the all-but-hidden presence of Regis and his horse. Then the stallion's gaze swung back and locked with Regis's eyes.

The mustang stallion stared for long moments, an unfelt breeze riffling his topknot. He flicked his ears, snorted once, and stomped a foreleg. The splashing alerted the other drinking horses, and the entire mass of them—brown, fawn, black, gray—swung their dripping muzzles upward and seemed to stare at him.

Regis felt at once awed, at home, and unnerved, a combination of feelings he'd not experienced since the war's battles. The herd wasted no time in stomping up and out of the river. In moments, there was little more to prove that their presence had been real but dissipating swirls of mud that soon the river carried away.

He guessed the water for what it was—the Santa Calina, a flowage of clear, cool water that fed live oaks and anaquas along its banks. Those trees gave way to the waist-high grasses of the prairie he'd been admiring.

He took the mustang herd's advice and guided his horse through the grasses until they broke through and emerged along the muddy creek's bank. He slid from the saddle but held the reins as the horse sipped long and deep, glancing often at the spot where the mustangs had been across the river but moments before.

When the horse had slaked its thirst, Regis squatted low upstream and lifted his hat free. He squinted—the sun had been given free rein to annoy his sight—and scooped the refreshing liquid onto his face, down the back of his neck, and finally over the top of his head.

It felt so good that he remained squatting at the edge of the water and let his eyes close as he breathed in the lush, verdant smells surrounding him. A kiskadee called out, and another answered, somewhere up in the high, blue sky.

With a sigh, he stood and mounted up and kept riding, spying turkeys, quail, antelope, and deer, all eyeing him with interest and perhaps a twinge of suspicion as the wayward breeze carried his strange scent to them. They would scatter in all directions, coyotes as much to blame as Regis's presence in this otherwise seemingly untouched place.

It wasn't so much a valley as a wide, endless sea or rolling green cut through by the Santa Calina. Rough, wild, vague thoughts formed in his mind, drifted out again, and reformed, telling him little more than one thing. He knew, somehow deep in his guts and bones, that he wanted to be here for longer than just the duration of this pleasant ride.

He surprised himself by realizing he wanted to live here, to possess it somehow. But how? And why? Did he not have a life, a thriving business, friends, several women—prominent young things themselves the daughters of men of society—who wished to impress him? Why here, then? What was it about the place, other than its obvious raw beauty?

In this manner, Regis's thoughts rambled and ricocheted off one another as he rode, much of the time at little more than a leisurely walk, the horse in no hurry, either.

It wasn't until he heard a crashing and a stamping in a thicket to his left, between him and the river, from which he'd strayed, that something happened that would alter forever the course of his life, the lives of countless others, and the very land on which he rode.

For Regis Royle, steamship captain, saw cattle. A vast herd of them—feisty feral beasts little more than ornery goats with wide horns and blood-red eyes and burr-stickled hides. Cattle that fought and stomped one another and rubbed their rank hides raw against mesquite trees. But they were cattle. And in that moment an idea came to Regis Royle almost wholly formed. He would ranch this very land.

He knew instinctively that if it weren't him, someone would, for it teemed with life. And what gave life its very essence? Water, the tincture of life itself, for without it life will not last. But here in the midst of this hot-as-sin place known as South Texas, there was ample water and lush green grasses, and massive herds of wild mustangs, hundreds, perhaps thousands strong, barely outmatching herds of balky, crazy-eyed cattle. And that wasn't to mention the wild game.

Here a man could own land, good and valuable land—though he knew some might debate those descriptions—and never go hungry. And more than that, he could raise beasts, horses, and cattle and sell them to others for profits that one day might far exceed the solid earnings he'd made from plying the waters of the Rio Grande.

And here, here it all was. He might be no landman, but he, by golly, knew opportunity when he saw it. And this was it—prime ranching land, water and all.

That had been three days prior, and thoughts of the place throughout his long, slow trip had leeched into his mind, his heart, the marrow of his very bones, and would not let him be.

He'd been poor company, he knew, to his kind friends in Corpus Christi, but he'd been haunted by the place, and he had cut short his trip by a day in order to repeat the journey from north to south, half expecting the mystical place to have been little more than some fiendish trick of the brain, some devilish whim sent from on high to torment him, for what purpose he knew not.

But it had not been the case. Instead, he had been, if possible, even more impressed with the sights and smells and sounds and feel of the Santa Calina range. All of it had been repeated—the stretches of lush grasses, gamma near water, the ample game and stock roaming the hills, the very creek, the Santa Calina itself.

Only this time his thoughts of it were anything but vague. They were sharp and shrewd and calculating, all the things that had made him a solid businessman now came into play, and he knew he had made a decision. Or maybe some unseen hand had made it for him. No matter, he was a practical man and now was the time for action. He would have the Santa Calina range.

He knew he would be bullish, ruthless if need be, in his pursuit of it. He'd not intentionally cause anyone harm, but neither would he mince in his pursuit of his goal. To the devil with anyone or anything that might get in his way.

Regis knew there would be plenty who would dare to stop him. This region was famous for Apaches and Mexican and Texas outlaws, all eager to lay low newcomers with blind ambition and money to burn.

Regis snorted. They'd not have reckoned on Regis Royle, for once he set his mind to a task, let alone his heart and his wallet, it would take all the Indians, outlaws, and the US Army, too, to peel him from his dream.

He'd just have to convince his pard, Cormac Delany, to back his play in laying claim to the Santa Calina. Regis wasn't exactly sure how much this land was selling for, but he doubted a place like this would come too dear. On the other hand, what did he know? How much land had he bought? Exactly none. So it could well come hard, and his own coin purse, while healthy, wasn't what he'd call fat.

Yet somehow he knew that Cormac would be intrigued, too, and not just because he'd want to humor Regis. He'd been a father figure to young Royle when he had been little more than a skinny starving stowaway on one of Delany's steamers.

Delany could have tossed him overboard and been well within his rights to do so. Instead, the seemingly surly Irishman had scowled at Regis, told him he was too thin to be of use to anyone, and fed him.

He'd plied him with more food than the kid had seen since the Christmas before, when his mother's family back in Maine had hosted dinner for her and her two young boys, a kind but charitable gesture given that Regis's philandering father had gambled away their savings some months earlier.

Cormac had then made Regis a cabin boy, and he'd worked his way up, year after year, with Delany teaching him to read and cipher at night by light of an oil lamp.

Yes, Delany would back his play because he'd trust Regis and his intuition, in part because it was his own teaching that guided Royle. And it had paid off handsomely in the past. It had landed them shipping contracts that had rewarded the pair well, allowing them to expand their holdings.

Regis also knew he had to have Cormac in on such a deal because the older man's cultured ways would more than compensate for Regis's own reputation for a distinct lack of tact when it came to protracted negotiations.

And so, wedged in his rocky nest, Regis had smiled and nodded, caught in his blissful dream of the future despite the grim situation in which he now found himself.

And that's when the bullets, which had trickled to a random but steady flecking on him with rock chips that stung and nicked, poured on him once more. Through the long hours, the bandits never seemed to gain any ground, nor did they seem to lose interest in him.

They'd lobbed insults and sneers and jeers and hoots, and twice he heard glass shatter. So they'd been drinking. That was a two-edged sword. Good because their senses might be dulled, but bad because they would be emboldened for even more of this fool's fight.

"Well, let's get to it," he mumbled. He had decided to shuffle to his knees and prairie-dog up to see if he could size up one of the rats, when a fresh voice shouted from afar, and it kept shouting.

It was a yip—no words, but it sounded an awful lot like a man trying to imitate a drunken coyote. Or maybe the other way around. But curiously, the awful yowling was accompanied with the increasing loud sound of pounding hooves and, most important, fresh shots. Sounded as if it was coming at him fast and from the northeast.

Regis bent low and risked a peek around the base of the rock, hoping he'd not get a third eyehole for his trouble.

It was definitely a crazy rider, barreling pell-mell into their midst. Puffs of blue smoke from three directions told him the rider was not one of his attackers. Whoever he was, he was still yipping and howling and cranking off shots with a revolver and what looked to be a shiny new rifle. And he was tugging along a second horse behind. Hmm.

The man seemed to be pounding at everything in sight, except at Regis. Maybe his luck had turned. He resumed his own firing, measuring his shot and taking his time. Regis heard a scream and saw the back of a man as he emerged from behind the rock pile he'd suspected the first shots came from, thanks to the bird. The man bolted for a ground-tied speckled horse and leapt on, one hand held to the side of his head.

Regis saw spatters of blood on the man's white tunic. He also saw that the man wore an unusually tall blue-banded sombrero and a bright red sash about his waist. Regis aimed for the man's back, raised his barrel to adjust for distance, and . . . he held his shot. He'd not fired at many men in his life, and he'd certainly not shoot one in the back, marauder or no.

That didn't seem to bother the man who'd apparently ridden to his rescue. Friend or foe, he'd yet to find out. But the man wasn't bothered by shooting at the retreating bandits.

Regis risked a wider peek and counted four, five of them. He looked again at the man barreling on in. He was still smoking the blue blazes out of the pan-hot afternoon. And what he saw surprised him almost as much as the events of the previous hour. It was most definitely his own horse lined and trailing behind the newcomer.

Regis stood, visoring his eyes with his left hand and holding his cocked revolver on the slowing howler with his right. The man raised the rifle and butted the stock on his thigh as he trotted up.

The sun was in Regis's eyes, but he swore there was something familiar about this fellow. Then the newcomer spoke and removed doubt.

"That any way to treat kin, Mr. Royle?"

No, couldn't be, thought Regis. He goosed his neck forward and peered up at the mounted man now but three paces from him. "Shepley? That you?"

"The one and only, big brother!" The newcomer slid from the saddle and landed with a plunk, his boots raising dust.

If a full-bore circus troupe had wandered at him out of the shimmering landscape, Regis Royle could not have been more surprised. And yet, the impossible had just happened. Before him stood his very own little brother, his only sibling, one Shepley Royle, who until that moment Regis had assumed was still a student at that Quaker boarding school in Connecticut he'd been paying for.

"What . . . But how . . . What are you doing here?"

The younger man doubled over as if he were choking on a hunk of cheese, laughing and smacking his leg with a palm. "To think . . . Regis Royle at a loss for words! Hooboy, I never thought I'd see the day!"

Regis shook his head and strode forward and stuck out his hand. "Shepley, I . . . I don't know what to say!"

"Start with thank you, you big ninny! I come all this way, show up in time to save your sorry hide, and all you can do is shake my hand?"

Before Regis could react, the kid jumped up and locked his free arm around Regis's neck. "Good to see you, big brother!"

They smacked each other's backs for a few dusty pats, then stood back, Regis holding the youth's shoulders. "Let me look you over." He saw little and yet everything of the youngster he'd last seen four, five years prior? "Still the whip-snap, hell-raisin', risk-taking kid brother, I see."

"And a good thing, too, from the looks of it. I'm not sure how you ever got along without me all these years."

"Oddly enough, I managed." Regis smoothed his moustaches. "Question is, What are you doing out here? And at just the right moment, too."

"Oh, I come looking for you, of course. I had your address in Brownsville from that last letter you sent a few months back. Talked with a huge man, funny name . . . Big Jaw? Something like that. Anyway, he said you'd ridden out this way, but he forbade me to go after you."

"That'd be Lockjaw. And how'd you get away from him? He's not an easy man to disobey."

"He made a big mistake when he told me not to do something. Cause then I just had to do it! It's as certain as the moon and stars coming out at night or the sun rising and baking our heads off out here in this cursed wasteland! It's just the way it is with me, Regis. Can't explain it."

"I believe you just did."

Shep shrugged and smiled. "So I hopped my horse and rode on out. And the rest, as they say"—the kid looked around him as he untied Regis's horse and led him over—"is now history."

"Or dumb luck on both our parts. No matter, I see you are as humble as ever," said Regis, still smiling. He didn't think he'd ever smiled so much all at once in all his days. "Funny thing. I promised Ma I'd look out for you."

"Well, looks like you got it backward, big brother."

Regis worked his jaw muscles. Nobody in the world could be as exasperating to him as Shepley, and that included a pile of annoying, ornery old businessmen of his acquaintance. By gaw'd, but he'd forgotten how the kid could set him off. And this, despite the fact he was mighty glad to see him.

"Won't happen again." He stabbed his left boot into the stirrup and paused, looked up, then over at his brother. "Thanks, Shep. Appreciate it."

The younger man nodded. "Of course, brother."

Regis scanned the distance where the banditos had ridden. He fancied he saw puffs of dust growing fainter with each passing second. Whoever they were, they were not interested in a second dose. "I best find my hat. Oh, by the way, I'm pleased to see my rifle worked for you."

The kid raised the long gun and nodded. "Yep, just fine, just fine." He admired the blued barrel and rich walnut stocks. "Course it's tricky to load and ride fast, so I switched to my revolver." He patted the gun on his belt.

Regis nodded and mounted up without asking for the rifle back. "Where'd you learn to shoot like that, anyway?"

"That fancy school you sent me to," said Shep as they rode eastward. "Best part about it was the riding and shooting lessons."

"I thought they were Quakers."

"Oh, they are, but that doesn't mean I didn't pursue the more practical arts on my own time."

"Uh-huh. So you still didn't tell me what you're doing here. South Texas is a long ol' way from Connecticut, unless I'm forgetting something about maps."

Shepley smiled and sighed. "Mighty thirsty work saving your hide."

Regis didn't say anything but slid from the saddle and retrieved his hat. He held it up and poked a finger through a fresh bullet hole angling from left to right across his topknot.

"Yep, mighty good to have me around, huh, big brother?"

Regis felt the twinge, the momentary urge to clout, playfully, the kid on the ear. Instead he nodded. "Doesn't mean I don't want answers from you, boy. But thanks again."

They rode in silence for a few moments, then Shep cleared his throat. "Course, this means you'll stand the first beer."

Regis, slightly ahead, cracked a smile. "Only if you beat

me to it." He tucked low and spurred his horse into a hard gallop, knowing Shep's brown eyes were wide and a growl was already crawling up out of the kid's throat.

Regis glanced back and saw his younger brother jam heels into his buckskin. Then the kid's old beaver topper, more hole than hat, whipped off his head. He didn't slow a hair. Time for hats later. Regis grinned and looked forward again. He had a brother to beat—and a beer to drink. A free beer, or he wasn't fit to wear the name of Regis Royle.

CHAPTER 2

It was close to dark by the time they rode down the dusty main street of Brownsville. All about them, squares of light shone long across their path. Bawdy, bold shouts from men, laced with good-natured shrieks from their fair counterparts, filled the night air, still warm but with an edge of ease only night in the desert can bring.

Piano music, pounding and urgent, leaked from over and under a set of poorly hung, puckered batwing doors.

"How about that beer, brother?"

Regis looked over at the slouched youth riding beside him. "I guess one for celebratory purposes wouldn't hurt."

"One?"

The kid's bald disappointment made Regis smile. "Unless you'd rather have milk?"

"Oh no, anything but that. I ever have enough money I'm never going to drink milk again."

"Thought you liked growing up on the farm back in Maine."

"Ha!" Shepley shook his head. "You're confusing me with you."

"Wasn't me! Why do you think I made for the coast?"

"Yeah, and left me to . . ." The kid's words pinched out, and he looked ahead at nothing. Regis didn't question him.

"How about here?" said Shep.

Regis eyed the cantina. "The Lucky Dog? Nope, too rough for the likes of us."

"After what we've been through?" The kid angled his horse toward the hitch rail out front.

"Nope, Shep. I mean it. There's a decent place down the lane. You go in there, you'll come out poor and dead. Place is filled to brimming with card sharps and worse."

Regis noticed how the kid watched through the open doorway, his gaze lingering on the dimly lit action taking place at the games tables.

Shep pulled on his wide smile and said, "Okay then, lead on, oh fearless brother of mine."

A half-minute later, Regis stopped his horse before a quiet, well-lit establishment.

"Millie's?" said the kid, reading the sign. "This a . . . bordello?"

Regis chuckled. "Not that I'm aware of. And don't let Millie hear you say that. But they do make a sinful apple pie, and I'm about ready to indulge. Figured we could fill our bellies before that beer." He looked at Shep, who eyed him back with the same dark-eyed stare. "I'm sorry to disappoint you, little brother, but if I don't eat something soon, I'm not going to be fit company for man or beast."

Shepley climbed down out of the saddle and sighed, then clapped a hand to his waist and offered a short bow. "To err is human, to forgive divine."

Regis regarded Shepley. "Well, sounds like something from that school stuck."

"Yep," said the young man. "The sap from that pine I climbed down to make my escape from their dastardly clutches." He laughed as he looped his reins around the rail and strode toward the diner's front doors.

It was apparent to Shep that Regis was a regular customer at Millie's. A thick-waisted German woman a good decade beyond Shep's seventeen years batted her eyes at him and fanned her shining face as she took their order. Regis barely had to speak when she let loose with a giggle that seemed never to end.

"Good girl," said Regis after she'd left. "Can't understand a lick of English, but she manages to bring out something tasty every time I wander on in here."

"Mmm, I'll just bet she does," said Shep, looking everywhere but at his scowling big brother.

"Don't let Millie catch you talking like that," said Regis.

"That wasn't Millie?"

"Nope." He leaned over the table. "She's even bigger."

The youth's eyebrows rose, and he looked toward the closed swinging door that led to the kitchen.

The feed was true to Regis's words, and despite Shepley's initial hesitation, Shepley tucked in with a vigor only a Royle could muster. "Only person I have ever seen put away that much food at once," said Regis wiping his ample moustache with his napkin and reaching for a last swallow of coffee, "is Lockjaw. Or maybe me."

"What about Pa?"

Regis's grin slid from his mouth. "I guess." The old man hadn't been the easiest critter to get along with and was much of the reason Regis left home. "I'm sorry I left you back there like I did all those years ago."

Shep shrugged. "I'm tough. I could take it. Besides, Ma kept the worst of it from me. Then the old man left us, and we were better off. Then we heard he up and died, but you knew that."

Regis nodded. *Good riddance*, he almost said, then cleared

his throat. "How about that school, then? You on a break? Odd time of year for it."

Shep looked away, his face reddening. Then he looked back at Regis. "I haven't been going."

"What?"

Shep sighed. "I don't go there anymore."

"But . . . I've been sending the money. It's a good school, Shep. You'll get a good education there. More than I had. Ma wouldn't let you up and quit. What's she say about this?"

Shep looked away, then at Regis's eyes. "She doesn't have a thing to say about it."

"What do you mean?"

But even before Shep replied, Regis knew. He could tell by the misting of the kid's eyes, the tuck of the kid's bottom lip. "She's . . . dead. Ma's dead."

They didn't talk for long minutes. Finally Regis said, "How long since?" His voice sounded hollow and old to him.

"Four, five months now."

The air left him. "How?"

"Doctor said pneumonia. I . . . I was there. Got home in time. I was with her." The kid cried, shame reddening his face as he dragged the back of his hand across his eyes. He wadded his napkin and coughed into it, then scrunched his eyes and wiped them.

"I been meaning to write again." Regis clenched his own red-and-white cloth napkin in his big fist. "So busy these days."

Shep didn't say anything.

"I'm so sorry, Shepley. Truly. I'd always meant to get back home before this."

"I know. Didn't help, though, did it?"

"Why didn't you tell me? Someone could have sent for me."

"Tried. I sent a couple of letters but never heard back."

Regis sighed. "I've been busy. Shipping . . . new steamer." He couldn't finish. Anything he said was a pathetic excuse not worth uttering.

After he paid the bill, Regis clapped a hand on his brother's shoulder. "Okay, I'll get us a couple of rooms at the Brownsville Arms. Maybe grab that beer before we turn in. I'll meet you in an hour or two in the lobby, okay? I have business to tend to. You're welcome to come along."

"That's all right," said Shep, yawning.

"Okay, if you're as tuckered as I am, I imagine you'd like to make it an early night. We can catch up more later. Sound good?"

"You bet."

By then they were on the sidewalk. "Good." He handed his reins to the boy. "Then you can take these two nags to Bowdrie's yonder." He nodded at a livery stable diagonally across the street. "Tell Tom I'll catch up with him in the morning. We go way back, helped each other out in the war."

Regis would later question why he didn't take his brother's enthusiasms for taking on a chore in stride. Maybe he thought the boy was growing up. He was, after all, seventeen now. He'd come to regret his lack of scrutiny.

But for the moment, he was headed to the office of his and Cormac's shipping company. He intended to leave Cormac a letter explaining what he'd found and his intentions for the Santa Calina range. He didn't want to waste any time in getting the purchase in the works, but he also didn't want to roust Cormac at his house. The man worked hard, doubly so while Regis had been gone. No need to bother him at home, despite the sense of urgency Regis felt. He was confident Cormac would back his play on this. He'd find out for certain in the morning.

After he did that, Regis turned left from their office and made for Joplin's boarding house, where he suspected his friend, one Jarvis "Bone" McGraw, would be holed up in the kitchen, trying to finagle his way into Mrs. Joplin's good graces and, with any luck, out of her knickers.

He grinned and shook his head as he strode up the street and two lanes over. As it turned out he didn't need to make the full journey to the boarding house. From somewhere inside Barnard's Tonsorial Parlor, all windows alight, he heard a boisterous, deep-throated braying he knew could come from only one man. He stepped up onto the boardwalk and opened the door.

A man looked up at him from over a checkerboard. "Regis Royle, as I live and breathe."

"Bone, Mr. Barnard, how are you both on this fine evening?"

"Fine?" said the proprietor of the barbershop, a squat, bald, fat man with huge ginger muttonchops and a Donegal brogue as thick as the drifts of hair piled up in the corners of the room.

The man did not like to tidy up much, Regis noted—not for the first time—with a suppressed grimace.

The barber mopped his sweating red face with a voluminous handkerchief. "The last time the weather in this hellish hole of hell was fine, the Good Lord himself was in knee pants and all was right with the world."

Bone was a tall, lanky, raw-boned man roughly Regis's age. He stood—still not wobbly, Regis noted—and shook Regis's proffered hand.

Royle prided himself on his solid handgrip when greeting folks, but Bone, without trying to, had a way of commanding a situation with that one grip and looking you square in the eye every time. It was one trait among many that Regis admired about his friend.

"What brings you into town on such a night, Regis?"

"Oh, this and that, that and this."

"Uh-huh," said Bone as if reading his mind. He stretched

and yawned. "Well, Barnard. Much as I like your company, you ain't getting any prettier, and I suspect it will be a cold day well south of here before you're a comely woman, so I'm going to take my custom elsewhere. And besides"—he inclined his head toward the portly Irishman—"you told me an hour ago that Myrtle had supper on the stove. I don't want to take the blame for you missing a meal. Lord knows you can't stand that!"

He raised his eyebrows and reached for his hat—a mammoth, wide affair. He pinched the brim and walked out, ignoring the muttering Irishman. "He's just sore because I licked him at checkers. Again. Man will never learn."

"I heard that!"

Bone winked at Regis and said, "I know, you Irish devil. Now get on home!"

"Sure, this lousy Texas Ranger thinks he can throw his weight around my shop, tellin' me what to do. If I were a fightin' man, I'd . . ." Barnard's muttering drifted to silence behind them.

"Man never changes," said Regis. "Hey, how about a quick beer? I have a notion I'd like to float your way."

"Sounds serious," said Bone. He stopped and tapped his chin. "If a conversation's going to take place, then we best do it somewhere we can hear each other. How about Stump's place?"

Regis considered the suggestion, nodded, and led the way across the street. Once the two men found a table and seated themselves with glasses of warm beer before them, he leaned forward. The place wasn't as empty as he'd have liked, but it was better than the alternatives—loud bars with louder people getting louder as their evenings ground on.

He sized up Bone, one of his oldest friends, a swaggering, womanizing Texan through and through, and a Texas Ranger to boot. And, Regis knew, one hell of a cattleman.

"I just got back from a few days up Corpus Christi way."

Bone nodded. "Decent town, growing like a weed in a rainstorm."

"Yep, but it's not what impressed me most."

"Oh?"

"It was the Santa Calina range."

"Ah, should have known. She got to you, too, huh?"

"You know of it?"

"Who doesn't? Oh, there ain't much of this region I haven't ridden through. It's surprising what you'll find down there flanking the creek."

"That's what I want to tell you about. I aim to buy it."

"You don't say?"

Regis nodded, noticing Bone didn't seem overly surprised. "Yep, and run cattle all over it."

"What do you know about ranching?"

Regis smiled and shook his head. "What I know of it could fill this beer glass." He emptied it, then said, "But you, Bone, know more about such endeavors than any other fellow I know."

"If you're buttering me up for something, you'd have more success with whiskey."

Regis ordered a bottle of their finest and poured them each a shot. "What I have in mind is a partnership, Bone. I aim to buy that range. There's fine water, ample cattle, horses, game, all just waiting for someone to put shape to it."

"And that someone is going to be you?"

Regis shook his head. "Not just me. You too. That's what I meant by a partnership. You have the experience running a ranch. You know cattle and cowboying and the land better than anyone I know."

Regis's voice rose, then he looked around at the few patrons aside from themselves in the dark little hole of a place. "I have my commitments with the fleet, but I'll work with you as I can."

"That's just what we need—a greenhorn rancher with

one foot in the water!" This struck Bone as humorous, though Regis could not see why, and the former Ranger guffawed.

Regis looked around. Any more of that and he'd have to tell him to keep it quiet. He didn't want to tip his hand, not when the plan was so fresh.

"What?" said Bone, seeing his chum scanning the room. "You think you're the first to have this harebrained idea, Regis Royle?"

"It's not harebrained, and no. Well, I don't know. Hadn't really thought on it." He leaned forward and poked the tabletop with a ramrod finger. "There's a big difference between dreaming and doing, Bone. I haven't failed at much I've turned my hand to. Why do you think Cormac partnered up with me?"

The Ranger lost his smile then and got that windburned crinkly look about his eyes as he studied his friend. "You're serious, ain't you?"

"Serious as a frigate full of gunpowder."

"By gaw'd." Bone nodded and drummed the tabletop with his fingertips. He was silent a few long ominous moments. "It'll take a pile of cash to get started, you know."

"I know it."

"I mean"—Bone drummed his chin with his fingertips—"got to build corrals, hire a passel of men, the works. Then there's a cookie for chuck and such, quarters for them to live in, can't expect them to hang their hats in the thin air!"

"Never thought I would."

"You saying you're serious? All in on this?"

"Yep." Regis nodded solemnly.

"Cormac in on it too?"

"He will be, soon as he reads the note I left him. The idea's solid. Just have to track the deed, find out who owns it, and make it happen."

"Hmm. That'll take some doing, if I know anything of it.

I expect you'll be dallying with old Spanish land grants and such. But it's probably nothing that money can't handle."

Regis leaned back and shook his head when Bone offered him a second shot of whiskey. "That's for you. Paid for the bottle. Figured it might help you think this thing through. But I would like to introduce you to someone, if you have a few more minutes to spare."

Bone's bristly brown eyebrows rose, and the shot of whiskey stuttered in midair halfway to his face. "You get yourself hitched to a woman in Corpus Christi, Regis Royle?"

"God no!" Judging from Bone's reaction, Regis knew his face wore a mask of horror. Maybe one day, but marriage now? No, no, and no.

"Okay, then. I reckon whoever you're about to spring on me can't be all that bad."

Regis shook his head and shoved back from the table. He waited to rise while Bone gathered the bottle and tamped in the cork.

Behind him, at the far end of the bar, a thin man in a colorful serape that barely concealed a blood-spattered tunic slid off a barstool and turned toward the door.

Had Regis been looking, he would have seen that the man's dark hair bore thick wrappings of muslin, with a brown stain along one side of his head.

He also would have seen a red silk sash about the man's waist. And in his hand the man held the brim of a distinctive sombrero with a wide, bright blue band. He also wore a smile that lifted the corners of his wide, bristled mouth as if he had just overheard very interesting news. Because he had.

Had Regis been paying attention, he also might have heard the man chuckling softly as he left the cantina.

As they walked to the hotel where he'd told Shep they'd meet up, Regis wondered just what sort of person his younger brother had become. It wasn't as if Regis really knew the kid. When Regis had left home, Shepley was less than a shaver. Then they'd seen each other, what was it? Three, four times in all those years, not counting today.

Regis groaned to himself. What did the kid want with him now? Best to get him sorted out, then send him back to that school in Connecticut to finish his education. *I guess a little interruption—of a few months of traveling solo—never hurt anybody*, he mused. As valuable as sitting in a classroom, in its own way.

But Regis always regretted not having had more formal schooling. With Cormac's help he'd been able to get a leg up on reading, and within a couple of years of being taken under the man's wing, Regis was tallying accounts books like a professional money man.

As soon as Regis entered the lobby of the Brownsville Arms and didn't see his brother, he frowned. The woman at the desk, a perky young thing he knew to be the daughter of the owners, likewise wasn't helpful. She'd not seen anyone answering to Shepley's name or fitting his description.

"Your brother, huh?" said Bone, not working too hard to tamp down a smile. He cradled the half-filled jug as if it were a child. "Why not let him have the run of the town? Never did me any harm."

Regis said nothing, but his raised eyebrows told his opinion of that idea. "Kid's seventeen—a mighty young seventeen—and fresh off the trail. Or stage. Or boat or train. I don't know which he took to get himself out here. But he's my charge now, and I won't have him come to harm, nor cause it for others." A twinge of guilt stabbed him in the gut as he said it. Thoughts of his old mama dead these five months threatened to upset his apple cart.

"You okay?" said Bone.

"Yeah, yeah. I got an idea where the kid might be. Passed the Lucky Dog on the way in. He seemed keen to test it."

"If he has a half dime in his pocket, it'll go amiss in that rat hole." Bone took a pull on the bottle. "We best make certain he's not in there. That's not a place even I choose to frequent."

But Regis was already legging it back up the street toward the loudest spot ahead. "He's there."

"How do you know?" said Bone.

"That's my horse and his, tied out front. Likely half my gear'll be missing, too. Told him to take them to Bowdrie's, dammit." He ended his sentence with a growling, groaning sound that caused Bone to pop the cork on the bottle once more.

Regis glanced at Bone and suspected his friend was secretly thankful he wasn't Regis's kid brother at that moment. Regis knew enough about himself to know that when his back was up, he was one wild-haired mountain lion.